"COOPER MacLEISH HAS A LOT OF ROBERT B. PARKER'S SPENSER IN HIM . . . HE IS AN ALLURING BLEND OF KINETIC FORCE AND INTELLECTUAL HESITATION . . . THE HARD-BOILED FRATERNITY HAS A NEW MEMBER, AND HE'S A GOOD ONE."

Booklist

"CRIME FICTION HAS ADDED A PROMISING NEW AUTHOR TO ITS RANKS . . . THE CHASE IS A FINE ONE AND REAVES KEEPS THE SUSPENSE HIGH THROUGHOUT"

Boston Herald

"FOR SLAM-BANG ACTION, REAVES CAN'T BE BEAT."

Ocala Star-Banner

"NEW VOICES ARE ALWAYS WELCOME AND SAM REAVES' IS EXEMPLARY"

Los Angeles Times

"THE ACTION IS ALMOST NON-STOP"

Mystery News

"SAM REAVES WRITES WITH A TAUTNESS REMINISCENT OF A JOHN D. MacDONALD OR AN ERNEST HEMINGWAY."

Muncie Star

"AN OUTSTANDING MYSTERY WRITER"

Stuart Kaminsky, author of *Red Chameleon*

Other Avon Books by
Sam Reaves

A LONG COLD FALL

FEAR WILL DO IT

SAM REAVES

AVON BOOKS NEW YORK

AVON BOOKS
A division of
The Hearst Corporation
1350 Avenue of the Americas
New York, New York 10019

Published by arrangement with G.P. Putnam's Sons
Library of Congress Catalog Card Number: 91-32820
ISBN: 0-380-72034-5

First Avon Books Printing: January 1994

Printed in the U.S.A.

RA 10 9 8 7 6 5 4 3 2 1

Once again I must thank a number of people whose expertise remedied the author's ignorance: Septimus Paul of the fair isle of Trinidad, Richard Ramker of Miami, J. L. Smith, Dave Salter, Lawrence Leveque, Terry Smith, Mark A. Bandy. Thanks to you all. As usual, any mistakes are my fault.

No author could receive greater help and support than I do from Kim, to whom the book is dedicated with much love.

AS THE JET banked ponderously, deliberately, bringing the vast constellation of lights slanting up at the window, Tommy smiled at Chicago. He could see the endless rows of lights stretching back toward the nothingness of the lake; he could see the skyscrapers clustered in the distance, glittering.

A new town to conquer. Tommy liked the feeling. He liked getting into new towns, stepping off a plane or a bus or a boat, not knowing where he was going to sleep or what adventures he was going to have. He liked having a clean slate in a place.

Tommy checked his seat belt, felt with his toe for the carry-on bag under the seat in front. He felt the old familiar flutter in the gut. There had been a lot of new towns in the last fifteen years, a lot of adventures, a lot of nights on the street or the beach or somebody's floor, a lot of good gigs and bad gigs and full pockets and empty bottles. And there had been a few quick exits, a few last flights out.

It was good to get into a really big town, knowing that if things worked out he could rest for a while. He'd never been in Chicago but he felt he knew it, the way musicians know New Orleans or Manhattan. He wanted to see mean streets and smoky taverns and old black men biting into the blues. Tommy had heard Chicago in a thousand hard-driving tunes; now he wanted to see it. He was going to have a good time here.

He had a clean slate in Chicago, too. With a little luck he'd leave it clean, too. Give it a couple of weeks and go take a good long break.

It would be nice if he could find Slim. Having Slim to help would make it a lot easier and a lot safer. Tommy mused, wondering if and how much Slim had changed, and then the jet was leveling off; everyone was quiet in the nervous silence that comes just before the landing. Things on the ground were rushing by, starting to look real again and then there was the jolt of touchdown and Tommy smiled, because he had arrived.

Cooper heard the woman's cry before he saw anything. He was walking up Glenwood in the cool of a May evening that hadn't quite started to believe in summer yet. The dingy shuttered shops on his left opened onto the narrow sidewalk, with the high concrete wall of the El embankment on his right, trees hanging over with their new leaves. He was still a block away when the cry came down the street, a single note of alarm. Cooper looked up toward Morse Avenue and saw legs kicking.

He had already started to run when she came out with the first real scream, and now he could make out individuals: two men were trying to stuff the woman into a car. They had the rear door of an old battered Galaxy open but the woman was hanging on to the door frame for dear life and kicking while one man held her by a thigh and the other pried at her fingers, taking shots to the body from her feet. "Bastards!" she screamed.

Cooper was a hundred feet away and starting to think tactics when an old man stepped out of the doorway to a bar. He said something Cooper didn't hear and the man who was working on the lady's hands turned and snapped something at him. Then the old man took two steps forward and collared him.

They peeled away from the car and a wide sweeping hook glanced off the old man's head, sending his baseball cap flying. The old man held on and they went to the sidewalk; arms started windmilling. The other man jerked hard on the woman's leg and hauled her out of the back seat, dumping her on the sidewalk. She rolled over, winded or dazed, long hair dragging on the concrete. The man reached into the back of the car and came out with a tire iron.

The old man was getting the worst of it when Cooper arrived. Cooper planted a foot in the back of the man with the tire iron and sent him headlong up the sidewalk. He hauled his partner off the old man and spun him against the Galaxy, and things suddenly got a lot scarier. When the man came off the car he had a blade in his hand and gleaming light-colored eyes focused on Cooper.

"Try me, fucker. You'll need a bucket for your guts." He was dressed in basic biker: bandanna holding long greasy hair out of his eyes, denim vest over black T-shirt, tattooed arms.

Cooper had backed off; it wasn't worth getting cut. He looked to his right to see the woman rising unsteadily from the sidewalk. She was a fashion match for the men and Cooper wondered if he'd walked into a domestic dispute. "Take off, sister," he said. The woman didn't wait; she went south fast.

Cooper saw that wasn't going to end things; the man with the knife was interested in him now. He held the knife like he'd used it before and he circled to Cooper's right, low and balanced. Cooper was ready to concede the point and take off, but he heard footsteps behind him and knew his escape route was closed.

He took a quick look behind to see the man with the tire iron coming. Cooper was starting to think about scaling the car that blocked his way to the street when the old man came up off the sidewalk.

The old man drove a fist hard into the second man's belly and Cooper whirled to look for the knife again. The man was almost on him and he had to kick the blade aside, finding reflexes he'd forgotten he had. He got his balance back and circled away from the street, watching the blade. He heard ferocious scuffling to his left. The man with the knife didn't give him much time; he was determined to put that blade in him.

Cooper circled and kicked, willing to take a few cuts on the leg but intent on keeping the knife away from his torso. He kicked for the knees, kicked for the stomach. Somewhere down the block the woman was screaming for help. Cooper was landing kicks but they weren't expert ones; they weren't going to disable anyone. The point of the knife caught in his jeans and tore; just cloth, no flesh yet. The screaming was getting to the man with the knife and he was getting wilder, slashing down at Cooper's legs now, lowering his defenses.

Cooper waited for a downswing and then planted his foot and came inside with the one-chance uppercut, hoping it would be good enough. It was good enough to jar him up to his shoulder and put the man against the storefront, the knife up in front of him again but the eyes unfocused. He was wide open and Cooper finished him with a right cross that bounced his head off the planks. Cooper pulled the knife out of limp fingers and turned to look to the old man.

The old man was on his back, shielding his head with his arms and kicking wildly enough to keep the tire iron from landing too solidly. The second biker gave him one more impatient and not too effective whack along the side of a thigh and wheeled toward Cooper. This one had black hair in a ponytail and a thick beard; he took a step toward Cooper and then saw the knife in his hand.

"Good luck," said Cooper.

The man with the tire iron looked at his partner on the sidewalk and then into Cooper's eyes. He thought about it for a second, just a second, and then ducked out into the street. He went to the driver's side of the Galaxy and tore open the door. "Motherfucker," he said. He threw the tire iron in and slid behind the wheel. Cooper kicked the rear door shut and walked to the back of the car while the engine whined and turned over; when the Galaxy squealed away from the curb he was memorizing the license number.

The old man had risen to one knee. "Ya bastard," he said. Then suddenly it was quiet. The Galaxy screeched around the corner under the El viaduct; the woman had stopped screaming and disappeared.

Cooper stood with the knife in his hand, reeling just a little. He took a couple of deep breaths and laid the knife on the sill of the bar window and stepped to the old man.

His eyes were bleary and blood dripped from his nose onto the cracked concrete. A few damp wisps of hair were streaked across his mottled bald pate.

"You OK?" said Cooper, hauling him upright.

"Shit no, I ain't OK. Motherfuckers pounded lumps on

me." He put a gnarled hand to his nose and then shook blood from it onto the sidewalk. "All over my fuckin' jacket, look at that." The old man seemed steady enough on his feet and Cooper turned to the faces that had appeared at the door to the bar. "Anybody in there know how to use a phone?" he said.

A squad pulled up before too long, blue light bouncing off the wall of the enbankment, and a crowd gathered. Cooper went over it all with the impassive cops, the old man snarling his part of the story. The biker was still woozy when they cuffed him and threw him in the squad. Cooper and the old man signed complaints and the cops left, almost forgetting to take the knife with them. "I wanna buy you a drink," the old man said, clutching Cooper's arm and dragging him toward the door of the bar.

Cooper had been in the place before. Once in a long while he tired of Burk's, his regular place farther up the street, and took refuge in here. It was a long dim room hidden behind a rough wood-paneled storefont with a neon beer sign filling the single small window. There was no jukebox, just a TV, and the air was thick with tobacco haze. The average age of the clientele was, Cooper estimated, well over fifty. The long polished bar stretched forty feet back from the door and the rear of the place was filled with discarded boxes. There were Bears and Hawks posters on the wall along with the usual beer company cheesecake, and an impressive collection of whiskeys behind the bar. Most of the cushioned barstools were ripped and repaired with duct tape or gutted completely. It was a place for people who wanted to drink and didn't worry about decor, run by an elderly Japanese American who served the drinks with silent efficiency.

The old man still held a wad of paper towels to his nose but the bleeding seemed to have stopped. There was a scrape over his left eyebrow that didn't look too serious and the beginnings of a shiner under his left eye. He limped a few steps, wincing, testing the battered legs, complaining of bruises that would be spectacular in the morning. He held court perched on a barstool for a while but Cooper was mildly surprised at how quickly the stir died down and the patrons returned to their drinking.

The old man turned to Cooper. "You saved my ass out there." His voice had been broken beyond repair some years back; it was a ragged snarl with an underlying hint of respiratory distress.

"I'd call it the other way around," said Cooper. "If you hadn't guarded my back I'd be lying out there bleeding right now."

The old man shook his head. "Most people would have walked on by," he said.

"Most people would have let them get her in the car," said Cooper.

"Yeah, and that's why they get away with it." The old man took the paper towels away from his nose, dabbed at it with his fingers and tossed the wad on the bar. "What are you drinking tonight, my friend?"

Cooper ordered a beer and watched as the old man paid for it. The blood-spattered jacket had been hung on a hook on the wall and the old man hobbled over to fish in the side pocket for a handful of singles. He was short, not more than five-six, and bandy-legged. He wore a dirty white T-shirt and ancient brown corduroys. As he reeled back to the bar Cooper saw that he'd already had quite a bit to drink. He smelled it, too, as the man pulled up onto the stool beside him. He wore a greasy, faded Cubs cap on the side of his head and white stubble covered his cheeks. "I want to shake your hand, friend," the man said, holding out a paw with broken and dirty nails. "Norman's the name but most everybody calls me Stumps."

"Stumps?"

"On account of the short legs. If I had normal legs I'd be six feet tall." He grinned at Cooper, blood scabbing already in the whiskers beneath his nose, breathing whiskey at him.

"OK, Stumps," Cooper said, shaking his hand.

The beer was set in front of Cooper along with a shot of bourbon for Stumps, and the old man shoved across a couple of bills. On the pale flabby forearm stretched across the bar Cooper saw an old tattoo in faded blue ink, the globe and anchor going blurry in the aged flesh. "What the hell, I owe myself one more after that," Stumps said, tossing off the bourbon.

"You owe yourself a trip to the hospital, you mean," said the Japanese bartender, shaking his head glumly. "You take a knock on the head like that, you want to see a doctor."

"Nah, hell with that." Stumps flapped a hand at him. "Next time they get me back inside the VA it'll be for an autopsy. You're just worried I'm gonna keel over dead in here and you'll have to clean up."

The bartender gave Cooper a quick glance and a shake of the head and moved on.

Three stools down the bar, an old lady with tight gray curls and a red jogging suit raised a slurred, gin-sodden voice. "Least you didn't get cut this time."

"That'd make you happy, wouldn't it?" growled Stumps.

"I never seen anyone get beat up as much as you do." The old lady listed precariously toward Stumps as she gave vent to a thick unhealthy cackle.

"Hell, I'd rather get my ass pounded than sit and watch, like all you old corpses in here."

The old woman's laugh fought its way out of a congested throat. "And you're Tom Cruise, are you? Go look in the mirror back there, honey."

"I ain't dead yet," said Stumps. "Not till they nail the coffin lid down."

She leaned toward him, serious now, as serious as an alcoholic haze would permit. "You gotta stop trying to be a hero."

Stumps wheeled on her, hands planted on the bar. "The day I need your advice, I hope somebody'll put me out of my misery." He turned back to Cooper, watery eyes fierce. "Used to be, hero was something you wanted to be. You got balls, mister, and here's to you." Stumps raised the shot glass in a toast and scowled at it when he saw it was empty. He turned to find the bartender. "Kenny, fill me up here."

Cooper hadn't even touched his beer. He didn't want to spend the evening in here watching an old wreck drink, but he thought of the way the old wreck had reached out to collar the biker and then held on, and he had to admire him just a little. He slapped Stumps lightly on the shoulder. "This one's on me."

"Thank you, my friend, thank you. You handle yourself pretty good. I'm glad you're on my side."

Cooper gave a little half-shrug. "I'm like you. I can't just go on by."

"Then here's to you, by God," Stumps said, raising his refilled shot. They clinked glasses and drank. "What's the name again?" Stumps said, leaning back a bit to look up at Cooper's six-one on the stool next to him.

"Cooper. Friends call me Coop."

Stumps nodded and frowned in concentration. "I think I seen you around the neighborhood some."

"Yeah, I've been here for a while."

"Got a family?"

Cooper smiled. "Sort of. I have a son I didn't even know existed till he was fourteen. Fortunately he's got a rich grandma to take care of him."

The old man nodded as if he heard it every day. "I had a family, but they got a little tired of me. Or maybe I was the one got tired of them, I don't remember. That was a ways back. What do you do for work?"

"Drive a cab."

"Ah, yeah. I did that for a while, long time ago. Before all the foreign guys come in. You must be the last American cab driver left."

"Just about," said Cooper.

"You ever get stuck up?"

"A couple of times. If it happens again, I get out."

"Get out now. Next time might be too late."

Cooper smiled into his beer. "That's what the girlfriend says. But I don't think I'd ever be able to go back to working regular hours."

"Tell me about it. I was never too good at regular hours. 'Course, that's why I never had no money." Stumps laughed his ragged laugh and picked up his empty shot glass. He looked down the bar toward Kenny, but seemed to think better of it and came back a bit unsteadily to focus on Cooper again.

"Where'd you learn to fight?"

Cooper stared at him for a moment. "Here and there."

"You handle yourself pretty good. You ever do any boxing?"

"Not really."

"You musta learned the same place I did, then."

Cooper's eyes flicked to the old tattoo. "Not exactly."

"Army?"

"That's right."

"Yeah, I figured you'd been in the service." Stumps looked at him, appraising, whiskey breath whistling out of his half-open mouth. "You get in on that Vietnam shit?"

Cooper took a drink of beer, slowly, and nodded. "Spent spring and summer of 1969 with the 101st Airborne in the A Shau Valley. Worst time of my life."

"Tell me about it." Stumps shook his head, staring at the bottles on the shelves behind the bar. "I know."

After a moment Cooper said, "Let me guess. Back when you were in the Corps it would have been the Japanese."

Stumps grinned. "Yeah. I was over shooting at all of Kenny's cousins." He looked down the bar but the bartender had either not heard or decided to ignore him. He turned back and his face had fallen, a grizzled wreck of a face. "You ever hear of a place called Bougainville?"

"Yeah. In the Solomons."

"That's right." Stumps picked up his glass again and started to clink it against Cooper's but saw it was empty and set it down. "You know, ain't many people around who know what the hell Bougainville was. They all heard of Guadalcanal, but can't nobody tell you about Bougainville."

"All I know is the Marines took it in what, forty-three?"

"Yeah. November and December. I was eighteen years old. I went ashore with the 21st Marines, 3rd Marine Division."

Cooper took a drink of beer, not really wanting to swap war stories.

But Stumps just sat staring watery-eyed at the bottles behind the bar, then shook his head like a dog shaking off water and passed a dirty hand over his face. "Long time ago," he said. "Lotta water under the bridge."

"Uh-huh," said Cooper, thinking that the two decades plus that had gone by since he came out of the A Shau had been long enough and wondering if he would be like Stumps in another twenty-five years.

"Aw shit," said Stumps, looking down into his lap. "I'm bleeding again."

"So I wound up taking him to the emergency room." Cooper nestled lower into the sofa and cradled Diana's feet in his lap. "And now I got a friend for life, I think."

"How badly was he hurt?" Diana had her crooked little smile in place, lifting one corner of her mouth, the one she always put on when hearing about Cooper's misadventures. Cooper had not told her about the knife.

"Not bad. A poke on the nose, but nothing broken, no concussion or anything. He's a tough old customer. The biggest problem they're likely to find with him is alcohol poisoning."

Diana shook her head, her auburn tresses flashing in the lamplight. "Sounds like a delightful man."

"All right, he's an old drunk. Still, how many old drunks would have gone for that guy the way he did?"

"I'm not knocking him." Diana reached for her wineglass on the low cherry table by the sofa. "He sounds a lot like you."

"I figured you'd say that." Cooper smiled and his eyes drifted from Diana's sleek form in the dark blue robe, out over the room with the plants filling the front window and the shelves lined with books. It struck him suddenly that if he and Diana did move in together, they'd have trouble finding room for all the books. Half of hers were in languages he didn't understand, mainly Spanish. He ran an eye over the spines, seeing the names: Vargas Llosa, Borges, Pérez Galdós, Unamuno. Cooper had learned a little street German in his army days in Mannheim, but the ability to read a foreign language still awed him. "You'll have to teach me Spanish someday," he said.

"OK. If you teach me philosophy."

Cooper gave a little snort of laughter. "Teach you? I'm just starting to get the basics."

"You work on your book today?"

"It's not a book. It's just therapy. Yeah, I stared at it a little today. But I think I have to read this eight-hundred-page book I found. It's a history of the twentieth century by this irascible English historian who seems to have been influenced by Popper."

"Popper again. You're getting a little far afield, aren't you?"

"I told you, it's not about Vietnam anymore. I'm way past that."

"Well, don't give up on it. Parts of it at least are bound to be worth publishing."

Cooper shrugged. "There's no hurry."

Diana was looking at him over the rim of the glass, dark Latin eyes a little sad, the smile almost extinguished. "You know what I think," she said.

"Yeah. Get out of the cab and back into school."

"It's what you were made for. You're an intellectual. An intellectual manqué, anyway."

"An intellectual what?"

"You missed your calling, it means."

Cooper smiled at her. "I'm too damn old to go back to school."

"You're only eight years older than me, and I'm going back just as soon as I can scrape up the money."

"So how were the tips tonight?"

"OK. Wow 'em for a couple more years and I'll have enough."

"Wow 'em, huh? You're that good."

"That's an acronym. W-O-W for Waiting on the Wealthy. A dirty job, but somebody has to do it. They can't take care of themselves."

Cooper laughed and looked at her, a sharp, smart, trim tawny animal resting at the end of the couch, and he felt lucky. He felt suddenly that all the risks and all the compromises were going to be worth it. He lifted her feet from his lap, reached out to take the wineglass from her and set it on the table, and stretched out on the sofa to take her in his arms, a thrill of desire welling up at the feel of her body beneath him, a rush of affection taking him at the sight of her high-cheeked cat's face. "Nobody but you," he said.

"Nobody but you," she repeated, softly. Cooper could

see sun in her golden face with the faint freckles, long reaches of sea in her Caribbean eyes.

"Forever," he said.

"Forever," she breathed, just as his lips descended on hers.

TOMMY STOOD ON the balcony of the Holiday Inn and looked at the town. He could hear the deep constant murmur of traffic, with occasional plaintive honks drifting up from the street. He could look south and see the eruption of skyscrapers in the Loop; he could look east, just to his left, and see the flat shimmer of the lake melting into a pale sky at the horizon.

It does look like the ocean, he thought. He'd never really believed a lake could be that big. It looked like a cold northern sea. Tommy was a creature of the tropics; he shivered and came in off the balcony. He went over to the desk and looked again at the open Chicago phone book.

Froelich Cezar, Froelich Dave, Froelich D. And then on to *Froelich Jayne*. The *D.* had to be Slim. Unless she had left town, but Rusty had said she'd heard from her last year and it sounded like she had put down roots. Tommy copied the number onto a card he pulled from his wallet, then sat down at the desk and pulled the phone toward him. He smiled again at the thought of a Puerto Rican with a German name. He punched the number into the phone and sat with his heart pounding just a little while it rang at the other end. Come on Slim, time to be up and about. Worlds to conquer. After four rings there was a click and the recording came on. "You have reached 339-2678. I'm sorry I can't come to the phone right now, but if you'll leave your name and number I'll get back to you as soon as I can." A pause, and then the beep. Tommy hung up, smiling. That was her voice, for sure. Still being careful. She wouldn't leave her name on the tape, not Slim.

She'd be sleeping in and ignoring the phone. Or maybe she had a straight job after all and had to be out early. The recording suggested she was living alone, and that was good. Tommy told himself there was plenty of time. He sat looking out the window at the bright spring day over the city, hoping it would work out with Slim, not least because he couldn't afford another night at the Holiday Inn. Mostly, however, he hoped he could persuade Slim to help him, because it sure would be a lot safer. He figured he could get her to help him without too much trouble. He and Slim went back a long way.

Diana's idea of a place to drink was more genteel than Cooper's. Under her civilizing influence he allowed himself to be steered a couple of times a month to what he thought of as the Yuppie Chinese Place. It was a semi-elegant restaurant a bit out of place in the unassuming lakeside neighborhood where Cooper and Diana lived. Featuring a sort of Chinese nouvelle cuisine, it was softly lit, furnished with old wood and with nary a red tablecloth in sight. The bar was, Cooper had to confess, a pleasant spot to drink. It was decorated in cool grays and midnight black, with anything from Back to Brubeck coming in just loud enough over the sound system and a long bar with a padded rail and comfortable tall chairs. Cooper liked to sit in the place with Diana on her nights off and watch her toy with a tall drink and unwind. This was the crowd she'd run with since long before he'd known her; there was a circle of young and prosperous Asian-Americans, the generation Cooper figured might just keep the U.S. from sliding into the Third World, all of them doctors and biochemists and the like. There was an intersecting circle of half-familiar faces Cooper saw around the neighborhood, and a couple of old well-dressed men who drank at regular times and in solitude. Cooper still considered a shot-and-beer type of place like Burk's his natural habitat, but he liked the Chinese bar more than he would have expected.

Tonight he was talking to Barry, with Diana between

them, mediating with a carefully chosen word or two when necessary. Barry was a lawyer, tall and for a lawyer unexpectedly mild and quiet, with an air of innocence that didn't quite fit with the gray of his thick curls. He was fortyish, Jewish, highly educated, civilized, and soft-spoken. He had spent most of his twenties in Toronto, preferring it to either jail or Vietnam.

"All I'm trying to get across," Cooper was saying, "is that for all our mistakes and all our crimes, 'cause yes, we did commit crimes, you can't say we were on the wrong side."

"We came in on the wrong side, yes." In his quiet earnest tone Barry delivered the statement apologetically, as if it painted him a great deal to have to say it, but he delivered it firmly. "We betrayed the Vietnamese. Ho Chi Minh came to us first, because he admired our principles."

"He couldn't have admired them too much, seeing how he turned out."

"He wanted independence and he assumed we would support him. We turned hm away and ultimately tried to crush him."

Cooper eased back on the barstool, shaking his head, frowning at his beer. "And none of that conferred any kind of sacred unshakable rightness on him. So we fucked it up. OK, Dr. Frankenstein fucked it up too, but a monster's a monster. You have to look at what's happened since. If the Cong and the North Vietnamese were the right side, then why the boat people?" Cooper stabbed at the bar with his index, holding Barry's eye now. "And you can't put it down as the bourgeoisie fleeing to creature comforts anymore. The poor, the peasants are risking their lives to get out. They risk pirates, sharks, drowning, starvation to get out. The sheer numbers of people who have risked their lives to get the hell out of Vietnam since the Communists took over are proof we were the right side, man."

"Ask the people in My Lai if we were the right side."

Cooper's mouth twisted in a grim smile. "Yeah, My Lai's a tough one, isn't it? Look, My Lai was a crime. A war crime. And people were prosecuted for it, probably not enough of them and probably not high up enough. But it sure as hell wasn't the only war crime committed over there. Got any idea how many civilians the Communists killed?"

Barry sat holding a cocktail straw, twisting it meticulously into pretzel shapes. "We took sides in a civil war and just made things worse. It was a struggle for the soul of the country, and we tried to impose the solution we wanted. In the process we almost certainly killed thousands more than would have died without our intervention. We corrupted a society and multiplied the killing a hundredfold. What gave us the right?"

"Maybe nothing. Sure, they told us we had to save Vietnam because our security was involved. Well, we didn't save it, and we're still afloat, so it was a fucking waste. I grant you that. Nobody's more aware of the waste than somebody who was there, believe me. But we weren't the wrong side. The war's been fought all over the globe in the last fifty years, and it should be clear which is the right side by now. Eastern Europe at the end of eighty-nine should make it clear. People hate communism for good reasons, man. They hate it because everything the communists touch turns to shit."

"So let people work it out for themselves."

There was plenty more to say but Cooper knew he couldn't say it all. "Look, my only point is that the twenty years since we lost Vietnam should have proved to everyone's satisfaction that we were the right side."

"Despite My Lai."

"Despite My Lai. If atrocities automatically discredit the cause in which they're committed, I think you'll have a hard time finding a cause to support in this world. Whatever I may have on my conscience for what we did over there, at least I'll go to my grave knowing those little fuckers in the pith helmets really were the bad guys, 'cause what they were fighting for is what Vietnam got. Now let me buy you another drink and let's forget all that, because it was a long time ago."

Barry smiled at him then, sadly, and his mild eyes went from Cooper's face down to the twisted straw and then out across the room. After a brief silence Diana rescued them by snaring a passing acquaintance, and a new and innocuous conversation ensued. After downing the drink Cooper brought him, Barry took his leave and shortly after that Cooper and Diana did the same.

Cruising home in Cooper's old Valiant, they were silent until Diana said, "So what do you have on your conscience?"

"From over there, you mean?"

"Uh-huh."

"Nothing like My Lai, if that's what's been worrying you."

"I'm sorry. I couldn't help wondering."

"I know. But you can rest easy. The only people I ever shot at were NVA regulars."

"That's what I thought."

"But I want you to understand something, too."

"What?"

"I can't guarantee that if I'd been with the unit that went into My Lai I wouldn't have participated. I can't guarantee that." He drove in silence for a few seconds, through the empty streets, feeling Diana freeze on the seat beside him. "See, I can understand how it happened. Ever seen a bunch of teen-age guys get a little drunk or just over-exuberant and do something stupid, break windows in an old house or something? Something none of them individually would have done but that they'll do in a group, reinforcing one another, once someone has broken the first taboo? Well, that's what that rifle company was. A bunch of teenage guys, tired and scared and pissed off at these alien people who they figured were setting the booby traps they stepped on every day, or at least hiding the people who were. A bunch of teen-agers with unlimited firepower and license to use it. And their officers and non-coms abdicated, and somebody broke the first taboo, and that was all it took."

"Now you are making excuses for them."

"No. Just explanations, and explanations are never excuses. All I'm trying to tell you is that there but for the grace of God go I. I can't guarantee that I would have been . . . I don't know, good enough, strong enough not to participate. I just don't know."

"I'd still love you."

Cooper reached for her hand and squeezed it. "I want

you to understand who it is you're loving. I found out what people are capable of, what I'm capable of, and it wasn't very pretty. All I can say is that it's made me think about right and wrong an awful lot since then."

"Then I think you should rest easy, too."

"I'll never be able to do that. But that's all right. That's life."

Cooper parked a half block from Diana's place and they walked back hand in hand. Cooper felt a sudden quiet lifting of the spirit, knowing she really did love him, that things really were going to be all right, after all.

A cigarette glowed in the dark on Diana's doorstep. Cooper saw it from a hundred feet away, and as they approached, the figure smoking it grew distinct. It was a man, lounging on the doorstep, legs stretched out along the walk and crossed, back against the doorpost, profile silhouetted against the light inside the door as he lazily blew smoke into the cool night air. Diana's end of the neighborhood was fairly sedate and Cooper wasn't inclined to worry too much about midnight idlers, but he gave him a careful eye as he and Diana turned up the walk. The long legs were in jeans and the feet sticking out wore square-toed cowboy boots. He wore a black leather jacket against the spring night chill. The face was pale and narrow in the dim light from the street lamps. The man watched them come up the walk and smiled.

Diana stopped short and her grip tightened on Cooper's hand. "Tommy!" Her voice was something above a whisper and below a gasp. Cooper glanced at her and saw only the clear signs of astonishment.

"Hey, Slim. You're kind of hard to get in touch with." The man uncrossed his legs and pulled them back, grinding out the cigarette on the concrete step. "I've listened to that phone message of yours a dozen times today." The smile shone even in the half-light.

"What in God's name are you doing here?" said Diana, her voice recovered.

"Hell, you're in the phone book. I hoped you wouldn't mind a little visit from an old friend."

Shaking her head slowly, the corner of her mouth going up in the crooked smile, Diana released Cooper's hand and took a step forward as the man rose from the step. He and Diana embraced for a second or two, just a quick hard squeeze, and he pecked her once on the cheek.

Diana stepped back and turned to Cooper. For a moment her lips were parted with nothing to say; Cooper wasn't sure what he saw on her face. Then she said, "This is Tommy Thorne, a historical relic. The last time I saw this man was in Miami in 1981. From the look of him he hasn't changed a bit." The smile was back now as she looked at him.

"We all change, Slim." The man grinned at her from a height somewhere above six feet.

"That name's a relic, too. You know my real name."

"See? I told you we all change. OK, Diana from here on out. Now introduce me." Tommy's voice was deep and clear, a good strong speaker's voice.

"This is Cooper." Diana eased back to Cooper's side and slipped her arm through his. The embrace and the peck on the cheek hadn't particularly bothered Cooper, but he was obscurely glad of the gesture. He stuck out a hand and Tommy shook it with a brief firm squeeze.

"Cooper? I'm glad to meet you." Tommy turned to Diana and said, "I'm sorry to drop out of the sky like this, but you know the way I travel. I was hoping you could put me up, but if I'm in the way you can just point me to the nearest motel."

Diana hesitated for a moment, the briefest of moments. "Come on upstairs. We'll sort things out," she said. She pushed into the entryway, where an old army duffel bag, a hand grip and a guitar case were crowded into a corner. "Traveling light, huh Tommy? There's a few guitars missing, aren't there?"

"I'm just scouting a trial. I left most of my stuff with a partner in Lauderdale. Things work out up here, I'll haul it all up."

With Cooper's help he got his bags up to Diana's place. Installed in the armchair near the front windows, Tommy stretched out his legs again and beamed at Diana. "You don't look a lot different. Slim as ever. Maybe a little wiser looking."

"Older you mean, huh? Well, I'm not the only one. But wiser too, I hope."

"Ain't we all," said Tommy. His long tanned face came to a point at a sculpted chin; his nose was long and thin, his mouth a firm stroke when the broad smile wasn't in place. His straight brown hair was long in the back and standing up on top, just spilling over the ears. He had good looks of the show-biz variety, camera-ready good looks. Cooper put his age somewhere in the late thirties. Tommy's gaze ranged over the room, avoiding Cooper at the end of the sofa. "Now this is a home. This is a nice solid dry-land kind of place. You remember those little cabins on the *Bismarck?*"

"I remember. You couldn't stretch your arms out far enough to fold a towel." Looking at Cooper she said, "We called it the *Bismarck* because after a while we wanted to sink the damn thing."

Cooper had pieced it together, remembering things Diana had told him. "You two were on the cruise ship together."

"That's right," said Tommy. "That lady over there is the ace blackjack dealer of the Caribbean."

"Was. Let's keep it in the past tense."

"What the hell was the name of that band? The Cruisers or something."

"No. The Ramblers. Wasn't it the Ramblers?"

"Yeah. The Ramblers, that's it. I've moved on to better bands, believe me, Slim. Sorry. Diana."

"Tommy played lead guitar in the dance band," Diana tossed in Cooper's direction.

"Four hours a night, the same people for a month on end. Trapped on a boat with these characters. Retired accountants, spinster secretaries in wolf packs. Get a couple of secretaries from Des Moines drunk on a cruise ship and watch out."

Diana laughed. "I remember. The lady pounding on your cabin door at four in the morning."

"Groupies, occupational hazard. And the music, Jesus. Material that was stale when Hendrix died. How many times can you play 'Born to be Wild' and keep it wild?"

"Dues paying."

"If those were dues, I was overcharged. Meanwhile, Diana's up a deck or two in the casino, making sure nobody gets ashore with any money left."

"I'm ashamed of it now, but it was a living, I guess."

"Hey, don't be ashamed. They had the money or they wouldn't have been there. And tell me they didn't enjoy losing it to the likes of you." Tommy looked at Cooper. "The company only hired beautiful women as dealers. They'd sign 'em in Miami, give 'em a couple weeks' training and take 'em out. What Diana took off those old New York scarecrows probably paid the food bill for the cruise."

"We didn't see too much of it, that's for sure."

"No, but we had room and board, remember? Meals down in the hold. With the other peons, the dishwashers and waiters and so on. All those Cuban and Puerto Rican guys who were trying to make you."

"Yeah, that's right. Once they found out I was from San Juan I was fair game."

"Diana and a guy or two from the band and me used to meet back at the stern after everything shut down. Four, five in the morning, sit back there and smoke a J, watch the water slip by under us, talk about the idiots we had to put up with and wait for the sun to come up."

"That was nice. That's the part I remember. Just sitting back there in the cool watching the sea, seeing the horizon turn pink."

"And when they let us off the ship it wasn't too bad. Those boats do take you places."

"I can't remember them all now. Aruba, Martinique. Where the hell did we go?"

"Aw, I could tell you the whole itinerary, but I'd have to think."

"That was a different lifetime."

"It was a living. Playing music, going places."

Tommy felt silent and smiled at Diana across the room. Cooper needed a role so he stood up and asked Diana if she had anything to drink. He went to fetch the wine from the refrigerator while the reminiscences resumed. When he came back with the bottle and three glasses Tommy was talking.

"Best band I ever played with, only one I had a chance to get somewhere with. We had an L.A. agent interested, big times ahead. Then the bass player and the lead singer went off a bridge into the water down in Key West, probably coked out of their minds. Didn't pull 'em out until the next day. That did in the band. I did some studio work around Miami for a while after that, then went to L.A. after all, just on my own. I called the agent, he didn't want to know me. I hung around there playing a little music for a year or so, just kind of getting by. Then I went back to Florida. I ran into this piano player I knew and he told me about a hotel on Guadeloupe that was looking for a band, so off we went. And I've been island-hopping ever since. Play a little music, live cheap, lie in the sun. It's not a bad lifestyle, but it gets old. Thanks, man." He took a glass of wine from Cooper.

While Cooper poured her a glass, Diana said, "So answer my question. What are you doing here?"

Tommy shrugged and a half-smile crossed his face. "Looking for music to play. If you ever try to play the blues, you wind up wanting to check out Chicago."

"So you're going to settle here?"

"Who knows? I want to get a place to stay for a while, hear a lot of music, try getting into a band. What the hell. It's a new town for me. And I got tired of the tropics, I guess."

"God, I miss 'em," said Diana. "Someday I'm going to take Cooper to Puerto Rico, get him out of Chicago for the winter." She smiled at Cooper as he filled the third glass, plunked the wine bottle down on the table and sank onto the sofa.

"Sounds good to me," Cooper said. "I got nothing against the tropics."

"They're great for vacation," said Tommy, "but you get tired of vacation after a while. And tired of other things."

"Like large and unpleasant vermin," said Cooper.

"You've been there." Tommy grinned at him.

"Southeast Asia."

"Peace Corps?"

Cooper shook his head. "War Corps, I'm afraid."

"Ah." Tommy looked at him blankly for a second and

turned back to Diana. "So listen, Slim. Sorry, I mean Diana. I don't want to be in the way, but if you could put me up for a night or two until I could find a place of my own I'd appreciate it. All I need's a floor."

"Sure. I may dump you here and go over to Cooper's if you don't mind."

"Cool. It's a great place. How long you been here?"

Cooper sat and listened while Diana brought Tommy up to date on her life. He had never met anybody else from the pre-Chicago phase of Diana's life and he was amused to watch a specimen of a period Diana had described to him as a cross between *Fellini Satyricon* and *Miami Vice.* Tommy sat with one leg hooked over the other and sipped the wine. He went solemn when Diana told him about her marriage to a Miami cop and subsequent widowhood, and he flashed the broad smile when she told him about the restaurant, about dealing with rich idiots, just like on the *Bismarck.*

Cooper watched Diana, too. Every once in a while she would cast him a glance, a quick flick of the eyes, touching base, maybe apologizing, once holding his eyes for a second with a look he couldn't read. When Cooper started to yawn, Diana roused herself, got Tommy squared away for the night and prepared to take her leave.

"Tomorrow morning we can talk about finding you a place. Help yourself to breakfast. I'll be over around nine. OK?"

Tommy stood planted in the middle of her living room, arms akimbo. "I'm glad I hung around. You're an angel, Slim."

Driving across the neighborhood, Cooper said, "He takes favors well, doesn't he?"

Diana said nothing for a moment and then, "That's his lifestyle. Don't worry, I'll have him out as soon as I can."

Cooper laughed softly. "Look, I'm not jealous or anything. I was fascinated. As you would be if any of my old girlfriends showed up, God forbid."

"What makes you think he's an old boyfriend?" she said sharply.

"I don't know. I just assumed."

"I used to hang around with all kinds of men. Precious few of them were ever boyfriends or anything close."

"Sorry. I jumped to conclusions."

In bed at last in Cooper's bachelor redoubt, they lay in each other's arms in the dark. "I didn't mean to snap at you," Diana murmured. "It's just awkward, Tommy showing up like this, and I was embarrassed, I guess."

"Forget it." Cooper kissed her on the forehead, right at the roots of her hair. "I got no problem with the guy. As long as he doesn't stay too long or anything."

After a moment Diana said, "No. Tommy never stays in one place for too long."

FROM WHERE HE sat in the bare holding room the prisoner could hear the sounds of freedom, faintly. He could hear car horns bleating, women calling to one another, distant distorted strains of music from overtaxed speakers. He could close his eyes and see it, the sun beating on the walks, glinting off windshields, glittering on the bay far below. The prisoner had heard the sounds and imagined the sights every day in the harsh gloom behind the high walls topped with wire; now that he was on the point of walking out into their midst, an uncomfortable thrill washed through his entrails.

He had not imagined that simple formalities could take so long. He had been sitting on the hard wooden chair in the little bare room for an eternity. He kept his eyes closed until he heard footsteps in the passage outside. He opened them to see the sergeant swing into the room, clutching the papers, the eternal scowl in place on the round black face.

"On your feet."

The prisoner rose slowly. The sergeant came to a halt in front of him, stiff and straight in peaked cap and starched khaki, scowling. The prisoner met the scowl with the empty look he had perfected in the dank corridors of the Royal Gaol.

"I'll be sorry to see you go," the sergeant said, with a very small smile that was not warm.

The prisoner made no response. He was listening to the street sounds again.

The sergeant reached slowly for the prisoner's light cotton jacket. "Cheap bloody clothes they give you," he said. He grasped the seam at the shoulder with thick thumb and index and gave a quick hard jerk. The stitching gave way and a two-inch tear appeared. "Bloody rags," the sergeant said. "But you've never had better, have you?" He was still smiling.

The prisoner looked into the sergeant's face with his placid stare, knowing what the sergeant wanted him to do but determined to walk out into the beating sun today, no matter what.

The sergeant's smile faded. "Here are your papers." He handed over the folded sheets and wheeled toward the door. "Follow me."

The prisoner followed the sergeant down the hall and into the yard outside. He took one look through the gate to the left and saw the catatonic shuffle of inmates in the exercise yard. A dark figure near the gate stiffened and threw up a hand in farewell. "Cecil!" the figure called.

The prisoner ignored the call. He followed the sergeant to the guard post by the main gate and presented his papers. The guard who came out of the booth glanced at them and refolded them and handed them back.

"Don't come back," he said brusquely.

"He'll be back, a bad john like this one," the sergeant said, his smile broadening in the sun. "He'll be back before we've given his bed away."

The prisoner was already looking through the gate into the street. His heart was beating faster.

"Out with you then," said the sergeant.

The ex-prisoner stood on the sidewalk outside looking at people, looking at the women in their bright dresses, weak in the knees to be seeing women again. He looked left and saw the green open spaces of Queen's Park Savannah above, looked right and saw the street plunging down into the crowded sweating hustle near the port. Above, the tropical sun shone unimpeded by clouds.

People were staring at him. Cecil began to walk down toward the port, overwhelmed by the noise, by the color, by the heat and by the absence of walls. He began to come to his senses. He had a long way to go but he wanted to walk; he could walk where he wanted now. He wanted to walk for a while, just to rediscover his city, before he began to look for the people he needed to find. He hoped he would find them where he had left them, back behind the bridge. It was going to take some time, he expected.

Cecil had a lot of work to do.

Tommy had no trouble locating coffee, eggs, bread and all the necessary utensils in Diana's kitchen. He scrambled the eggs and toasted the bread and sat at the table eating, looking around the room. It figured that Slim would have a tidy kitchen, all the pots hung in order of size on the wall, everything scrubbed, no roaches. Tommy put the dishes in the sink, poured a second cup of coffee, and went ambling slowly through the apartment.

The living room was dominated by the plants in the front bay and by the books along the wall. Tommy remembered Diana with her books, curled up on her bunk or stretched out on a beach, reading. Reading things he'd never heard of—things in English, things in Spanish, things in French. Tommy stepped over the worn sepia-colored rug toward the bookshelves, shaking his head. He was suddenly suffused with a rush of affection for her. He shouldn't have let her go.

He sipped coffee, turning slowly to take in the whole room. She'd put together a warm, comfortable space with furniture that hadn't been new when she'd gotten it but was solid, cared-for stuff. On the walls hung a couple of bright prints, museum-shop stuff, and an original oil, a luminous seascape. She had a little portable TV discreetly concealed in a corner and a stereo that had been state-of-the-art maybe back when Beck was still with the Yardbirds. Slim was not into expensive things; he remembered that about her. Not a material girl. A bookish, intellectual kind of girl inside the easy-to-look-at exterior. The exterior hadn't changed much in ten years, Tommy reflected; she still had the firm sleek look of the natural athlete and the natural beauty, the dark gold sun-nourished tones of the Caribbean.

Tommy moved like a cat over the carpet, toward the doorway into the hall. He stood at the door to the bathroom, looking at the bright white tiles and the old bathtub perched on squat legs. Everything was tidy in here, too. There was a clear plastic shower curtain and towels of many colors folded neatly and stacked on a set of shelves next to the tub. There were two toothbrushes in the holder over the sink. What's the guy's name, Cooper, odd name, the guy was spending nights over here. Good for you, Slim. Got yourself a man, never be a shortage of them around you. Seemed like a solid type of guy, strong silent type with his scraggly, weathered blue-collar look, curly brown hair going gray, straggling over the ears, moustache drooping around the corners of his mouth almost into Fu Manchu territory. And those skeptic's eyes.

War Corps, for Christ's sake. Probably one of these professional veteran types, march in all the parades, get his picture taken staring moodily up at the wall in Washington, wearing his old fatigues with medals pinned to them. Gimme a break. Not smart enough to stay out of the service, then spends the rest of his life bitching about how unappreciated they all were.

Tommy went into the bedroom and stood looking, sipping coffee. More books, for God's sake. The closet door stood open, revealing a riot of color, a well-stocked woman's wardrobe. Slim looked good in anything; she was that type of woman. Tommy looked at the bed, carefully made, with the deep green comforter on it. He tried idly to picture Diana rolling in the bed with Cooper and was abruptly overtaken by carnal memories.

He'd almost forgotten that part of it. Tommy had had a lot of women before and since, but Diana had been special, with that passion that had always seemed part desire, part fear. Or maybe he was just idealizing it. She'd been just a girl back then. That had been part of the charm, the way she was so smart and so well traveled and still so young. Young in bed, anyway.

Yeah, he should have held on to her. For a couple more years, anyway. Everything ended, Tommy had learned, but Diana really hadn't lasted long enough for him.

Tommy moved back into the living room. He smiled. It was good to see he again, and he was starting to get confident. He had known the first meeting would tell, and the first meeting had gone well.

Tommy finished the coffee and put the cup in the sink. He went into the living room and opened the guitar case and pulled out his Stratocaster and a pick. He sat in the armchair and ran his fingers over the steel strings, tuned it just a touch or two, and ran through a riff, just working through a basic blues progression, the faint twang of the unamplified strings wafting through the sunlight. In between all the business he had to do, Tommy wanted to go hear a lot of blues. He'd get Slim to take him around; hell, he wouldn't even mind if Sergeant Rock came along. Go hear Willie Dixon, Lefty Dizz maybe, if guys like that were still playing. Hear some legends.

Tommy smiled again. He had a feeling he was going to like Chicago.

"Maybe give me a day or two to take care of Tommy," Diana said. "I mean get him started looking for a place, stuff like that. Show him the ropes a bit. Unless . . ."

She paused, and Cooper looked up from the paper and smiled. "Unless I don't trust you?"

"Unless you want to come along for the ride, I was going to say. I thought I'd take him to hear some music or something."

Cooper shook his head, turned the page. "Have fun with the guy. I wouldn't mind tagging along for a drink or something, but I can do without the music. Elbow-to-elbow, breathing smoke for three hours isn't as much fun as it used to be. Go ahead and take the guy out, catch up on old times. I'm not jealous."

He felt Diana's eyes on him and looked up again; the corner of her mouth curled up to soften the gaze. "I know.

I like that. But I want you to know there's no reason to be."

"I know it." Comfort, Cooper thought. That was comfort, caring enough about someone to be hurt by them, but being confident they weren't going to hurt you.

"I'll be back here tonight. I'm not going to stay over there with him."

"Shit, stay over there if you want. It's your place, he's your friend. I'm not worried about it, Diana."

"I'm glad. But I'll be back here." She kissed him quickly and was gone.

Walking home in the cool gray May morning, Diana thought, I lied. She scowled at a squirrel, glared at the dirty sky. Not overtly, but a lie was a lie. She wondered why she had felt it necessary to mislead Cooper.

And she wondered why Tommy had come to Chicago. She wanted to take him at face value, to believe what he said about it. But she knew Tommy. She'd learned a lot about Tommy in those fast hard six months in the Caribbean and then later, in Miami. Tommy was never an easy read. Diana wanted badly to believe that he was just an old pal looking for a place to sleep for a few days, that he had no desire to rekindle or excavate or even to reminisce very much, but she wasn't sure. There would always be things about Tommy that bothered her, even though he'd been a good sport when she'd left him. There had been no hard feelings; that was the way Tommy lived. Tommy took everything easy.

Diana unlocked the door of her building and trod up the stairs, suddenly dreading to go into her place and find him there. She hoped he wouldn't want to monopolize her time today, or any other day. Tommy was history and she wanted to keep him that way. She turned her key in the lock and pushed into her place and saw Tommy in the armchair, fingers flying over the neck of the guitar, smiling at her. She said hi and closed the door behind her, wondering again as she did: what did Tommy want?

"The son of a bitch is probably still around the neighborhood," said Stumps. "You could have walked past him on the sidewalk today." He gave a quick deploring shake of the head and picked up his glass.

Cooper watched him suck the beer in past his white stubble. "You don't think it was an outsider, huh? If I was going to knock over a store I'd go farther afield."

"Yeah, well you're not stupid," said Stumps. "Your brain ain't fried. Ten to one they find the guy, he's a dope-head. Needed the money fast, remembered the store down on the corner. And killed the guy and his wife 'cause they'd seen him before."

"Could be." Cooper shook his head. He'd come into the old-times' bar on an impulse after calling it a night with the cab, curious to see how Stumps had weathered his thrashing. He'd found the old man drinking in solitude, as far as he could tell none the worse for wear. The talk had turned quickly to a recent atrocity in the neighborhood, the killing of a Korean shopkeeper and his wife.

"They know who they're looking for," Stumps went on. "No more'n twenty years old, puts everything he gets up his nose. Hell, I bet I can tell you what building he lives in. One of those dumps down around Ashland, Pratt, Farwell, in there. And black as the ace of spades."

Copper looked past Stumps, back into the dark recesses of the bar. "That's an easy guess, considering the demographics of crime in this city," he said. "But don't get too fixed on it. There's plenty of white people who'll kill you for what's in your wallet."

"Hell, yeah." Stumps looked at him hard for a moment and then said, "Look, don't get me wrong. Man could be purple, it don't make no difference to me. I got no problem with nobody because of the color of their skin. Or because they come in here from somewhere else. Hell, I walk around this neighborhood sometimes, could be south of the border for all I can tell. I don't have no problems with that. What gives me a royal pain in the ass is how you can kill somebody in this country and they give you six years in jail." Stumps shook his head and swayed a bit, staggered by the thought. "That ain't right. Murder's too cheap anymore."

"I'm with you there. But the jails are full. What are you going to do?"

"Start frying a few of 'em, clear out a few cells."

"Or stop putting people in there who shouldn't be there."

Stumps cast a suspicious glance at him. "And if you try and defend yourself, you're the one who's the criminal."

Cooper shook his head. "Yeah, I guess I finally decided the Second Amendment means what it says."

"Damn straight it means what it says. You keep a weapon around?"

"No." Cooper shook his head. "I haven't felt threatened enough. Or ready to take on all the responsibilities that come with it."

"Get yourself one. With these drug gangs bringing in the automatic weapons, get yourself a fuckin' machine gun if you can."

"Jesus, it's not a war yet, Stumps."

"It's getting close." The old man leaned close to Cooper, plucking at his sleeve. "I'll tell you a secret."

"OK."

"Over there in the church. Where I stay, you know?"

"The church?" Cooper frowned at him.

"St. Stephen's. I keep the place clean, fix things up, lock it up at night. Father Doyle lets me sleep in a little room in the basement over there. They got storerooms and places they don't know what to do with down there."

"Uh-huh."

"And we been broke into at least five times. I finally got tired of it." Stumps glanced over his shoulder, breathed alcohol fumes into Cooper's face and said, "I got me some firepower." The ravaged face receded a bit, the eyes narrowing in a wicked smile.

"What kind of firepower?" said Cooper.

"I got me an old Browning shotgun used to belong to my brother. He loved to hunt ducks but he couldn't shoot worth shit, so he got an automatic. He figured he'd have to hit something if he put enough lead up there. Half the time you couldn't eat what was left of the birds, there was so much shot in 'em. Anyway, I snuck it out of his closet when he died. Hauled it over to the church, got a hacksaw and sawed off the barrel and the stock. That son of a bitch lays down real nice between the mattress and the wall, where I can get at it fast, and it'll put out almost as much lead almost as fast as a submachine gun."

Cooper smiled, faintly. "If the Medellín Cartel decides to invade the church, you're all set."

"I hope I don't never have to use it, but if I do, there's gonna be some very surprised criminal types laying on the floor."

"Father Doyle doesn't know it's there, I take it."

Stumps shook his head, still grinning. "Father Doyle thinks he was smart to find the whiskey I keep down there."

Cooper shook his head slowly. "You're a public menace, Stumps."

"No, I ain't. I just ain't gonna let the bastards walk away with everything, that's all."

Cooper waved a couple of bills at the bartender. "Well, I'm like you. I hope to God you have to use it." He slid off the barstool.

"If I do," said Stumps, "I won't be the one to regret it." He waved an unsteady hand in farewell.

Cooper stood at the door of the bar looking up and down the street. It was just past eleven and he wasn't sleepy; he could move up the street to Burk's and try and get in a game of pool, or he could go home and tackle the stack of books on the old oak desk, or just put his feet up on the windowsill and look out at the trees and wait for Diana.

She could be out a while, if she'd taken Tommy down to the Halsted blues bar or someplace like that. She'd ring his bell in the wee hours, come in smelling of smoke, breathe beer in his face as she kissed him. He felt it for a moment, just a twinge of jealousy, thinking of her with big handsome Tommy, bar hopping, maybe even dancing together.

Aw grow up, Cooper told himself. Diana was embarrassed by the whole thing, anxious to get rid of the guy. She'd asked Cooper to come along, for Christ's sake. Cooper meandered up the street toward where he'd parked the taxi, reproaching himself for not taking her up on the invitation. He would have enjoyed the music and it would have averted these petty suspicions. But then wasn't it better to show her he trusted her? He'd wanted her to know she could deal with Tommy however she felt best without worrying about him. But maybe she had felt it best that he come along and had been disappointed when he'd said no.

Hell, the only thing to do was go home and wait for her, act as if he hadn't given any of this a second thought. Cooper unlocked the cab and got in and started it. He glanced at his watch again. They might have gone to an early show, if Diana had wanted to get it over early and get back to his place, just to show him she wasn't going to have too much fun with the guy. She might have come over, or more likely called, while he was in there drinking with Stumps. If she hadn't found him, she'd have gone back to her place with Tommy. It was worth a spin by there to see if they were there, killing the bottle of wine.

Cooper nipped over to Ashland and sped north, making the lights. It was interesting to see a chapter of Diana's past, the distant past, the part Cooper had never quite gotten straight. He knew about college in the States and her unhappy return to San Juan, looking for a place where the daughter of a German painter and a Puerto Rican doctor could be happy. And he knew all about her doomed marriage to a Miami cop. But between the two there was a part she'd skated over a bit quickly, the Caribbean adventure period. A period that had included Tommy Thorne.

Cooper smiled at the thought of some faces from his past showing up on his doorstep. There were people he'd run with in L.A. whom he'd *pay* to stay away.

He turned onto Diana's street and grabbed the first parking place he saw. He had to walk another couple of hundred feet to get to her place, and as he approached it he slowed and finally stopped. Diana's apartment was on the second floor, and from the sidewalk he could see the upper half of her living room. The curtains were not drawn and he could see in the side window of the bay, past the fringe of plants on the sill, to where a tall figure stood silhouetted against the soft light of a lamp. Tommy stopped talking and took a drink of something in a glass. Cooper could see the ice cubes glinting in the lamplight. The glass was lowered out of sight and then Tommy bent over, almost out of sight, only the back of his head and his broad shoulders visible as he leaned over somebody in the armchair in the bay. After a moment he stood up and Diana rose into view from the chair. Cooper stepped off the sidewalk onto the grass and moved close to the trunk of a tree. All he could see above the plants was Diana's head and shoulders; she was staring intently up at Tommy as he spoke. She was backlit and he couldn't make out her expression, but he could see the stillness of her bearing. Suddenly she was gone, away into the depths of the room, and after another sip from the glass Tommy followed with an unhurried step.

Cooper stood leaning on the tree looking into the empty bay, waiting to see more, debating whether to ring the bell. He wasn't sure what he'd seen, but he didn't think it was catching up on old times. Finally he told himself he trusted her, and went home.

Well past midnight the doorbell roused him from an uneasy doze on the couch, and Diana came stealing in from the landing with a smile and a kiss. "Sorry to wake you," she said.

"That's OK." He was still groggy and he went back to the couch and watched her shed her jacket and purse. "How'd you spend the evening?" he said.

"We went down to Lincoln Avenue to hear some blues band I'd never heard of. Tommy said their guitar player was a hero of his."

"Huh." Cooper rubbed at his eyes and looked at his watch, feeling a malicious desire to ask for details.

"I'll tell you all about it tomorrow," Diana said, a gentle hand on his cheek. "Let's get you to bed now." She smiled and Cooper calculated that if they'd gone out right after he'd seen them at Diana's, they had paid a hefty cover charge for no more than an hour's stay. He supposed it was just barely possible. He let Diana lead him into the bedroom, resisting the urge to tell her that she didn't smell like smoke.

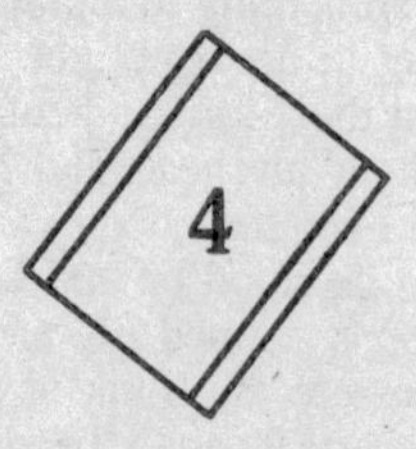

COOPER DROPPED A Personage in a Dark Blue Suit at the Hilton downtown and then got flagged down by a Lady on a Shopping Spree; she wanted to go up Michigan to Water Tower Place even though she could barely carry the packages she already had. Her eyes were glazed with the effort. Cooper fought his way slowly up Michigan, chafing. There were days when he was in the groove and the worst traffic in the world wouldn't bother him, and others like today when he wanted to pull the thing over at the curb and leave it, just walk away and let the lady stare after him.

He fought his way to the curb at Water Tower Place and was rewarded with a long suspicious stare at the meter and no tip. A Boy Wonder in an expensive raincoat commandeered him and wanted to go north; that was fine with Cooper, who was sick of fighting his way around the Loop.

Pushing toward the tunnel to Lake Shore Drive, Cooper glanced up at the hotel. He could see the windows of the very pricey restaurant, and he wondered if Diana was at work. No, not for an hour or so yet. The tightness in his stomach returned.

He'd convinced himself that she hadn't lied to him, that what he'd seen through her window was entirely innocent. But the doubt lay deep down, stirring occasionally. Today she'd planned to take Tommy out for some pavement-pounding, find him an apartment. When Cooper had said that Tommy was a big boy and could probably find one all by himself, she had shrugged and said of course, but she didn't have much else to do and he didn't know the city and it would be easier with her car. There had been a moment of tension, the first little perceptible clash, and then she'd run a hand through his hair and smiled her crooked smile and promised to get rid of Tommy as soon as she could.

Speeding north along the Drive, with the vast cool grays of sky and lake opening out on the night, Cooper sighed and told himself that the green-eyed monster was a sly one. Trust had to be strong enough to resist nonsense like this, some oddball from the past landing square in the middle of things. It put her in a difficult position, and Cooper had to allow for that.

So trust her. Cooper started whistling softly, feeling suddenly that all this was going to pass quickly, whatever it was. Diana was solid; he was a fool to doubt her.

Tommy polished off the riff and looked across the room at Diana. "Di-an-a." He smiled as he said the name slowly. "See? I'm working on it. No more Slim. Got to change with the times."

"You want a change that would really make me happy? Go back south and leave me alone." Diana smoldered on the couch, arms folded firmly at her breast, eyes fixed on him.

The thin metallic notes came across the room as he plucked at the strings, frowned, tried it again. He twanged insistently at a string, tuned it, played some more. He shook his head. "This old axe doesn't want to play in tune any more. I may have to take it someplace and have it looked at." He looked at Diana, held her gaze for a while. "Don't tell me you're getting old and conservative on me, Diana."

"What I'm getting is pissed off."

Tommy pursed his lips, rocked forward, and laid the guitar carefully in the open case at his feet. He put his hands on his knees, stood up. "Diana." He came slowly over the rug, padding softly on stockinged feet, shaking his head with a faint bemused grin. "You still don't really have the right perspective on this."

She watched him come, glaring. "My perspective is that I like the way my life's turned out here. I'm happy here, I got nothing to do with you anymore, nothing. I owe you nothing. And now you come crashing in and want me to risk it all for another Tommy Thorne special. That's my perspective. Tell me how that's wrong."

Tommy moved a book aside and sat on the coffee table, facing her, leaning toward her with his elbows on his knees, the smile fading to a wise sad fatherly look. "Here's how it's wrong. One." He ticked it off on his left index finger. "You do owe me something. You owe me for some very high times you couldn't have lived without me."

"You got paid. Whose bed did I share all those months?"

Tommy shook his head sadly. "Don't make yourself out to be a whore, Diana. I never did. What happened with our emotions was a separate thing. I'm talking about the life-style. That was an expensive ride, baby."

"I didn't like it. That's why I bailed out. That's my prerogative, isn't it?"

"Sure. But I'm talking about gratitude, that's all."

"Tommy, don't talk bullshit to me. I'm a big girl now."

"All right, let's go on. Two. I'm not asking you to risk anything here."

"You're asking me to take all the risks, goddammit." Diana rose from the couch and brushed past Tommy's knees to stalk over to the window.

"The risks are minimal."

"For you, yeah. You know what you are? You're a coward. You need a woman to run the risks for you, do the hard part."

Tommy shifted to the couch, taking Diana's place, looking at her back. "Call me names, Slim, I don't care. I'm the one who's run all the risks so far."

"And left the dangerous part for me."

"You don't know half of it. You don't know what risks I've run up to now. But listen. The main reason your perspective is all wrong is because, like I keep on saying, there's financial benefit in this for you. I'm talking windfall here, I'm talking gusher, gold in the pan. Let that in your perspective, see if it doesn't change things a little."

"I don't want your money."

"It's not my money. It's somebody else's money."

"It's theft then."

"Of course it's theft. I told you that from the start. But there's theft and there's theft. You steal an old lady's pension money, that's one kind of theft. That's not what I'm talking about. Diana, for Christ's sake, you know me. The kind of theft I'm talking about is different. I'm talking about the kind of theft where some son of a bitch has piled up so many coconuts from just being a son of a bitch that he won't miss the few you get off the pile. He'll still be rich, and he'll always be a son of a bitch. Hell, I'm talking Robin Hood stuff here."

Diana turned to face him, the corner of her mouth lifted. "You're going to give it all to the poor, huh?"

"I'm offering half of it you, and you ain't exactly Jackie Onassis, baby." Tommy flapped a hand at the room.

Diana spun to face him. "I like it here. It's my home. I put it together with my two hands and my money. Money I *earned.*"

"You'll earn this."

"I don't want it. I have enough."

"Enough to go back to school? That's not what you told me."

That stopped her for a second, just a second. "You're asking me to stick my neck out."

"I'm offering you a job, for a hell of a lot of money. An easy job, a couple of phone calls, a meeting. You don't take it, I'd call that dumb."

Diana stared at him mutely, dumbly, with a sudden desolate need to cry but bitterly determined not ever to cry for Tommy again. She was backed into a corner but he didn't own her, never had and never would. "The answer's no, Tommy," she said.

Tommy sighed and rose to his feet. "Now that pains me, Diana. I'm real sorry to hear you say that." He took a few steps toward her and stopped, shaking his head, looking at her with the same sad wise look. He said, "I was kind of afraid you might say it, though. So I went to the trouble of poking through some old papers I had lying around."

Diana swallowed and felt a long slow sinking inside because she knew it was coming. Here came Tommy's trump card.

The phone rang close to midnight and it was Diana. "Tommy picked me up after work 'cause I lent him my car today and he wants to buy me a drink. We'll make it a quick one and then I'll drop him off at my place and come by. Is that OK?"

Cooper settled onto the couch. "That's fine. You don't have to check in, you know."

"I wanted to let you know, that's all." There was a brief pause, both of them feeling for irritation in the other. "How was the driving today?" she said in a softer tone.

"Tedious. I'm still seeing tail lights when I close my eyes. How was the waiting?"

"The same. But reasonably profitable."

"Good. Have a drink for me. Say hi to Tommy."

"Will do. I won't be long. Wait up for me."

Cooper tried, but he had dozed off again when the bell jarred him awake. Diana swept in from the landing in her long black skirt, fancy waitress clothes. She planted a long probing kiss on his mouth, tasting of liquor. "Meet me in the bedroom," she said.

Cooper woke up a bit. While Diana was in the bathroom he prowled around the place, turning off lights. He needed to use the toilet himself and he sat on the edge of the bed with his shirt off, scratching, wondering how many drinks she'd had.

When Diana came out of the bathroom she was halfway out of her clothes, down to the sheer bra and bikini panties, her sleek limbs golden in the lamplight. She tossed her clothes in a heap on the chair and said, "Tommy went looking for a place today. He'll be out of our hair before too long."

"You're more worried about it than I am," said Cooper, not entirely truthfully. He looked at her body, seeing it anew tonight, lithe and strong and warm.

"It's weird, having him here." She shook her head absently and Cooper saw stress or irritation or something else he couldn't pin down.

"Forget the guy. There's nobody here but you and me."

She relaxed visibly and came and stood in front of him where he sat on the bed. She took his hands and pulled him to his feet. "You're overdressed," she said.

"Give me a minute."

When Cooper emerged in his turn he halted at the bedroom door because the sight was breathtaking. The sheet was peeled down to the foot of the bed and Diana lay in naked splendor in the soft glow from the lamp, her hair spreading tongues of flame across the pillow, one hand resting on her concave belly, the other thrown out across the white sheet, long supple legs converging at a geometrically precise triangle of hair, breasts rising and falling gently with her respiration. She had been staring at the ceiling, but she turned her head to look at Cooper in the doorway. "You don't seem to have lost any of those clothes," she said.

Cooper managed to lose them between the door and the bed, clumsily. He smiled, thinking that he probably owed Tommy Thorne a word of thanks; he figured it was partly Diana's guilt at running around with the guy that had brought her in like this, anxious to please.

As soon as he hit the mattress she had him, rolling him over, pinning him beneath her. "I can taste you already," she breathed, her lips very close to his, and he could taste her, too: a whiff of liquor, a breath of passion. Her tongue came into his mouth and he was her captive for a long suspended moment, and then she was moving down, tasting other parts of him, biting, teasing, tenderly exploring throat, chest, nipples, stomach, the pale twisted scars left by flying metal, the thin trail of hair leading down from his navel.

She rose above him on all fours and he looked at the play of the muscles just beneath the lightly freckled skin of the shoulders, the small round breasts with their dark nipples, the hair falling through the lamplight. He held his breath at the beauty of her and grasped her wrists and wrestled her onto her back. She was his captive now, and he felt for words to tell her of the desire she aroused in him and how the desire was enriched by all the rest of it, but he gave up; there were no words for that. She watched him from the depths of those bottomless Iberian eyes, silent, while he ran a hand slowly down the length of her. With the soft, hidden swell of the pudendum cupped in the palm of his hand, he thought once again that he was the luckiest man on the face of the Earth; fortune had smiled on Cooper MacLeish, in the person of this woman.

Diana turned the key as softly as she could, trying to mute the clicking of the lock. She eased in through the door, peeking into the living room, hoping. She closed the door but didn't lock it, not wanting the noise. The floor creaked as she stepped into the living room and there was a rustle from the sofa and Tommy sat up, a tousled head appearing above the back of the sofa.

"Sorry to wake you," Diana said sourly. She put her purse on the table, next to the phone, and took off her jacket.

Tommy swung his feet to the floor and rubbed his face. "No problem. I was awake. Just lying here daydreaming about good times to come." He yawned.

Diana scowled at the back of his head. "You could sleep in the bedroom, you know. I'll put clean sheets on if you want."

"Naw, the sofa's fine. Don't want to make trouble."

Diana stalked to the bay windows and wrenched open the curtains. "Save the irony."

Perched on the edge of the sofa in his jockey shorts, Tommy watched her move around the room. "You got up on the wrong side of the bed this morning, huh?"

"Put some clothes on." She went back into the kitchen. At least he wasn't making a mess, she thought, surveying it. There was a beer bottle and a single plate in the sink; the counters were clean. She pottered around, making work for herself: scrubbing the stovetop, sweeping the floor. She heard Tommy go into the bathroom, heard the toilet flush, scowled when she heard him come out again.

Tommy was right about her morning; she was as jumpy as a cat, guilt-ridden for splitting too soon from a comfortable intimate breakfast with Cooper, explaining it with more lies.

Stop lying to Cooper, she told herself. That's the worst thing Tommy's done, the worst he could do, to make me lie to Cooper. She froze with the broom in her hands, suddenly resolved to level with Cooper, come what may.

Come what may? Jesus, dear God, there were dangers she just couldn't risk. She had one chance left, the chance that had brought her over here. She heard Tommy rummaging in his things out in the living room. Take a shower, you stinking bastard.

Her heart began to beat quickly when she heard him go back into the bathroom, heard the water start to run. She gave him two minutes, then set the broom aside and walked quickly, softly, into the living room. Clothes spilled out of his duffel bag against the wall, next to the guitar case. His jeans were draped over the back of the straight chair in the corner; wallet and keys were on the seat of the chair. Diana went swiftly over and picked up the wallet. She rifled it with a few quick strokes of her fingers, whisking out and replacing licenses, business cards, stray slips of paper, a few bills, none larger than a twenty. She dropped the wallet back on the chair and went to the duffel bag. She pushed her hands deep into it, rummaging, listening anxiously to the distant plashing of the shower.

Pay dirt. She felt leather and pulled at it, freeing it from the clutch of clothing deep in the bag. It was a large, stiff leather wallet, bound with a clasp. The clasp was held with a small lock. Diana whirled to look at Tommy's keys lying on the chair; as she did so she saw Tommy standing in the doorway from the hall, shirtless, a bath towel around his waist.

"Diana." He said the name slowly, as if trying out the sounds. He came forward into the room, completely dry; he'd never stepped into the shower. Diana straightened up, meeting his grave stare, heart pounding but determined to stand up to him.

Tommy came across the rug slowly and took the wallet from her, shaking his head, starting to look concerned, puzzled. "I don't understand you, Diana," he said. He held the wallet in both hands, looking down at it. Suddenly he brandished it in her face. "There's more in here than just what you're looking for," he said. "What's in here is going to make us rich. Can't you understand that? It's going to make us rich, Diana. Me and you. What I'm offering you is a fifty-fifty split. That's generous. Hell, that's Christmas morning for you. I don't understand why you can't look on the bright side of it. Shit, I don't want to pressure you—all that was just insurance. In three days you can tear it up or burn it or flush it down the john. I was hoping I wouldn't even have to pull it out. But I need your help, Diana. And I'm offering you the world. Just like they used to tell 'em on the *Bismarck,* remember? The world, baby, with the kind of money I'm talking about. You can call me a blackmailer if you want, but hey—this is your ship, Slim, and it's come in."

Diana stared at him for a long time, looking into those blue eyes, thinking about things long past, things to come. Finally she said, "OK Tommy, you win."

Tommy smiled, that great charming smile that had won him friends from Curaçao all the way to L.A. "Naw, we're both winners now. And I promise you one thing, Slim. You won't be sorry."

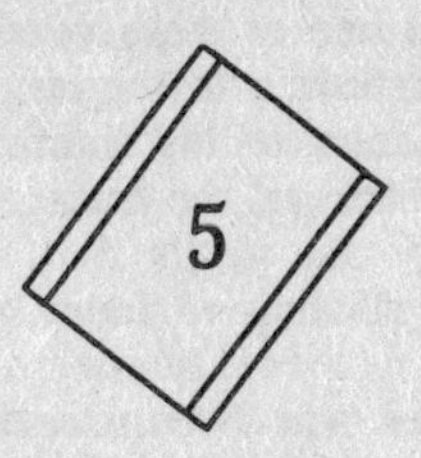

MAJOR TORSO TRAUMA, thought Cooper, that's what we've got here. The diaphragm is about to tear loose from its moorings. Slow down, for Christ's sake. No reason to kill yourself. Especially not this early in the year, only the third time out . . . but then if you push it through this last lap, burn it all the way to the end, you can dog it on the way home.

Wheezing, pounding, lurching, Cooper labored through the last turn and saw the homestretch ahead, one hundred yards of dark red all-weather track and fifteen seconds of agony. He ran with a terrible fixed gaze and the slightly lopsided stride of a man who long ago took two 7.62mm rifle rounds in the right thigh, but he ran.

Just put one foot in front of the other. You can throw up later. And dog it all the way home. . . . Christ, hit the wall. Hit that wall they talk about, where the legs get leaden and the lungs . . . give . . . out! Cooper leaned across the finish line, pressing the button on the cheap plastic stopwatch, and lumbered to a halt, running out of track and fetching up against the fence.

Sucker. Got you again.

No matter how often Cooper resolved to take it easy on himself when he headed down to the track, the fear of growing old and lazy and the sight of the final stretch of track ahead always brought out the kick, the need to wring himself dry. He staggered away from the fence, gasping for air. He did feel like throwing up, but he knew it would pass. He looked at the watch. 15:03, slow. Cooper shook his head, wondering if it was time to admit he would never again break thirteen minutes in the two-mile.

Hell, it's early in the year. Come July I'll be there again.

Cooper knew that one of these years he wouldn't, that it would be time to lower his sights, to concede something to the completion of his fourth decade on Earth. He walked slowly back up the track under the gray sky, buffeted a little by the winds that had made the run harder, the nausea starting to fade, his diaphragm still functioning.

Hell, four decades was two more than he'd had any right to expect at age nineteen. Cooper was still feeling lucky today. Lucky to be alive, lucky to share his bed with the woman who'd come sweeping in from the landing last night. And that had brought him down to the track today, the thought that he owed it to that woman to take care of the battered old body she seemed to take pleasure in—keep it running, keep it strong, keep it for God's sake under a hundred and eighty pounds at least.

He left the track and started jogging, dogging it just as he'd promised himself, but knowing he would push it again down the last block to his place, because he would have to. Dodging co-eds, he left the Loyola campus and headed up Sheridan Road, feeling good. For past forty and been shot up and kicked around a little, he was in pretty good shape. Cooper picked up the pace a little.

He saw Diana's car as he crossed Albion. Even as a pedestrian, Cooper automatically scanned traffic on the road, from long habit. The old white Volvo was coming down Sheridan toward him at a fairly good clip. He had time to recognize it and start to raise his hand in greeting, hoping she'd see him, and then the car was flying past, with Tommy at the wheel.

Cooper spun around and ran backwards for a few steps, seeing the back of Diana's head in the passenger seat, watching the Volvo disappear. Tommy driving, Diana in the passenger seat. He shook his head a little and went on up the street.

He pushed it even harder than he usually did down the last block to his place. Recovering, he shambled up and down the sidewalk with his hands on his hips, wondering why the hell Tommy was driving. If Diana had lent him the car, OK, but she was with him. Why would she let the son of a bitch drive?

Maybe he was dropping her off somewhere before taking the car to go apartment hunting again. In which case, Cooper heartily approved. The sooner he was in his own place the better. The guy was starting, just a bit, to get on his nerves, and he'd only talked to him once. He wasn't even intruding really; Diana wasn't spending any less time with Cooper than before. And what she did with her time was her business.

Give it a rest, then. Cooper mounted the steps to his front door, looking back toward Sheridan Road as if expecting to see the old white Volvo again. He paused with his hand on the door, wondering why the image of Tommy speeding down Sheridan at the wheel of Diana's car bothered him.

It was an image of control, he decided. It looked like Tommy was in control, and he didn't like that. But then there had to be an innocent explanation. He pushed the door open.

Had to be.

"OK, you've seen the place, you know how it's going to work." Tommy looked steadily at Diana over the rim of his glass. The bar they had picked at random was empty but for them, and the street beyond the big etched-glass windows was quiet in the midafternoon lull. Diana could see tree branches tossing in the wind against a thick gray sky. It was a calming view and she wanted to walk out of the place and take a long solitary ramble through quiet unfamiliar streets. But here in the aqueous light at the back of the bar, Tommy was looking at her.

"Yeah, I've seen it," she said, barely audible.

"Then it's cake. You talk to the man and you split."

"Having made a mortal enemy." Diana stared back at Tommy, keeping her face free of expression.

Tommy shrugged, a little movement of the head, a little raising of the brows. "I never said there was no risk. Just that the rewards outweigh the minimal risks."

"Minimal for you. Like for any pimp."

Tommy's smile widened slowly. "You're losing perspective again."

"Tommy." Diana shoved her drink aside with a finger

and put her arms on the table to lean closer to him, glancing at the bartender bent over his paper at the far end of the place. "I have to live here. It's all very well for you to say the man won't know me from Eve, but consider this. If this guy's as rich as you say he is, then I've probably waited on him. Or else I'm going to, sooner or later. What do I do two months from now when the man I helped blackmail walks in and sits down at my table? Blush and bat my eyelashes at him?"

"Two months from now your waitressing days will be ancient history. You won't have to live here. You'll be able to live anyplace you want."

There was tightly reined fierceness in Diana's voice. "I like it here. This is my home. The man I love lives here. An itinerant good-for-nothing like you may never put down roots, but a lot of people do. And you're trying to tear mine out."

"Take Sergeant Rock along, for Christ's sake. With the kind of money you'll have, both of you will be able to set up anywhere you please."

It was futile, Diana knew. She leaned back again, and her eyes left Tommy's. She looked out the window for a long time while Tommy sat sipping beer and tapping a foot to the tune coming softly over the stereo system.

"So who is this guy?" she said finally.

"You never heard the name?"

"No, I told you."

"That's good. The less you know about him, the safer it is for you."

"How the hell is it safer for me? He'll *think* I know, whether I do or not."

"Nah. All you have to do is tell him you're just a messenger."

"And he'll believe me."

"Maybe not. But it's still safer if you really are just a messenger."

"Safer for you, for sure."

Tommy cocked his head at her. "Perspective, Diana."

Diana sipped her vodka and tonic. "What if I can't get through to him?"

"You'll get through. He's in town—I found that out with all the phoning yesterday. And if you use the name Gladstone Drake, that'll get him to the phone. Then you just say you're a friend of Gladstone's, in town for a couple of days and you'd like to talk to him. That'll get him to the bar, especially if you use your come-up-and-see-me voice, with a bit of the accent maybe."

"He'll see through it all right away. He'll find out I'm not saying at the hotel . . ."

". . . and he'll call Drake and find out he doesn't know anybody like you," Tommy said wearily. "I told you. It doesn't matter. All of that's just to get him to a table across from you, so you can give him the envelope and set your terms. Then you book, fast and clean. Like I showed you."

"What if he investigates a little beforehand, calls this Gladstone before he decides to show up?"

"He won't. He'll come running. But even if he does, remember I'll be watching. You check with me before you even walk in. If anything smells, we stand him up."

Diana went back to staring out the window, wanting to cry again. She wondered where Cooper was and what he was doing and if he would be able to help her if she disobeyed Tommy and told him about it.

She decided she was on her own. She couldn't risk it, not with Tommy holding that trump card, and if things went as Tommy said, it might even work. Tommy had made a career of this, after all. Her eyes flicked to his again. "You better be right, Tommy."

"I'm right, Slim." Tommy raised his glass. "Right on the money. And here's to you. To the Pirate Queen of the Caribbean."

"It's a matter of principle," said Barry. "In a world where war is capable of ending all human life, pacifism is the only principled position."

Cooper shook his head. "The *only* principled position?" He took a drink of Guinness and glanced down the bar toward the door, looking in vain for Diana and Tommy. Diana had said they'd meet him at the Chinese place at nine, but when Cooper had shown up the only person at the bar had been Barry.

"It's the only position that can in principle end war. Prepare for war, you'll get war."

"Maybe. But don't prepare for war, and you'll sure as hell lose the next one that comes along."

"Declare your refusal to participate in war, and you will remove a necessary condition for war. It takes two to make a fight."

"Yeah, but it only takes one to make a victim."

"Sometimes there's strength in that. Look at Gandhi."

"OK, let's look at him. He wasn't facing armed attack from a hostile power. Colonization is a different kettle of fish. And I'll grant you, his way of resistance was pretty damn good against that. I got nothing against Gandhi. But remember, he was dealing with a relatively enlightened British government. OK, accent the relatively. But if Gandhi had been dealing with Hitler, he would have been a grease spot in the road, and they'd be speaking German in Neue Delhi today."

"That kind of speculation isn't really an argument."

"OK, here's an argument. I'd argue that the Jews in the Warsaw ghetto were perfectly justified in shooting as many Nazis as they could. Shooting to kill."

Barry smiled, sadly as always. "I may have to concede that. But we're hardly the Jews in the ghetto. We're the world's greatest military power, with the ability to destroy the Earth."

"Stop a second. You conceded all I'm trying to get you to concede. You're not a pacifist."

"Not an absolute pacifist, perhaps. But definitely an opponent of the military culture. Definitely opposed to the maintenance of a military establishment. Military power corrupts. You have to brutalize people to make them into soldiers."

Cooper smiled into his beer. "Nobody knows that better than me, pal. But here's the thing about soldiers. You never know when you're going to need 'em. I know, you keep them around for years, take these young guys and teach them to kill people, brutalize them, and all they do is burn money and corrupt the garrison towns and tear up the landscape. And they get used for the wrong things a lot, too. I'll give you that. But every once in a while a Hitler comes along. Or a Stalin. Or an Idi Amin or an Abu Nidal or a Pol Pot. And then you've got to have 'em, Barry. You've got to have those guys who are prepared to pull the trigger without asking questions, because people like Pol Pot don't wait for questions."

Barry stared at him for a moment, very still, sadness spreading over his long soulful face under the salt-and-pepper hair. "You know what I just can't understand?" he said. "I just can't understand how you could hate a person enough to point a gun at him and kill him. I just can't understand that."

Cooper opened his mouth but couldn't find words, seeing that Barry really didn't understand the basics. "You don't have to hate anyone, Barry. Hate may be one reason to kill but it's not the only one. Look . . . walk up to a mother with a small child, try and snatch the child—I guarantee you'll have a homicidal lady on your hands. I didn't hate those little fuckers in the pith helmets, not at first anyway. But they scared the living shit out of me, and that was enough. You don't need hate at all. Fear will do it. Fear will do it every time, man."

Cooper didn't know how long Diana had been standing behind him; he felt a hand on his shoulder and then she said, "Don't let me break things up, but could we squeeze in here?" Tommy was with her, and Cooper was glad to see them. He kissed her lightly with relief and said hi to Tommy, resplendent in a black velvet jacket over a green T-shirt. Cooper and Barry made room for Diana and Tommy between them, introductions were made, and Diana said, "Sorry we're late. Our dinner was delayed by criminally incompetent service."

"Don't ever take a waitress out to dinner," said Tommy. "It's like sitting down to listen to records with Toscanini." He settled easily onto his stool, smiling his photogenic smile.

"No, really. This girl was bad," said Diana. "I doubt if she can get her own breakfast to the kitchen table in the morning." After an account of their tribulations at dinner,

Diana looked at Cooper and said, "Want to come with us and hear some music?"

Cooper blinked at her. "You just got here. Have a drink for Christ's sake."

"I mean later. We're going downtown to hear some blues. Thought you'd want to come along this time."

Cooper had a moment to ruminate while Diana and Tommy ordered drinks and Barry faded away. He really didn't have the slightest desire to go, but he thought perhaps Diana wanted him along. He shrugged and took a drink of beer. Tommy was looking at him. A bit maliciously, Cooper said, "How's the apartment hunt going?"

"Slow." Tommy tossed a bill on the bar and shook his head. "I'm still feeling out the town, figuring how much I can afford."

"Where are you looking?"

"Here and there. Looking in the paper, checking out places all over." He busied himself stirring his drink.

Cooper decided not to press him. He could feel Diana looking at him. "Rents must be a lot higher here than where you've been."

Tommy shrugged. "What you'd expect."

"What's Guadeloupe like?"

"Hot. Colorful. Smells. You know the tropics."

"Yeah. You said you'd been island hopping. Where you coming from now?"

Tommy looked at him for a moment before answering. "Trinidad."

"Next to Tobago."

"Right."

"Which is fairly far down the chain towards Venezuela, if I recall. And that's all I know about it. What's it like?"

Tommy shrugged and Cooper expected him to say hot, colorful and it smells, but after a sip from his drink he said, "It's different. It's wild." He paused, his eyes drifting from Cooper's face, remembering. "Rain forest, beach, mountains. Incredible wildlife. Sixty different kinds of bat. Rain like the end of the world, and then a sun so hot you have to hide from it. The most beautiful seascape there is.

People everywhere, most of 'em black and most of 'em poor. But cool—the people are cool, laid way back. You can live cheap, live like a king. Terrific music, all the time, everywhere. A rhythm connoisseur's paradise. And food. Seafood, tropical fruits you never dreamed existed. Good things for your head. Maybe too good. As much rum as you can hold and unbelievable dope." Tommy shook his head once, the glass at his lips. "You sit out on the porch and watch a storm sweep across the bay and never want to come back."

After a pause Cooper said, "Why did you?"

Tommy shrugged. "I used up all my money. Ran out of jobs and the energy to hustle for them. Just gave in to the place. Woke up one day nearly broke and tired of the tropics, like I said."

"There are worse ways to use up your money, I suppose."

"Probably better ones, too. But I guess I needed the rest."

"Yeah, sounds like a rough life down there." Cooper wasn't really trying to bait him, not consciously at least, and he was startled by the quick hard look Tommy shot him. Conciliatory, he said, "I could probably use the rest myself."

"I'd recommend it," said Tommy, "for a while anyway." He smiled again, looking at Diana.

Cooper turned to her and said, "How about it? Want to head down there, oh, say come December?"

Diana was staring at Tommy and it took her a second to disengage. She looked at Cooper and smiled softly and said, "Sure. Sounds great."

It lacked conviction and Cooper was suddenly annoyed again by the feeling that there were things going on that he wasn't privy to. He took refuge in his beer, suppressing the irritation.

"Make a real holiday of it," said Tommy. "Take a whole year. Charter yourselves a boat, start at the Virgins and work your way down. That's the only way to do it."

"Charter a boat?" Cooper said. "Who do you think you're talking to, Aristotle and Jackie?"

"You never know when you might come into some money." Tommy smiled at Diana again.

"You never know," she said, deadpan. She turned to Cooper and said, "So, you coming with us?"

He tried to read her look but he couldn't. He was on the verge of saying why not, but then he weighed a couple of hours of being polite to Tommy against going home to bed and hesitated. What tipped the scales was just the slightest touch of malice, the desire to show Diana he wasn't going to run after her if she was trying to make him jealous. "No, you two go on. I drove all day and I'm whipped. I'm going to hit the sack. You got the spare key, right? I won't wait up."

He saw just a hint of pleading in Diana's eyes, which made him uncomfortable, but he was too stubborn to waver. Diana took a drink and said, "You're not going old and conservative on me, are you Cooper?"

"NOW THAT IS an unbelievable piece." Moss Wetzel shook his head in reverent wonder. "Where in the hell did you find this girl?"

The shirt-sleeved production manager stood looking at him with a bored expression. "She's an L.A. whore like the rest of 'em, Moss. Agencies out there got hundreds of these broads."

"No, but I mean really. Those eyes." Moss swept a hand over the glossy proofs laid out on the desk. In the photos, a young woman of arresting beauty sprawled on a couch, bent over a chair or writhed on a bed, mostly without clothes, sometimes in lingerie of dubious utility.

"It's not the eyes I notice first," said the production manager.

"That raven hair. That skin. What is she, Mexican?"

"Probably. Who the hell knows, out there? Could be Filipino or something."

"These are good. These are real good." Moss sifted through the photos slowly, feeling a stir of arousal. These were good enough that he might just have to have the girl flown in. He could have Dunlap locate her through the agency, bring her in for a week or so. "Christ, look at the curve of that ass, just that bit of black hair peeking out there. Now that's artistry. That's a Pornography Hall of Fame shot there. That'll put hair on some palms this month, huh?"

"It oughta do that, yeah." The production manager gathered up the pictures as Moss shoved them across the desk. Moss watched him leave the office, thinking with satisfaction that while other men would have to sneak off to the bathroom with those pictures, he, Moss Wetzel, could have the real thing flown in at the snap of his fingers. He stirred in his chair, wondering if he ought to cancel the next hour or so of appointments and have Nora come up for a while. That was the kind of option he had—he, Moss Wetzel, publisher of *Maverick* magazine, a captain of industry.

That was really what he was, Moss thought, a captain of industry. He smiled at the thought, toying with his gold-plated Mont Blanc fountain pen, looking across his broad teak desk out the window at the lake beyond the manic geometry of the Loop. Moss prided himself on not having any delusions about the industry he was in. Moss knew he was a captain of the great Masturbation Industry, a billion-dollar gold mine. He was the Lee Iacocca of cooze. There were at least 50 million slobs out there who needed a little fantasy in their lives and, not incidentally, were willing to pay exorbitantly each month for it.

But he, Moss Wetzel—he had the real thing. He had a harem, for Christ's sake, just like an Oriental potentate, whatever the hell a potentate was. Moss sat in his plush leather executive chair and felt the stirring in his loins and smiled more broadly at the thought that he could have Nora up here in two minutes or, if he was willing to wait a bit, Jessie or Kareema or Sally or Brandy or shit, just about anyone he had a taste for, to take care of him. He glanced at the long gray leather sofa on the opposite wall and sighed and looked at his calendar. He decided he would restrain himself, exercise his iron will, and take care of business for a while.

Moss rose from behind the desk to his full five feet six inches, absently smoothing the sides of his tailored wool gabardine jacket, running a hand lightly over his thick brown exquisitely cut hair. He strode to the window and took a look down at the distant silent commotion in the streets, thinking of all the copies of *Maverick* that were being purveyed (one of this favorite words) in the several-block area he could see. He raised his eyes to the haze-masked farther reaches of the city.

Fuck you all, he thought, silently addressing the greeting to the hapless residents of the Southwest Side neighborhood where his unhappy childhood and adolescence had been played out. I made it, you sorry bastards. I'm sitting on top of a gold mine, dressed in the finest products of the tailor's art, dining on the creations of the city's finest chefs, chauffeured each night to an Oak Brook estate populated by the kind of women you losers would kill to get a close look at.

Or pay to drool over in the pages of *Maverick,* my magazine. The rag I rescued eight years ago with the money I made in cutthroat real estate. The magazine I made over, slicked up, juiced up, smarted up. Coming up fast on *Penthouse,* leaving the sleazier stroke books behind, challenging the Big Two for preeminence in the sophisticated pornography market. And making a fucking bundle.

Moss thought for a second he might reward himself after all, but then his iron will asserted itself and he went back to the desk. He took a Barclay out of the inlaid cigarette box on the desk and lit it with his gold Italian lighter. He blew smoke in a stream out over the desk and surveyed the papers there. He did have a couple of things to attend to. He had to get on Murray's ass about the First Amendment Alert column thing—if they were going to start it in the August issue they had to get moving. If Murray couldn't find some bright son of a bitch who could write a few hundred words in defense of the right to purvey good old-fashioned snatch, he'd write it himself. And

Rickett had promised him the proofs of the Neighborhood Nymphs layout later this afternoon. But the main thing was to get old Butt-face the accountant in here and go over these figures. That would take a little time. Moss sighed again, a captain of industry at the helm, and settled onto his chair again.

The phone on his desk buzzed softly and he answered it. "Mr. Wetzel," cooed Janet from the outer office.

"Mm," growled Moss. Janet irritated him because she was old, at least thirty-five, and distant and efficient. Moss had grudgingly given up his experiment with Nora when Rickett had pointed out that they needed somebody in the damn office who could type a letter.

He frowned out the window as Janet spoke. "There is a call for you from a rather persistent woman who refuses to identify herself. Apparently the girl downstairs transferred the call despite instructions because the woman would not be put off."

"Well, what does she sound like?" Moss said. "Does she sound nubile and willing?"

Janet's tone was neutral. "I couldn't judge for certain." No, you wouldn't know, would you, thought Moss sourly. "She did say to tell you she's a friend of a . . . Mr. Gladstone Drake."

The name froze Moss for a few seconds. "Gladstone Drake?" he said finally.

"I believe that's the name she gave."

"Yeah, yeah, I know the guy." Moss hesitated a second or two more, his thoughts racing. "If she's a friend of Gladstone Drake's . . ." It was a toss-up, Moss decided. ". . . then sure I'll talk to her. Put her on." In the moment it took to transfer the call, Moss thought hard and decided Gladstone couldn't know anything about all that shit. God knew what this was all about, but if Gladstone was sending him a woman, odds were he would enjoy meeting her.

There was a click in his ear and a woman's voice said, "Hello?"

"Hello there," said Moss at his most jocular. "I understand you come special delivery from my old friend Gladstone."

"I guess you might say that." She certainly sounded

nubile; voices could fool you, but this one was promising, with a bit of a purr to it. "I used to work for him, actually. I do hope I'm not inconveniencing you. My name is Alba Torres and Mr. Drake suggested I call you."

Moss's hand went to the knot of his silk tie and gave it a little tug. "Well, well. I'm glad you did. It's nice to get a bit of a Caribbean breeze up here in the frozen north."

"Not so frozen, really," she said with a nice lilt. "A bit cool comparatively speaking, but rather nice."

Promising, yes. Moss was starting to like the voice. He could detect just a hint of an accent, Spanish. "What can I do for you, er . . . Alba?"

"Well, to come right to the point, I've decided to relocate in Chicago and Mr. Drake said you might be helpful."

"Uh-huh. You worked for Gladstone did you? In what capacity?"

"Several, really. Among other things I used to deal in one of his clubs. Blackjack, I mean."

"Ah, super. Uh . . . I didn't know Gladstone was into anything like that."

"In a small way. I tended bar and did various other things for him as well. Mr. Drake suggested you might find me useful somehow."

"I see, I see. Well." With the promise of that last sentence Moss's misgivings vanished and he was suddenly smitten with gratitude toward that old cannibal Gladstone, for sending him this little present. He could see her, raven-haired like the girl in the pictures probably. He leaned forward, intent now. "Listen, why don't you come on up to the office and we'll chat? I'm sure we'll be able to work something out."

After a brief pause she said, "If you'll excuse me, Mr. Wetzel, I just now got in from the airport and I'm lying down in my hotel room. I was going to suggest that you meet me here for a drink later. I'm sure you're busy now anyway."

"Nothing that couldn't wait, but OK, if that's the way you want it, we'll do it that way. Where are you?"

"I'm at the Palmer House. I saw they have a nice quiet bar downstairs and I thought we could meet there."

"The tavern, you mean, in the Steak House? I know the place. Sure, that's fine. What time?"

"How would five-thirty be? I'm sure you have lots of things to do, so please tell me if this is inconvenient."

"Not at all, Alba. It will be a pleasure. I'll see you there at five-thirty. You sure you wouldn't rather I call for you in your room?"

"Oh no thank you, I'm sure I can find my way down there."

"OK, so how am I going to recognize you?"

"Oh, that's a good question, isn't it? I tell you what, I'll put on my black dress, how's that?"

"I can't wait to see it. Till five-thirty then. Bye."

After he hung up Moss sat with his hand on the phone, staring out the window. When it rains it pours, he thought. Moss my boy, this must be your month for Latin poontang. He remembered the silky voice with the trace of Spanish in it and he could already feel that dark skin next to his. He had to get up and walk to the window.

Holy shit, old Gladstone. Moss had thought he'd heard the last of Trinidad or anybody on it. What a fucking vacation that had turned out to be. But hey, here some good had come of it, right out of left field. A favor from Gladstone Drake, the old cannibal chief himself.

Still and all, Moss couldn't help feeling just a bit uneasy for a moment. That had been very weird, that business down there on the island, and it still gave him the willies a bit to remember it. But Gladstone couldn't know about any of that. Moss had gotten out clean. Better to forget about it.

Moss stood at the window, hearing Alba Torres's voice again and feeling powerful.

Powerful and yes, potent.

Cooper got a cheeseburger and fries at a place on Sheridan and headed out to the park. He drove out along the breakwater at Montrose, parked the cab pointing down toward Indiana and sat on the hood eating and thinking. It was a clear bright day, a respite from the dirty wool skies of the past week. Cooper chewed slowly and thought about Diana.

She'd come in around four, waking him as she crawled in bed, smelling of genuine stale smoke, affectionate in a sodden beery way and then quickly asleep. She hadn't stirred when Cooper had arisen and she had still been asleep when he'd gone out to drive.

In this whole business he was nettled by minor things, like the spare key. For all the nearly two years he and Diana had been together, they hadn't exchanged keys; it had been a symbol of their closely guarded independence, of their respect for the other's privacy. They'd talked of moving in together, stepping warily around the topic of marriage, but they hadn't nerved themselves up to it and they'd gone on ringing each other's bell. Cooper had long considered giving her a key but wanted to wait for some occasion of symbolic importance; to have been forced into it by the importunate visit of a stranger bothered him.

He wanted Tommy gone. He was ninety-nine percent sure there was nothing untoward going on, but he wanted the guy elsewhere. Cooper couldn't really put his finger on anything Tommy had done that had gone over the line, but he had an uneasy feeling about the man. Tommy seemed to have a talent for making himself at home.

Cooper stuffed his trash back in the paper bag and tossed it on the seat of the taxi. He crossed his arms on the roof of the cab and stared down the shore of the lake to the familiar skyline of the Loop. He liked this town, warts and all. He belonged in Chicago, a great blustery town on a cold northern sea. Hearing Tommy talk about the Caribbean had woken him to one reason for his jealousy; Tommy and Diana were both creatures of a mysterious lush south. To Cooper the tropics had meant pain and terror, and he'd never had any desire to go back. But Diana's tropics were something else, and Cooper now wondered if on snowbound Chicago nights she pined for old times under a Caribbean moon.

He'd have to show more interest in it. He'd spoken lightly the night before, but now that he thought about it, it would be good to get away come winter, let Diana take him to San Juan, to the magic island places she remembered from her childhood. Find her roots. He'd gotten a bit set in his ways maybe, resistant to change. So OK, take off.

Things would be good again. As soon as Tommy Thorne was gone.

"I'm sorry, sir, we have no one registered by that name."

Moss scowled, irritated by the unruffled patient female voice. "Gotta be. I talked to her an hour ago. She had just gotten in. Check your recent arrivals."

"I have, sir. No one by the name of Alba Torres has registered today, and that's right up to the last minute."

Moss held the phone away from his face and looked at it in distaste. He took a deep breath and let it out, slowly. He spoke into the phone again. "All right. I'll take your word for it, sugar. You have a terrific day." Moss clapped the phone back on the hook and sagged back on the chair. He glowered out at the lake for a while, his right hand balled into a fist on the desk.

So what the hell does this mean, Moss asked him self. Either the dumb bitch at the desk made a mistake, or Señorita Alba Torres is playing games. Moss started to chew at the thumbnail of his left hand but remembered it would ruin his manicure. He swore softly and bitterly.

After a couple of minutes Moss reached for the phone again and punched out a number. He said, "Send Wes in here, will you?" He hung up and looked for something on his desk to fiddle with, to look busy.

There was a knock on the door and Moss barked "Yeah!" A compact man with short muscled arms hanging from broad shoulders under a red and black batik shirt came into the office.

"You wanted something?" he said.

Moss tossed aside the sheaf of papers and laid down his pen. "Have a seat. Want a drink?"

"I thought I was working." The man sat down on the chair opposite Moss's desk. He leaned back and crossed one leg over the other.

"Yeah, OK, that's great. I forgot you don't drink on

duty. I'm glad you take it seriously and all. Look, I got a weird thing here I wanted to bounce off you."

"Uh-huh." The compact man stared at Moss, unblinking.

A fucking robot, thought Moss, looking at the snub-nosed, pitted round face under the close crop of Brillo-pad hair. "I got a call earlier today from a Spanish broad who said she was a friend of that guy Drake's, down in Trinidad, you know?" Moss paused to let Wes nod or say uh-huh or anything, but he got no response. "She gave me the big come-on, told me Drake had sent her up here to make herself useful to me, she actually said that. Said she was staying at the Palmer House and she wanted to meet me and she suggested the Steak House Tavern there in the hotel. I said sure. Well, a while later I figured what the hell, do it right, I'll come by and get her at the hotel and take her out to dinner. I call the fucking hotel just now asking for her and they tell me there's nobody there under that name."

"What name?" said Wes abruptly.

"Uh, like I said, Alba Torres."

"You didn't say," said Wes.

"All right, all right. Anyway. What's the first thing comes into your mind here?"

Wes stared at him for a moment and said, "I don't know. What's supposed to come into my mind?"

"Well, shit. After what happened down there, the first thing that comes into my mind is, does this have something to do with . . . all that shit."

Wes finally blinked. He has snake eyes, thought Moss. Those goddamn gray snake's eyes. "I don't think so," said Wes. "Drake wouldn't know anything."

"No, I know that." Moss reached for his pen. "I guess just anything about that fucking place makes me kind of nervous. I mean, I'm potentially vulnerable there, you know?"

"I took care of it, Mr. Wetzel."

Moss tapped the pen irritably on the desk. "So why did this broad lie to me?"

Wes's eyes went to the view out the window. He blinked again. He doesn't even look like he's thinking, Moss thought. He looks like a fucking rock sitting there. After a long moment Wes looked back at him. "Probably because she can't really afford the Palmer House but she's trying to impress you," he said.

"Hm." Moss tapped the pen on the desk a few more times and tossed it aside. "OK." Of course, he thought, that has to be it. "Wes, you do good work. You take care of business and you set my mind at ease. Listen, all the same, I want you to come over there with me, just kind of sit and keep an eye out while I'm talking to her, you know?"

"That's what I get paid for."

"Yeah. OK then. Thanks. I'll be ready to go in about half an hour. Meet me downstairs, OK?"

Wes gave him one more stone-faced look and stood up and turned toward the door. "Sure thing." As Wes walked out of the office and closed the door behind him, Moss looked for a bulge under the loose batik shirt. The only place it could be was at the small of the back but Moss couldn't really make anything out since the shirt hung loose there, the tail out.

It gave Moss a thrill to have an armed bodyguard around; it was another sign of who he was and what he was worth. Early on, he'd learned that when you got into the sex business in any form you had to deal sooner or later with gentlemen of Italian descent, and it paid to have a large shadow. Wes had come highly, though vaguely, recommended, and Moss had never had cause for complaint. And he sure had come in handy down in Trinidad.

He wished he could read Wes better, though. The guy could make him feel uncomfortable because he never showed a human reaction. Moss had watched Wes's reaction to some of the goings-on at parties out at the house, unbelievable pussy buck naked and up for grabs; Wes had just watched, not batting an eye, like he was bored. Once Moss had shown him some proofs, just trying to get a flicker of interest out of the guy, and Wes had looked at them like they were the blueprints for the new cafeteria or something and given him that snake-face look, the look that made Moss feel he must have said something stupid. If Wes had appetites, he sure as hell kept them under wraps; Moss sometimes wondered what turned Wes on, if anything.

But then the guy was a pro, and maybe the stone face went with the job.

Tommy slewed over to the curb and put his foot on the brake, keeping the Volvo in drive. "All right Slim, break a leg. Give me ten minutes before you come in. And remember, no need to linger over the cocktails. You give him the package and split."

Diana paused with her hand on the door and gave Tommy a brief look that he chose to take as one of quiet assent. She pushed open the door, swung out her sleek nyloned legs and was away, and Tommy was swinging back into the traffic under the clattering, roaring El tracks. He glanced at his watch and saw there was plenty of time; it wasn't quite five yet. He worked his way through the creeping traffic down Wabash to Jackson and turned left. He fought his way into the left lane and swung abruptly into the alley that was halfway down the block. A narrow, dirty passage between two enormous buildings, it ran past loading docks back up toward Adams. Parking was strictly prohibited but Tommy wasn't worried about tickets and he was pretty sure they wouldn't tow him, not in half an hour, anyway. Other cars were parked at intervals along the way and the Volvo wasn't going to stand out. The biggest potential snafu was if there was a cop or an officious janitor or something in the alley to scare him away, but Tommy saw no one.

He left the car halfway up the alley, nestled between two trash dumpsters, and hiked back up to Adams and over to Wabash again. As he drew near the Palmer House his heart accelerated a bit; the lights were about to go up.

The entrance to the restaurant and bar was a modest revolving door just north of the grand canopied entrance to the hotel complex with its uniformed doormen. Tommy pushed into the dim quiet interior and wandered toward the back. The tavern was long and narrow, with the dark gleaming bar on the left and a door into the restaurant on the right. A passage went farther back past the johns, through the nether reaches of the restaurant and out into the hallway beyond, which connected with the central passage of the hotel-and-shop complex. The tavern was moderately full of the Friday afternoon crowd, as Tommy had hoped. He went all the way down the bar slowly, looking around as if he were uncertain where he wanted to sit, sliding politely past business-suited types, letting his eyes adjust to the gloom. He paused at the end of the bar, appearing to make up his mind. Tommy hiked himself up onto the last stool and ordered a draft from an elderly bartender with a Spanish accent and settled down to watch. He had a clear view down the bar all the way back to the street end of the place, where a partition next to the door made a little alcove, filled by a Chesterfield-type banquette nestled beneath a bogus medieval tapestry.

After three or four minutes he was pretty certain the place wasn't crawling with Moss Wetzel's men; nearly everyone in the place was in a pair or a group, drinking fast to unwind after another day of making or losing money. The groups were all focused on themselves and the only man who was alone was absorbed in the clear liquid in his glass. Nobody was watching anybody else except Tommy. He took a drink of beer, pulled *The Christian Science Monitor* out of his jacket pocket and laid it on the bar. The alcove up at the front was still empty.

When Diana walked in Tommy saw her right away out of the corner of his eye and looked up, naturally, as any man would. Their eyes met just briefly and he had to resist the temptation to wink. Hers went down to the paper spread out on the bar, the OK sign, and then were away again. She looked superb in the slinky black dress and her gold earrings, with that dark-gold hair hanging free about her face. For just an instant, Tommy felt a distant pang, remembering.

Diana turned a few heads as she made her way down the bar, walking slowly and haughtily on her high heels. She had come in through the back, from the central hallway, and she headed toward the street end of the bar, making for the alcove under the tapestry. She set the copious shoulder bag on the seat and slipped in behind the table, her back to the wall. Tommy went back to lazily turning pages, sipping beer and checking the other drinkers. The bartender ventured out to take Diana's order and came back and made her what looked like a whiskey sour.

A couple of new groups came in, and one of the old ones broke up and drifted off. There was another solitary drinker down the bar now, and Tommy stole a couple of looks at him. He was a broad-shouldered plug of a man with iron-gray hair and skin that had not been pretty to look at in his adolescence. He was wearing a sport jacket over some kind of wild print shirt but he looked uncomfortable in it. He looked like a steelworker on vacation. He took one look at Diana down by the window but didn't seem too interested; he took a drink of beer and proceeded to stare at the bottles across the bar. Tommy thought he was a maybe.

When Moss Wetzel came in from the street, Tommy knew him at once. He'd seen a photo in the copy of *Maverick* he'd bought, and he would have known him anyway by the way he stood looking around just inside the door and then fastened on Diana when he saw her just to his left in the alcove. He was a little sawed-off runt of a man, no more than five-six or so, with carefully tended hair. He was wearing a double-breasted gray suit and a dark red tie. Tommy couldn't hear anything of what was being said, but he could have written the dialogue as Wetzel leaned over the table and clasped Diana's hand in both of his. Diana smiled at him, that smart tough catch-me-if-you-can smile that had driven Tommy wild, and murmured something. Wetzel released her hand, waved at the bartender and took a seat with his back to Tommy.

Tommy drained his beer and laid a couple of bucks on the bar because he knew it wouldn't take long now. By the time the bartender had made Wetzel's drink and taken it over to him, Diana had the thick manila envelope out on the table. Wetzel froze; Tommy could see only the back of his head but he could see he wasn't moving. Diana was saying something to him, leaning forward over the table with that little crooked smile. Then she rose, picking up her bag and stepping deftly out from behind the table. If things worked as Tommy had planned, Wetzel would open the envelope and stare at what was inside long enough for Diana to hustle out through the back. By the time Wetzel got over the shock and realized that she wasn't just going to the ladies' room as she had said, she should be all the way down the central passage and about to step out onto State Street a few feet from the subway entrance.

Tommy made sure to look down at the paper as Diana passed. What happened next would be the interesting part. He waited a few seconds and then looked up, making himself look around in feigned boredom before he chanced a look down at Wetzel. He was just in time to see Wetzel shove something back into the envelope and come up out of the chair like a jack-in-the-box and turn wildly to look toward the back of the bar. Then Wetzel was moving fast, dodging chairs, clutching the envelope. Before he got to the bar the vacationing steelworker had slid off his stool and gone to meet him; Wetzel grabbed him by the arm and leaned close, his lips moving. The compact man nodded once and moved fast toward the rear entrance. Tommy was on his feet, folding the newspaper back into his pocket. Wetzel had moved fast and Tommy was silently urging Diana to hurry, hurry her ass into that subway station. He started to move away from the bar as Wetzel's man went by him, very close, taking no notice of him. Tommy followed him at a leisurely pace, watching him trying not to break into a run as he went past the restaurant tables toward the exit, and was immensely relieved to see him turn right when he got to the passage, toward the Monroe Street entrance. There was no way he would catch Slim now. Tommy walked out into the arcade with his hands in his pockets and turned left, not even deigning to look. Wetzel's man passed him when he was halfway to the big central passage, going at a good clip. Tommy saw him stop and look both ways, and then come back slowly, walking with his short powerful arms held out a bit from his body, like a weight lifter. Tommy chanced a direct glance at him when he passed, expecting to see consternation, but the blunt pitted face was devoid of expression.

Tommy went left at the central passage and out the Wabash exit. He walked slowly down to the alley and retrieved the car, keeping the lid on his elation. Things had worked perfectly, but then the hard part would be next time.

Diana. A woman in a thousand. A performer, a pro. Tommy eased into the traffic on Adams and turned down Wabash again. At Van Buren he went right and drove over to Dearborn, where he stopped in front of the deli at the corner and honked. The traffic behind him honked at him in turn but he didn't give a damn. Diana came out of the place, wearing the raincoat she'd had in the bag, her hair now clasped behind in a ponytail, the earrings gone. She jumped into the car and Tommy pulled away.

"An Oscar for you, sweetheart. The man is hooked." Tommy wrestled with the wheel and Diana stared out the windshield. "He had a gorilla in there, but the guy had no idea where you went."

"A gorilla." Diana was looking at him with a blank expression.

"Yeah. A goon. But like I say, you got away clean. The guy was heading back to say sorry boss when I left. I'm telling you, you tied them in knots."

Diana said nothing for a while but when Tommy looked over again she was still staring at him; Tommy realized it was shock. She was just staring, hands clutching the bag in her lap. Tommy reached out and clapped her on the thigh. "Relax, Slim. This is gonna be the easiest fortune you ever made."

Diana finally turned her head away from him. They drove in silence for a while and then she said, "You better be right, Tommy. You better be right."

FRANK FUDGE LOOKED up from the *Sun-Times* when Wes slid into the red plastic-upholstered booth. Smoke rose from a cigarette in Fudge's right hand and at his elbow sat an oval plate smeared with egg yolk and littered with hash browns. Fudge parked the cigarette under his moustache and shook Wes's hand across the table. "Top o' the mornin' to you," he said. Fudge looked as if mornings were hard for him. He was a poorly kept fortysomething, short of money, sleep and optimism.

"What's in the news?" said Wes.

"The usual. I think they're recycling the stories along with the paper these days."

"Always have been."

Fudge closed the paper. "So what's going on? You still working for the *Maverick* guy?"

Wes nodded. "If you can call it working."

"He ever float any tail your way?"

"There's a lot of it lying around out there."

Fudge shook his head. "So where does the work come in?"

Wes gave a perfunctory smile. "Well, we've got a little problem right now we could use some help with."

"Nice of you to think of me."

"I think we're going to need your kind of skills."

Fudge took a pull on the cigarette and peered at Wes, heavy-lidded eyes narrowed against the smoke. "Which ones in particular?"

"You used to be good at looking for things. Things and people. We've got some people we need to find, and they have some things we need."

Fudge nodded. "And you can't really go to my former colleagues."

Wes looked blank and said, "That's why we came to you." The waitress came and shoved a menu at Wes, but he waved it away. "It's a sort of collection job really, but it's got to be very, very, quiet," he said.

"That's all I've got left to sell. I'm quiet."

"Yeah. I know. You want the job?"

"I need the job. Talk money to me."

"What do you usually get?"

"One hundred bucks a day. Plus expenses, like they say in the books. I'm cheap, Wes."

"I'll give you two-fifty. With a bonus for hitting pay dirt."

Fudge raised an eyebrow and stubbed out the cigarette. "Deal."

"We're going to need one more man," Wes said. "Not a brain, just muscle. You know some nice quiet muscle?"

"You'd be more likely to know somebody like that than me. I'm a legitimate businessman. A small businessman."

"You're a legitimate as a shaved deck, Frank."

Fudge smiled. "I know a kid. He's no brain, that's for sure."

"He doesn't have to be Einstein, but he has to be smart enough to do his job and keep his mouth shut."

"I think he can do that."

"I'll leave it up to you. I'll pay whoever you pick the same as you. And I need to get started today. You can get me at either of these numbers." Wes dropped a slip of paper onto the table next to Fudge's coffee cup and started to slide out of the booth. "We have to move fast, Frank."

Fudge folded the slip of paper and looked up at Wes. "That kind of a thing, is it?"

"It's that kind of a thing,"

Cooper awoke to the drizzle, rain touching the windows on a dark weepy May morning. Diana had risen before him; he could hear her making distant breakfast sounds in the kitchen. He lay for a moment trying to sort out his feelings. The night before, he'd come in past the witching hour from driving, to find her drowsy and warm in his bed. Now, trying to put his finger on what was different, he realized that it was the first time in memory Diana had gotten up without him and proceeded with breakfast. Normally they lay together until fully awake and rose together, starting the day at their leisure, the priceless privilege of people who don't have to work in the morning.

Hearing the domestic clatter a couple of rooms away, Cooper felt almost married. It was good to lie in bed and hear somebody making coffee for him, but then he wasn't sure he wanted Diana to stop being a lover and start being a wife. Lovers stayed in bed together, he thought. Having had Diana around the house the past few days had changed things a bit. Again he felt the little stab of resentment that their relations had been affected by the descent of Tommy Thorne upon them.

He got up and put on T-shirt and jeans and followed the coffee smell into the kitchen. Diana had the percolator going on the stove and was beating eggs in a bowl. "I hope I didn't wake you," she said, looking at him over her shoulder.

"If I've got to be woken up, this is the way to do it." Cooper ambled to her and put both arms around her. "You don't look like you slept real well." He kissed her behind the left ear.

"I didn't." She gently disengaged and went back to flailing at the eggs. Cooper stepped over to examine the old battered percolater, a hopeless anachronism and his most treasured possession. "Did I do it right?" Diana said.

"Smells like it." Bubbles appeared in the glass knob on top and Cooper turned off the heat. "You worried about something?"

Diana set the bowl aside and opened the refrigerator. "You don't have any onions," she said.

"Hell, is that all. I can run out to the store if it bothers you that much."

She was smiling in spite of herself as she turned back to him. "No. I'm not worried about anything in particular. Au contraire. Tommy's out of my hair as of today."

"Found a place, huh?"

"Yeah. A studio someplace down in Wicker Park. He's moving today."

"He need any help?"

"I think he can handle it." Diana smiled her crooked smile and went back to the eggs.

The omelette was a success without onions, and with toast and ample fresh coffee and the *Tribune,* Cooper came as near as he ever got to unabashed hedonism. There was just enough rain feebly spotting the panes to make him wish he could lie in all day. He'd had a good night moneywise and wouldn't have to hustle too hard today, but he did have a few hours left with the cab and rainy days were good for making money. He had worked his way back to the sports section when Diana spoke.

"Cooper, I want to ask you something. I hope you'll understand."

He looked up and she was holding her mug in both hands, gravely regarding him over the rim. He stared for a second, trying to anticipate.

"Sure. What is it?"

"Now that Tommy's going to be gone, I'd like a couple of days to myself. I need some elbow room for a while." Her expression didn't change, and after a moment he realized he was still staring. "OK?" she said.

"Sure." Cooper answered quickly, with a shrug. He looked back down at the paper, turned the page. "You mean completely to yourself?"

"Just for a couple of days. I need to get to know my house again. I need some head room, maybe."

"Yeah, OK. I understand."

"You're not disappointed?"

Cooper looked up at her again, considering. "Well, sure. A little, I guess." What the hell, he thought. Women always asked you that kind of damn fool question, wanting you to spell everything out. He said, "But I understand. I guess."

Diana put down the mug and reached for his hand across the table. "I'm sorry. I've just been feeling crowded. Because of him I mean, not you. Understand me. I just need to reclaim my place, have some time to myself there. Then I'll want you back in it. Monday. Let me call you Monday, OK?"

She squeezed his hand, imploring, and Cooper thought about his own intermittent cravings for the lost Eden of bachelorhood and smiled. "OK. Monday. I'll get in a lot of pool this weekend."

"Thanks." Her eyes dropped from his quickly and she reached for a section of the paper. Cooper contemplated his feelings for a moment longer and went back to the baseball scores, uncertain.

Taking her leave half an hour later, Diana put her arms around Cooper's neck and drew his lips to hers. Her kiss lingered and then she put her cheek to his and said softly, "I'll miss you." Cooper was about to remind her she wasn't going off to spend two years at sea when she pulled back and added quickly, "But that will make Monday sweeter." She kissed him once again and was gone, across the landing and down the stairs. She waved as she swung around the newel post and out of sight.

Fudge found the house halfway up the block and pulled over to the curb. The house was a narrow two-story frame job painted yellow, with a front porch four feet off the ground like all the other houses on the block. Fudge eyed the house while going up the walk; it needed a new roof and some new yellow paint, and the porch was shored up at one end by a sloppily erected pillar of cinder blocks. Fudge climbed the steps and rang the bell.

The woman who opened the door was not a lot over five feet tall. She had gray hair that had once been jet black and dark eyes in a battleworn face. She wore a black cardigan over a black dress. She ushered Fudge into the living room with an anxious scuttling walk. "Jimmy, he's get up now. He coming down now," she said, with more than a trace of her origins somewhere toward the eastern end of the Mediterranean. "He's asleep late, you know. He's have a job at the night." Mrs. Poulos stood wringing her hands in the middle of the room, and Fudge was struck with how rare it was to see people actually wringing their hands. He smiled to try to relieve her nervousness.

"No problem," he said.

"Sit, please. Sit here." The woman waved him toward a high-backed wing chair by the front window, upholstered in a musty green fabric that reminded Fudge of his grandmother's house. He sat and smiled again. Mrs. Poulos hurried to the foot of the stairs in the hallway and shouted up them. "Jimmy! Here is Mr. Fudge!" She ducked back into the living room to say, "He's come now. I'm have work in kitchen." She beat a retreat and Fudge was left to look at the lace-draped furniture, the fading family photographs on the mantelpiece and the framed print of the Acropolis on the far wall.

The stairs creaked. The man who came down them and into the living room was about five-ten and over two-hundred pounds. The weight was in the broad shoulders and the barrel chest and thick arms that showed under the T-shirt, as well as in the ample waist and thighs. Fudge got up and stuck out a hand.

"Sorry to roust you so early," he said.

"That's OK." Jimmy had the head of a fighting dog screwed firmly down between his shoulders. A moustache split a broad face framed by a square unshaven jaw and tousled brown hair and dominated by suspicious dark eyes. The hair stood up on top every which way like a storm-swept cornfield and was shaggy at the nape of the neck. His broad thick hand gave Fudge more of a shake than he had bargained for. "How you doing?"

All right. Grab a shirt and some shoes and I'll buy you breakfast."

Jimmy Poulos nodded. He went to the hallway and shouted toward the kitchen. "Mama! Get me a shirt." There was a scuttling noise at the rear of the house and words Fudge didn't catch. Jimmy pulled a pair of expensive white leather basketball shoes from a pile by the front door and sat on a couch to put them on. "What's the job?" he said.

"We'll talk about it over coffee," Fudge said.

Mrs. Poulos came hurrying up the hall with a carefully ironed chambray work shirt trailing in the breeze. Jimmy took it in silence and put it on. His mother hovered.

"You listen what Mr. Fudge say you. Is no good, you work in bar all the time."

"Why don't you mind your own goddamn business?" Jimmy said, concentrating on the buttons.

Going down the walk to the car, Fudge said, "I ever talked to my mother like that, she'd a walloped me."

"She tried it once," Jimmy said, shortly.

Hissing through the drizzle up toward Lawrence Avenue, Fudge said, "Still bouncing, huh?"

"It's a living."

"Where at?"

"Gooner's, place way out on Irving."

"Plenty of action?"

"Just the Friday night fights. Had a good one last night. Turned over a few tables."

Fudge made a left onto Lawrence. "I heard you were going into the service or something."

Jimmy sniffed. "They wouldn't take me 'cause of that shit when I was sixteen."

"What, because of your record?" Fudge shook his head. "Seems like they'd want somebody like you. I thought kicking ass was what the army was all about."

"That's what I thought too. Far as I'm concerned, they can go fuck themselves now."

In a Greek diner on Lawrence Jimmy dived into a pile of corned beef hash while Fudge fired up a cigarette. Fudge glanced at the empty booth behind him and said, "Well, I got a job for you if you want it," he said.

"So what is it?"

"It's not strictly legal, to begin with."

The big square jaw worked a few times. "That don't bother me."

"I didn't think it would, too much." Fudge took a drink of his sixth cup of coffee of the morning. "I'm supposed to find somebody. And they might not be too happy to see me when I do."

Jimmy washed down a mouthful with a swallow of orange juice. "You going after bad debts now?"

"Something like that. And I might need you just to flex a little, you know?"

"I can do that."

Fudge smiled. "I'll tell you one thing, if I owed somebody money and I saw you at the door, I'd pay up fast."

Jimmy reached for the ketchup. "They always do," he said.

Cooper was back in the cab by ten-thirty, squeezing the last few dollars out of it before the twenty-four-hour lease was up. He got a Late For His Plane out to O'Hare in the nick of time with a masterpiece of Grand Prix expressway driving and came back in with a Flying Expense Account he dropped at the Hyatt. He had a couple of short hops around the Near North Side and called it a day.

Driving home in the old army-green Valiant, wipers beating hypnotically, Cooper tried again to decide if he was hurt. He had anticipated that Diana's reclaiming her home would involve reinstalling him in place of Tommy. He decided at last that he was a big boy and would survive until Monday.

Late in the afternoon Cooper shoved his chair away from the old oak desk in the corner. The books lay in precarious stacks on the desk: *Modern Times, Human Action, Objective Knowledge.* It was all there, Cooper thought, if he only found time to read them all. He leaned back, put his feet on the corner of the desk, and looked out the window. The rain hadn't gotten any more assertive; it seemed content to settle gently onto the quiescent city. Cooper stared into the diffuse gray afternoon, thinking about the catastrophic century that was grinding to an end, thinking maybe he was starting to understand it, starting to come to terms with his participation in the catastrophe.

He rose and went into the kitchen to dump his mug in the sink. He'd reached the limit of his intellectual endurance for the day. He wandered back into the living room, absently surveying the place. His eye fell on the battered furniture, the books piled on makeshift shelves everywhere, the faded reproductions of Gauguin and C. M. Russell, torn from magazines and curling at the corners where the thumbtacks had fallen out, the Louisville Slugger standing in the corner by the door. It was the den of a rumpled, incorrigible bachelor. Cooper realized he was looking for traces of Diana.

He wondered if it was time. He wondered also if it was too late, if this old dog was beyond new tricks. He loved Diana but he had been a bachelor for a long time.

"He'll be sitting by the phone, believe me. With what you showed him he hasn't been farther than ten feet from the phone since yesterday. You won't have any trouble getting through." Tommy put the Volvo in park and nodded at the bank of pay phones outside the 7-Eleven. "Just make it quick, lay out the terms and get an answer."

Diana opened the door and got out without looking at him. The light rain in her face woke her up a bit and she turned her mind to the task at hand. She ducked under the overhang of the roof and ransacked her purse for a quarter. She plugged it in the first phone she came to and punched out the number she'd memorized the day before. Standing with her back to the phone while it rang at the other end of the line, she looked out over the rain-slicked colorless cityscape and wished she were far, far away. She saw Tommy watching her through the whisk-thump of the windshield wipers.

"Wetzel Enterprises, may I help you?" said a woman's voice.

"Put me through to Moss Wetzel," Diana said tonelessly. "This is Alba. He's expecting the call."

It worked just the way Tommy had said it would. After no more than five seconds of indeterminate noises over the line, Wetzel's voice snarled. "That you?"

"It's me, Mr. Wetzel."

"Call me in ten minutes at 260-8649. Got it?"

"Got it." Diana hung up and wrote the number on the heel of her hand and went back to the car. "He wants me to call back," she said as she slid onto the seat.

"What'd I tell you," said Tommy. "Time to find another phone." He put the car in reverse. "I'd be surprised if he had the means to trace it but you never know."

Tommy drove over to Broadway and turned south. Diana looked out the window, remembering rain on a beach near San Juan, a long time ago. Tommy pulled in at an Amoco station with a phone on the side wall, exposed to the rain. "You couldn't find me one with a roof over it?" said Diana.

"Ten minutes are almost up."

This time Wetzel himself answered after a single ring. "Yeah."

"Let's talk money," said Diana.

"No, let's talk sense. You want to live a long time?" The voice was different from yesterday's. It sounded as if Wetzel were keeping it on a tight rein.

Diana said, "How about you? You could live a good thirty years or so in a jail cell. If you're lucky maybe Trinidad has the death penalty."

"Now listen, *bitch.*" Wetzel articulated the word carefully. "Blackmail is a very unhealthy business to be in. I employ people who can make you very sorry you got such unwise ideas."

"I'm sure you do. Now let's talk money. I think half a million is a fair price for what I have to offer. You can get five thousand one-hundred-dollar bills together by tomorrow, I'm sure."

She could almost hear him turning red in the ensuing brief silence. When he came back on he sounded more than ever as if he were hunched over the phone, trying to keep someone in an adjacent room from hearing him. "You're out of your fucking bimbo mind. There's no way in hell I can get that much together on a weekend."

"I guess you better start running then. The police in Port of Spain may be corrupt, but with the American media all over the matter, even they'll have to come after you."

"You'll be dead before one fucking word hits the papers."

"Let's cut out the bullshit, Mr. Wetzel. You don't have the slightest idea who or where I am. And you can imagine what the police will make of the objects you saw in the photographs yesterday."

"You'll spend the rest of your life running. Half a million won't take you far enough to get away from the dogs I'm going to put on your trail."

"We're agreed on the price then, are we?"

"We're not agreed on a fucking thing. I . . ."

"I'm sorry to hear that," said Diana, and hung up. She ran a hand over her rain-spotted hair and pulled her jacket closer about her throat. She turned and gave Tommy a venomous look. He made a shrugging gesture, asking her what the hell was going on. Diana made no response, enjoying the feeling of keeping two men in acute suspense. She turned back to the phone and produced another quarter and dialed again.

"Don't hang up on me again." He was starting to sound desperate, Diana thought.

"Then don't bullshit me anymore. You put the money in a suitcase and wait to hear from me tomorrow evening between four and six. Give me a number to call."

"Half a million's too much."

"Too much to keep you out of jail? I doubt that. I'm giving you a bargain price, Mr. Wetzel. You're worth a lot more than a million, but I'm not greedy."

"You know what happens to cunts like you?"

"That's not a very nice word."

"There are lots of ways to hurt a woman, you know."

"I would imagine jail inmates in Trinidad can hurt people too, Mr. Wetzel. Now give me a number to call and start getting the money together."

"I can't do it, for Christ's sake. The fucking banks are all closed."

"You're a man of influence. Use some of it."

"I can't do it. Give me till Tuesday."

"I'll call you at this number, shall I? Tomorrow between four and six."

"Wait!" Diana waited, hearing the man crumble. "All right, call me here again. Call at four on the dot."

"I can't guarantee when I'll get to the phone. You be waiting."

"I want you to remember something, little lady. I want you to remember this when you're looking a very bad death in the face. Remember I warned you. Because I will catch up with you, bitch, you can put that in the bank along with my money. I will find you."

"Till tomorrow, Mr. Wetzel." Diana hung up and stood in the rain for a second or two, a slow chill seeping through her from diaphragm to sphincter. Then she walked slowly back to the car, mentally phrasing her report for Tommy.

"You guys had it easy," said Stumps. He stood next to Cooper with his hands on the bar, leaning against it as if trying to keep it in place. A half-full stein of beer and an empty shot glass stood on the bar in front of him. The Cubs cap was in place at its rakish angle, the red watery eyes wide beneath the bill. "The helicopters and all that. Us, we fuckin' walked into the jungle and walked back out, if we was lucky. Through two feet of mud most of the time."

"We did our share of humping," said Cooper through his grin. "I had my boots held together with tape after a couple of months in the valley. Infantry's always going to be infantry, I don't care if you put them in spaceships."

Stumps cocked his head and looked skeptical. Behind Cooper the television was blaring incoherently; farther down the bar past Stumps two old men were poking fingers at one another in debate. Cooper was again the youngest person in the place, and he wasn't quite sure why he was there. He'd taken a late walk out by the lake and gone past the Chinese place on his way back. It had looked inviting through the big front window with the atry neon, but he had suddenly seen things in terms of a choice between talking to Barry and talking to Stumps, and something had brought him down the narrow brick street to the old folks' joint.

"And them plastic rifles you had," growled Stumps. "What'd they weigh, five pounds?"

"Around six and a half, without the magazine."

"Hell, an M-1 weights almost ten pounds. Now there was a rifle, my friend. That son of a bitch could get heavy, let me tell you. Try swinging one of them around in a hurry to draw a bead. You had to aim those. Couldn't just point and pray, like you guys. We had the lost art of marksmanship. The Marines in my day could shoot."

"Yeah, and they found out later half of you didn't even fire your rifles in combat. That's why they went to the automatic rifles."

"Now don't you believe that shit, son. You think we could have taken Bougainville and Guam and Iwo if half of us wasn't firing our rifles?"

"The last real men. OK Stumps, you got me beat." Cooper smiled and took a drink of beer.

Stumps nudged him on the arm. "Aw hell, I'm just blowin' smoke. I don't figure it got any easier for you. But they did get you home faster."

"That they did, yes."

"And the one-year tours. Hell, there was men that spent three years in the Pacific in my day."

"Yeah, I guess we had it easier that way, for sure. Although our unit morale wasn't for shit with guys rotating in and out all the time."

"Well, let me tell you. I think we'd have swapped a little unit morale for a chance to get home after a year."

"How long were you out there?"

Stumps was silent for a moment, his eyes going aimlessly over the bottles behind the bar, settling on the TV for an instant and then away to the far end of the bar. "Well, see . . . in my case . . . That was a little different, see." He picked up the stein and drank deeply, then thumped it back onto the bar. "I was on Bougainville for fifty-seven days. In combat. Fifty-seven straight days, and then they shipped me out." He gave one quick shake of the head. "With combat fatigue." He flashed a quick furtive look at Cooper.

"Huh." Cooper took refuge in his beer, not finding anything to say.

"All's I remember is the mud and no sleep at all and bullets coming out of the bushes. And then I wake up and I'm on a hospital ship. I got back to the regiment and went in on Guam but . . . first night on Guam I kinda . . . froze up and they shipped me home for good. It was the nights gave me trouble, see, on Bougainville. I wasn't never scared of the dark till then, but on that island . . . well, shit. You don't want to hear it. When they let me out of the hospital they discharged me. I kinda . . . I had kind of a rough time for a while." Stumps looked away, shaking his head.

Cooper nodded, twirling his beer glass slowly on the coaster. He knew what combat fatigue was. Fatigue was too kind a word for it, a polite word for the breakdown that came when any rational human was subjected to endless stress and horror. Cooper had looked into that hole himself, and while he hadn't slipped in, he would never look down on anyone who had. Anybody who had been in sustained combat knew what that hole looked and smelled like.

"That was when I took to the drinking," Stumps said. "Off and on anyways, at first. I had a little trouble . . . handling things."

"I know what you mean."

Stumps shook his head. "I doubt it."

Cooper looked sideways at him until the old man turned ravaged eyes to him and held his gaze for just a second. "There was men went on from Bougainville to Guam, the Marshalls, Iwo Jima, Okinawa. Spent the whole fuckin' war out there. Me, fifty-seven days on Bougainville and I ain't good for shit anymore. That works on your mind a bit."

"It's no disgrace. Don't let anybody who hasn't been out there judge you."

"No. But the ones who was. That's who I think about. You know what I wanted? All I wanted? I wanted to come back with the rest of 'em, on a ship, through the Golden Gate at the end of the war, lining the rail, waving at the people on the docks. I wanted to come back with the rest of 'em or else stay out there under a little white cross. Know where I was when the war ended? West Madison Street, living in a rented room above a tavern, 'cause I was ashamed to go home. I read about the ships coming back in the paper. I'd been back for a year and a half when the war ended, a lot of it in the hospital. They let me out and I hit the street. And the bottle."

The TV filled the silence. Cooper said, "Maybe your fifty-seven days were rougher than their three years."

"Naw, that won't cut it. I just wasn't strong enough."

Lamely, Cooper said, "Well shit, Stumps. The war's over. Give yourself a break."

Stumps shook his head slowly. "It ain't over. I fight that war again every day of my life."

Cooper drained his beer and slid off the barstool. He said, "You're like the old Japs who hid out in the jungle for forty years after the war. Time to come out of the jungle, Stumps."

"Yeah, all right. Get a little booze in me and I can't shut up. See you around." Stumps was already waving at Kenny for more whiskey as Cooper left.

The rain had stopped and Cooper emerged into the cool air with relief. He paused for a moment in the doorway, looking up at the clearing sky, watching a car hiss by on the freshly washed brickwork. He wished he'd gone to the Chinese place.

He made his way up the street to Burk's, where he chalked his name on the board and drank another beer, slowly, while waiting for his turn to come up. Cooper usually avoided Burk's on Saturday night because he didn't like the crowds, but tonight he didn't mind the noise and the jostling and the smoke. He leaned on the wall and drank and waited for the good tunes to come up on the jukebox: "L. A. Woman," "Crossroads," all the classics. When his name came up, he held the pool table for an hour, whipping all comers, playing well but finally getting bored with barroom eight ball on a small table.

He pissed in an alley on the way home, a simple atavistic pleasure. The streets were empty; it was nearly one. Diana would be home from work by now, he figured, sipping wine in her plant-filled living room, reading one of the books in a foreign tongue. Upstairs at his place Cooper scanned the TV channels and tried four different books and finally turned out all the lights and sat on the couch looking out the front window at the surreal glow of the street lamps on the gently waving trees.

He needed Diana in his life because he didn't want to be like Stumps when he was old. He was in a lot better shape than Stumps, had had a better war apparently, but nothing in the old man's character was all that foreign to him, and it scared him a little.

He fell asleep on the couch and awoke sometime in the dead hours, needing to piss again and drink some water.

He stripped and flopped on the bed and wondered where his life was going, if anywhere. The past twenty years were very close to him in the dark; there were parts he was glad were gone but others he would give a lot to have back. Twenty years seemed like a long time to go through without doing very much. A siren flared and died away in the distance.

In the morning he was at a loss, since Sunday mornings were a tradition with him and Diana: leisurely breakfast out someplace, ramble in the park, often a bedroom tryst in the early afternoon before she left for work. Alone, Cooper rattled irritably about the apartment, wanting to eat out but not wanting to do it alone, angry with Diana for not being there and angry with himself for wanting her there. He cooked a half-assed breakfast and drank too much coffee and finally said hell with it and went out to the park.

It was cold and foggy: weird primal weather with the lake lapping sinisterly at the edges of the invisible city. Cooper stood for a time with his back to the water, shivering, looking across the sand at the ghost trees in the park. After a hike along the beach he came back down Sheridan Road, stopped in a coffeehouse and listened with contempt to the prattle of undergraduate philosophers, then went home.

He dragged himself out to the track for a run, had nothing in him, and came home drenched with sweat and mist. After a shower he willed himself over to the desk and sat down with the books again.

At four he gave up. He stood up and breathed on the windowpane for a minute or two and then went to the phone. Diana's number was hard-wired in his fingers by now and he was hardly conscious of tapping it out. He would just catch her before she left for work, just time enough for a hello, reassure me.

After a single ring the phone was picked up and Tommy Thorne's voice said, "Diana's in the shower, this is the butler speaking."

Cooper sat still while Tommy said hello once more, and then he hung up, softly. He sat on the edge of the couch and stared at his feet for a while, his heart pounding absurdly. "The butler," he said out loud. He rose to his feet and went and got his jacket from the closet doorknob. He turned and looked at the phone. "The butler, huh?" he said. "Well, you really did it this time, didn't you?"

GLADSTONE DRAKE HAD the air-conditioning on, not so much to cool the office as to drown out the throb of the steel band in the hall next door. Gladstone liked music, but there was nothing quite so disruptive to thought as the sound of a bad steel band just practicing, and Gladstone liked to concentrate when he was thinking about money. He cut a fine figure in his chair, with the face of polished ebony above the gray pin-striped suit with the silk handkerchief blossoming from the pocket and the rich crimson tie with the pearled tiepin. Gladstone was a man who liked to dress well.

He looked up from the bank statements in annoyance when the door opened, letting in the clamor of the band. The irruption of noise was quickly cut off, however, as the man who had opened the door slipped into the office and shut it behind him.

Gladstone stared for a moment and then said, "Who in the hell are you?" in his resonant bass.

The man at the door smiled. "I'm Cecil," he said. He was the color of unsweetened chocolate, with a lean hungry face. There was a ragged fringe of beard at the tip of the jutting chin. He was dressed in a cheap lightweight sport jacket, torn at one shoulder, over a limp and graying white shirt with a thin tie in bright blue and orange. Dangling from the ends of long fingers was a plastic shopping bag. He had country written all over him, Gladstone estimated. Or perhaps even Grenada, fresh off the boat.

"If you're looking for employment you'll have to speak with Mr. Tompkins behind the bar," Gladstone said. He raised one eyebrow in a gesture of authoritative disapproval that had never failed him.

"No, man. I have all the employment I need," Cecil said in a soft voice. He didn't sound like a Grenadian. He had stopped smiling.

Gladstone stared at him for a couple of seconds and then shouted a name. "Jojo!"

"Jojo kyan' hear you. Not with all the noise dey making next door, my friend."

"How did you get back here?" Gladstone growled, irritated.

"Was no problem, not in the middle of the day, before the place open. Nobody watchin'. Jojo, he drinking cold nut on the sidewalk outside. Ain't nobody here to stop me."

"And no money, either," said Gladstone, easing back in his chair, hoping to intimidate this creature of the barrack-yards or the hills. With his carefully honed Oxbridge speech and his patrician manner, Gladstone was a man to be reckoned with. "Each night's receipts are taken to the bank immediately."

"But yuh have ah safe," said Cecil. "Ah sure it ain't empty. And nobody here to guard it. Not at lunchtime. Foolish to come here at noon to rob, 'cause no money here. But I ain't greedy. Ah go take what in the safe."

Gladstone's broad features settled slowly into a scowl. Deliberately, he reached for the phone. He had it off the hook and halfway to his ear when a rustle of plastic drew his eyes to the intruder and he saw the revolver emerge from the shopping bag. "No, man," said Cecil. "Not if yuh want to live." He leveled the revolver at Gladstone.

Gladstone replaced the receiver. "What do you want?" he said.

"Open the safe," said Cecil.

Gladstone nodded, a look of disgust on his face. He placed his hands on the desk and rose to his feet, then glanced at the revolver before turning and pacing off the three steps to the safe in the corner. Cecil came away from the door, the revolver steady in his hand. "Nobody go hear a shot back here, either," he said. "Not with the music goin' on like that."

Gladstone nodded briefly and turned to the safe. Very carefully, he twisted the dial. He made no attempt to shield it from the intruder's view, thinking it wasn't going to matter if he could read the combination or not. He turned the dial right, left, right again. He eased back a step and turned the handle and then moved so as to obstruct the other man's view as he pulled the heavy door open. Quick, he thought.

As Gladstone spun away from the safe with the automatic in his hand, Cecil shot him once in the chest. The report of the gun was quite loud, but Cecil showed no signs of nervousness as he watched Gladstone slide to the floor, gasping, unable to raise the automatic.

"Dat's the oldest one in the book," Cecil said. "The gun in the safe." He stepped over to where Gladstone lay with his breath bubbling out, blood starting to foam at his lips. He stood on Gladstone's wrist, just in case, and looked into the wide black eyes, which were frantically searching for something to hope for.

Cecil opened his mouth, about to speak, paused and then closed it again. A very long three seconds passed, during which Gladstone finally abandoned all hope. And then Cecil shot him in the forehead.

Cecil put the revolver in the right-hand pocket of his jacket and stepped away from the body, moving quickly now. He reached into the safe and pulled out a manila envelope. He glanced inside and stuffed it into the shopping bag. He rummaged in the safe, raking out stacks of papers bound with rubber bands, finding other envelopes, checking them and stashing them in the bag.

He was happy to find U.S. dollars, lots of them. He had known Drake would have dollars. There were also a few TT dollars and even some pounds. He took all the cash, left everything else and stepped to the door, leaving the safe open. He opened the door to the flood of sound from the steel band, glanced to the left and walked briskly to the right. He went down a flight of steps and out a door into a narrow alley. He trod over garbage, making his way toward the street ahead, seeing just a slice of the noontime crush on the pavement, under the tropical sun.

He turned down Ajax Street and made his way back to Wrightson Road. He turned left and strode quickly toward Independence Square. Above the noise of traffic he could hear the steel band, still practicing. As he passed the facade of the Chaconia Club he saw that Jojo had gone inside and wondered how long it would be before somebody looked back in the office. He was sweating in the noontime heat. Ahead the vista opened and he could see the port, a tangle of cranes, and beyond it ships riding at anchor out on the steel-bright waters of the Gulf.

Cecil turned into Independence Square, looking at his watch. He had time. He made his way along the Square, through dreadlocked and turbaned and uncovered heads, past vendors' stands and the mouths of cafés. In the cafés men lounged, liming, looking out at the world passing by. Cecil looked at them and thought that he would never have time to join the lunchtime lime again. Cecil had a feeling that a fast-moving period of his life was beginning. He listened to the music, coming from everywhere, from radios and cassette recorders in the vendors' booths, and wondered if it would be quieter in Florida.

Midway down the Drag he slowed, looking for a face in the milling of people with things to sell and things to buy. He found the face in a ramshackle booth and spoke quickly, and was ushered into the darkest recesses of the booth. Money changed hands, and when Cecil emerged the weight in his jacket pocket was gone and he was carrying nothing that would stop him from getting on an airplane.

His eyes were drawn to the hills of Laventille rising ahead, then to the entire circle of mountains around the city, and he wondered briefly if he would ever come back to Port of Spain. He made for the point along the Square where he would find a pirate taxi for Piarco. He felt in his pocket for the British West Indies Airways ticket and felt a flutter in his stomach.

Cecil had never been on an airplane before.

* * *

"Have a drink for Christ's sake, Wes. I know you're on duty but we got some serious things to talk about here." Moss opened the mahogany cabinet in the corner and went straight for the Chivas. "You can't discuss serious business with a dry throat. You want some of this? Some Stoly maybe? Or I can get you a beer if you got simple tastes. Name it." Moss took down a glass and stopped to open the mini-fridge nestled in the bottom half of the cabinet.

"Nothing, Mr. Wetzel. Thanks a lot." Wes sat in the ox-blood tub chair at the corner of the desk, his legs crossed, watching with the same blank expression.

Moss straightened up with a grunt, plopped ice cubes in the glass and shrugged. "OK. Suit yourself." He splashed some scotch over the ice. It looked so clean and bright and potent he could hardly wait to sip it, and he fumbled with the cap a little while putting it back on the bottle.

"All right. So that's pretty much what it looks like." Moss took a drink and pursed his lips and then sidled back behind the massive mahogany desk and sat with his back to the drawn brocade curtains. "It looks like hell. It looks like shit. It makes me sick to think about it. Any time I gotta get involved with Infante again it makes me nervous. But I have no choice here because who the hell else is going to be able to float me a half million dollars in cash on short notice on a fucking weekend?"

Wes shrugged. "If it bothers you, don't do it."

"It's done. It's sitting over there in the safe. Infante brought it over in person this morning. I could see the son of a bitch salivating, thinking about the interest he's going to gouge me for, for one fucking day. He'll get repaid tomorrow one way or another. I can raise it when LaSalle Street opens up, but what I'm hoping is I won't have to. I'm hoping we can hand him back the same suitcase and all I'll have to raise is one day's juice."

"I think I can take care of it. I don't think you should even take the money."

Moss shook his head once. "I can't risk it, Wes. You know I can't risk showing up empty-handed. I have to have that stuff."

Wes watched him with his reptile eyes for a couple of

seconds. "You won't be really safe as long as the broad and whoever's with her are still breathing."

Moss paused for only an instant. "I know. That's your part of the job. Cleanup. Just like with the guy down there. And getting the money back."

"I can do it. But I have to know as soon as they get in touch."

"The bitch is supposed to call between four and six. I gotta be downtown to take the call. You come with me, and as soon as we know what the deal is, you can go to work. Who'd you get to back you up?"

"I did a little subcontracting. Two men."

"OK, how much are they going to cost me?"

"Nothing you can't afford. Two-fifty a day apiece, the bonus you mentioned for actually coming up with the material."

"Ah . . . what about the uh . . . disposal problem?"

"I'll try to take care of that part of it myself."

Moss nodded, absorbed in his drink. "Tell me about these two guys."

Wes blinked. "They're competent and they don't talk."

"They fucking better not. Who are they?"

"The less you know, the better, Mr. Wetzel. I'm like any other tradesman. I have associates in the business, people I've worked with or seen work. I'll vouch for these two."

Moss nodded a few more times and finally looked up from his scotch. "Just how in the hell did you get into this line of work, Wes?"

Wes didn't exactly smile, but Moss thought the reptile eyes looked amused, just for a moment. "I'm like you. I just found a way to get paid for doing what I like to do."

Moss stared at him for a moment, chewing his lip. "OK. Listen, don't tell these two guys anything beyond the job at hand."

"I know my job, Mr. Wetzel."

"Sure you do, Wes. I know you do." Moss drank deeply of the scotch and let out a long sigh, looking around the walnut-paneled study with the old dark oils on the walls and the wide fireplace opposite the door. It had cost him an arm and a leg to have the room decorated this way, but he had always wanted a study with a fireplace and a drinks cabinet and oxblood leather furniture and somber oil portraits on the walls. It was a little hard to enjoy it today, because Moss was too conscious of the possibility of losing it all. He had been swinging back and forth all morning between sudden silent rages that shot his blood pressure up into the stratosphere and bouts of icy panic.

Moss knew he would never be able to do time. He liked to talk tough and act tough and think though, but sitting in the chair across from a genuine tough guy, he knew that jail was beyond his capabilities, in Trinidad or anywhere else. Moss knew he wouldn't last a week in jail. "You get me out of this, there's a nice bonus in it for you," he said, raising his glass in salute to Wes.

"I'll get you out of it, Mr. Wetzel. You want to know the truth, it's really kind of hard to pull off a blackmail scam. Especially for amateurs. And I got a feeling that's what we got here."

Diana came into the living room, zipping up her shoulder bag. "Who was that on the phone?"

"Some deaf-mute, just practicing I guess." Tommy sat in the armchair, flipping through a copy of *Vanity Fair*, tapping his foot in time to the beat coming from the radio. "He hung up."

"Why'd you answer? That's what I got the machine for."

Tommy looked up and shrugged. "I was sitting right here and the damn thing went off. Reflex."

Diana shook her head and went to the closet. "Let's get going." It was Cooper, she thought, and now he knows I lied.

The sudden urges to cry were getting easier to fight down. Diana shrugged into her raincoat, thinking that in twenty-four hours it would be over, all over.

Tommy tossed the magazine on the floor and stood up. "Hey, Slim."

"Don't call me that."

"Diana. I have to say, for a lady about to come into a substantial sum of money, you don't seem real cheerful. You been dragging around like a zomboid the last day or two."

Diana turned to face him. He stood in the middle of the rug, thumbs hooked in the pockets of his vest, head cocked on one side, a faint mocking smile in place. Diana said, "Don't worry, Tommy. Inside, I'm having the time of my life."

"Deadpan she does it. You're a natural comedian, sweet thing. Listen." Tommy caught her arm as she tried to slide past him. "Look me in the eyes for a second here. Yeah, you. You're going to be rich tomorrow. Provided one thing. Provided you play the game." He met the hostility in Diana's dark eyes head on, staring back and thinking what a magnificent animal she was. "It's just like dealing twenty-one all night, just like playing a gig. You get prepared and you concentrate. I've played with some shitty bands, babe, but I always played the best fucking show I was capable of, 'cause if you don't value your craft you embarrass yourself and things go all to hell. And you've dealt enough hands of blackjack to know that if you let that concentration go for a second, if you stop playing, you lose. Big, sometimes. So I know I can count on you to play it out, right? Tell me I'm right now, Slim. You're a player, aren't you?"

Diana looked into Tommy's long handsome face and let the tension go out of her shoulders. She exhaled and smiled her crooked smile and said, "I'm a player. But after this hand, I'm out. After this gig, I retire."

Tommy let go of her arm. "You're gonna have a very comfortable retirement, Diana my lass. You'll be able to afford the best shuffleboard set there is."

Cooper sat at the wheel of the Valiant, looking out at the lake, or what little he could see of it through the trees. He had fetched up in a park, as close to the lake as he could get in the closely guarded preserves of the North Shore. The park was deserted in the chill gray afternoon. Cooper had intended to get out of the car but had not found the initiative.

For the first time, he was afraid. He'd tried putting the most charitable construction possible on it, that Tommy had come back to get a last load of stuff, that he'd dropped by to take Diana out for lunch to repay her hospitality, other scenarios. He knew that Tommy didn't have that much stuff and he wouldn't have stuck around after a luncheon date while Diana took a shower and got ready for work.

Cooper was afraid. Diana had been lying to him, and that led to worse thoughts, thoughts he could hardly admit to his consciousness. In the course of what his mother had once quaintly referred to as an irregular life, he had experienced a good many vicissitudes, but he had never been flat-out betrayed. The notion that that was what was happening now filled him with a deep cold dread, as deep and cold as the unquiet lake waters in front of him.

He could be wrong. He would love to be wrong. Dear God let me be wrong, Cooper thought, appealing to a deity he no longer believed in. Let it all be a stupid misunderstanding. Let Diana come back to me unchanged tomorrow, let the trivial and obvious explanation come out without my having to worm it out, let us get back to loving each other with no trace of Tommy Fucking Titmouse in our lives.

As he prayed to be wrong, Cooper felt the slow leaden certainty sinking in, the numb queasy paralysis of fear. Maybe she was punishing him, punishing him for not going with them to hear music that night, for not being more jealous. Perhaps for not asking her to marry him. But Diana wouldn't play those games—would she? Diana wasn't a game player—she was as true as a clear night sky.

Or so Cooper had thought. He kept trying to face it, to imagine confronting her on the morrow, getting at the truth. The thought of hearing her confess terrified him. He would rather live with the doubt, almost.

Cooper started the ignition. It was time to drive back into the city, find a place to drink. The lake and the sky and the fog and the solitude had all gone sour on him.

If Diana could betray him, what was there to count on in the world?

* * *

This time Tommy sneaked down back streets to the Loyola El station and sent Diana in to make the call. He had rehearsed her coming down, making sure she had the rap down tight, because this was the crucial one. Tommy put the flashers on and watched Diana push through the door into the station and go over to the phones, the tail of her raincoat floating out behind her, showing the long black skirt of her waitress's uniform. She'll never have to work another night after this one, he thought. The first phone was vacant and she disappeared behind the stand, only her legs showing beneath it. Tommy watched her shift from foot to foot, trying to infer the words from her posture. He could see her stiffen a bit, about when Wetzel would be answering; he watched her remain still after that. His heart had accelerated again, as it always did with the excitement.

Diana. Old Slim. What a piece of luck to have found her again. And what a job to get her to play along. But Tommy had always been good at that; he'd always had good people skills. And the luck to find good people, for sure. Diana was a hell of a woman, and he wished, would always wish, he'd held on to her longer. Ah well, no hard feelings, Slim. You'll be able to buy Sergeant Rock all the beer had can hold now.

Diana had been still long enough to deliver the instructions; Tommy saw her shift her weight, stand sideways to the phone for a moment and then emerge into view again, walking swiftly, her head down. She came across the street and ducked into the car and said, "All right, let's go. I'll be late for work."

Tommy put it in gear and rolled up to the light at Sheridan, smiling. "You want me to ask how it went, OK. How'd it go?"

Huddled over by the door, as far as possible from him, Diana said, "Fine. He sounded a bit chastened this time. He'll be there. With the money."

"Sure he will. Damn bet you he will. You got the man twined around your little finger." Waiting for the light to change, Tommy looked over at her and saw her sulking, arms folded tightly over the bag on her lap, staring out the windshield, looking like a petulant schoolgirl in her cute uniform with the black bow. "Come on, Slim. Think positive. You can count the time you got left being poor in hours now."

Without looking at him Diana said, "I'm counting, believe me."

Cecil emerged from the air-conditioned terminal into the warm damp air. He took in a lungful, glad to be free of the oppressive bright lights and hard stares inside. The plastic bag still hung from his fingers, and the fact that that was his only luggage had seemed to enrage the hard-eyed men at the customs station inside. However, they had found nothing on him because he had nothing on him, and the passport with U.S. visa he had purchased for an exorbitant sum a week ago in the back room of a shop on Nelson Street in Port of Spain had passed muster. They had finally expelled him into the tumultuous Florida night.

He heard nothing but Spanish around him, and he worried briefly that he had somehow taken the wrong plane, landed in Venezuela or Mexico instead of the United States. He was reassured by the sight of an unmistakably American policeman, blond and muscular in his brown uniform, sweeping by in a patrol car. On the shield stenciled on the side of the car Cecil caught sight of the name MIAMI and decided he had arrived after all.

There were cars at the curb, with families clustered around them heaving luggage into trunks, exchanging embraces and prattling in Spanish, but there were no taxis or buses in sight. Cecil began walking to his right, dodging the people who came hurtling through automatic doors into his path, looking for someone to talk to. He finally saw a middle-aged man stranded at the curb with two heavy suitcases, looking peeved and very American in his pallid skin and straw Panama.

The man shot Cecil an angry glance as he approached, but Cecil was not deterred. Mustering his best Yankee accent he said, "Excuse me, sir. I would like to go to Fort Lauderdale. Can you tell me how I might get there?"

The man scowled at Cecil but softened a bit as he listened, a faint smile replacing the scowl. "Get over to ninety-five and go north about thirty miles," he said. He looked Cecil up and down and said, "Got a car?"

"No, sir."

The man smiled, as if at Cecil's naivete. "Well, then I'd say your best bet is to rent one."

"There are no buses?"

"Probably, but I wouldn't begin to know how to direct you to one."

"Is it too far to take a taxi?"

"Not if you're an oil sheikh. Or a cocaine baron. Or Jean Paul Getty." The man smiled again. "First time in the States?" Cecil nodded. "Well son, I wish you the best of luck. I hope you got lots of money, 'cause you're going to need it. Try the rental counter back inside the terminal there." He pointed and then stooped to pick up his bags as a Cadillac slid over to the curb in front of him.

Cecil went back inside, thinking of the dollars he had taken from Gladstone Drake's safe that afternoon, so long ago already, and deciding he could afford to rent a car. At the Hertz counter they informed him with exaggerated regret that he must have a credit card to be entrusted with one of their cars, and he thanked them softly and turned away.

Outside again, Cecil wandered, pushing through crowds, seeing taxis fly past but always full. The airport was enormous and Cecil began to feel the least bit daunted.

"Hey, brother." Cecil looked at the man who had called to him. The man was black, a little shorter than Cecil, with hair trimmed close to a round skull and a moustache that went straight across his upper lip and swelled to tufts at the corners of his mouth. He wore a lightweight light-colored sport jacket and shiny alligator boots with pointed tips. He was leaning on the hood of a car. "You lookin' kinda lost, my man. Fresh off the boat?"

Cecil smiled uncertainly. "Yeah, man. A big boat with wings."

The man laughed, flashing white teeth. "Where'd you come from?"

"The islands, man. Trinidad."

"Yeah, you don't sound like you're from around here. And you're wandering around like a little lost puppy. I seen you go by three times already. Where you tryin' to go?"

"Fort Lauderdale."

"Fort Lauderdale, no shit. That's where I'm goin'."

"Oh yeah?" Cecil looked around, nodding. "Then maybe you can tell me how to get there."

The man looked at Cecil for a moment and then at his watch. He said, "I tell you what, my man. I'll do better than that. I'll take you there."

Cecil stared. "You going to Fort Lauderdale?"

"I sure as hell am. This is your lucky day, my man."

"I don't want to trouble you, man."

"Shit, it ain't no trouble. I gotta go back there anyway, don't I? I was waitin' for a lady friend, but you want to know the truth, I don't think she's comin'. Get in." He slid off the hood and pulled open the door on the passenger side and waved at the seat. Cecil got in slowly while the man went around to the driver's side.

"You got people in Fort Lauderdale?" the man said, speeding away from the airport on a wide, brightly lit highway. Cecil said nothing for a moment and the man prompted, "Huh?"

"Ah got a friend there," Cecil said. He had to raise his voice to make himself heard above the synthesized beat from the radio.

"What part? What's the address?"

"Ten forty-five Southwest Twenty-sixth Street," Cecil said from memory.

"Hell, that ain't hardly out of my way at all," said the man. "I can drop you right there."

"Thanks, man," said Cecil, clutching the plastic shopping bag on his lap with two hands. He was watching the lights, endless rows of them, in a city that went on forever. He could see houses passing by in the night, flat bungalows in infinite rows. He could see a jet leveling off on its approach, lights winking. "It's a big city," he said.

"You talk good American. You been here before?"

"Never," said Cecil, flattered. "I was in Venezuela one time."

"Well, I hope you like it here," the man said. "And I hope you got a job lined up. 'Cause if you don't, you gonna have a rough time."

"My friend said he could get me work," Cecil said.

"He from down there too, on the island?"

"Yeah. He been here a long time."

"Well, he'll tell you. It's a mean town, brother. This is a white man's town. Even the Cubans make out better than a black man here. You talk any Spanish?"

"A word here, a word there."

"Well, you gonna need all of 'em, 'cause the fuckin' Cubans are everywhere. This is a mean town for black folks, my man."

They cruised in silence. Cecil was still watching the lights, thinking that they'd already crossed Port of Spain two or three times over and there was no end in sight. The man at the wheel put on his turn signal and drifted over a lane. Cecil looked up, too late, at the brightly lit green sign that was flashing by overhead. He saw it for only a fraction of a second, but was certain it said nothing about Fort Lauderdale. The car eased out of traffic and onto the off-ramp.

"Have you there in no time," the man said. "Gotta go north a ways now."

Thirty miles, Cecil almost said, but didn't. They went north along a brightly lit thoroughfare, longer and straighter than any street Cecil had ever seen. He watched car dealerships, real estate agencies, hamburger restaurants, shining glassed-in spaces he couldn't even identify slide by under bright street lamps, block upon block of them.

"What's it like down there where you're from, Trinidad you said?"

"Yeah." Cecil thought before replying. "It's hard, man," he said.

The man laughed. "Shit. It's hard here too, Jack. If you was hoping to find the streets paved with gold, somebody sold you a bill of goods."

They slowed and turned east, then north again, and

Cecil was looking at blocks of shabby buildings, shop windows covered with grillwork, vacant lots. The people on the sidewalks were black. "We're almost there," the man said.

Cecil saw a large yellow plastic sign ahead, lit up from within. It said LIQUORS. "Do you fancy a drink?" he said.

"Huh?" The man turned to look at him.

"I want to buy you something to drink. To thank you."

"Shit, you don't have to do that."

"Please," said Cecil. "It's a Trinidad custom. To share a drink with somebody who help you."

The man shrugged. "What the hell." He slowed and pulled to the curb in front of the liquor store. Cecil got out and went in, leaving the plastic bag on the seat of the car. Inside, he stood looking at the shelves beyond the counter while the old leather-faced man behind the bullet-proof glass stood immobile, watching him with a frown. Cecil looked at all the sizes and shapes of bottles and finally pointed to a $3.25 bottle of Mogen David. He carefully extracted a five-dollar bill from a fold he pulled from his trouser pocket, shoved it through the window in the glass and took his change and the bottle in a brown paper sack. "Thank you," he said.

Back in the car, he unscrewed the cap on the bottle as they pulled away from the curb. "Please," he said, offering it to the driver.

"That's mighty nice of you, brother," the man said. He held the bottle, still in the paper bag, and took a quick pull. He handed the bottle back and put on his signal for a left turn. "Gettin' close," he said.

Cecil took a drink of wine and looked out the window at grassless yards and cracked windows. "Are there no white people in Fort Lauderdale?" he said.

"Hell, yes," said the man. "But not this part."

They drove several blocks farther north, and then the man turned right again. This block was darker than the others; something seemed to have happened to the streetlights. There were houses, and in some of them lights burned behind shades. But there were gaps in the block where no houses stood, like gaps in a mouth where teeth have been knocked out. The man drove slowly down the street, looking at houses. "What did you say the address was?" he said.

Cecil repeated it. Then he said, "I'm disappointed. It sounded much better in my friend's letters."

The man at the wheel braked the car to a smooth stop. It was suddenly very dark; there were vacant lots on either side. "Well brother, let me tell you how it is." He put his right hand inside his jacket, at the belt.

"What do you mean?" said Cecil.

"I mean that money belt you're wearing kinda spoils your waistline, know what I mean?"

Cecil nodded and said, "I see how it is."

"You do, huh?" The man's arm shifted slightly, starting to come out of the jacket.

"Yes," said Cecil. "It's like this." And he whipped the wine bottle into the man's face with a firm backhand stroke, making sure to lift his elbow high enough to clear the back of the seat. There was a cracking, tearing burst of noise and the man's head snapped back and his hand came up with a gun in it but without any firmness of purpose. Wine was dripping everywhere and the man was making a gurgling noise as Cecil snatched the gun and reached across the man to open the door on the driver's side. He got it open and started pushing the man out.

The man began to recover as he was going out the door and Cecil had to put his shoulder into him. He heaved and the man fell onto the pavement. Cecil started brushing glass off the seat, glad that the paper bag had contained the breakage to some extent. The man had a hand on the door frame and was pulling himself up, starting to growl.

Cecil shot him through the open doorway, in the chest, twice. The man fell back onto the street with a final gurgle and Cecil finished picking bits of glass off the seat and closed the door and settled into the driver's seat. He could feel wine soaking into his trousers but thought that it couldn't be helped.

He put the car in gear and left the dark shape on the pavement subsiding into stillness. He laid the gun on the seat beside him. At the end of the block he turned north again. He drove for a long way, making several turns but always tending north, heading for lights. He became aware of water on his right and he slowed to look. Cecil stopped the car and got out by the bank of a canal, shining darkly in the light from street lamps. He looked around and saw lit windows but no people on the street. He leaned into the car and took the pistol off the seat and walked to the edge of the water and tossed it in. It made a quiet splash.

Five minutes later Cecil found a Texaco station at a brightly lit intersection. He parked the car next to the garage entrance and went into the office. A black man behind a desk looked up.

"I want to go to Fort Lauderdale," said Cecil.

COOPER KNEW HE'D played his fish just right. It had taken patience and time and a small investment of cash, but it was just about over. In fact it had been over when Cooper, with just the right note of sullen desperation, had proposed quadrupling the stakes. The sailor had smirked and agreed, and Cooper had known it was over.

He leaned over the table, lining up a straight shot into the corner and thinking three shots ahead to victory. He saw where he had to leave the cue ball, calculating the English. He breathed out and stroked and the six dropped square in the corner pocket. The cue ball came back just right to line up with the seven and the side pocket. As Cooper straightened up he saw the sailor glowering at him, just at the edge of the light. "I'll try and make it quick," Cooper said.

"You been sandbagging me," said the sailor, trying to look mean but failing with the red bandanna tied over his shorn head.

"I couldn't resist, pal." Copper chalked his cue. "People like you have a special function in life. They make other people rich." He could feel the heat coming from the kid as he bent to line up the shot. He potted it and moved around to draw a bead on the eight, already feeling the touch which would leave him a foot from the nine, sitting primly at the lip of the far corner pocket. Breathe, stroke, watch it fall—breathe, stroke, game. "Thanks for the practice," said Cooper.

The sailor didn't move; he just watched as Cooper stepped around the corner of the table and faced him in a relaxed but significant stance that said "Pay me." Cooper knew he'd transgressed against poolroom etiquette by taunting the kid, but he was enjoying himself. "I hope you got a way home," he said.

By the very slight freeze in the atmosphere of the room Cooper knew people were aware of what was happening. Over the sailor's shoulder he could see Derrick watching from behind the counter. Cooper wasn't worried about anything the kid could do, but he did want to avoid a ruckus. Derrick turned a blind eye to cash transactions unless they were too obvious or they started trouble, and Cooper didn't want to be told to stay home for a while.

"I believe that'll make it eighty you owe me," he said. "I know you got it, 'cause you were careless when you paid me the five bucks way back when. You got to learn to keep your cash hidden."

The sailor wasn't in a mood to take lessons, which for Cooper made it all the more fun to give him one. The kid just rocked back and forth very slightly on his heels, giving Cooper the heavy-lidded look. "Suppose I just say 'fuck you' and stroll," he said.

Cooper nodded toward the front. "See those two large black gentlemen on table one? All I have to do is raise my voice a bit. I think you'd prefer to pay. With your back to the counter, please."

The sailor finally paid, dragging out his wallet as if it were made of cast iron and pushing the four twenties into Cooper's hand in slow motion. "Choke on it, motherfucker," he said.

"Learn some manners," said Cooper. "And take off that rag, for Christ's sake. A military haircut's nothing to be ashamed of. You look like Aunt Jemima in that thing."

He left the kid standing at the table and went to settle up with Derrick. "You wouldn't be gambling in here, would you?" said Derrick deadpan, taking Cooper's cue from him and putting it in the rack he kept for players who didn't use fancy ones but paid to have a good house cue kept safe for them.

"It's only gambling if there's an element of chance," said Cooper.

Wes could see the guy crumbling fast; he was going to have a weeper on his hands soon. The guy was backed against the wall between the dumpster and the light pole, huddled like a scared six-year-old, not knowing what to do with his hands. He held them a little out from his waist, curled into ineffective fists, waiting for blows and trying not to cry. His eyes shone in the sulphurous light from above. He was shivering a little, maybe from the cold clinging fog, maybe from something else.

He'd lost the cocky show-biz look he'd had inside at the bar, flashing that Hollywood smile and tossing that expensive haircut whenever he blew smoke at the ceiling. That look had faded fast when Wes had clapped a hand on his arm. It hadn't taken much to herd him quietly out the back door into the alley.

"You're an amateur, aren't you?" Wes said.

"You'll get it back," the guy squeezed out, just able to talk. "She's got it."

Music came faintly through walls from a basement jazz joint. There was a distant honk from the direction of Rush Street. The guy's eyes flicked out over Wes's shoulder and Wes could see that the guy knew who he really had to worry about. Wes turned to look at Poulos. The kid with the stupid haircut was standing just a couple of feet behind Wes, looking bored but shifting his feet a little, edging closer, as if he couldn't wait.

"He sounds a little nervous, doesn't he?" Wes said to the kid.

"I think he sounds like a queer," Poulos said.

Wes turned back to the guy, shaking his head. "You got a key?"

"Yeah." The guy finally did something useful with his

hands, digging in a pocket and pulling out a key. Wes took it from him and looked him in the eye. "You'd be a lot better off somewhere else," he said. "Another country. Another planet maybe."

Wes saw hope dawning in the scared six-year-old eyes; the guy had been sure they were going to kill him out here. The hands dropped to his sides and his shoulders slid a couple of inches up the wall. "But we want you to remember your stay here," Wes said. He moved aside, not needing to signal to Poulos.

The guy watched Poulos as he stepped in, trying to scrape together some resistance, coming away from the brick wall, the hands going up again in that half-assed way. He looked like a little kid scared of a mean dog, Wes thought.

Poulos squared off in front of him. "Hey faggot," he said. "You want to suck me?"

The guy knew there was no good response to that and he firmed up a bit, the lips sealed shut and the hands going to Poulos's chest, but it was too late for effective resistance.

"I don't like queers," Poulos said, and drove his right fist hard and fast into the guy's stomach.

Poulos stepped away and the guy sagged in silent agony, away from the wall and onto his knees, eyes wide open looking for air anywhere he could find it, arms hugging his collapsed midsection. "See?" said Poulos. "He loves being on his knees." The head went down to the asphalt and the guy rolled onto his side, still not finding any air. Wes was starting to move, ready to motion Poulos away with a toss of the head, but he looked at the kid's broad face and saw he wasn't finished.

Poulos hauled the guy to his feet, the guy drawing his first long tearing breath after the blow, wobbling on his pins. Poulos took a calculating look at the dumpster against the wall and shoved the guy half-heartedly against the side of it, not much of a push. The guy bounced and started to slide and caught the side of the open dumpster to support himself. Poulos reached around him to the lid standing open against the wall and whipped it shut with as much force as he had.

The lid slammed home with a CLANG and what Wes saw were the guy's eyes over the top of the dumpster, as wide as eyes can get, looking at Wes for help. The lips were stretched back over the perfect teeth, wanting to scream but not finding the air. The face changed, going from surprise back toward agony, and with an effort the guy pulled his right hand free. The left hand was caught back closer to the hinge, under the knife-edge of the lid, and wasn't going to be pulled free. The guy made a sound that reminded Wes of freight trains grinding to a halt.

"Let's get comfortable," said Poulos, and put his hands on top of the dumpster. He hopped and pulled himself up onto the lid, planting his thick haunches there and wriggling back until he was firmly seated, feet dangling over the front. Wes heard bones cracking.

Poulos looked down at the guy, slowly sinking to his knees again, pushing at the lid to the dumpster with the heel of his still-functional right hand. The guy's eyes were pleading, offering anything.

"Looks like you got your hand caught there," Poulos said. "You oughta be more careful."

"Aaah," said the guy, tears spilling out of the wide eyes, still slowly sinking.

Wes looked at the kid and saw him smiling up there, grinning down at the guy on his knees. "Let's go," he said.

Late on a Sunday night there weren't too many people on Sheridan Road; a few cars sped by but the sidewalks were nearly empty. Cooper came out of the liquor store with a flask of Jim Beam, because that was the kind of mood he was in. On the sidewalk again, he stopped to peel off the seal and get the flask open and take a swig out of the brown paper bag. He cast another glance back toward the pool hall and saw the sailor standing in the doorway glaring at him. As Cooper watched, the kid turned slowly away and marched south toward the El stop, his cue case under his arm. Cooper shook his head and went north.

Are we going back to the bad old days? He pondered the question as he hiked up toward the park. Taking candy off babies in the pool hall, pushing for a fight, was something Cooper had thought he'd outgrown. He'd left it behind in the bad old days of the middle seventies, when the anger he'd gotten up with every morning had sabotaged two romances and half a dozen jobs, had driven him to the bottle and nearly to the brink. Cooper took another swig of whiskey, grimacing with the burn going down his throat and enjoying the slow radiance from his stomach. He stopped and turned suddenly, scanning the sidewalk behind, looking for the red bandanna. He saw nobody but a bent old man in the door of the liquor store.

He turned down Pratt toward the lake. The evening was damp and cool, and the lights in the park were blurred by a clinging mist. Cooper picked up the pace, impatient to be clear of the lighted streets, the confinement of the city. In the clean darkness out at the end of the Farwell pier there was a breath of wind, bringing the heavy wet lake air into his face. The distant skyline of the Loop was a dim smear of light beyond a fogged windowpane. The lake lapped at the concrete in the blackness below him.

Maybe I should kill Tommy, Cooper thought. It's been twenty years since I killed anybody. Though not for lack of trying, a couple of times. He drank again, slowly, savoring the bourbon as it washed over his tongue. It would be the first time I killed anybody who wasn't trying to kill me, though. He stuffed the flask back in his pocket and kicked at the stanchion at the edge of the pier, knowing he wasn't going to kill anybody.

Diana. Cooper put both hands on the restraining cable and leaned, reeling a bit from the bourbon kicking in. Christ, Diana, what are you doing? Nobody but you, we said.

Let it be a mistake, let it all be a ghastly misunderstanding. If it's all a mistake I will tear out my heart and hand it to you, bleeding, in penance. I will take you to San Juan, I will buy you a house on the beach, let your tropical soul drink in the sun. Just come back to me tomorrow unchanged, unsullied.

As insistent as his heartbeat, Cooper felt the fear stirring underneath, the fear it was no mistake. Cooper knew it would be the bad old days again if he lost Diana, and he wasn't sure he could take any more of that. He had the flask to his lips again when he thought of Stumps. He lowered the flask and stared at it for a while, seeing the two thirds that were left and wanting to down it but not wanting to be Stumps some day.

After a minute he upended the flask and poured what was left into the lake. Happy fish, he thought. Then he pitched the bottle as far out over the black water as he could, losing sight of it immediately, waiting forever before he heard a faint distant splash.

He wasn't going to lose Diana without a fight. If she was punishing him, he'd take his punishment. He'd kick Tommy Thorne's ass all the way back to Trinidad; maybe that was what Diana had wanted him to do all along. He'd change whatever she wanted him to change and get it all worked out and maybe they'd be stronger than before. Starting tomorrow.

Weaving a bit as he went back down the pier, Cooper was glad the cables were there to keep drunks like him from falling into the water. For a moment he regretted throwing away the rest of the bourbon; hell, there was never a better night to get wasted. His gaze swept over the water to the far skyline and back up the shore past the high-rise condos to the scattered lights among the dark shapeless trees in the park. A hundred feet in front of him, blocking his path, he saw the sailor.

The bandanna was gone; that was why Cooper had failed to pick him up checking over his shoulder. The kid was getting smarter. He stood in the middle of the path, feet spread. There was just enough light out on the pier for Cooper to see him pull the butt end of the cue out of the bag and toss the bag behind him.

Cooper had slowed, but kept walking. He was wired now and he was looking at options. To the right was beach, abutting the breakwater just beyond the cables. To the left was a six-foot drop into the lake. Cooper knew he could duck through the cables onto the sand and beat a retreat and stand a chance of getting away, if he could outrun the kid on the uncertain footing.

Forget it, he thought. As far as he could tell, the kid didn't have a knife or a gun, which were the only things that would really worry him. Cooper kept his hands in his jacket pockets as he approached. Up for it, he thought, hell yes. I'm up for it. He came to a stop ten feet from the sailor.

"I want my money," the sailor said in a cold flat tone.

"It's my money now," said Cooper.

"You sandbagged me," the sailor said. Cooper could make out his wide eyes in the dark. The sailor was running on anger, which made him dangerous but not as dangerous as if he had smarts.

"There's no law against it, friend. The only people it outrages are the ones dumb enough to fall for it. If you're going to play for money, you got to know the game. All the parts of the game. Eighty bucks isn't that much to pay for a lesson."

"You want to hustle me, you gotta be prepared to back it up. Now cough it up, motherfucker."

"You're a disgrace to the Navy, boy." For a moment Cooper considered trying to lull him, sliding by, ready to hit back if the sailor hit first. But he didn't know how fast the kid was, and that could be disaster. "Think for a second," he said. "You're fighting for eighty bucks. But if you come at me with that thing, as far as I'm concerned I'm fighting for my life. And you don't want to make somebody fight for their life if they've done it before. 'Cause when you've done that you know what it takes to win. And I guarantee you I'll win."

It gave the kid pause, but just for a second. "Yeah, suck me. Toss the money on the ground and back off and I won't split your fuckin' head."

Cooper smiled and took his hands out of his pockets. "Come and get it, junior," he said, raising them and half turning, shifting his feet.

The kid's shoulders relaxed perceptibly and then suddenly he crouched and circled, coming at Cooper low, left hand forward, palm out, club hand out to the side. Cooper waltzed with him, wary, certain of winning but not of the price. He knew he had to protect his head and he wasn't going to be hampered by the Queensberry rules, but then he doubted the sailor was either.

They circled until Cooper's back was to the land and the

kid feinted. Cooper reacted but stayed contained, concentrating on defense, knowing time was on his side. The kid feinted, jabbed, feinted and swiped low, at his knees. Cooper got a foot up and caught the sailor on the wrist, disrupting the blow. Immediately there was another feint and then hard on its heels a real one, and Cooper took a whack on his forearm. The sting hurt but Cooper was locked on; he skipped back a step and got balanced again.

The kid wasn't bad; he made Cooper worry about the grasping left hand to distract him from the money pitch in the right. Cooper knew it was time to stir the pot. Winning meant fighting dirty and fighting dirty meant closing in. He put out a quick left jab which just glanced the kid's cheek. He was ready for the comeback; when the kid grabbed his right arm he spun away to his left and then planted his back foot and ducked back in as the club came whistling down in a fast hard overhand. The club missed his head and landed with lessened force high on his back as Cooper butted the kid hard in the face with his forehead. The kid's head snapped back and Cooper followed it up fast; he came up wickedly with the heel of his right hand and caught the kid's jaw and snapped the head right back again. Two in a row was too many and the kid obligingly stepped back just far enough to allow Cooper room to wind up again and double him over with a solid right to the stomach. The butt end of the pool cue rattled onto the concrete.

Cooper was afraid for a moment he'd killed him after all, until the kid keeled slowly over from his knees onto his side and took in air with a long sucking moan. Cooper stepped clear of him, breathing hard. The kid gasped a couple of times and rolled onto his back. There was a smear of dark blood on his upper lip and his eyes were squeezed shut.

"A fucking disgrace," Cooper said through his teeth. "You got so much to learn I wouldn't know where to start." He bent to pick up the cue. He took one fast step toward the edge of the pier and flung the club spinning out over the black water. Possessed, he strode to where the canvas case with the other pieces of the cue lay on the pier and snatched it up and threw it as far out as he could. He didn't wait to hear the splashes. He walked back to where the sailor had made it to his hands and knees, head drooping. There wasn't enough hair to grab so Cooper grasped the kid under the jaw and forced his face up to the feeble light from the park. "You learning, son? You paying attention? Next time bring your brains along with your cue. Now go crawl back in your hole." The sailor's eyes focused on him, wide now with something other than anger, and suddenly Cooper was disgusted. With himself, with the kid, with everything. He released the kid's jaw and the head dropped again. "Grow up," Cooper said, as much to himself as to the sailor, and spun on his heel and left.

The cop's spotlight hit him as he reached the walk at the shore end of the pier and Cooper said softly, "Shit."

"Take your hands out of your pockets," said the voice through the loudspeaker. Cooper raised his hands and walked slowly toward the light, eyes lowered, hearing car doors come open. The bad old days, he thought.

"He came at me with a pool cue," Cooper said with his hands on the hood of the squad car, a cop methodically patting him down.

"I don't want to hear it," said the cop, stepping back.

And Cooper realized he had just thrown the evidence into the lake.

The white Volvo sat across the street, a lifeboat on a tossing sea. All Tommy wanted out of life was to make it to the car. All he had to do was to make it to that lifeboat before the sharks got to him. He couldn't see them anymore, but he knew they were close.

Tommy held the handkerchief gently in place around his shattered hand, his heart going like the bass beat on "Mean Town Blues." He wasn't sure he could drive, but he had no choice. The street looked about a mile wide. There wasn't a lot of traffic at this time of night and Tommy didn't even look; he just stepped out into the street on a beeline for the car.

He was too scared, too badly hurt to think about Diana anymore; all he wanted was to get into her car and drive, to someplace where they could fix his hand. He mustered his concentration, knowing his life depended on it. He wished there were more people around. It was a sorry-ass excuse for a town that couldn't put more people than this on the streets, even at midnight on a Sunday. He was half-way across the street now, trying not to break into a run. Trying to suppress the awful knowledge of the damage done to him, he let his useless hand fall to his side and started rooting with his hurt but working hand in his trouser pocket for the key, anticipating getting the door open and plopping down on the seat and getting the key in the ignition without fumbling. The raft was right there and there were still no sharks in sight. Tommy began to think he had a future.

He got the door open and got behind the wheel, the bloody handkerchief coming loose and falling to the pavement. He lifted his hand gingerly to his lap, groaning a bit with each breath; he tried to move calmly and deliberately as he felt with his good hand for the ignition on the steering column. The key slid in; Tommy had never taken more pleasure in sex than he took in the entry of the key into the ignition. He pumped the gas and flicked his wrist and the engine turned over, and just then a shadow stirred in the side mirror. Tommy's heart nearly kicked out the front of his chest and he snapped his head to the left and saw the man, his hand bringing iron out of a jacket pocket, the lizard's eyes still unblinking.

Tommy had time to think it was unfair; he'd made it to the raft. After that he had time only for a brief but intense child's longing for comfort in the night before two 9mm slugs punched through the window and his forehead and put out the lights on Tommy Thorne forever.

CECIL WONDERED IF it was time to abandon the car. Most likely, he thought. Noon at the latest. He tried to weigh the convenience against the danger. Convenience won out and he kept driving until he found the street he was looking for.

The house was a bungalow on a street of bungalows. There was yellow grass dying in a coating of dust on the front lawn. Cecil watched the house for a moment from the car and then got out and went up the walk. He noted the name on the mailbox with satisfaction and touched the knot of his tie. He rang the doorbell and waited what seemed a long time, standing on the porch and watching small brownish children fight over an enormous plastic tricycle across the street. He rang once again.

There was movement behind the door and it was yanked open. A man stood there, wearing cut-off blue jeans and nothing else. He had dark blond hair that crawled around his ears and down his neck and just missed getting in his eyes. He had a flat chest with a light covering of limp hairs. He needed a shave and probably coffee too, judged Cecil. His eyes were blue and penetrating and Cecil thought he was remarkably pale for someone who lived in such a sunny climate.

"Yeah," said the man.

Cecil tried his most winning smile. In his soft voice he said, "Mr. Beckett?"

"Yeah. What do you want?" The man leaned on the doorjamb as if for support, looking at Cecil through the screen.

Yanking again, trying out the accent, Cecil said, "I'm looking for a friend of mine. A man called Tommy Thorne."

The man stared at Cecil for a long moment. "Who are you?" he said.

"My name is Cecil," said Cecil. "I became friends with Tommy when he was in Trinidad."

"Trinidad," the man said. "Oh yeah. Trinidad."

"I play music. Tommy and I played together in Port of Spain."

"Uh-huh?"

"Tommy said I was to look him up if I ever came Stateside. He said I might find a gig here, playing music."

"He did, huh?" The man's head drooped for a moment. When it came back up he was smiling. "Well, old Tommy pulled a fast one on you. He's not in Florida anymore."

"Ah." Cecil looked down at his neatly clasped hands. "I see. You know where I could find him?"

"Yeah." The man peered at Cecil through the screen as if trying to decipher something in his face. "How the hell did you find me here?"

"I talked with a neighbor of yours on Twenty-sixth Street. He remembered you and Tommy. He didn't know where you were, but he gave me your name. It wasn't hard finding you in the telephone book. All you have a good telephone system here."

The man was nodding slowly. "Uh-huh. Well, like I say, Tommy took off again. He wandered in out of the blue about a month ago, dumped some stuff with me and took off again. For Chicago."

"Chicago?"

"Yeah. He said he wanted to learn to play the blues."

"I see." Cecil's gaze drifted out over the dying yard, past the children, down the street. "I was hoping Tommy could put me in the know with the right people."

"If you're counting on making a living playing music around here, lots of luck," said the man. "I been at it for years, and I'm barely getting by. You can see the lifestyle I'm accustomed to." He was smiling again.

Cecil nodded slowly. He turned back to the door. "Maybe I should call Tommy. Might you have a number for him?"

"Nope. All I know is he was going to try and track down an old girlfriend of his."

"In Chicago?"

"In Chicago." The man paused. "I can give you her name."

"That would be very kind," said Cecil, smiling his spectacular smile.

"What's the holdup?" said Cooper. "I've been in here for twelve hours."

The cop shrugged as he pushed a baloney-on-Wonder Bread sandwich through the bars. "You ever been arrested before?"

"Once. In Germany, a long time ago."

"Well, if they don't have your prints on file it takes 'em a long time to check. Germany, huh? You get around."

"Military. In the bad old days." Cooper went back to sit on the stainless-steel platform that served as a bunk. He took two bites of the sandwich and set it aside; it had more value as relief of monotony than as food.

Cooper sat without shoelaces or belt, anger having long since given way to a shamefaced melancholy and above all the crushing boredom. The cell in the back of the modern Twenty-fourth District station was spotless, fluorescent-lit, mind-obliterating. There were two of the metal platforms, a stainless-steel toilet and nothing else. A TV camera kept watch on him from the corridor beyond the bars. Cooper had finally slept a little, fitfully, in the wee hours, waking up stiff and hung over. After that the boredom had overpowered even his anxieties of the evening before. Three other men had been brought down the corridor to other cells during his time there, one of them an old and obstreperous drunk. The drunk had finally fallen asleep and the other two men had made bail and been released.

The cop on duty had let him out twice to use the pay phone just outside the cell. Cooper had tried to call Diana both times but had gotten no answer. With a brief resurgence of anger he had written her off and called Emilio's wife and told her the story, with some embarrassment; an hour later Emilio had come down with a hundred dollars cash for the bond. Now all he needed was for his fingerprints to clear.

He heard the door at the end of the corridor open and he slipped off the bunk and walked hopefully to the bars. A tall, broad cop in a lieutenant's white shirt and gold-banded cap came down the way and stopped in front of his cell. Cooper shook his head and laughed briefly. "The dungeonmaster," he said.

"I saw a familiar name on the sheet," said the lieutenant. Valenti had more gray at the temples every time Cooper saw him, but the moustache was still black and trim and the cop's swagger even slower and more imposing. He looked at Cooper without smiling. "Let me guess. You're going to tell me the same thing you always tell me, aren't you?"

"That's right. I didn't start it." Cooper leaned on the bars and had to smile. It was good to see a familiar face, any face.

"You sure as hell finish strong through, don't you?"

"I try. Don't tell me the guy's really hurt."

Valenti shook his head. "Nah. Treated and released. Simple battery's what you're charged with, huh? Half of these cases, the other guy never shows up in court. Too ashamed of being whipped."

"Let's hope that's the way it goes. He really did jump me, you know. With a pool cue." Cooper waited for Valenti to say something about eighty dollars and accusations of theft, but the policeman only shook his head.

"You know something, MacLeish?" he said, starting to turn away.

"What?"

"A man your age needs to take a hard look at his lifestyle."

"I'm with you there, a hundred percent," Cooper said to Valenti's back.

At two in the afternoon they let Cooper out. He reclaimed his possessions, including the eighty dollars. He had feared the sailor would try to make a mugging out of it, but apparently the kid had decided to take his lumps and retreat to the safety of Great Lakes Naval Training Center. The thought gave Cooper little satisfaction. He was given a slip of paper with a court date a month away on it, and he emerged into an unseasonably cold day with a thin overcast diffusing the light over a dilapidated stretch of Clark Street. He walked slowly away from the station, profoundly grateful for his freedom, feeling old and tired and depressed. He went straight to the garage on Lunt where Emilio worked and left the eighty dollars plus twenty more with him, along with a sheepish explanation. Then he hiked up to Morse Avenue and sat in the window of his favorite Korean place, eating poolgogi and looking out the window. The day was like his mood; cold, gray, quiet.

At his place he tried to call Diana once again but still got no answer. He took a shower and shaved. Afterwards he tried calling again and then lay down on the couch, faintly troubled but too tired to deal with the collapse of his personal life. He fell asleep quickly.

Sudden awakenings still gave Cooper trouble even after twenty years, and when the harsh rattle of the doorbell tore into his dream he came upright flailing. For a moment he sat still, not knowing what had woken him. His head hurt and his heart was kicking at the walls. Then the doorbell went off again and he swung his feet to the floor, thinking Diana.

As he leaned on the button which opened the door downstairs it occurred to him to wonder what Diana had done with the key he'd given her. But when he pulled open the door and listened to the feet coming up the stairs, he knew this was no Diana; there were two pairs of feet and they were heavy male ones. He sent a tentative hello down the stairwell and the answer came back "Police."

And Cooper watched with a familiar unease as two big men barely contained in suits came around the landing and up the final flight; he'd had enough dealings with detectives in his life to know a dick when he saw one. The lead dick was bald, with the remnants of his blond hair trimmed close around the sides of his skull, as if he wanted to keep it from showing up the shiny dome on top. He had a neat little blond moustache and a thick neck and fish-colored eyes. The second man was taller, gray-haired and long-faced and predatory behind rimless glasses. "Are you Cooper MacLeish?" said the bald one, reaching the door.

Cooper stared, looking from one man to the other and back. All he cold think of was that they had come to take him back to jail. "Yeah. That's me," he said. He retreated into the room with a dull sensation of things crashing down around his ears. The sailor, he thought. He must have gone with the robbery story. "What's the bad news?" he said, trying to think of a lawyer he could call.

"What makes you think it's bad news?" said the bald one.

"That's the only kind of news cops bring, isn't it?"

"Sometimes we're just looking for news. I'm Detective Peck, and this is Detective Hunt. Area Six Violent Crimes."

Cooper stared at him. "Hunt and Peck? Is that how you type your reports?"

Peck did not look amused. "No, that's how we get answers. We hunt you down and we peck you to death. Got a minute?"

"Sure." Cooper waved at the canvas director's chair by the window and the armchair in the corner. He walked slowly to the couch, rubbing his eyes, trying to think. He sank onto the couch and watched as Hunt, the lean and hungry one, moved past him to look down the hall and then into the dining room.

"You alone?" said Hunt from behind him.

"Take a look," said Cooper.

"I'm just asking you a question." Hunt sounded bored.

"I'm alone," said Cooper, waiting for the axe to fall.

Peck sat heavily on the director's chair. "I understand you were a guest of the city last night."

Cooper blinked at him. "What do you want me to tell you?"

Peck shrugged. "Just making small talk. What happened?"

"I took some money off the guy playing pool. He tried to take it back and I creamed him. I thought it was all over for now. I got a court date, I'll be there."

"Relax," said Hunt. He had moved back into Cooper's line of sight. He went to the front windows and looked out, then perched on a corner of the old oak desk, long-limbed and long-beaked like a carrion bird. "That's not what we're here about."

After a moment Cooper said, "OK, what are you here about?"

"You know a woman named Diana Froelich?"

Cooper had a very bad feeling suddenly. "Yeah. Is she all right?"

"What makes you think she might not be?" said Peck.

"Cops show up, my first thought is, who got hurt?"

"When did you last see her?" said Hunt.

"Saturday morning. Here. What happened to her?"

"We wish we knew. What about a guy named Thomas Thorne? You know him?"

Cooper's eyes went back and forth between the two detectives. "Yeah, I know him. He goes by Tommy, like he was ten years old. What do you mean, you wish you knew what happened to Diana?"

"Just that. Tell us what you know about Tommy."

Cooper scowled at him. "He's an old friend of Diana's. He showed up here out of the blue about a week ago. He's been running around with her."

"Running around with her."

"Yeah. He was staying with her until he found his own place."

"Uh-huh," said Peck. "You and Diana an item?"

Cooper swallowed, getting riled. "Yeah. Do you mind?"

"Don't get bent out of shape here. We're just trying to get the picture."

"Me too. I'm not getting much of a picture from you two, though."

Hunt said, "How'd you feel about Thorne staying with Diana?"

Warily, Cooper answered. "I didn't think much of it at first. They were old pals and I don't get jealous too easily. But then I started getting the impression they were carrying on behind my back. I got a little bothered then."

"How bothered?"

"Bothered enough to get drunk and get in a stupid fight. Now you mind telling me what the *fuck* is going on?"

Hunt cast a quick look at Peck before he answered. "We found her car last night."

"Yeah, and?"

"And we found the stub of an old electric bill on the dash. With a sketch map on one side and your name and address on the other.

Cooper sat still for a moment, thinking. "Yeah. I drew the map for her. She was going to meet me at a party after she got off work. That was weeks ago. Why were you looking at her car?"

" 'Cause that's what we do, we look at things." Peck gave him a blank stare.

Cooper smoldered for a moment. Finally he said, "OK, you two are from Violent Crimes. What's the crime and who's the victim?"

The two men exchanged a look. Hunt said, "The crime is shooting somebody in the head a couple of times, if you consider that a crime. After nearly severing a couple of fingers. The somebody is Tommy Thorne."

"Jesus Christ," said Cooper softly.

"Yeah," said Hunt. "Jesus H. Christ."

"On a crutch," said Peck.

"What about Diana? Where is she?"

Peck crossed one leg over the other, settling in. "That's what we'd like to know."

"You've been to her place, I take it?"

"Yeah. It was quite a sight."

"What do you mean?"

"Either she's the world's worst housekeeper or somebody got over there during the night and turned it upside down."

"And shook it a couple of times," said Hunt.

Cooper exhaled and leaned back on the couch, reeling. "Wait a minute. Tommy was in her car?"

"All over it. Your lady friend's going to have to get the seats cleaned, let me tell you."

"And then somebody went through her place looking for something?"

"Before or after the killing, we don't know."

"When was all this?"

"Just about the time you were getting arrested last night. Fortunately for you."

"Huh?"

"I mean if you didn't have the best alibi in the world, we'd be tempted to think you did it. Tommy was carrying on with your girlfriend, you got pissed off and did 'em both."

Cooper blinked a few times. "Except you know I didn't."

"Yeah. I guess you couldn't have," Peck said, wistfully it seemed. "But I bet there's a lot you can tell us. About you and Diana and Tommy. From the start, OK?"

Cooper parked the Valiant across from Diana's place on Fargo. He sat in the car for a moment, looking at her windows, with no sign of life behind them. Finally he got out and crossed the street. For form's sake he rang the bell a couple of times, but he got what he expected and gave up and went around to the back.

Cooper had told the detectives everything he could. He had given them the names of Diana's closest friends and her employer and told them all he knew about Tommy and everything else he'd thought might help. When they had finally left him alone with his fears, he had considered for a moment just sitting by the phone, but decided that if she were still going to call, she would have done it in the hour or so he'd been home. He knew he had to take a look at her place.

Walking down the gangway, he ran over what he knew. That she had wanted him out of the way for the weekend. For playing around with Tommy, he'd thought at first. Now? For whatever it was that got Tommy killed. Cooper felt certainty running through his fingers like sand. There was a cold dark hole in the center of his knowledge about Diana.

Walking up the back steps, he wondered if the place was still open. He hadn't thought to ask the detectives whether whoever had searched the place had broken in or had had a key. He found the back door intact and locked; through the window he could see disorder. Cooper went to look for the janitor.

He found him in the garden apartment; the hard part was convincing him to let him in. "You talked to the police, right?" said Cooper.

"Yeah, but they don't say nothing about letting other people in." The janitor, like all Chicago janitors, was a southern Slav. He was a short powerful man and he spoke with a thick accent. Children teemed darkly behind him in the basement apartment.

"You know the lady's disappeared, right? She's in trouble. Well, someone has to notify her family, and I'm the guy. You've probably seen me with her."

"Yeah, yeah."

"See, I need the phone numbers. Her mother, her friends, people like that. You can come with me, watch me. All I need is to find her address book or something."

The janitor shook his head, but he went to get the keys. "You gonna have hard time finding anything in there," he said, leading Cooper up the back steps. "I don't know how they get in. I don't hear nothing. Nobody hear nothing."

The second the door swung open Cooper could see why he was going to have a hard time finding things. On the kitchen floor was a litter of dishes, pans, towels, onions and potatoes, ripped-open boxes, washtubs, other detritus. Cupboards hung open, the shelves cleared. The mugs and jars and plates that had been in them were scattered along the counters. Drawers had been pulled out and emptied on the floor or the counters. The doors below the sink were ajar, revealing pipes and an empty laundry basket. The oven stood open.

Cooper waded through the wreckage, looking through to the dining room. There he could see the sideboard open, empty. It had been pulled away from the wall. The table had been shoved to one side of the room and the rug rolled up and thrown in a corner. The contents of the sideboard were on the table: the punch bowl, the fancy champagne glasses, the good napkins. The pictures had been taken down and removed from their frames, then laid on the floor. "They look at a lotta stuff, I don't know what they took," said the janitor. "The TV, stereo, that stuff, all still here."

"I don't think it was a burglary." Cooper stepped gingerly into the living room. In the living room he could not see the floor. Instead there was a layer of books, cushions, prints, pens, photos, papers. Mainly books, all of Diana's treasured library. By the bay windows lay the plants, uprooted from their pots, the dirt scattered over the floor. The TV sat on the floor.

Similar chaos met his eyes in the bedroom and bathroom. Cooper came back into the living room and looked at the janitor, who stood shaking his head. "Big mess," he said. "Big mess."

"It could have been worse," Cooper said, scanning the room. "There isn't really a lot of breakage. They were . . . careful."

"Looking for money, maybe."

"Maybe. This took time. They must have been in here all night. That's why they were careful. They couldn't make much noise. Look how all the furniture's moved out from the walls. There must have been more than one of them. A whole crew."

"I don't hear nothing," the janitor said. "Too far, on the other side of the building."

Cooper shook his head. He was looking for hopeful signs, wondering if the shape of the place told him anything about the shape Diana would be in.

OK, it wasn't a burglary. It had something to do with Tommy getting shot. What did that mean? The fact that they had a key was not good, he thought. He felt anxiety pushing at the surface, wanting to mutate into full-blown panic.

"How long you gonna be here?" said the janitor.

"Give me a couple of minutes." Cooper was trying to scan the wreck on the floor, realizing how nearly impossible it would be to find an address book or anything else. Clues, he thought. I should be looking for clues. "Did the cops search through the place?" he said.

"They stay here maybe five minutes, just look and make sure your friend's not here. Not long time."

Cooper kicked at a sheaf of papers that looked as if they had come from the desk drawer where Diana kept bills and the like. Somebody's going to have to sort through all this, he thought. He stepped toward the windows.

The telephone was still in place, sitting neatly on its stand, though the stand had been moved away from the wall. Cooper's eye fell on the answering machine on the shelf below the phone. A tiny red light was blinking. He looked at the phone machine for a moment and then knelt and pressed the MESSAGES button. There was a whir as the tape rewound and then a female voice came out of the machine.

"This is Rachel . . . My God, I saw the paper. What is going *on* with you? Why didn't you say something? Call me. If you need to stay here, if you need anything at all, *call me.*" There was a succession of beeps and another whir as the tape rewound. Cooper rose to his feet.

Rachel. Of course she would go to Rachel. "Did the cops hear this?" he asked the janitor.

"No, they don't touch nothing."

Cooper was pawing at the debris. Leeds, he thought was the name. He found the phone book fairly quickly, not too far from the phone. He founds *Leeds R* on Elmdale at about the right address.

The phone rang five times before she answered. "Rachel, it's Cooper," he said.

"Cooper. Oh, God. Is Diana all right?"

"I don't know. I'm looking for her. From your message on her machine I got the impression you've seen her recently."

"She stayed here last night. You know about the guy they found in her car?"

"I know. Can I come over and talk to you?"

"Please do."

Cooper thanked the janitor and told him to keep an eye on the place. He hopped in the Valiant and pointed it south through the descending evening.

Rachel lived on the top floor of a three-flat on a tree-shaded block of Elmdale, not too far from Broadway. She ushered Cooper into a room that had been put together with taste but not a whole lot of money. The floor was bare and polished, the front windows shielded with rice-paper shades. There were few books, but things to look at everywhere: a tapestry in earth colors on one wall, an array of paintings on another. Light came from a frosted globe on an old wooden cask in the corner.

"What is going on with that woman?" Rachel Leeds was thin and tightly wound. Her light brown hair fell in disarray from a hastily gathered knot on top. She had the wiriness of an athlete and the intensity of a neurotic or an artist.

"I don't know, the cops don't know, nobody knows. Except her, I hope."

"You talked to the cops?" She pointed Cooper to a rattan chair.

"I told them what I knew, which was nothing. You say Diana stayed here last night?"

"She called me about one, one-thirty in the morning, woke me up. She said she was sorry to bother me but her place was a mess because there had been a leak or something, some kind of water catastrophe. She had just gotten home from work and found it. She asked if she could crash over here and I said sure."

"Was she all right? I mean, did she seem nervous or scared or anything?"

"Sure, she seemed kind of shaky and pissed off, but I thought it was 'cause of her place being a mess."

"I was just over there. The place is a mess, but not because of a leak. Somebody trashed it."

"Trashed it? You mean like on purpose?"

"They were looking for something."

"My God." Cooper watched Rachel go another couple of turns tighter. "She didn't say anything about that."

"She was lying to you. What else did she say?"

Rachel was still trying to digest the idea of having been lied to. After a moment she threw up her hands, giving up. "Not much. We talked about work and stuff, she complained about her neighbors, the ones she said had the leak or overflow or whatever. She sure didn't say anything about a guy being shot to death in her car. I almost *died* when I saw it in the paper."

"You have it? I haven't seen a paper today."

She snatched a *Sun-Times* from a futon on the floor and leafed through it before handing it to him, open to the Metro page.

FLORIDA MAN SLAIN ON NEAR NORTH SIDE was the headline. Cooper scanned the brief story rapidly. The facts were much as the detectives had given them to him. Thomas Thorne of Fort Lauderdale, Florida had been found shot twice in the head in a car parked on Oak Street. No mention was made of witnesses, but the police were said to believe the shooting had occurred shortly after midnight. The car, the article reported, was registered to Diana Froelich of Chicago.

"Her name like jumped *out* at me when I saw the article. I almost dropped the paper." Rachel stood with her arms folded tightly, wide-eyed. "Do you think she's all right?"

Cooper folded the paper and handed it back to her, frowning. "If she made it over here last night, I think she's probably all right. But I don't think she's having much fun."

"She tried to call you this morning, just before I left. She was going to stay here a while, then go home and deal with the mess. She seemed like irritated when she didn't get you on the phone."

"Yeah. I was kind of tied up all day."

"I found a note from her when I got home. Just 'Thanks, I'll call you,' you know."

Cooper passed a hand over his face. "Shit. I got a bad feeling about this."

Rachel was staring at him, standing in the middle of the room. "Who is this guy they found in her car, anyway?"

"An old friend of hers, from her wild youth down in Florida."

"Oh shit, you mean it could be like drugs or something?"

"I don't know. But I'll tell you one thing—whatever it is, Tommy Thorne started it, and I can't say I'm sorry he got shot. Now can you think of anything else she said about where she was going, what she was thinking, anything like that?"

Rachel shook her head, tossed her shoulders. "No, I mean—we didn't talk much about it after she told me the story, about the leak I mean. I didn't have any reason not to believe her, you know?"

"Uh-huh." Cooper stood up. "All right. I guess I'll go home and chew some more nails. Listen, let me know if you hear from her, will you? And if you want to be a good citizen, you might call Area Six police headquarters and leave a message for a couple of detectives named, uh, Peck and Hunt. I'm not sure what good it'll do, but they'll want to know. You can look it up in the book, it'll be seven-four-four something."

At the door Rachel shook her head with a little spasm of tension. "This gives me the creeps."

"If the creeps are the worst we get," said Cooper, "we'll be lucky."

11

THE LIMO EASED over to the curb and from the back seat Moss saw Wes and two other men sitting at a table in the window. The two other men were unknown to Moss; he thought they looked like they were having a bad time. Maybe the service was bad.

Wes had seen the limo and risen from the table. As Moss waited for him to come out and join him in the back seat, he said to the driver, "Go take a walk, Omar."

"But I ain't supposed to park here," Omar said. "What if a cop comes?"

"Don't go too far. You see a cop, come back and move it." Moss snapped at him a bit harder than he'd intended to, but he wasn't in the best of moods. Omar switched off the ignition and got out of the car, and a moment later Wes was climbing into the back seat beside Moss.

"So where is she, Wes?" Moss was looking for signs of

fatigue or worry or anything at all on Wes's face but didn't find any.

"Could be anywhere," said Wes, slamming the door and closing out the street noises. "But odds are she's still in town. That stuff's her meal ticket. She'll want to try another exchange soon."

"She won't be scared off by last night?"

"I don't think so. As long as she thinks she can take a bite out of you, she'll stick around."

Moss shook his head, mouth set in a hard line. "She's not going to go to the cops about last night, is she?"

Wes was looking straight ahead, out the windshield. "Not unless she's stupid. She'll go down for extortion *and* have to look over her shoulder for the rest of her life if she does."

Moss was starting to want a drink. He opened the little locker in front of him and swore because somebody had forgotten to restock it. "So this little piece of tail isn't from Trinidad after all, huh?"

"She may have been there, but her residence is right here in town, up on the far North Side."

Moss was silent for a moment. "I had a look at the papers today. The guy in the parked car on Oak Street. That's our guy, huh?"

Wes gave him a snake look, sidelong. "Mr. Wetzel, you do not want to know. My job is to protect you, and not knowing is part of the protection."

"OK, Wes, you're right. I'm in your hands. But you've got to find the broad."

"She'll come to us eventually, I'm telling you. But we're not just sitting on our hands."

Moss nodded, staring moodily out the window. "Those two earning their pay?"

"You're getting your money's worth. We were up half the night searching the girl's place, and we've been working all day. We'll find her, we'll get the items back."

"How the hell are you going to find her? This is a city of three million people."

"But the number of places she could be hiding are limited. First, we're checking motels and places like that. One of those men in there is an ex-cop, he knows how to find people."

"You've got an ex-cop in on this? Jesus, Wes, it's the cops I have to worry about."

"Ex is the operative word with him. He's only worried about the price."

Moss gave a skeptical shake of the head. "One guy checking all the motels in the city?"

"That's not our only lead. She's got friends. She'll try and hide with them, and we'll get her."

"How the hell are you gonna find her friends?"

"We got her address book last night, when we went through her place."

Moss gave a little toss of the head. "Well, it sounds like you're on top of things. But you damn well better find her. I got one hell of a lot at stake here, Wes. Even if the courts down there are buyable, there's no guarantees. We gotta put a pillow over this right now."

"That's one thing I'm pretty good at, Mr. Wetzel."

Cooper sat at the end of the couch, next to the instrument on which his sanity depended, the telephone. It was dark outside and he had turned on the floor lamp by the armchair, casting shadows in the corners. His fourth cup of coffee sat on the steamer trunk in front of him, half drunk and lukewarm. He was paralyzed, waiting.

He had come straight home from Rachel's, believing that Diana was out there somewhere, in one piece, trying to call him. He had eaten cold ham and a can of soup and then made coffee and waited. At intervals, tired of waiting, he had picked up the phone and called people, friends of his, friends of Diana's, asking after her. Some of them had talked to the police; none had heard from Diana. It was mid-evening and the anxiety was building. Reading was impossible, television an irritation. The phone had rung twice: a wrong number and a sales pitch.

When it rang for the third time Cooper had gone to the front window and opened it to the nighttime cool. He had raised the storm window and had his head and shoulders outside, staring fiercely up and down the empty street. He banged his head on the sash pulling back in, swore and got to the phone on the second ring.

"Cooper?" The voice came from far away.

"Diana! Jesus Christ, are you all right?"

"I'm in trouble, Cooper. I've been trying to call you all day." She spoke quickly, quietly, the faint trace of accent in her voice.

"Where are you?" Cooper had sunk to the couch, weakened by relief.

"I'm in a motel, over here on Ridge."

"I'll be right there."

"No, listen. Be careful. Has anyone come around asking about me?"

"Yeah, two cops. They found Tommy."

"Nobody else?"

"Nobody else, but I was gone most of the day."

"I know. You know how many times I've dialed your number in the last twelve hours?"

"Long story. What the hell is going on with you?"

"That's another long story. Listen, I'm worried they'll come after you."

"Who?"

"The people who killed Tommy. Cooper, I'm in bad trouble." The voice wavered on the last sentence, just a touch.

"I'm coming to get you. You mean that place just off Peterson, the Chicagoland Inn or something like that?"

"That's it. Room two-thirteen, on the upper level. Be careful. Watch your back, be careful going out. I think Tommy might have given them your name."

"Give me fifteen minutes. You know how glad I am to hear your voice?"

"Oh God, me too. Hurry."

"I'm flying."

And Cooper flew, looking up and down the street as he left, daring somebody to try and stop him. He wasn't too worried about anyone watching him, figuring he would have noticed them from the window, but he did keep a watch in the rearview mirror as he sped down Glenwood and then went west on Devon. By the time he turned south he was sure nobody was interested in him.

The Chicagoland Inn was a survivor of an earlier age, when there were no interstates and the flow of U.S. 41 up through the city had supported dozens of motels. Most of the Lincoln Avenue motels had fallen on hard times and had to sell themselves like the women who now worked in them, but the Chicagoland Inn still sat in an unremarkable neighborhood, in apparent decorum and prosperity. It was an L-shaped fifties-era structure, painted robin's egg blue, with a walled-in parking court and two levels, with Coke machines and ice machines on each level just as a motel should have, and a flashing neon sign hovering over the street. The neon subscript to the sign said VACANCY.

Cooper pulled into the court and put the Valiant on the opposite side from the office. From the upper walkway, approaching Diana's door, he could see the entrance to the court and a stretch of Ridge Avenue beyond. He reached two-thirteen and knocked.

When he slipped inside and into Diana's arms, they clung to each other without speaking for a long moment. Finally Cooper pulled away and looked into her lamplit face, seeing a sleepless night and a long, long day in her dark-rimmed eyes. "You OK?" he breathed.

"Barely. I think." She replaced the chain on the door and pulled him toward the rumpled double bed. Cooper hardly noticed the room: standard motel. Diana was in jeans and a lavender sweatshirt, her shoes on the floor by the bed. An overnight bag, open with jumbled clothing spilling out, sat on an upholstered chair with wooden arms in the corner. Both the *Tribune* and the *Sun-Times* lay on the bedside table beside empty pop cans.

"You been here all day?" He sat beside her on the bed and she slipped both her arms under his and held on tight.

"Since about two. Where the hell have you been?"

"In jail."

"What?" She stiffened, pulled away from him, staring.

"I got in a fight last night and won by too big a margin."

She stared for a moment longer and then collapsed back onto the bed, letting go, giving in to a long shuddering spasm of laughter, finally drawing a rasping breath and curling up in a fetal position, her back to him, shaking again. "In jail," she managed to get out. Cooper laid a hand on her back and waited for it to stop heaving. When she had been silent for a moment she sat up slowly and wiped her eyes, slipping one arm through his again. "I thought they'd gotten you," she said. Suddenly she was sagging against him, wrung out. "I'm in deep shit, Cooper," she said.

"Lie down." He disengaged himself and started to swing her legs up onto the bed, but she stopped him with a hand to his chest.

"I'm all right. You sit down."

Cooper obeyed, dumping the overnight bag on the floor and hauling the chair over to sit at the bedside like a doctor on a house call. Diana put her feet up on the bed and leaned back against the headboard. In the light from the bedside lamp she was pale, dark eyes accented in a feline face. Cooper sat on the edge of the chair and said, "OK, talk to me."

Diana heaved a long sigh and said, "It starts with Tommy. I lied to you about Tommy."

"So I gathered. You two were getting pretty tight there."

"Cooper, that was part of his scheme. There was nothing else. What I lied about was the past."

"The past?"

"Yeah. See, we were lovers all right, way back when."

"On the *Bismarck?*"

"And afterwards. For about a year."

"Huh. There's a year of your life you never talked about."

"Not that part of it, no."

"So what the hell was Tommy up to?"

"He was trying to blackmail somebody. They killed him, and now I think they're looking for me."

"I'd say that's a safe bet, judging from the condition of your apartment."

Diana froze. "They found the place, huh?"

"You didn't see? I thought that's why you went to Rachel's."

"I went to Rachel's because I was scared they'd come after me. They must have been right behind me. How bad is it?"

"It's bad. But it's mainly a pick-up job, not much broken. What were they looking for?"

"The stuff Tommy had on this guy."

"And now you have it."

"No. I don't know where it is."

Cooper sat still, digesting. "I see. Why do they think you have it?"

"You got a while?"

"I got all night. You want to stay here?"

"I don't know where else to go. Listen to the story, you'll see why I'm not sure even your place is safe."

They looked at each other for a moment and then Cooper smiled, still feeling the great good fortune of finding her safe. "Well, if you have to be in deep shit, it's nice to have company."

Pale and drawn, Diana smiled her little crooked smile. "I was hoping you'd take that attitude."

They conferred in the parking lot, standing between Wes's LeSabre and Poulos's battered Trans Am. "Think about it," said Fudge. "She's scared and needs to hide out. Where does she go?"

"Anywhere in the fuckin' country," said Poulos. "I think we're wasting our time." Poulos leaned on the car, arms crossed on his thick chest, eyes roaming out across the parking lot. His massive head was set directly on his shoulders without the intervention of a neck.

Fudge shook his head. "We gotta assume she's staying in town. Now if she has good enough friends, she goes there. Real good friends might not be in her book, but you never know. And most of the Chicago addresses are right around this part of town, so the odds are that's where the real good friend is. That cuts down the number of places to check." He stuck a cigarette under his reddish moustache and cupped his hands to light it.

"Can you check them without setting off alarm bells?" said Wes.

"Don't worry, people trust me," said Fudge, smiling. He gave his loosened tie an absent tug. "All right. And if she doesn't hide out with friends, where's she go? She's not going to have a lot of money to spend, judging by her apartment. So she won't be at the Whitehall. She's in a motel somewhere, and there aren't that many around this part of the city."

Poulos looked at Wes. "And when we find her. Same still goes?"

"Same still goes. Make sure you get the material."

"And?"

Wes looked at him for a moment without speaking. "And call me. Just keep her quiet and call me."

Poulos's eyes flicked away, out over the parking lot. "It's that kind of deal, is it?"

"It's that kind of deal," said Wes.

"Tommy had this scheme, like always." Diana sat on the bed, knees drawn up to her chest, arms clasping them. "It started down in Trinidad. He wouldn't tell me anything about how he got the stuff, but somehow down there he got something that could put this guy in jail."

"Who's the guy?" Cooper had taken his jacket off and leaned back in the chair, intent on her words.

"A man named Moss Wetzel. I'd never heard of him. Turns out he publishes this magazine, *Maverick*. It's like *Playboy* or something."

"I've seen it around, yeah."

"Well, Tommy had something on him. That's why he came up here. All that about wanting to play the blues, that was bullshit. He came up here to blackmail the guy. And he wanted me to be his messenger, because it was safer for him."

"A real gentleman, huh?"

Diana gave a little whiff of laughter and shook her head. "He said it was a great deal for me. He offered me half the take. Half of half a million. I don't know if he really would have come through."

"What did you tell him?"

"I told him no, of course. What do you think?"

Cooper stared at her for a moment. "So what did he have on you?"

Diana's head dropped just a fraction and she stared at the worn blue bedspread. "Stuff that could put *me* in jail."

After a moment she looked up at Cooper. "Potentially, at least. I decided I couldn't take the chance."

Cooper was frowning at her. "I have lots of questions all of a sudden, but here's the big one. Why the hell didn't you tell me what was going on?"

She took a breath before answering, eyes looking into his with the exhalation. "Number one, I wasn't sure you wouldn't kill him, and I didn't want to see you go to jail for the rest of your life."

"Jesus, Diana. Give me credit for a little more brains than that."

"Number two, he said if I told you anything, the Feds would be knocking on my door the next day."

Cooper shook his head. "And I thought I knew you. What the hell did you ever do to interest the Feds?"

She closed her eyes briefly. "This all has to do with another time in my life, about ten million years ago. It has to do with why I split from Tommy in Miami."

"I'm listening."

Diana's smile was distant, faint. "You have to understand, Cooper. I was twenty-two years old and innocent as a lamb. This guitar player I met on the ship was handsome, fun, talented. . . . Tommy could make you laugh when you were down to your last dime and stranded in the rain. He was shrewd, he was funny, he had that ironic view of life. . . . It was the first time I really fell in love, my first real adult love affair. Those nights at the stern of the boat we were telling you about? We would sit there with one or two others, and I would just feel this . . . this current flowing between us. I would sit there wishing the others would fall overboard, wishing Tommy would give me some sign he liked me. This went on for a couple of weeks and then . . . the night he took me back to his cabin for the first time I remember telling myself over and over, 'I'm a woman now, I'm a woman.' He was all I wanted in the world." Diana's head lolled back against the wall as she looked at Cooper. "Don't be too hard on me. I was a sheltered child." She looked away and went on.

"Besides, I wanted adventure. I had told off my parents, dropped out of school, got this job on the boat. I wanted to see the world, I wanted to make money, I was tired of being the well-behaved little girl. And for ten months Tommy gave me the wide world." Diana gazed into the shadows for a few seconds, absent, before shivering suddenly and casting a haunted look at Cooper. "He's dead now. And I don't feel a damn thing. Except scared."

"Why should you?"

"I don't know. Because I really loved him, I guess. Or thought I did. For the first few months I was in heaven. We worked hard, sometimes at least, but we had plenty of time for all the other stuff I'd wanted, especially after we quit the boat gig. The sailing and the diving and the pub-crawling in Kingston and the bungalow on the beach in Martinique. And the whole time, lots of sex, very intense, and other stuff too—Tommy could be gallant, romantic. He could dress up and take me out for dinner and treat me like a queen. He had charm in bucketfuls. He could get people to eat out of his hand. And I guess that's what he did with me. The sun and the sea and the romance and everything went to my head, and I would have done anything he said. By the time I started coming out of that we were back in Miami and I'd already started doing things for him."

Cooper waited through a silence and said, "What kind of things?"

"Tommy always had his schemes. He was a pretty good guitar player, but unless you hit the big time there's no real money in that. So he did other things. In Miami you can guess what he did. Tommy made a little investment."

"An imported product, I'd guess."

Diana nodded. "He always knew the people he needed to know. He had a pretty good gig in Miami for a while and put everything he made from it into these deals, as kind of an investor, not actually peddling the stuff. For a while I was basically supporting us waiting tables while he speculated. But the rate of return is fabulous on that stuff and before too long he had to think about what to do with all the cash. That's where I came in. He got himself into a sort of money-laundering syndicate, with a few other relatively small players, where he could hand over sacks of cash to somebody who would put it in a bank, have it wired to some phony corporation in Panama, and bring the money back as loans and salaries and so forth, all looking perfectly legal. And the only place where a paper trail would exist, he had me to leave it. My part was to collect a regular paycheck from this fake setup in Panama City."

"I see. And somebody's got your name down somewhere."

"Yeah. The precaution I took was to get paid and deposit the money as Diana Vela, not Froelich. See, with the usual confusion over the two surnames we use, I was able to set up an account, with real ID but a fake address and all, under my mother's surname. And all I did was deposit these twenty-thousand-dollar paychecks that came in the mail from Panama every month or so, and then be sure to keep drawing out cash to support my lavish lifestyle, meaning to hand the cash back over to Tommy. Of course, he spent a lot of it on me, so who was I to complain?" She gave Cooper a veiled look, asking perhaps for absolution. "I never used the product. I never saw any, except at parties and stuff. The only thing I did was deposit those checks. I guess that helped me rationalize the moral issues away. All I knew was I was having adventures."

Cooper nodded slowly, absorbed. "But you got tired of it."

"I got tired. And scared. When it finally dawned on me that I was a criminal, I told Tommy I wasn't going to help him with that business any more. He shrugged and said OK, it was nearly over anyway. He'd made a quick killing and he was smart enough to get out. I closed the account and he stopped investing. I heaved a great big sigh of relief. But things changed after that."

"What do you mean?"

"Once I was no longer in a position to control his money, the cooling started. He wasn't quite the same lover. I started to catch on after a while."

"I guess you would," Cooper said quietly, frowning at her. "So you split."

"Not right away, no. I carried on a little internal war. Because you see, it tore me up to leave him. I had realized he was fundamentally . . . a pimp, but he was still the man who had made love to me on the beach in Guadeloupe, run off with my heart. There was a rough couple of months."

Diana was speaking slowly, irony protecting her. She shook her head and closed her eyes. "I finally left, not when I saw him purring at this other woman in the bar where he used to play, but when I realized my first impulse had been to make excuses for him, blame her. The anger finally outweighed all the rest and I flew back to San Juan the next day and went into a shell at my mother's place for a couple of months. And at the end of that time I said, OK, now. *Now* I'm a woman."

After a silence Cooper said, "You told me about other lovers. How come you never mentioned him?"

It looked to Cooper as if Diana had to struggle a little to meet his eyes and answer him. "Shame, I guess. When you're that intimate with someone, completely devoted, and he turns out to be a shit, it takes some restructuring, some suppressing, to rebuild your self-esteem. I never even told Roger, not the whole story anyway, and I was married to him. I think I would have told you eventually, but when Tommy showed up like that it was too much. My first reaction was to deny, hide it from you at all costs."

Cooper stirred on the chair, shifting stiff limbs. "OK. So Tommy had something that connected you with the drug business, right?"

The look in Diana's eyes was positively haunted. "He had some old deposit slips and a bank ID for the Diana Vela account. A picture ID, for God's sake. I don't remember what happened to it, why I didn't burn all that stuff. I was young and stupid, I guess. But he had it. And it's easy to show that I'm Diana Froelich Vela."

"So?"

"So he said the outfit in Panama had been blown by the DEA, wide open. With all the records, presumably."

Cooper shook his head. "I don't know. Whoever handled things in Panama would have been stupid to keep records of who they paid out to. That sounds a little weak to me."

"Can I take the chance? With this drug war in full swing? They just threw some guy in California in jail for ten years for giving his friend a ride to a drug buy. Cooper, I voluntarily aided in laundering proceeds of drug transactions. Not to mention evaded taxes on this so-called salary I was getting. Would you risk having some guy turn over that stuff to the Feds?"

"Hang on a second. Wouldn't he have been slitting his own throat? It was his own damn scheme."

"I pointed that out to him. He said there was absolutely no evidence to connect him with any drug deals and no one would take my word for it. He dared me to call his bluff. I didn't."

Cooper gave a single grim nod. "I bet he was a hell of a poker player. OK, so you agreed to help him. What happened?"

A long breath escaped her. "So Tommy tells me one day that we can make a half million dollars off this man Wetzel. He had something Wetzel would give an arm and a leg to get back. So he had me call the guy and set up a meeting. Tommy said it was a lot better to work something like this through a cut-out, and I was the cut-out. From my point of view it just looked like I was taking all the risks, but Tommy said he was being generous giving me half the money. Anyway, Tommy had done a little research and he said I could get through to the guy fast by using the name of someone he had associated with down in Trinidad. And he said Wetzel was a sucker for a skirt and if I sounded available he would come running. That was Tommy the pimp at work again. So I talked to the guy and gave him the lines Tommy had rehearsed me on, and it worked. We set up a meeting at the Palmer House and I gave him a sample of the stuff and got out of there. Tommy was there watching, and when we rendezvoused afterwards, he said Wetzel had had a man there watching. That's when I really started to get scared."

"What was this sample? What did Tommy have on the guy?"

"He would never tell me. He said it was safer for me not to know. All he would tell me was that it would put Wetzel in jail for a long time down in Trinidad. He just gave me a sealed manila envelope and said give him that. But I cheated. I looked. When Tommy dropped me off and went to park, just before the meeting, I went past a stationery store there on Wabash, and had an inspiration. I went in and got an identical envelope and opened the first one and looked at the stuff. Then I put it in the new envelope and went on to the Palmer House."

"And what was in the envelope?"

"Weird stuff. A map, I mean a Xerox of part of a map, with a little red X on it. And a Polaroid photo of a scrap of cloth lying on a table. It looked like the bottom part of a necktie, torn off about halfway up and real dirty, all wrinkled and stained. There was a monogram but I couldn't make it out. That was all."

"Could you tell what the map was?"

"Not from a quick glance. But it looked hilly, or mountainous, with a bit of coastline at the top. There were place names in French and Spanish, I think, and one in English—The Saddle. That's all I can remember. I'd bet it was in Trinidad."

"What did the X mark?"

"I couldn't tell. It was just an X, in the middle of nowhere, as far as I could tell at a glance."

"Huh. And a piece of a tie?"

"Looked like it. But only a picture of it. Not the tie itself."

There was a long silence. Cooper frowned into the dark corners of the room. "I can make guesses," he said.

"Me too. The piece of cloth looked like it might have been underground for a while."

"So this guy, what's his name . . ."

"Wetzel."

"He kills a guy down there and Tommy finds out about it, finds the body or something. Is that about the shape of it?"

Diana shook her head. "You know as much as I do. Tommy wouldn't tell me. But if that's right, I can see why the stuff in the envelope would throw the guy into a panic."

Cooper's frown had deepened. "And why he would kill to get it back."

Ray didn't look up for a second or two when he heard the door to the office open because the count was full on Salazar and the Reds pitcher was into his windup. When

Salazar fouled it off, Ray looked up to see a man with brown curling hair and a reddish moustache standing above him at the counter. "Ball four," said the man, nodding at the TV.

Ray shook his head as he got out of the chair. "That's a Latin ballplayer for you," he said. "Swing at anything moving." Ray gave the man the eye as he ambled over to the counter; giving people the eye was second nature after thirteen years in the motel business. He saw a tired-looking white guy in a very ordinary suit, mid-forties. In the first instant Ray guessed salesman-on-the-road, but then something about the authoritative way the guy stood at the counter, hands in his trouser pockets, chin raised a bit, giving him the eye right back, made him doubt. "What can I do for you?" Ray said.

"Police. I'm Detective Reilly, Area Six Property Crimes." The man held out his right hand and Ray reached for it slowly, wavering between two reactions. Reaction number one was alarm, and reaction number two was a sudden eagerness to please, because Ray liked cops.

"What'd I do this time?" he said, a hearty smile in place, alarm taking over for a moment.

The cop smiled back. "That's between you and your confessor. I'm looking for somebody else tonight."

Ray relaxed, recognizing a kinsman: Chicago working-class white guy. The alarm vanished and Ray was immediately part of a two-man conspiracy: Chicago working-class white guys against the world. Ray had wanted to be a policeman long ago, but they didn't take just anybody; Ray hadn't even made the waiting list. He had swallowed his disappointment and after a while he had recovered even from the envy; Ray loved cops. He loved the way they wore their authority, walking tall and keeping the lid on the mean streets. He loved the trappings, the radios and sticks and cuffs and big heavy revolvers. He loved watching a tac unit tear down the street in the unmarked car, racing off to do battle. He loved seeing black punks with their hands spread out on the hood of a squad, looking worried as an officer went methodically through their pockets, doing the job patiently and right. He loved talking to detectives, giving them the facts in a clear, well-organized manner, doing his best to help. He loved watching them as they moved, trying to catch glimpses of the heat lurking under their jackets.

"You mean a guest?" he said.

"Possibly." The cop inclined his head a little to one side, as if trying to decide if Ray could be trusted. "We're looking for a young lady."

Ray blinked at him. "This place is clean as a whistle. We don't rent by the hour, we never had no problems with . . . that kind of client."

"Relax." The cop shook his head patiently, and Ray's alarm receded again. "The lady we're looking for is wanted in connection with a confidence game somebody was running on old folks up in Rogers Park. You know the type of thing—all I need is that five hundred from your account and I can make us both rich." Ray nodded, following intently. "We got these characters wrapped up yesterday, but the girl got a phone call in time or something and she split. Except we're sure she's still around. She's not going anywhere without her share of the proceeds, which she thinks is still safely hidden in the basement of a house up there."

"And you think she's hiding out in a motel."

"Or the Y or something, yeah. Not under her real name, of course."

"Sure. What's she look like?"

Detective Reilly from Area Six Property Crimes reached inside his jacket and pulled out a photograph. He laid it on the counter and slid it over toward Ray. The photograph showed two young women with their arms around each other's shoulders, beaming big white smiles at the camera, with greenery in the background. One of them had dark hair and big dark eyes, and the other had auburn hair and faint freckles. "The one on the right there, the brown-haired one," said Reilly. "That's our girl."

Ray just stared at the photo for a moment and then looked up and stared at Reilly. His heart had started to beat faster, because for once in his life, Ray realized, he was really going to be in on something, was really going to help the police. In a hushed voice, looking into Reilly's suddenly interested eyes, he said, "That's her."

Reilly said, "That's who?"

"She checked in here today. She's up in, I don't know, two-thirteen I think. I should have known something was funny. I mean, something *was* funny. I just didn't think . . ."

"Whoa, slow down. What do you mean something was funny?"

Ray regrouped and leaned closer to the detective over the counter. "She came in here and told a big sob story about how her purse and stuff had been stolen, so she didn't have any ID, see? She said she was trying to get in touch with her family or someone but she wasn't sure when she could do it and she might have to stay here a day or two. She had some emergency cash she'd managed to hold on to and she paid for a night in advance, so I checked her in. Look, I'll show you the card, she gave her name as . . ."

"That's OK, that's OK." Reilly stopped him with a hand on the arm. "Look, you gotta be sure. You're sure this is the lady?"

"That's her, absolutely. Jesus, I should have figured."

"Not necessarily. Remember, this is a pro. She's an actress, she's good at telling stories. You didn't do anything wrong. Now listen, do you have any idea if she's up there right now?" The cop was in charge, brisk, efficient.

"As far as I know. But she could have slipped out. She didn't have a car. She said she was on a bus trip or something. Boy, I really fell for it, didn't I?"

"Good thing you did. Now we've got her. You're sure it's two-thirteen?"

Ray glanced at the registration card. "That's it, two-thirteen."

"Are the rooms on either side of her occupied?"

Ray was brisk and efficient now, too, riffling through the cards. "Yeah. Both of 'em. Just rented two-fourteen a couple of hours ago."

The detective rewarded him with a nod. "OK. Now the best thing you can do is nothing. I'm gonna go call for some backup. You just go on doing what you do on a night like this. We don't want any unusual activity to warn her, if she's still up there."

"Right, right, OK."

"No standing at the window here or anything. It won't be much of a show anyway, a nice quiet arrest if everything goes all right."

"You got it."

"You just watch the rest of the ball game there and take care of any customers who come in and I'll let you know when it's all over." Reilly's voice had taken on the same hushed quality as Ray's.

"OK, good luck." Ray wanted badly to rush to the window as soon as the detective left and watch, but he wanted even more to do exactly what he was told.

"There is one more thing you might do for me," the detective said, pausing by the door.

"What's that?"

"You got a passkey?"

12

"IT WAS SUPPOSED to be a dry run." Diana had risen from the bed, her limbs stiff, and was slowly wearing a path into the rug, from the bathroom door to the foot of the bed and back again. Cooper had leaned back in the chair and hoisted his feet up onto the bed, watching her move through the dim lamplight. Outside, traffic ebbed and flowed with the changing of the lights.

"Tommy knew I was scared, and I think he knew I had good reason. He said Wetzel would be planning to bring his goons along but we could get rid of them. So he came up with this plan. He picked a place on Rush Street for the fake exchange, right down the way from the bar where I go after work sometimes. He had me call Wetzel and tell him to bring the money. I gave him all the details of the switch, just as if we were really planning to do it. But what was supposed to happen was that Tommy would be at the bar, watching, like before at the Palmer House. I would go straight from work to my usual place just up the street. Tommy would let Wetzel wait while he tried to spot his people. Then he would call me at the other bar and fill me in on who was with Wetzel. Then I was supposed to call Wetzel back at the first place—Tommy had gotten the number and everything—and tell him the swap was off and he was to leave his men at home next time. I would describe the men Tommy had spotted to show him I knew what I was talking about. And I would tell him I'd call him in the morning with new instructions and he'd better be ready to roll, alone, because I wouldn't give him much time. Then I would go meet Tommy at the car. That was the way it was supposed to work."

"Huh," said Cooper. He watched as Diana sank onto the bed again, passing a hand over her forehead and back through her hair. Fatigue was showing in her face, in her movements. "Where was the real switch supposed to happen?" he said.

"At the new Greyhound station, down on Harrison. He had it all worked out. I would be there waiting, like I was going to catch a bus. Wetzel would come in with the suitcase full of money and sit next to me. After a while I would get up and take the suitcase into the restroom and count the money, and if it was all there I would come out and give him the envelope. Then I would get on a bus for Indiana, and get off in Gary, where Tommy would meet me with the car. He had the schedules and things worked out. He said doing the exchange in a public place was our best insurance. That didn't reassure me a whole lot, even if he could spot Wetzel's gorillas. I wasn't convinced Wetzel would do as he was told and leave them at home the next day."

"No. Doesn't seem likely." Cooper mused, frowning across the bed at Diana's still figure. "What did you tell Wetzel about the exchange in the bar? What was the plan there?"

"Essentially the same as the real plan for the bus station. Go into the john to count the money, come out and give him the envelope. I'm glad that's not how Tommy was really going to do it, because I don't know how the hell I would have gotten away with a suitcase full of cash."

"Really. Did Wetzel say anything about hauling a suitcase full of cash into a crowded bar? The bus station's one thing, but it would have been a little conspicuous in a bar, wouldn't it?"

Diana stared for a moment. "If he didn't like it, he didn't say anything. I guess either he was ready to go along or he had his own plan by that time."

"Huh. So what happened?"

"I don't know." Diana shook her head slowly, pulling her legs up onto the bed and sitting cross-legged. She made a half-hearted shrugging motion. "Before I even left work I got a phone call from him. He must have been at the bar by that time—I could hear music and talk in the background. He was brief—he just said forget it, everything's off for tonight and go home and wait for me. That's all. He had the car, so I hiked over to Clark and Division and hopped the El. I knew something was pretty wrong, but I kept thinking maybe it meant I was free. The first thing I did when I got home was to look for the stuff, the evidence Tommy had. He'd been keeping it in a big leather folder he had, along with the stuff he had on me. I found the thing and got the clasp open with a screwdriver, but it was empty except for a little cash."

"That's interesting," said Cooper.

"Yeah. I thought he must have taken it with him, except . . ." Diana paused, trying to work it out.

"Except if it was Wetzel who killed him, he would have gotten the stuff from him, so why did he have to search your place later?"

"Yeah. I *guess* it was Wetzel or his men who killed him."

"Who else? They must have spotted him. He made a break for the car, they got him."

"But what happened to the stuff?"

"I don't know. How did they spot him?"

"I've been thinking about that. I think he must have run into Wetzel down in Trinidad. Tommy was pretty close-mouthed about what went on down there, but he must have known him, been associated with him somehow.

How else would he have gotten this evidence? Or one of Wetzel's men knew him and spotted him last night."

"Could be." Cooper was lost for a moment, absorbed in the oil landscape that hung over the head of the bed. "How did they find your place?"

"Tommy must have told them where I lived. I guess when he saw they had him he tried to bargain. He must have told them I had the stuff or something."

Cooper shook his head. "He was a low form of life."

"I was worried he would have told them about you, knowing I might try to hide with you. But whatever he told them it doesn't seem to have worked."

"Mm." Cooper was trying to picture it. "So after you saw the evidence wasn't there?" he said.

"So I got out. I called Rachel and went over there, and today I came here. I didn't want to get anybody else mixed up in this. I gave the guy here a false name and a story about being robbed so I wouldn't have to show ID, and I kept trying to call you. It's been a very long day."

Cooper took his feet off the bed, leaned forward, rested his elbows on his knees, clasped and unclasped his hands. Outside in the night somebody honked. Cooper raised his eyes to Diana's face and said, "Why haven't you called the police?"

Her face registered something, briefly—surprise or affront or perhaps just acknowledgment. "Think about it," she said. "I was actively trying to blackmail the guy. I can't imagine they'd be too lenient."

"You were coerced."

"Prove it." Her gaze challenged Cooper's. "That's the first thing they'll say. Prove it. How can I?"

"Tell 'em the story. You come forward and help them bag the guy who shot Tommy, they'll be more likely to believe you. Or cut a deal even if they don't."

Diana was looking at him from beneath lowered brows now, as taut as a trip wire. Her voice had ice at the edges. "Cooper. I've had a lot of time to think about this in here today. If I go to the police, they will see a small-time extortionist who got scared when the going got rough. If I explain what Tommy had on me I'll have the federal government down on me. Even if the police believe me about who killed Tommy, they won't have any proof of anything. Just my word. Wetzel and his people will still be out there, and when I get out on bond or whatever, I won't be able to go near a window for the rest of my brief life. I cannot go to the police, you understand?"

Cooper stared at her, seeing things in her eyes he'd never seen. Finally he said, "You have to, Diana. Don't be an idiot."

For a moment he thought she was going to throw something, the pillow, the lamp maybe. She rocked forward on the bed, rigid with tension, eyes locked on his. "Yeah, that's the word, isn't it? I've been an idiot from the start, haven't I? Well I'm sorry. But no more. No policemen, Cooper. *That* . . . that I can't have."

Cooper was on his feet, pacing, speechless for a moment. He wheeled to face the bed. "The cops are not going to put a bullet in your head. They will put you through the mill, growl at you, call you a lair, laugh at you, insult you, make you feel like shit. They're good at that. Maybe—just maybe—they'll charge you with something. But they aren't going to kill you. I'm sorry I used the word idiot, but you've got to see clearly what your choices are here. There's only one smart one."

Without a word Diana rose from the bed and snatched the overnight bag from the floor. She stuffed clothes back in it, zipped it, reached for her shoes.

"What the fuck are you doing?" said Cooper.

"I need help, Cooper. I don't need a goddamn lecture. Call me stupid if you want, but either help me or get out of my way."

She was heading for the door when Cooper came out of his stupor. He grabbed her wrist as she reached for the latch and held her, looking into those fierce eyes and seeing a stranger. He let her arm drop and leaned on the door.

"So what are your options?" he said after a moment.

"I don't know." The words were said slowly, evenly spaced, and behind them was desolation. "I was hoping you'd have some ideas." The ice was gone and the tone was a hair's breadth from pleading.

Cooper turned and stepped absently toward the window, reaching for the curtain, then hesitating. He went to the bedside lamp and bent to turn it off. In the darkness he returned to the window and moved the curtain aside. He could see the lit walkway just outside, the parking court below and the street beyond it. Lights burned behind closed curtains in the perpendicular wing of the motel, but there was no movement. Cooper let the curtain fall shut. He stepped carefully to Diana, feeling for her in the darkness. His hand found hers and he led her to the end of the bed. They sat down and there was silence for a while. Cooper could hear her breathing.

He thought for a long time, not liking anything about the position, not one thing. "Sounds like we need to get a hold of Tommy's stuff," he said finally.

Seconds passed, and Diana squeezed his hand gently. "What do we do with it? If we find it."

A long slow breath escaped Cooper. "What were you going to do with it, if you found it?"

"I hadn't thought that far. Last night I was thinking on the run. I had some idea of giving it to the police, getting Wetzel put away. But I hadn't really thought it through."

Cooper shook his head in the dark. "I still think your instinct was right. Get yourself a lawyer and deal."

"I'm looking at years of legal trouble, Cooper." In the dark Diana's voice was disembodied, distant.

"Any way you cut it you're looking at trouble."

"I can run. Help me run, Cooper."

"I'll run with you to hell and back if that's what you want. But think about it first. Sit here for a minute and think about it and then tell me what you want to do, and we'll go and do it."

Cooper waited. The wait stretched on, and he could feel the fear and the resistance through Diana's hand. His eyes were growing accustomed to the dark, and he could make out her profile in the light coming around the edges of the curtains. She stared wide-eyed into the mouth of the night, unmoving, and suddenly Cooper was looking at the frightened Puerto Rican girl who had been tossed into a fourth-grade class in Florida without knowing a word of English. He wanted to pull her to him and hold on for dear life, but her hand on his was saying "don't move."

The sound of a key sliding into a lock dropped into the

silence like ice down their backs. Cooper felt Diana's hand tighten as he twisted to look at where he knew the door was, hearing the key turn. He was unable to move until the door came open six inches and thumped as it hit the limit of the chain, and then he swept Diana onto the floor behind the bed.

Everyone waited. Perhaps three seconds passed in silence. Crouched on top of Diana, Cooper could crane around the corner of the bed and see the door; through the six-inch gap he could see the rail at the edge of the walkway but nothing else. Then there was a shuffling outside and something came into view: what looked like bolt cutters, the jaws going around the chain that held the door fast.

"Who is it?" Cooper shouted, for lack of anything better to shout.

The bolt cutters were withdrawn and there was silence again. Cooper saw things happening fast: people coming through with guns, himself charging the door, trying to slam it shut again and get the bed against it before they could regroup. He was aware of Diana's hand, clutching his shirt in a vise grip. He was rising to charge the door when he heard footsteps outside, more than one person, fading away down the walk to the right.

Cooper had time to think of the window he'd noticed at the rear of the room; it was small and high up and he wasn't sure how much of a drop there would be or where to. He had time to think that the men with the bolt cutters had wanted to do things quietly and hadn't expected him to be there. Then Cooper thought that when you were trapped it was time to take the initiative. "Stay put," he whispered and disengaged himself from Diana, tearing at the laces to his shoes. He got them off and yanked his shirttail out of his waistband and lost a couple of buttons getting the shirt off. Then he went to the door and undid the chain and burst out onto the walkway, doing up his belt buckle, the picture of an irate guest interrupted in slumber.

He saw them right away, two of them, at the head of the stairs to the lower level. One of them had the bolt cutters hanging at his side. Noise, thought Cooper. That's the last thing they want. "What the fuck?" he shouted, as loudly as he could.

One of the men gestured to the other, who started down the stairs. The remaining man came slowly back along the walk toward Cooper. He was medium height, stocky, wearing a suit. He walked with his hands in his trouser pockets, as if he had all the time in the world to cover the fifty feet of walkway between him and Cooper. Cooper watched him come and wondered briefly if this was a cop.

"Who are you?" he said, not shouting but louder than polite conversation required.

The man stopped in front of him. "Management," he said quietly. His eyes took in Cooper from head to toe.

"Management?" The skepticism in Cooper's voice was genuine, but for a moment he was thrown off, doubting.

"Yeah. And you're hitting the road, Jack, and the broad with you."

Cooper gaped for a moment, catching up. "What broad?" he said stupidly.

"Let's cut the shit, huh? We don't rent by the hour here. You want a quick piece of ass, try Lincoln Avenue. We're legit here. Now grab your clothes and clear out. I'll deal with the broad."

"There's no woman in there. You got the wrong room, or a dirty mind." Cooper had caught up enough to know that management wouldn't operate this way, or if they did they wouldn't back off just because they heard his voice in the dark.

"There's not, huh? Can I take a look?" The man was an inch shorter than Cooper but broad and solid-looking under the jacket. His chin rose just a bit, challenging. His eyes were tired-looking, slightly watery, but they didn't blink.

Cooper had been in a lot of stare-downs and he didn't flinch from this one. He knew the man was lying, and the man had to know he knew. But for form's sake there was a role to play. "I ought to deck you and call the cops," he said. "But I'll make a deal with you."

"What's that?"

"You come and look in the room. If you find a woman

in there, you can have us both arrested. If there's no woman in there, I get to deck you after all."

Seconds passed while they stared at each other, two feet apart. Cooper was seeing it all in advance, following the man into the dark room and cold-cocking him before he could turn on a light, getting the piece he would have on him and calling the cops, over any objections Diana might have. "Deal?" he finally said.

Just perceptibly, the man relaxed. Either he wasn't sure, or he wasn't going to let Cooper take him into a dark room. "I'll take your word for it," he said. "My desk man said he saw the broad come up to the room. I guess he must have called it wrong. My apologies. The room's on the house for tonight, OK?"

Cooper just watched as the man spun and went away down the walk toward the stairs. He glanced out over the parking court, looking for the other one. He didn't see him, but he would be close. Cooper knew he'd won nothing but time. He went back to the open door of the room, seeing a curtain fall back in a lighted window across the way, a figure in a darkened doorway three rooms down. He stood in the doorway of two-thirteen and watched the courtyard, hearing nothing behind him, wishing he had good news to take to Diana.

A dark car, maybe a Trans Am, eased out of the parking lot onto Ridge Avenue and went away east. At least one of them will stay, as long as necessary, thought Cooper. And maybe more will come. He thought frantically about possibilities and decided that there wasn't really any choice except to persuade Diana to throw herself on the mercy of the court. With only one exit and at least two unfriendlies out there, they needed police help. He stepped back into the room and closed the door, feeling for the chain.

When he had the door secured he went to the end of the bed again. "Diana," he called softly.

He was answered by the breath of wind that came through the little window high up in the back wall. He felt briefly on the floor where she had lain and then turned on the light in the bathroom and saw the chair sitting below the open window. With visions of Diana lying in the alley with a couple of broken legs, he stood on the chair and looked out. He saw the wooden light pole next to the window and a clear, well-lit stretch of perfectly empty alleyway below.

Cooper sat on the bed and thought. Outside there were only traffic noises, a murmur in the night. Cooper thought until he was sure he knew what had to be done. After a few minutes he retrieved his shirt, jacket and shoes. Dressed again, he picked up the bag Diana had left on the floor and turned off the light in the bathroom. He slipped out onto the walkway, pulling the locked door shut behind him. He made his way to the stairs and went down. A look around the court showed only parked cars, but he knew at least one of them had somebody inside. He spotted somebody sitting in what looked like a Chrysler Imperial on the far side as he walked slowly toward the exit onto Ridge Avenue.

He moved a few feet away from the motel gate and took advantage of a red light on Ridge to jaywalk. A dark, tree-lined residential street shot north from Ridge opposite him. Cooper left the bright lights with relief and headed into the shadows.

If they were interested enough to come after him, he didn't want them to know what kind of car he drove. The car could get picked up later. He wasn't sure they'd come; if they thought they really had had the wrong room they'd let him go, and if they thought Diana was still back there they'd sit and watch or maybe go in again. If anyone did try to follow, they'd either have to do it on foot or be conspicuous in a slowly moving car. Cooper resisted the urge to turn and look until he was well up the block. When he turned he saw no one on the street behind him, either walking or driving.

The street, it turned out, was Hermitage. Cooper followed it all the way up to Devon, hoping, flinching a bit when cars went by, resisting the urge to look back every five steps. At Devon he went right and hiked to Clark Street and pushed into the dark shabby bar on the northwest corner. The bar was full of old men like Stumps. They watched Cooper in silence, sullen or indifferent or just tired. He sat at the end of the bar, near the door, and ordered a draft and waited, wondering what to do if he was wrong about what Diana would have done. *I'm so lonesome I could cry,* said the jukebox.

Diana walked in two minutes later, pausing on the threshold for a second before spotting him. Cooper felt muscles unclenching, anxiety letting go. She came to his side and he put an arm around her waist, searching her face. Her face was vacant but her eyes held his.

"Are you damn sure nobody saw you?" Cooper said.

"I'm damn sure." He could barely hear her over the music. "I cut through a couple of back yards and circled around to Ridge by the Ravenswood tracks, then came back down Hermitage in time to see you come out. You went right by me, halfway up the block."

"You're a pro."

Diana clasped her hands on his shoulder, that wide-eyed stare still locked on him. "They were going to kill me, weren't they?" she said.

"Probably. After they made you tell them where Tommy's stuff was."

"I couldn't have told them."

"Then it's a damn good thing you got away."

Diana's eyes finally left his and danced for a moment out over the static gloom of the interior, neon reflecting off the bar and the bottles ranged behind it. "How did they find me?"

"I don't know. Maybe just checked motels."

She nodded vaguely. "What do we do now?"

Cooper shifted his untouched stein a half inch on the dark wood and then scratched at his ill-shaven neck. "We get you a lawyer and go to the police. Tonight."

He felt Diana shiver in his embrace, a long tremor that seemed to run all the way down her trunk. "I can't," she said, barely audible.

"Then you go someplace far away. For a fairly long time. Either way, your life is going to be severely disrupted. Normality is gone for a while anyway. The cops are your safest option. You have to know that now, don't you?"

"They'll send me to jail."

"No they won't. Not if you cooperate. You walk in and hand them Wetzel, they'll believe you about Tommy coercing you. The drug stuff, they'll forget. That's how they work. Quid pro quo."

She was silent for a time, rigid against him. A bent and swollen old bartender made his way down to ask if she wanted a drink. She shook her head absently and he walked away grumbling. The jukebox fell silent. Finally Diana put her lips close to Cooper's ear and said, "They'd be more likely to believe me if I had that stuff Tommy had on Wetzel."

After a moment Cooper said, "I have a feeling I'm destined to lose this argument. If you're not scared enough to go to the police now, I don't know what it'll take."

She put a hand on his chin and turned his face to hers. Her eyes were as deep as the midnight sky. "I'm scared all right, Cooper. I'm scared of getting killed if I don't go to the police and I'm scared of getting killed if I do. Remember, I don't have *item one* of evidence for my story. Nothing on Wetzel at all. Just a story. The cops'll shake their heads, Wetzel'll laugh it off, and he'll get to me. On the street if I don't go to jail, in jail if I do. Yeah, I'm scared. But I'm not ready to go to the police. Not yet."

"Then get the hell out of town."

"Where? Where do I go?"

"San Juan, Paris, Berlin, Hong Kong. Pick one."

"Without you? For how long?"

"Long as it takes for things to get quiet."

She considered it; Cooper could see her thinking about it as she stared down the long lonesome bar. "Not yet," she finally said.

"So what in the name of God do you want to do?"

"Help me find that evidence. Tommy hid it somewhere, and we can find it. And with it is the stuff he was holding over my head. I have to get my hands on it before we go to the police. Then, if they can nail Wetzel I'll be safe. Maybe."

Cooper took a drink of the beer and stared out the window past the neon Old Style sign at the traffic easing by on Devon. "All right," he said, trying to ignore his better judgment. "We'll need to park you someplace."

"No more motels."

"No. Not my place either, 'cause the cops may be back. And no friends, either."

She shivered again. "You think they could trace my friends?"

"Probably not. But your friends all know you're wanted by the police. Do you want to put them in the position of harboring a fugitive?"

"Where the hell am I going to stay?"

Cooper looked down the long bar, seeing old men's faces, thinking out the next twelve hours or so. "How about the basement of a church?" he said.

Cecil stood in the darkness at the edge of the parking lot. Three hundred yards in front of him lights swept past on the interstate. Behind him the diesel engine of the Trailways bus rumbled. Faint voices came from the doorway of the restaurant beyond the bus. Soon it would be time to get back on. The night air was cool.

Cecil didn't know where he was, except that it was a long way from the sea, the farthest from the sea he had ever been in his life. He looked at the stars visible overhead and tried to decide if the sky looked familiar. He knew the sky changed as you went farther north, but he had never paid enough attention to the stars to be able to tell if the change had begun. Cecil was farther north than he had ever been, and he wondered how many more hours of immobility he would have to endure. He had not thought there was any bus ride in the world that would take so long.

Cecil stood in the dark at the edge of a Georgia peanut field and thought about the size of the massive North American continent and about Chicago, which was only a name to him. He wondered if there were still gangsters in Chicago.

THE DOORBELL BROUGHT Cooper out of deep waters, and it cost him some effort to sit up and get his feet on the floor. It rang a second time, for a full five seconds, while he was zipping up his jeans, and to Cooper it sounded like the ring of authority.

Hunt was as lean as remembered, and Peck hadn't grown any more hair. They didn't pause at the threshold this time. Cooper got the feeling he was being backed into the center of the room as they advanced into it.

"Sleep OK?" Peck said.

"Till just now." Cooper was still shirtless, still rubbing sleep out of his eyes. For a frantic moment he couldn't think what his role had to be, what he would say to them if he had never heard from Diana. "What's the news?" he said.

"That's what we were going to ask you."

"No news here. You guys always catch me at my best."

"That's the idea," said Peck. "We like to talk to people when they're at the top of their form."

Cooper looked from Hunt to Peck and back again. "Want some coffee?"

Peck scowled at him. "Sure. We could go sit in the kitchen. I love talking in the kitchen. It's so homey, you know?"

They followed Cooper with heavy, unhurried steps. He rummaged for the percolator and the coffee. "Those are some mean scars you got there," said Hunt, leaning against the doorframe.

"Shrapnel's mean stuff," said Cooper. He put the percolator on the stove. "Let me go put a shirt on."

"Mind if I come with you?"

The detective trailed him to the door of the bedroom, where he surveyed the rumpled empty bed, the clothes draped across the chair and the books strewn on the windowsill and the shelves while Cooper pulled a T-shirt on over the scars. "No word from Diana, huh?" the detective said.

"Nothing." Cooper pushed past him into the hall. Cooper heard the door to the bathroom creak behind him before Hunt followed him back through the dining room. In the kitchen, Peck had taken a seat at the table and was drumming his fingers on it. Cooper looked at the percolator and then leaned on the counter and crossed his arms. "I haven't seen her," he said.

Hunt resumed his spot in the doorway. "That's kind of strange, isn't it? Considering?"

"Considering what?"

"How close you two are. I mean, everybody we talk to tells us that if Diana was in trouble, she'd come to you."

Cooper was silent, fighting with his better judgment again. "Yes," he said. "She would. That's why I'm worried."

A look passed between the two policemen and then Peck said, "Let me ask you something."

"Shoot."

"Did she ever use drugs?"

"Alcohol. Very moderately."

The answer seemed to annoy Peck. His eyes narrowed. "Level with me. She ever use coke? Smoke a little weed, maybe? Anything else?"

"Not since I've known her."

"What's that supposed to mean?"

"It means just about everybody I know has used drugs at one time or another. I had my wild youth, you probably had yours. It wouldn't surprise me if Diana had sampled the usual things, but since I've known her the hardest stuff she's done is an occasional whiskey sour."

"Here's why I'm asking, MacLeish." Peck held his head on one side, as if staring at a curious fish. "Somebody took her place apart looking for something. I can stay up all night guessing, but in my experience there's a narrow range of things people are looking for in a case like that. What I'm wondering is if your girlfriend had a little business concern going, whether she was moving some sort of merchandise she had to keep hidden."

"That's bullshit. You can ask anybody who knew her."

"Would you have known?"

"I'd have known."

"Would you have helped?" said Hunt abruptly from the doorway.

Cooper glared at him. "If I was in on it, I wouldn't be likely to tell you, would I?"

"No, I guess not," said Peck. "You know, this Thorne character had kind of an interesting background."

Cooper waited. "Yeah?"

"Yeah. Ten years ago in Miami he seemed to have a lot of friends in the cocaine business. That gets our attention right away. Getting shot's kind of common in those circles. I was hoping we could find out a little more about your girlfriend's relations with him back then."

Cooper felt his skin prickling. "She never told me anything about all that. She had her wild youth, just like me. I wasn't too curious."

Peck sighed, still drumming on the table. "I guess we're going to have to ask around some more."

"I told you everything I knew last night," Cooper said, truthfully. "I've cooperated all I could," he said, less so.

"And we appreciate it," Peck said. "We just want to make sure of one thing."

"What's that?"

"We want to make sure you're not hiding her. Or helping her to hide. Or advising her to hide, or to run away. You might be tempted to do that. But it wouldn't be a very good idea."

"Why would she want to run away?"

"If she killed Tommy Thorne, I think she'd want to run away and hide, don't you?"

"Why the hell would she kill him?"

"I don't know." He turned to Hunt. "Do you know?"

"I sure as hell don't know. I thought that's what we were here to find out."

"Yeah, it is." Peck turned back to Cooper. "On the other hand, if she didn't kill him, why the hell would she run away?"

"Maybe she didn't run away," said Cooper. "Maybe something happened to her."

"Maybe. But there doesn't seem to be any reason to think something happened to her. We've only got one dead body here. And it was in her car. So who am I supposed to be suspicious of? Now, I'll be very sorry if something did happen to her. Not just for her sake and yours. But because as far as I can see she's about the only one who can tell us what happened to Tommy Thorne. And I'd really like to know what happened to him. So." Peck stood up and came over to stand directly in front of Cooper. "If you know where she is and aren't telling us, or if you know what happened to her or to Tommy Thorne and aren't telling us . . ." He put a finger in the center of Cooper's chest. "Think twice, because obstructing an investigation is something we take very, very seriously. You understand me?"

Cooper looked back at him, blinking, understanding only too well. "You're leaning on the wrong guy," he said quietly. "I have enough to worry about without defending myself from you guys."

Peck took his finger away and leaned back, infinitesimally. For an instant he appeared to soften. "You got our number. Enjoy the coffee." He turned away, and the two detectives left Cooper leaning on the counter and listening to the soft hiss of the percolator.

"But I like women." Moss held his hands out in a palms-up appeal. "How could I be in this business and not like women?"

The broad wasn't going to buy that, he could tell. She shifted very slightly on the chair, just a short length of stockinged calf sticking out below the skirt, and gave that little superior smile. "I'm not sure lust and liking are the same thing," she said.

Moss was perfectly willing to joust with her. "Of course not. But they can coexist, can't they? Listen. You're trying to trap me into some kind of statement that shows all I do is exploit women sexually . . ."

"I'm not trying to trap you. I'm asking questions and you're answering." She was still smiling, like well-dressed frigid women always smiled, like they were a superior race.

"As I was saying." The smile was frozen on Moss's face; he was determined not to let her get to him. "What is exploitation? All the women who appear in my magazine are paid and paid well. Except for the ones who send in their pictures voluntarily for the Neighborhood Nymphs feature, which is one of our most popular. Ever seen it? You should take a look." It might warm up your juices a little, thought Moss sourly. "We publish their pictures no matter what they look like—fat, skinny, whatever. Women who want to feel sexy. It makes 'em feel good about themselves. That's what we're all about. Healthy erotica."

"I see." She had stopped smiling at least. She glanced at the little recorder running on the desktop and said, "I've looked at your magazine. I noticed you have a video review section? In which you publish stills from and review pornographic videos?"

"The latest adult videos, that's right. Can we talk about that word pornographic for a moment?"

"Suppose we talk about the videos. Two of the ones reviewed in your last issue portray scenes of rape. For, shall we say, titillating effect. Do you have any comment on that?"

"My comment is that I do not and never have condoned rape. Some of these videos are made to cater to certain . . . tastes I don't share and don't promote. We just review 'em. There are plenty of adult films nowadays that are for couples, produced to appeal to female viewers as well. You ought to take a look at . . ."

"Excuse me, but I'd like to linger on this point a little."

Now she was getting outraged, thought Moss. Getting that fiery look in her eyes. Tossing that nice head of black hair, pointing the goddamn pencil at me. He laid his hands on the desk, the smile subsiding a little.

"You call rape a 'taste,' do you?" the lady writer said.

"No, I'd call it a crime, of course. Look, I'm not gonna lie to you and say there aren't some sleazeballs in this business. But I'm asking you to take a fair look at the magazine and who we're trying to appeal to and what we're trying to promote. I think if you're fair you'll have to admit that erotica doesn't have to mean exploitation."

"I'd admit that. But the issue here isn't erotica in general, but your magazine. I'd like to talk about what's been called the 'pornographic aesthetic,' as displayed in the captions that accompany your picture spreads."

Give me a break, thought Moss, the smile almost extinct. The pornographic aesthetic?

"In your last issue a caption under one of the nude photos reads, and I quote, 'Jessica stays hot throughout the sultry afternoon, thinking of the moment when her man will come and she will be able to submit to his every desire.' Would you like to comment on that?"

"What's wrong with that? That's an image of a woman wanting to please her lover. You ever been in love? You must know the feeling, if you'll excuse the personal reference."

He thought he'd gotten to her, but after a blink or two she went on. "The point is, it's not exactly an image of mutual sexual gratification, is it? It's an image of sexual submission, as are many of the other captions. In your May issue there's one . . ."

"Spare me." Moss had to work a little to put a tight little grin in place. "I know what the captions are like. Yes, they are designed to arouse desire in the male. Look, it's a men's magazine. You want to get turned on, read *Playgirl.*" God knows what would turn you on, he added to himself.

"So there is then no pretense of being a magazine of healthy erotica, for couples."

Moss laced his fingers, professorial and authoritative behind the desk. "I'm not sure you speak for all women, you know. You know how many women send us their photos each month?"

"Quite a few, I'm sure. And I would never claim to speak for all women. But I'm sure I speak for many in deploring the tacit dehumanization of women that is the primary message of your publication, if not the explicit one."

"Did you major in sociology?" said Moss.

That shut her up for a second. When she recovered she said, "If you don't like the word dehumanization, let's just say that *Maverick* promotes the pornographic aesthetic, shall we? The emphasis on women's sexual availability to the exclusion of all else."

"You're giving the interview now, are you?" Moss delivered his best chuckle of weary amusement, showing he didn't care. "Look, write what you want. I've explained our philosophy to you, tried to communicate that we are not rapists, we value women as human beings. We are an erotic publication, yes, but erotica is a part of human life. We're not really bothered by feminist diatribes. We'll stand on our record. Any more questions?"

She shot him a little smile of triumph that made him run cold inside for a second, then looked down at her notes while he slowly unclenched his fingers. "No," she said, "I think that's all. I thank you for your time, Mr. Wetzel."

"I'll get a transcript of the interview to approve before you publish, will I?"

"As we agreed. I think your words speak for themselves, and in any event, I never deal in distortion." She had switched off the recorder and was shoving it into her bag. Moss watched her move, shaking his head very slightly, sadly. She really wasn't a bad-looking woman, he thought, one of these hard-driving professional broads that needed a good lay every once in a while to loosen her up.

"You should come to our big party next month, when we inaugurate our new offices up on Wacker. I'll introduce you to some people, some of the women who have appeared in our pages. You can get their view of things."

Standing in front of him with that prissy superior smile, she said, "That's very kind of you, Mr. Wetzel. I'll keep it in mind. I'll be in touch." She spun and marched toward the door. Moss watched her go, hips flouncing a bit under the loose skirt, thinking how much he'd like to pin her against the desk, hike that skirt up . . .

The minute the office door closed behind her he was on the phone. "Send Wes up here," he said. Moss slammed the receiver down and went to the window, where he looked out over the Loop and chewed on a fingernail, waiting.

Wes came in with a light tap on the door. He was wearing a navy-blue sweater that hugged his broad squat torso, and Moss wondered again where the hell he kept his weapon. "Have a seat, Wes," he said. Moss went around behind the desk and sank onto the deluxe chair with a grunt. He picked up the hundred-and-fifty-dollar fountain pen and said "So what's the situation?"

"We lost her," Wes said. He looked mean this morning, Moss thought. "I'm not going to bullshit you, Mr. Wetzel. We should have had her. But there is one new factor."

"What's that?"

"She had a man in there with her. We don't know who he is."

"So what happened? Why didn't you get 'em both?"

"I wasn't there when my men found her. They got me on the beeper but they didn't wait for me. I had a word or two with them about it, believe me. But they had the right idea. They knew they had to do it quietly. And they didn't know the guy was there until they had the door open. Rather than risk a fight, cops showing up and all, they backed off. The guy came out and tried to bluff, so my guy got a good look at him. We'll know him next time. But before I could get over there, the guy walked out, and when we went into the room again the broad was gone too. Out the window in back."

"Jesus Christ, Wes, you let her get out a window and get away?"

"We underestimated her, I admit it. We put a man in the

alley before we went in the second time, but it was too late."

Moss shook his head. "What about the guy? Did you follow him?"

"We couldn't spare anybody. We thought the woman was still up there, and that was the main job. But we'll be ready for him next time. We've got a couple of cards up our sleeve. Unless she completely loses her nerve, in which case you don't have to worry anyway, she'll stick around and she'll stay inside her network. Don't worry, we'll find her again."

"When?" Moss put as much belligerence into his tone as he dared. The office was very quiet for a moment, and Moss held Wes's gaze, watching it turn just a shade meaner, wondering if he'd been a little too belligerent, even if he was the boss.

"Soon, Mr. Wetzel. She's still not going anywhere. She'll be back for another try."

Moss frowned at the fountain pen, disconcerted and determined to play the boss. "I don't want to have to spend that money I got sitting in my safe at home. I've already lost on this deal, with what I had to pay Infante yesterday. You know what that little transaction did to my financial picture? I don't know how in the fuck I'm going to explain this to my accountant. So I'd really like to be able to put that money back into a bank, where it'll start working for me again. Every day it sits in that safe I lose money."

"Put it back in the bank. I'll take care of this, I told you."

"I can't risk it, Wes. If they call again I've got to be ready to go and deal, 'cause I can't have that stuff getting out. If you can get the money back for me, great. If you can catch up with them before they try again, even better. But I've got to be ready to deal if necessary, and I don't like that."

"You won't have to deal, Mr. Wetzel. We've got this woman on the run."

Cooper rapped hard on a pane of glass with a knuckle. Waiting, he turned to look up the street along the high somber brick wall of the church. The sky was a limpid blue and the air was clear and cool, washed by the gusts that had come sweeping across the lake from Canada all night long. Cooper was wide awake, showered and shaved and worried to distraction.

St. Stephen's was one of the enormous old Catholic churches that loom unexpectedly in quiet Chicago neighborhoods. Its dark red masonry rose to twin bell towers above broad front steps on a residential street just off Clark. The board in front announced masses in English and Spanish. Cooper had walked around to the side of the church, looking for a small locked door. He knocked twice more before he heard the shuffle of footsteps on the other side of the door and it was pushed open with a creak.

Stumps had survived the night, but barely, from the look of him. The Cubs cap was not yet in place on the hairless skull. The bleary eyes had sunk deeper into the flesh, and the grizzled lower jaw hung loosely, showing gaps in the line of yellowed teeth. With a wave of the hand, Stumps beckoned Cooper inside. A flight of stairs went up to the right, and another descended on the left. "Down here," said Stumps in a hoarse whisper, leading him to the stairs. The old man's breath rasped in and out as he put a hand to the rail to steady himself.

Cooper followed him down into a dank hallway lit by low-wattage bulbs in wire cages. The walls had been painted an institutional cream color, sometime in the reign of Pope John. The cement floor was painted barn red. Every few steps, Stumps turned to make sure Cooper was following, motioning him on with another flick of his mottled hand.

"What are you, like the Phantom of the Opera down here?" Cooper said.

Stumps shushed him and halted with a finger to his lips. "I think Father Doyle's upstairs," he wheezed, still in his stage whisper. "Don't get me in trouble."

Cooper nodded and they went on. Cooper caught glimpses through open doors: stacked chairs, a table with a coffee urn, a boiler room. Stumps took him around a corner and stopped at a closed door, cocking a thumb at it. Then he knocked softly, three times.

Diana's voice sounded, muffled and indistinct beyond the door, and Stumps opened it and waved Cooper in. The room was dark, lit by a single window high in the opposite wall. It was clogged with the flotsam and jetsam of a working church's discards: folded cots, battered tables, piles of books, splattered cans of paint. Under the window, Diana sat on a cot, blankets bunched at one end.

She rose slowly and came to greet Cooper. "I'll be in my room if you need me," croaked Stumps behind them.

"Get me out of here," breathed Diana, sliding into Cooper's arms.

They embraced, listening to the old man's footsteps fade away. "It's not forever," said Cooper.

"I want to go have a big breakfast, someplace where the sun comes in the windows."

Cooper released her and offered her the white paper bag he'd brought in. "Coffee and doughnuts. I'm not sure we can risk a public breakfast."

"I can't stay down here forever."

"You won't have to. Today we make decisions."

Diana sank onto the cot, looking into the bag. "Stumps gave me some instant coffee, but that won't do it. I think he lives on whiskey."

"And beer. A balanced diet."

Diana set the coffee on the floor and peeled a napkin away from a chocolate doughnut. "So what's going on up on Earth?"

"We need to think about how we're going to stay alive and out of jail."

"We?"

"The cops came back. They think I'm shielding you. I told them some lies."

Diana looked at him gravely, chewing. "I'm sorry, Cooper. Give me a day. If we can't find the stuff in a day, I'll go to the police."

Cooper could feel the fear, hear it in her voice. He had come in intending to put his foot down, but now he only stared at her. "I'll be right back. I need to talk to Stumps."

Cooper found him in his room at the other end of the hall. The door stood open, revealing a card table littered with spoons, cups, packets of instant soup, a hot plate. What had been another storeroom was filled with a folding chair, a mattress on the floor with bedclothes neatly arranged on it, an ancient steamer trunk upright and open like a wardrobe. Stumps was on the chair, sipping black coffee from a plastic mug. A faint whiff of bourbon reached Cooper's nostrils.

"Easy on that. I need you sober this morning," Cooper said.

Stumps looked affronted for a moment and then grinned. "This ain't but a pick-me-up. Just like putting 3 in 1 oil on a rusty hinge. I can't function without it."

"Can you drive?"

"Hell yes, I can drive."

Cooper pulled his key chain from his pocket. "Grab a cab and go down to the Chicagoland Inn on Ridge, near Peterson, you know? My car's there. It's an army green '74 Valiant." Cooper handed him the key. "Bring it back and park it somewhere around here. Here's a ten for the cab and your trouble."

Stumps was on his feet. "You got it, son."

"Can Diana get back in here any time she wants?"

"I'll give her my key to the side door here. I can get in upstairs. But she's gotta make sure Father Doyle don't see her. Whiskey he can put up with, but if he thinks I'm monkeying around with young ladies down here, I'm out on the street again."

Diana looked up from the second doughnut when Cooper returned. "I'm getting you in big trouble."

Cooper shrugged. "That's part of the bargain when you love somebody. You get into their trouble. But let's think about getting out of it. Where could Tommy have put this stuff?"

"I don't know. In my place, I'd have said. But then those people would have found it."

Cooper considered. "Yeah. I think if they'd found it they wouldn't worry too much about you."

"So I'm not safe until we find it."

"Or until they go to jail for killing Tommy."

"But we don't have any evidence they killed Tommy."

"We don't even know who they are, just that they're presumably working for this guy, what's his name?"

"Wetzel. Moss Wetzel."

"Wetzel. We've got to find out about this guy."

"Listen, Cooper. If it wasn't in Tommy's briefcase, and it wasn't on him when he got shot, then he hid it somewhere. Maybe somewhere in my apartment, somewhere those guys didn't think of or didn't have time to look."

"You listen to me. One. Your place is a mess. You couldn't find an armchair in there right now. Two. It's dangerous to go back there."

"They can't watch it all the time."

"Maybe not. I'd still steer clear."

"What am I supposed to do?"

"I told you."

"I know. Go to the police. And I asked you for a day. One day. Come with me and let's look at my place. I have to see the damage anyway, and maybe I'll think of where Tommy could have hidden the stuff."

Cooper looked at her, pale but unflinching on the edge of the cot. He wanted to kick something, put his fist through a wall, shake Diana until she saw reason. But his better judgment was losing again. "OK. We'll take a look."

POULOS CLENCHED HIS coffee mug as if he were trying to crush it. Neckless and sullen, he looked like a pit bull just after someone has snatched away the T-bone. Wes sat across from him, immobile. Fudge leaned against the window in the corner of the booth, smoking studiously. "Three main lines of inquiry," he said.

He fell silent while a passing waitress stopped to refill their mugs, then went on in his low unhurried monotone. "Since I had the bright idea about the license numbers, I get to go after the guy."

"What bright idea?" said Poulos.

"After you left last night. I figured the guy who was with her probably came by car and only walked out because he didn't want us to get a number. I went and talked to the guy in the office again, checked the numbers of the cars that were parked there against the registrations. There was one that didn't belong to a guest. That's got to be our guy. I checked it out already this morning. Name of MacLeish. He lives not too far from the lady. Gotta be a boyfriend, maybe in on the scam. I'll try and pick him up, see how he spends the day."

"Which leaves you and me to work on the address book," Wes said, nodding at Poulos, whose scowl deepened. "Frank's got things narrowed down a bit."

"I don't want to spend all day sitting in the fuckin' car, watching somebody's front door."

"You know something? You don't have enough patience for this kind of work."

Poulos shrugged. "How do we know she hasn't split?"

"Would you, with something the client's that eager to pay for? If she is planning on splitting, she'll leave the merchandise with the guy. This new guy. You find a record on him, Frank?"

Fudge sucked life out of his Marlboro and gave a single shake of the head. "Turns out he was just arrested the other night, battery or something, but nothing else. Another amateur."

"See? We'll get 'em. Now, anything happens, you find anything, buzz me. I'm off to fix up the janitor at her place now, then I got other things to follow up. I got the beeper, the car phone, you get in touch with me. Understood?"

"Aye aye, sir." Fudge touched his forehead with an index.

Wes slid out of the booth. "The man that finds her gets the bonus, but no grandstanding."

"I got a question," said Poulos.

"What?"

"Supposing I find her, and get the material. What do I do with her while I'm waiting for you?"

Wes looked down at him blankly. "Just call me, Jim. Just call me."

Cooper parked the Valiant a block away from Diana's place. "If somebody's watching, they're probably watching the front. But they could be watching the alley, too. Most likely the entrances to the alley. So we slip through a gangway in the middle of the block." Diana nodded, tense and quiet now that they were close, and they got out of the car.

The opposite side of the block from Diana's building was mixed, with a couple of large brick houses breaking the line of apartment buildings. They went down the block slowly, passing locked gates, until they came to a walk that led under an arch and all the way back to the alley. There Cooper paused, taking a look both ways, calculating chances again. Diana put a hand on his arm. "Let's do it," she said.

Cooper shook his head once and led her across the alley to the foot of her back stairs. Going up, he remembered ambushes he had walked into and hoped this wasn't another one. At her back door he motioned her to wait. He checked to make sure that the door was still locked and then silently took her key. He unlocked the door and pushed it open.

The wreckage hadn't shifted as far as he could tell, and the place was silent. Cooper retrieved a skillet from the kitchen floor and stepped carefully through to the dining room, listening, watching, giving the blind spots a wide berth. The living room was even worse than he remembered; he looked at the uprooted plants and dreaded bringing Diana in.

By the time he had checked the bedroom, bathroom and closets and returned to the dining room, she had come in on her own. She was standing frozen in the doorway to the kitchen, a waxwork figure. Cooper laid the skillet on the buffet and put a hand on her arm. "Like I said, you've got a hell of a pick-up job."

Diana stirred and shook her head. "The pricks," she said curtly and brushed past him. Cooper watched as she made her own tour in silence, hands jammed in her jacket pockets, halting in shock two or three times and then pushing on. Cooper moved to the bay windows and, standing well back, looked out at the street and waited. Finally he turned and saw Diana in front of him, an absent pensive look on her face. She said, "I don't know where to start."

"Sit down and look at it," said Cooper. "Try and see it like it was. And think. If you're Tommy, and you want to hide something from Diana, what do you do?"

Diana walked to the couch, stooped to replace one of the cushions, and sat. After a moment she said, "He had it in that leather thing. I took it into the kitchen to use a screwdriver to get it open, but like I said, it was nearly empty." She was frowning now, concentrating.

Cooper thought. "He would have moved the stuff after he showed it to you, wouldn't he? He would have been afraid of your doing just what you did, sometime when he wasn't here."

"I guess. So what did he do with it?"

"He hid it under a loose floorboard. He got your basement key and hid it down there somewhere. He buried it in the sugar. He hollowed out *Don Quixote* and put it in there."

Her eyes went to the pile of books below the shelves. There was a long silence, "I don't know," she said, and Cooper saw tears on her cheeks. "I don't know. The sugar's all over the counter in there. I have hundreds of books. If there are any loose floorboards, I never found them."

Cooper wanted to get her out of there, take her someplace and hold on to her for a while, but he knew there was a lot to do. "What about the basement?"

"I guess it's possible."

"Got the key?"

She had no heart for the search, he could tell by the way she moved. She came up off the couch slowly, as if weighted with fatigue or stupor.

"Before we go down there and look," said Cooper. "Think again. Look around and think. You're Tommy. What do you do with this stuff?"

She made a slow three-sixty, eyes sweeping over the devastation, in silence. "I don't know," she said again.

At the back door she stopped and wiped away her tears with her sleeve. Cooper leaned out over the rail of the porch and looked up and down the alley. Then they went down the steps. The basement was clean and had a fair amount of light coming in the large south-facing windows. There were laundry machines along the west wall and storage lockers opposite. Cooper paced slowly up the room, looking. "Tommy swipes your key and comes down here one day when you're not around. He needs to stash an envelope somewhere. What does he do?" Diana was silent behind him. Cooper reached the end of the space and turned around, seeing Diana silhouetted against the windows. "He doesn't put it in your locker, 'cause it has a combination lock. Does he slide it in there under the washer? No, he'd want to keep it off the floor." Cooper's eyes rose to the ceiling. "Is there a nook or a cranny up there he might have stuffed it into? We'd need a flashlight." He walked back toward Diana.

"Cooper." She had put her hands back in her pockets and was standing with her hips cocked, looking at him coldly. "We don't have a chance of finding it, I know."

He stopped in front of her. "Not much of one," he said. He looked into her dark eyes, watching her blink.

"I don't want to go to jail," she said.

"You don't want to get shot either, do you?"

He could feel the shiver as it ran through her. "Maybe I should just get out to O'Hare, jump on the first plane out."

"San Juan can't be too bad this time of year."

"Except when would I ever be able to come back?"

Cooper looked past her, through the windows out into the alley. He put his hands on her shoulders, pulled her gently to him. "No, running away won't do it, will it? Not long term." He felt her arms go around him. They stood holding each other for a time, and then Cooper said, "Here's what we do. Get some books, clothes, whatever you need from upstairs. I'll take you back to the church. You lie down on that cot and think. Close your eyes, see your place the way it was, go over every square inch of it. With Tommy's eyes. I'll go see what I can find out about the guy, Wetzel. And I'll talk to . . . I don't know, I'll talk to someone. Maybe come back here and give the place another going over. But tonight, if we haven't found it, I think we have to take our chances with the law. OK?"

It was like holding a statue in his arms, waiting for it to come to life. Finally Diana said, in a steady quiet voice, "OK."

Moreland wasn't at his desk, but he was expected back shortly. Cooper didn't want to waste time, so he hung up the phone and went out and jumped in the Valiant. By the time he got downtown and up to Moreland's desk in the newspaper building by the river, he had missed him again, but a man at a neighboring desk told him where Moreland could usually be found at lunch.

The bar was crowded with what Cooper supposed were newspaper types. Moreland was easy to spot, however; he had grown larger and balder than the last time Cooper had seen him.

"MacLeish, as I live and breathe." Moreland laid down an enormous and disheveled Reuben next to his beer stein and passed a napkin across his mouth. "Please tell me you're in trouble again. I need a good story to save my sorry-ass job."

"It warms my heart to know you care, Mel." Cooper shook the fleshy hand and looked for an opening to squeeze in next to the bar.

"Move, lard butt, my source is here." Moreland put a hand on his neighbor's shoulder and shoved.

"You ever heard the saying about the pot and the kettle?" Cooper said, sliding in.

"This is not lard. This is secondary muscle." Moreland slapped his ample belly.

"That's at least six months of hard work away from being any kind of muscle, I hate to tell you."

"You still play pool? They haven't broken your thumbs yet?"

"Close, but not yet."

"Then I challenge you. We'll see if you can stand the pace in a real aerobic sport."

"You're on. But not today. Today I need information."

"Ha!" Moreland set down his beer. "I knew it. Paco! A beer for the man with the hair here. He's buying. You are buying, of course."

"Of course."

"We journalistic peons have to supplement our incomes as we can. So who you blackmailing today? Daley? The Fields? Cardinal Bernardin?"

"Moss Wetzel."

Moreland blinked a few times and then picked up his sandwich. "The *Maverick* magazine guy?"

"That's the one."

"Let me guess," Moreland said through a mouthful of Reuben. "You're trying to steal one of his girlfriends."

"How many does he have?"

"Who knows? He styles himself after Hefner, I think. You see him around town with different bimbos attached. I think he has a harem or something."

"Huh." Cooper looked at nothing while Moreland chewed.

"What exactly did you want to know?"

"Tell me about the guy. Honest, dishonest?"

Moreland shrugged, sauerkraut spilling from the sandwich. "Who's to say? Is pimping an honest trade? You ever seen the magazine?"

"Seen it on the stands."

"Basic generic skin magazine, fancied up. Safe sex tips and financial advice in between the crotch shots. Short stories, too, but nothing really quality like in *Playboy.* Not too sleazy, though, either—the guy's aiming for a classier market. College guys, oh yeah, and Vietnam vets, too. There you go, you'd like that. They run stuff about veterans, Agent Orange victims and so forth, and reminiscence-type things. 'The day we kicked the Cong out of Phuc Yu province,' stuff like that. And lots of Moss Wetzel everywhere: Moss with a model on his lap, Moss at a party in L.A., Moss shaking hands with Eric Clapton, that kind of thing." Moreland eyed Cooper for a moment. "What do you mean, is he honest or dishonest?"

Cooper shrugged. "I don't know. Is he in with the mob or anything?"

"The mob? Boy, are you out of date. We don't use that term anymore. The *Outfit,* for Christ's sake. Actually, I think he's probably above that now. He's way beyond the peep-show level. Moss is big business now, almost respectable. But whether he ever was, I can't say."

Cooper drew on his beer and nodded slowly. "I heard he was down in the Caribbean recently, on vacation or something. You know anything about that?"

Moreland sputtered a laugh through his sandwich. "You always do this, you know? You come and ask me about people, and it turns out you know more than I do."

"I need background. I never heard of the guy until last night."

"What is it, MacLeish? Let me guess—it's drugs, right? You're busting a coke ring all by yourself and you think Moss Wetzel's behind it."

Cooper smiled. "Close. The story's yours if you can find out something about his trip to Trinidad."

"Trinidad, was it?"

"That's what I heard. And I heard he had some kind of trouble down there, what I don't know. That's what I'd like to find out."

"OK, I'll see what I can dig up." Moreland shook his head, looking mournfully at the remnants of his sandwich. "Where the hell do you get this stuff? With your talent for raking through other people's dirt, you should be in my line of work."

"I don't think I'm rude enough, Mel."

Moreland paused with the stein at his lips, considering. He drank and said, "No, probably not."

It was thinking time, and Cooper went home and put his feet up on the windowsill and looked out at the new leaves on the trees. He drank coffee until his stomach protested, and then he took his feet down and paced, resisting the temptation to go over to the church and sit with Diana in her cell.

At an impasse, he finally remembered his own business. He was going to need a lawyer himself, a cheap one. He sat at the end of the couch and thought until he remembered Barry. He knew Barry had a small office on Howard Street, where his practice was mainly criminal law of a routine sort and his clientele mainly poor. Cooper enjoyed the irony of a pacifist striving to keep violent people out of jail, and the price range sounded about right. Besides, he liked Barry, in spite of everything. A quick phone call found Barry in his office, mildly surprised to hear from Cooper, and Cooper told him he'd be by in fifteen minutes.

Howard Street was dreary even in the clear chill of the afternoon, a little slice of slum at the northern edge of the city. Trash scuttled along the pavement and blacks and Mexicans jostled for space in the doorways of Korean-owned clothing shops. Cooper parked at a broken meter and walked till he found Barry's office, almost in the shade of the El tracks, half a storefront next to a currency exchange, with LAW OFFICE—BARRY FRANK stenciled on the glass.

Barry was a long way in distance, time and maybe ambition from a paneled downtown office. The furniture had Salvation Army cachet and there were no impressive ranks of leather-bound law volumes, only a cast-aside *Tribune* on top of a gray filing cabinet. The woodwork was painted black.

Barry was on the phone when Cooper walked in, but he had wound things up in a hurry and hung up by the time Cooper settled onto the chair opposite his cluttered desk. "Hi," he said warily.

"Hi. You accept stovewood and hickory nuts for payment?"

Barry stared for a moment before saying, "Like Atticus Finch?"

"Just kidding. I can pay you."

Barry smiled uncertainly and settled back in his chair. "Just what kind of trouble are you in?"

"Battery. Court date in a month or so."

Frowning faintly like a concerned guardian whose worst fears for his ward have come true, Barry said, "What happened?"

Cooper told him, neither omitting nor embroidering. While he talked Barry examined a number-two pencil minutely. His eyes flicked to Cooper at intervals.

"If the guy wants to make an issue of the pool cue, I think I'm sunk," Cooper said finally.

Barry shrugged and put down the pencil. "I don't know. It seems to me the pool cue is something he'd try hard not to mention, if he used it to attack you. You could even file charges against him."

"The arresting officers didn't see it that way. I think they were too impressed with the lopsided outcome of the fight."

Barry's frown deepened and Cooper wondered if he'd made a mistake in coming here, if he was too much a representative of things Barry hated to have his sympathy. "I'm hoping the guy just doesn't show up," Cooper said.

"If he does, I think we have a pretty fair case for self-defense. Although you probably should have kept the pool cue, showed it to the police."

Cooper smiled. "Foresight in moments of stress has never been my strong point."

"It probably doesn't matter. You didn't resist arrest or anything, did you? At the worst, if the judge takes the police version at face value and isn't swayed by the assault with the long-lost pool cue, I think the worst you'll get is probation. Unless the guy was really badly hurt."

"I haven't heard."

"Well, we'll see."

"If I may ask an indelicate question, how much will your services set me back?"

"What did you put up for bail, a hundred?" He considered for a second or two. "They'll give it back to you in court. You sign the check over to me and we'll call it quits."

Cooper wanted to ask, even if the guy doesn't show up? However, he didn't want to quibble. "Fair enough," he said. He told Barry the court date and other particulars, and then listened to a brief lecture on courtroom procedure and decorum.

Cooper sat still when Barry finished, frowning at the wall behind Barry's head. "We're all set then," Barry said, waiting for him to rise, show signs of leave-taking. Cooper was thinking hard about Diana, one weakening inhibition away from telling Barry all about it. Here was a lawyer, and a friend to boot, the man they needed to guide them through the legal mine field. His eyes met Barry's and saw the inquiry there.

The inhibition that finally held fast was his word to Diana. "OK," he said quietly, and stood up. "Thanks." He held out his hand.

"See you in court." Barry released his hand and then grinned. "Tell me. Do you really hustle people at pool, like Paul Newman or somebody?"

Cooper shook his head. "Hardly ever. I was in a bad mood that night."

The smile lingered on Barry's face, and for a moment Cooper got a glimpse of a different Barry, one who yearned in secret for a more thrilling life of less rigid principle.

"It's not all it's cracked up to be," he said, and left Barry pondering the remark.

CECIL WALKED EAST on Harrison Street, dazed at his freedom from the confines of the bus, elated to be able to stretch out his legs, stunned by the size of the city. He climbed a long rise and went past a massive gray building that never seemed to end, which he decided was the post office because of the U.S. Mail trucks scurrying in and out of it. He went over a river with water the color of iron. He stopped on the bridge to look past a tangle of expressway interchanges at the sinister black shafts of a skyscraper in the middle distance. When he saw the tiny figures at the base of the tower and finally got a perspective on its size, his stomach fluttered just slightly, as it had when the airliner had taken off from Piarco.

He went on walking, down the long gentle slope into the south Loop, past warehouses and delis and taverns and small dark shops of indeterminate purpose, all constructed of ancient and begrimed red brick. He came to a halt on South State Street, watching buses grind by in the rattling canyons of the Loop, aware of his empty stomach.

Still dazed, Cecil made his way to the Burger King on the corner.

Fudge opened the door of the LeSabre and slid onto the passenger seat. Wes reached out to turn off the radio. In the silence Fudge thought, country music? The guy listens to country music?

"So he talked to a lawyer," said Wes.

"Yeah. He was in there maybe fifteen, twenty minutes."

Wes's gaze went out through the windshield to the quickening grass and the sheen of the lake. "That's not long," he said.

They were silent for a while, watching the water. "Long

enough," said Fudge. "Long enough to feel the situation out, get a reading, have the guy tell him to head for the border or whatever."

"Long enough to drop off an envelope." A faint plashing of waves on sand came to them inside the car. "I wonder if the guy has a safe," Wes said.

"If so, it's over as far as I'm concerned. There are things I can do and things I can't do."

"Can't you do your cop number on him, tell him you're conducting an investigation, you need the evidence or something?"

Fudge considered. He hauled out his cigarettes.

"Not in the car," said Wes.

Fudge looked blank for a moment, then shrugged and put them away. "No," he said. "Not with a lawyer. I can get away with it with your average dumbass, but a lawyer'd be too smart. And he would refuse to give it to me even if he bought the story." Fudge scowled at the bright clean day outside, wanting a cigarette, wanting out of the job.

Wes sat like a rock, staring out at the lake. Finally he said, "Where's the guy now?"

"He went home. Jim's camped there, ready to pick him up if he moves."

"OK." Wes turned to look at Fudge. "Go get something to eat if you want. Give me a call afterwards and we'll see how things stand."

Fudge had the door open and one foot out. He paused and looked at Wes. "I don't think there's anything we can do about the lawyer," he said.

Wes was looking out at the lake again. "Maybe, maybe not."

Diana slept. It was her only refuge from worry, from fear, from immobility, from the dank clutter of the storeroom. She slept fitfully, drifting back to semiconsciousness as noises filtered down from the vast empty reaches of the church above or as thoughts crystallized around images in her exhausted brain.

I can kiss my job good-bye; Mario never forgives an unexcused absence. Silence. Distant honking of a car horn, out where people are free to move.

My home. Decimated, defiled, maybe forever. Plants dying on the floor, books scattered, a life carefully built up over ten years shattered. Where did Tommy hide the envelope? Silence, rest.

Tommy. Dead, shattered, and a part of me with him. Everything shattered. Why am I not safe? Cooper, help me.

God help me. I remember prayers, I remember the catechism. I remember *el padre Angel y su sotana negra. Y el interior de la iglesia, oscuro, fresco, misterioso. Ay Dios, ayúdame si existes. Tan lejos estoy de tu gracia.*

The creaking of the storeroom door awoke her. She was baffled for an instant by the looming shapes, then panicked by the approaching footsteps. She lashed out and a cry escaped her, inarticulate.

"Whoa, little girl, whoa." The rasping voice arrested her and she managed to focus on Stumps, sidling crablike through the gloom. There was just enough light coming through the high window for her to make out the Cubs cap askew on the grizzled head, the sticklike arms protruding from the stained down vest, the sagging jeans. He carried a white paper bag in his hand. "It's Uncle Norman. I brought you something to eat."

Dazed, Diana sat on the edge of the cot and brushed hair out of her eyes. "I'm sorry. I was asleep."

"That's good. Sleep all you can. Sleep till your ship comes in." Stumps offered her the bag. "Cheeseburger with the works. Fries and a Coke. I got you extra ketchup."

Diana took the bag from him, recovering. "Thank you." She peered into the bag and saw handfuls of little ketchup packets. With a sudden pang she became conscious of hunger.

"Nobody's upstairs now," said Stumps. "The place should be empty for a while. You can come upstairs and stretch your legs a bit if you want. I'll show you around." He wrestled a chair from the corner and unfolded it. "Here. Use this as a table."

Diana extracted the cheeseburger from the bag, packets of ketchup spilling out, and unwrapped it. She ate hungrily while Stumps produced another chair and sat leaning forward with his elbows on his knees. Suddenly the silence seemed prolonged, and Diana was too conscious of the old man watching her. She smiled gamely. "I was starving."

Stumps scratched in the limp white hairs on the back of his head. "Cooper told me to keep you fed. If there's anything else you want, let me know." He settled the cap on his head and gave a racking cough.

"Did Cooper say how long he was planning to keep me down here?"

"Naw." He paused. "I didn't get the idea I was supposed to keep you from leaving, if that's what you want to do."

Diana shrugged. The food helped, but she felt deserted, infinitely forlorn. "I guess I'll wait for him to come back."

There was a longer silence. She stared at the floor while she chewed, waiting for him to move, to say something, to go away. She realized suddenly she wanted him there for the company, even in silence. She took a drink of the Coke, looked at him and smiled.

Stumps smiled back, bleak rheumy eyes crinkling. "Got yourself in a pickle, huh?"

"Yeah. A real pickle."

"Cooper didn't want to tell me too much, but I sort of figured it involved police."

"I wish it was just them. The police are the least of my worries."

The Cubs cap bobbed up and down as Stumps nodded. "That don't leave a lot of places to run to, huh?"

"Not many, no."

"Sounds to me like you need to get out of town."

Diana nodded, looking past Stumps into the shadows. "Maybe so. Except when do I stop running?"

"It's that bad a fix, huh?"

"I think so."

Stumps shook his head a couple of times and fell silent. Diana fished in the bag for french fries. The rustling of paper was very loud. She could feel Stumps watching her. After a while the old man said, "Don't like ketchup, huh?"

Guiltily, Diana froze with a fry at her lips. "I don't use

it that much." She flashed him what she hoped was a disarming smile.

"My little girl used to slather it all over everything."

Diana ate the french fry and said, "I didn't know you had a daughter."

"Yep. She'd be a little older than you. She'd probably be forty by now."

Diana's face must have shown her perplexity at his phrasing. He said, "I ain't seen her in thirty years."

"What happened?"

"Her mother took off with her. Left me a note, took off for California and never looked back. I wasn't too sorry to see her go, but I sure as hell missed my little girl for a while."

"My God, I bet. You never saw her again?"

"Talked to her on the phone once, in 1971. She didn't sound too happy to talk to her old dad. I think her mama kind of poisoned the waters there.

"I'm sorry."

"Ah, you get over it. They're better off without me anyway. I did hear the girl got married a few years ago. I think I got me some grandkids out there somewhere."

In the half-light from the high window Diana felt entombed. She had left the world of the living, the world of sunshine and high hopes for the morrow. She kept her eyes on the food before her, knowing that if she looked at Stumps she would cry. Come and get me out of here Cooper, she pleaded silently.

The phone was ringing when Cooper came in the door. He picked it up and heard Moreland's voice at the other end. "MacLeish. I figured I'd catch you at home. Must be nice, not having to work for a living."

"You call what you do work?"

"It's grueling, let me tell you. Listen, I got you some news and views on Moss Wetzel. About one beer's worth. You want any more, we have to draw up a payment schedule."

"Let's hear what you got. I'll see if I need more."

"OK, I talked to a couple of people here who know the business end and a couple of others who know the dirt.

I'm afraid I'm going to have to disappoint you, but there isn't a lot of dirt on Wetzel."

"Just tell me what you got."

"Well, Wetzel's nouveau riche. The guy's from the Southwest Side somewhere, local boy, never even finished college. Fifteen years ago he was selling insurance out of a little storefront way down on Western Avenue somewhere. Then he got into real estate. Ten years ago he was a hard-charging dealmaker, made a killing or two carving up Will County and building cardboard houses everywhere. Eight years ago he bought *Maverick* and started the make-over."

"A real entrepreneur, huh?"

"Oh yeah. The magazine took off big about three, four years ago. Remember when they ran the nude shots of that lady newscaster, the one who had to resign?"

"Vaguely."

"Well, that didn't hurt their sales any. They're right behind *Playboy* and *Penthouse* now, and Wetzel's starting to do his Hefner number, elbow his way into polite society, give money to the right liberal causes and all that. He's semirespectable now."

"Just semi?"

"Well, hell. You ever seen the magazine? Can you see Renée Crown or somebody like that sitting next to the guy at a dinner and saying, 'Mr. Wetzel, why ever do they call it a split beaver shot?' "

"I see what you mean."

"Yeah. So anyway, the guy's rich now. Major rich. Lives in a nice-looking pile of stone out in Oak Brook, which they tell me he has grandly rechristened 'Broadlands.' Owns property all over the city, keeps a high profile."

"No whispers? No rumors of anything shady?"

"Nothing definite. Just if you consider pornography shady, which you probably do, being a clean-living Hoosier and all. I mean, look. It's not the prettiest business in the world, is it? But has Wetzel ever had trouble with the law? Not that anybody knows."

"No drug scandals? No hints he might deal something besides houses and magazines?"

"Not that I heard."

"No Mafia connections?"

"Mafia connections. There you go again, using those ethnic slurs. Look, Wetzel's in the pornography business, right? A branch of it, anyway, and that's Outfit territory. The man has friends with Italian surnames. Rivals, too. In fact there's a story he and Victor Casalegno are not to be invited to the same tea party."

"Casalegno the guy they failed to pin the RICO thing on last year?"

"Yeah. Apparently he and Wetzel have been butting heads for years, going back to the Will County days. These guys can carry a grudge forever, you know. But it's never been a shooting war type thing. More of a competing business empire thing. Casalegno has lots of legitimate enterprises, too."

"The Feds have never wanted to take a look at Wetzel?"

"Not that anybody's heard. Shit, it's no crime to have Italian friends. Wetzel's dealt with Outfit people at one time or another. But he's not a dues-paying member. I'm telling you, the guy's pretty clean. Legally, anyway."

"Huh. What about the Trinidad trip? You find out anything about that?"

"There, the only thing I can tell you is that a couple months back the magazine ran a feature on the place. Travelogue kind of thing, places to eat and drink, lie on the beach, get laid. The fleshpots of Port of Spain, that kind of thing. I think they threw in Tobago, too. And of course a photo spread on the women of Trinidad. I'll tell you, at least the guy's no racist. There are some pulchritudinous females down there, of various colors. Just judging by the feature."

"I hope it wasn't too much trouble, doing all this research."

"It was a bit of a distraction, but that's OK. Anyway, there were pictures of Wetzel, too, fondling women, lying on the beach, stuff like that. Apparently he and his entourage spent a week or two down there."

Cooper grunted faintly and stared out the window. "I don't suppose there was any mention in the article of a man named—um, hang on—Gladstone Drake?"

There was a short silence. "MacLeish, you are the single most mysterious person I have ever had the dubious pleasure of knowing. Yes, it so happens there was. If I recall correctly, Gladstone Drake is the owner of a nightclub in Port of Spain. There was a little blurb for it in the article. Gladstone Drake, yeah, I remember the name. I guess they go in for those old British Empire names down there."

"The owner of a nightclub, huh?"

"Yeah. Looked like a high-class type of strip joint in the article. How in the hell did you hear of Gladstone Drake?"

"It's a long story, Mel."

"And I'm not going to get it, am I?"

"Not right now, no."

"Listen, MacLeish. God knows what you're up to, but if you're trying to bring down Moss Wetzel's empire or some damn thing, don't you think you need the services of a veteran investigative reporter?"

"I'm not trying to bring anybody down. I'm just trying to follow up on a rumor I heard."

"What's it to you, if I may put it bluntly?"

"That, my friend, is none of your business right now. But I'll make you a promise, Mel."

"What's that?"

"If there's a good story in this, I give you my word you'll get it before anybody else. OK?"

"MacLeish, you just might save my job yet. I'm counting on you, baby."

"You're not the only one."

Diana padded down the corridor on stockinged feet, her shoes in her hand. She paused at the closed door to Stumps's room, hearing nothing, and she paused again at the foot of the stairs. As far as she could tell, the church was empty. She put on her shoes and went up the flight of steps to the side door. She stood looking out at the sunlit street, her heart drumming. She needed that sunshine; she needed to get out of the catacombs. She wasn't sure it was safe to leave, but she knew staying here would drive her slowly mad.

And she needed to go home. Her home lay in ruins, and

the pain was as acute as if it were a friend lying wounded; she needed to be there. Diana watched and listened, remembering what Cooper had said, trying to gauge the chances that the wrong people were watching the right streets just now, the chances she could slip in and out with impunity again.

After a minute she pushed open the door and emerged into the cool of the afternoon. She walked north in the shadow of the giant church, wanting to cross to the sunshine but fearing obscurely that it would expose her.

She had changed clothes, washed up in the dingy bathroom Stumps had shown her, brushed her hair. Movement, light, noise, the sight of people near her revived her. She walked fast, alert, tensed, resuming the familiar mantle of fear that settled onto her in the open.

It was a quick six blocks north to her street. Two blocks away she was already plotting tactics, remembering the route she and Cooper had taken in the morning, thinking of alternatives. Finally, however, she slipped down the same gangway, went through the same gate. She had convinced herself on the way that they couldn't possibly maintain a twenty-four-hour watch on the place; nonetheless she looked long and hard at each end of the alley before emerging from the shelter of the gangway. She saw no one who might be watching. With hurried steps, she crossed to the foot of her back stairs.

On the first landing she started a little as she nearly stumbled over one of the janitor's feral-looking children, a mournful lank-haired girl of six or so in green corduroy pants who was perched on the stairs, one foot casually grinding a doll's face into the boards. Diana flashed a quick nervous smile at the girl and went on up. Arriving at her door, key in hand, she halted and looked through the dusty panes of glass and listened.

She could see the sprawl of destruction in her kitchen but having seen it once, was already steeled. Her only thought was to detect if the apartment was empty. When after a minute or two she had heard nothing, she unlocked the door and pushed it open. She stepped in off the landing and listened again, hearing only the drip of the faulty tap in the sink to her right. Slowly she closed the door behind her and locked it.

She made her way through the wreckage to the front door, checked to see that it was locked, put on the chain. She turned and took a deep breath, then made a slow careful circuit of the apartment, staying away from windows. As she walked, she suppressed a tide of despair and grief, already sorting and ordering, trying to see the ground-up remnants of her home as just a job.

When she had looked into every room, every closet, she stood in the doorway to the living room with her fists on her hips and thought about Tommy. You bastard, she thought. Where did you hide it? Diana knew of no cubbyholes, no nooks or crannies in the place where an envelope might lie hidden. In an apartment in Miami long ago she had kept cash in an envelope slipped between the wall and the side of a sloppily installed counter, but she had never discovered any such places here. Tommy had been alone in here enough to have found such a place if it existed, but before she was going to find any loosened floorboards she had to get the floor cleared.

Diana slipped her keys into her jacket pocket and laid the jacket on the sofa. She started with the books, since she could do them in handfuls. She slapped them back on the shelves with no attention to their place, figuring there was time to sort them later. She filled the shelves rapidly, stimulated by the exertion, the movement and the slowly emerging order cheering her. She paused, panting slightly, when the large bookcase on the east wall was full. She had hardly made a dent in the landscape of destruction, and her heart sank again. She roused herself and made for the kitchen.

She found the kettle quickly, shoved to a corner of the counter. She had to partially reassemble the stove, replacing the grease traps and the grates. She wondered again at the thoroughness of the search and decided that if they hadn't found Tommy's envelope, it wasn't here. She had to root through a litter of cartons on the floor to find tea, but the mugs were still, miraculously, hanging on the wall as usual. With water heating and the tea bag in the mug, Diana was comforted a little, and she felt ready to tackle the plants. She wrestled the broom out of a pile in the pantry, gave up on finding the dustpan and grabbed a cookie sheet instead, and went back to the living room.

She was pleased to see that most of the pots were intact; they hadn't wanted to make a lot of noise and they had simply uprooted the plants, spilling the dirt out onto the floor to see if anything was buried in it. Diana thought the plants looked salvageable, if she got them repotted soon enough. Sweeping and scraping with the cookie sheet, she got together enough dirt to fill in around the roots of the wandering Jew, which lay in a tangle at her feet.

She was bent over the pot when they key turned in the back door. She simply froze for a moment, long enough to hear the door come open, remembering too late the key she had given Tommy. She stayed frozen as the first tentative steps creaked on the old linoleum in the kitchen, thinking wildly that they would just go away if she never moved.

Then she knew that it was all over unless she did something, anything. She rose from her crouch and strode to the doorway into the dining room, where she could see all the way to the back door.

A man stood there, slipping a key into the pocket of his brown suede jacket. He was not tall but his wide shoulders sloped up to the base of a large head with a jaw that bulged at the sides. His hair was brown and cropped close at the sides with a shaggy tail in back and a rooster's crest on top. He had broad thick hands, strangler's hands. He and Diana stared at one another for two or three seconds and then the man smiled. "Hi, beautiful," he said.

"Who are you?" Diana said, remembering the chain and the two locks on the front door and thinking she would never get them undone in time.

The man pushed the back door shut and turned the dead bolt to lock it. He came slowly around the kitchen table, kicking a path clear. "I'm from the insurance company," he said. He looked up at her, dark brown eyes in a broad humorless face. "And you must be Diana."

Diana was thinking of weapons, thinking of frying pans and butcher knives lost somewhere in the junkpile. But in answer to his question, she said simply, "No." He froze for a second, and from somewhere the words came to Diana: "I'm her sister."

He chewed on it for a moment and said, "Her sister."

"Yes. She had to work today, and she asked me to come over and start cleaning up."

"Uh-huh." If he hadn't bought it, he was at least thinking about it. He came into the dining room, ten feet from her now, watching her the way a shark watches lunch.

"You mind telling me how you got a key?" Diana said.

"Janitor. I didn't think anybody'd be home."

"You should have called or something."

"Next time I will. Sorry." The man had come around the table, eyes darting around the room but always coming back to her. Diana moved into the living room.

"You can see what happened. Somebody really tore the place up. We can't figure out why. They don't seem to have taken anything." She stooped to pick up the broom.

"Yeah, they really went to town, didn't they?" The man paused in the doorway, eyes moving until they settled on the front door.

"Diana won't be home till tonight, I'm afraid." Diana flexed her grip on the broom, wondering how much of a fight she could put up against shoulders like that, hands like that.

"Lemme just take a look around, then. Don't mind me." He moved out into the room, thick arms swinging at his sides.

Diana took a couple of swipes at the dirt on the floor with the broom. What would Cooper do? she asked herself, panic pushing at the edges, unable to find an answer. He would stay calm, she heard her inner voice say distinctly. "I'm making some tea. Do you want some?" she asked.

"Huh? Sure." The man moved a cushion aside with his foot and skirted the end of the couch. Diana watched as he reached the front door, undid the chain and the two locks, opened the door and looked out into the hall. He shook his head once and closed the door again but turned away without locking it. "They came in through the back, huh?"

"I guess so," Diana said. "I wasn't here." She swept dirt

onto the cookie sheet and poured it into the pot around the wandering Jew.

"What's your name?" the man said. He had come away from the door and was stepping through piles of papers and photos that had come from the buffet drawer.

"Teresa," Diana said, her mother's name being the first that came to her lips.

"Sounds Spanish or something."

"It is." She watched as the man shifted papers with the toe of his Nikes. She leaned the broom against the wall. "I'll go see if the water's ready."

She heard him coming after her as she moved deliberately through the dining room. He wasn't moving fast, just staying close. When she got into the kitchen she took another mug from the wall and put it on the counter, then fished another tea bag out of the box and put it in the mug. "Orange spice OK?"

"Yeah, fine." Diana turned to find the man three feet from her. His eyes were fixed on her. He held a photograph in his hand.

Up in the living room the door creaked open and soft footsteps came into the apartment.

"Back here, Frank," the man called. He held up the photograph. In the picture Diana saw herself and Roger, on their wedding day, innocent and beaming. Footsteps sounded in the living room, coming back. "Nice picture," said the man at her elbow. "Diana." The brown eyes in the broad face were utterly empty.

Calmly, Diana took a pot holder from its hook on the side of the cabinet. She took the lid off the kettle and saw the surface of the water roiling, steam rising. She lifted the kettle by its wooden handle, supporting the bottom with her left hand, protected by the pot holder. "Here's your tea," she said, and flung a quart of boiling water into his face.

The scream shattered the midafternoon quiet as Diana spun toward the back door, catching a distant glimpse of a man in the dining room. She was at the back door in a bound, hearing the broad man pitch onto the floor in a clatter of pans. She spun the dead bolt and tore open the door and catapulted herself out onto the porch.

She went down the stairs barely under control, hearing screams and curses and thumps behind her. She took a whole flight in two leaps, nearly losing her balance, hearing steps thundering on the boards above her. Abruptly she was on the bottom flight of steps with a decision to make.

It got made in some way she could never have described, and she went left. Her first thought was to go back through the gate, out of sight, but she would have to deal with the latch and she could hear the man on the steps behind her, almost at the bottom already. Adrenaline took her down the alley effortlessly, and for a moment all she could think was distance. Then she wondered if he had a gun. To her right the high apartment buildings had given way to single-family houses, and between garages there were fences hiding back yards. She took one frantic look behind to see a man in a suit fifty feet away, coattails flying but no gun visible, chugging after her.

Keep running, she thought, and abandoned the idea of getting over a fence into somebody's yard. She reached the end of the alley and burst out onto Ashland Avenue, veering left and nearly into the path of a GMC Forward delivery truck. The truck slowed in a squeal of brakes and Diana saw a startled face looking down at her from the cab. She was running parallel to the truck now, on the driver's side, and she could hear the man in the suit coming up behind her.

"Help me!" she gasped at the driver of the truck. The truck groaned to a halt and Diana looked to see her pursuer coming across the street, a gray-haired man with a moustache. She dashed around the front of the truck to keep it between her and the man. Another man was climbing out of the passenger side of the truck.

"Help me! He's going to kill me." She gasped out the words, heaving from her sprint, watching the man in the suit circle around the truck after her, glaring. The driver was out of the cab now, and he put a hand on the man's arm.

"Hold it there, Jack."

"Police!" the man shouted. "Get your fucking hands off me."

"He's no policeman!" Diana screamed at them, feeling

a protective arm go around her. She shook it off. "He's going to kill me. He's my husband, he's a maniac!"

"Easy, easy." The driver was a big man, bearded and heavyset. "If you're a cop, I want to see a star."

"A star? You wanna see stars? You don't mind your own fuckin' business you'll see all the stars you want." The man in the suit had a finger in the driver's face, but he was still coming around the truck.

"Hey, we got a tough guy here, Dave." The driver looked at his passenger, who had moved in front of Diana.

"No shit. Come on, Dick Tracy, arrest me." The passenger was black, short and wiry. He took a step toward the man in the suit.

Diana waited no longer. She took off again, onto the sidewalk and heading south, hearing scuffling and a single explosive "Fuck!" behind her. She was conscious of people moving out of her way, cars slowing on the street. She made for the corner, hearing shouts and blows, blessing the working man's appetite for a good fight. Nearing the end of the block she took a farewell look, seeing the man in the suit on the ground flailing. Across the street someone called to her, "Atta baby, don't look back!"

Cooper found the side door to the church locked. He rapped on the glass and waited, rapped again and gave up. He went around to the front of the church and found the big front doors unlocked. He slipped into the dark vestibule and through open doors saw rows of pews stretching up to a distant altar, with a single bowed white head near the front. He stood for a moment listening and then went down a stairway from the vestibule into the bowels of the church, wandering in windowless passages until he found Stumps's room.

The door was open and there was light coming in from the window above the bed. Stumps lay on the bed, flat out on his back. The smell of bourbon lay on the heavy air. Cooper stood in the doorway looking at the old man for a moment, wondering if he was passed out. After a few seconds the grizzled hatless head turned toward Cooper. "I think she's sleeping," Stumps said, in an ancient cracked wheeze, no breath behind it.

Cooper stepped into the room. "That's good. She get something to eat?"

"Yeah."

Cooper sat on the single chair. "You teach her to play gin rummy?"

The head swiveled back toward the wall. "Ah shit, Cooper. She's scared to death of me."

"Scared? Of you?"

"I ain't the grandfatherly type."

Cooper frowned into a corner. "She's not having the easiest kind of week."

"She's in a hell of a fix."

They sat in silence for a time while car noises swelled and faded outside and the room grew darker. "You gonna marry her?" Stumps said.

Startled, Cooper shifted on the chair. "I don't know. Maybe."

"I hope you do better than I did." The old man coughed, writhing on the mattress, and finally sat up. He cleared his throat and said, "Just about have to."

Cooper found nothing to say.

"You want a drink?" Stumps had pulled a bottle of Old Crow out of somewhere.

"No thanks. I think I'll go see if she's awake."

"OK. You need anything, just holler. She gonna be here again tonight?"

"I don't know. I'll keep you posted." Stumps nodded and waved and wrenched at the cap on the bottle. Cooper left him.

When he opened the door to the storeroom there was a rustling in the dark and Diana's voice said, "Cooper?"

"Yeah, it's me." He made his way to the cot, eyes not adjusted to the dark, and stumbled across the chair Stumps had left there. He sat on the cot beside Diana and felt her arms go around him. "You been in here all day?" he said.

"No. For a while I was out running for my life."

After a couple of seconds he said, "Huh?"

"I went back to my place. I thought I was safe if I sneaked in like we did this morning."

"Jesus, Diana."

"OK, it was stupid. But I had to get out of here."

"So what happened?"

"I ran into the janitor's little girl. I think she told her daddy I was back, and he called these guys."

"What guys?"

"The same guys that were at the motel, I guess."

"What happened?"

He could feel her shudder beside him. "I parboiled one of them and took off out the back."

"You what?"

"I threw boiling water in his face."

"Jesus."

"The other one chased me down the alley and these guys in a truck helped me, held him up while I got away. I made a domestic dispute out of it."

Cooper leaned away from her to look into her face. "Are you sure you got back here without being followed?" he said finally.

"Yes. It took me half an hour to work my way down through the alleys. I have a whole new perspective on the neighborhood now."

"Christ." Cooper held her and pondered. "And you think the janitor called them?"

"Who else? I don't think they were waiting. It took them a while to get there."

"Yeah, that would make sense. They'd buy him off or something, so they wouldn't have to watch all the time. The son of a bitch."

"Maybe they told him they were cops."

"Could be." Cooper pulled her closer to him. "Ah, Jesus. Diana, this can't go on."

"Tell me about it."

"You could identify these assholes, right?"

"For sure."

"Then let's talk to some cops. Your chances are a lot better with the law, no matter what they do to you for that business with Tommy years ago."

A long exhalation trailed away into nothing. "I'm ready," she said. "How much worse than this can jail be?"

"You're not going to go to jail. I got a lawyer all lined up for you."

Ten minutes later Cooper was punching Barry's number

into a pay phone on the side of a restaurant on Clark Street, while Diana huddled in the car. "Barry, Cooper again."

"Oh." He paused a beat. "Yeah, hi. What can I do for you?"

"I got some more business for you. You want a hard one?"

"A hard one?"

"Something better than keeping a barroom brawler out of jail. Every lawyer's dream, Barry. I'm giving you the chance to walk a client into Eleventh and State downtown with flashbulbs popping all over."

After a pause Barry said, "What are you talking about, Cooper?"

"Diana's in trouble. You read the paper this morning?"

"Diana?"

"Yeah. Every cop in Chicago's looking for her, and some other folks too. She wants to surrender, but not without a lawyer. Can we come talk to you?"

Cooper waited while Barry caught up. "Sure. When?"

"How about now?"

"OK, the sooner the better, I guess. Uh, Cooper?"

"Yeah?"

"This doesn't have anything to do with billiards, does it?"

Wes parked the LeSabre on Paulina a couple of blocks south of Howard and walked. The sun had set and only the top of a single highrise to the east was still glowing. High up in the deepening blue, a 727 shone silver on its approach to O'Hare.

Wes's eyes came back to the litter on the sidewalk, the earth-colored brick, the battered autos parked at the curb, back to the problem at hand. He had reconnoitered earlier, and turned onto Howard Street and headed west toward the El without hesitating. He scanned the sidewalks and the street as he went, looking for anything that would make him go on past the lawyer's office and wait, maybe in the coffee shop under the El tracks.

He saw nothing disturbing, and he paused only for a glance at the storefront before pushing open the door. This was one very cheap lawyer, he judged. Inside, a man in shirtsleeves sat at a lamplit desk, his arm resting on a telephone, as if he were about to speak or had just finished. The lawyer looked like all lawyers. Wes felt about lawyers as he always had about the smart kids in class. This one was tall and thin with a woman's face and graying kinky hair. "Mr. Frank?" Wes said.

"Yes?" The lawyer took his hand off the phone and leaned back in his chair.

"I got a little legal problem I'd like to discuss with you."

"Uh, could it possibly wait till tomorrow? Actually the office is closed."

"No, it can't really wait." Wes turned and shot the bolt on the heavy door, then walked toward the desk. He saw he'd gotten the lawyer's attention. "A man came to see you today." Wes kicked aside the chair in front of the desk. "A man named MacLeish." He leaned on the desk, almost down on the lawyer's level.

The lawyer was staring at him with big bright eyes. He's already scared shitless, thought Wes. "Yes?" said the lawyer, like a question.

"He gave you an envelope."

There was a silence. Wes looked into the lawyer's wide eyes, watching him scramble for a way out. "No," the lawyer said finally. "He didn't give me anything."

Wes straightened up and reached behind him, under the jacket, and brought out the Beretta. The lawyer's eyes got even wider and his lips parted. Wes knew how the lawyer was feeling and it was with exquisite pleasure that he trained the automatic on his forehead and said, "Give it up. It's not worth it to you. Give me the material, there's no hard feelings, I'm out of here."

Finally the lawyer pulled himself together and said, "He came to see me about a battery charge. I agreed to defend him. There was no envelope." He was having a little trouble with his voice.

"He talked to you about a woman. A woman named Diana Froelich."

The lawyer's lips parted slightly and his eyes flicked

away for a second and then back. "I have no idea what you're talking about."

"When's he going to bring her in?" Wes extended his arm just a fraction, for persuasion.

The lawyer raised his hands in the universal don't-kick-my-ass gesture they all went to sooner or later. "Look, you're barking up the wrong tree here. Cooper MacLeish hired me today to defend him on a misdemeanor charge, and that's all he did. Somebody's given you wrong information."

Wes sighed, ostentatiously. "I don't really have the time for this." He glanced at the filing cabinet behind the desk. "Let's turn out the drawers, see what comes up."

The lawyer looked over his shoulder at the filing cabinet, then back at Wes. "There's no envelope. He didn't give me anything."

Wes motioned with the Beretta. "Move. Open it up, start spreading the stuff on the floor."

Very slowly, the lawyer put his hands on the arms of his chair and pushed himself up. He dug in his pocket for a ring of keys and went to the filing cabinet, his eyes flicking ceaselessly from Wes's face to the muzzle of the gun and back. He extracted a key from the bunch and inserted it in the lock at the top of the cabinet and turned. He pulled open the top drawer. "These are clients' documents, routine things. Take a look."

"I don't want documents. I want what MacLeish gave you."

"But he didn't give me a thing." It always happened, Wes thought. They always showed a little spirit when they got scared enough. The lawyer had turned from the file, spread his hands in appeal.

"Pull it all out."

After a moment the lawyer nodded, shrugged very slightly and began to pull files out of the drawer. "Spread 'em out," said Wes. The lawyer nodded again and set to work briskly, fanning the files out over the worn gray carpet, Wes stepping back go give him room. Wes knelt and quickly shuffled through the papers, looking for sealed envelopes, or for a map, or some Polaroid photos, keeping the automatic trained on the lawyer. "Now the other drawers," he said. The lawyer obeyed.

It took only three or four minutes to plunder the files. The lawyer stood by the empty cabinet, hands on his hips, looking a little less scared. Looking superior again, thought Wes. "See?" said the lawyer. He waved at the litter of papers across the floor.

Wes stood up and looked around the room. "Where's your safe?" he said.

"I don't have a safe," said the lawyer, almost whining. "Look. This is it. This is all there is."

"All right, don't cry. What's down the passage?"

"The bathroom. That's the bathroom back there."

"Show me." Wes motioned with the pistol.

Warily, the lawyer moved out from behind the desk and headed toward the back. Wes followed, knowing it was time to get moving, confident now the lawyer really didn't have the stuff.

The lawyer reached through a doorway at the end of the passage and switched on a light, then stood back to let Wes see. "The bathroom," he announced. Wes could see the corner of the sink.

"Inside," he said.

Now the lawyer was scared again. Wes backed him into the little bathroom, the gun pointing at his chest. The bathroom was about four feet square, lit by a single unshaded bulb over the sink.

I'll make it easy on you, thought Wes, taken again with the strange feeling of pity that sometimes came on him at times like this. After all, it wasn't really the lawyer's fault, none of it.

"Lift up the lid of the tank. I want to see inside," he said.

The lawyer blinked at him and then gave the little half-shrug and turned around, starting to lean toward the toilet. Quickly, Wes put the Beretta six inches from the back of his head and shot him, dead center.

He had backed out of the bathroom, the shot ringing in his ears, before the lawyer's corpse had settled into its twisted position on the floor, wedged between the toilet and the wall. Wes took a last look at the expressionless face and the blood on the wall and then slipped the Beretta into the holster at his back. He leaned in to scoop the spent cartridge from the floor and made for the door at the end of the passage.

Thirteen, he thought. Jesus, they mount up. He undid chains and bolts and opened the door and stepped casually out into the deserted alley, into the evening chill.

I've just killed my thirteenth man, he thought. Hope it's a lucky number.

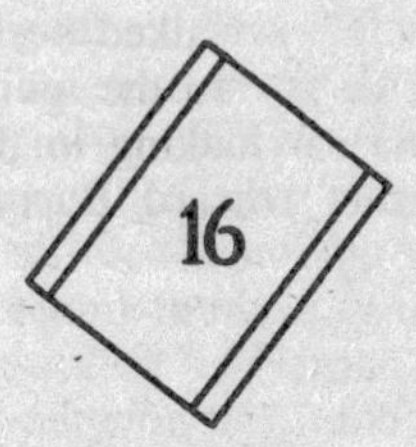

THE FIRST PARKING spot Cooper found was a couple of hundred feet past Barry's place. He switched off the ignition, glanced in his mirrors and looked at Diana. "All set?" he said.

"All set." Impassive, she reached for the door handle.

Cooper put a hand on her arm. "I don't want to frog-march you in there if you still have doubts."

She looked into his eyes for a moment and said, "What about you?"

"I don't have doubts. I have fears. And I have more fears about trying to guard you from both sides than about taking you to the cops. At least they're not going to kill you."

"No. I guess not." She shoved the door open.

Walking back to Barry's office, Cooper watched the traffic, pedestrian and auto, with a wary eye. He knew there was no way anybody could have traced them, but knowing was not enough to remove the feeling of exposure under the febrile glow of the streetlights. When they reached Barry's door he depressed the latch and pushed hard, anxious to get off the street.

He almost slammed his nose into the glass; the door didn't budge. He looked at the latch, tried again, shook the handle. He rapped four times on the glass with the knuckles of his right hand. While waiting for a reply he stepped to the right and tried to see through the blinds in the storefront window. He could see light inside but nothing else. Diana stood patiently with her arms crossed, shivering a little without her jacket. Cooper knocked again and waited another half minute. "Well shit," he said softly.

Diana just looked at him. Cooper scanned the sidewalk; there were plenty of people around, which was comforting. "Let's go," he said. They walked back to the car. In the driver's seat again, he started the ignition, but instead of putting it in gear he sat looking in the rearview mirror, back down the street toward Barry's office. "That's strange," he said.

"Yeah," said Diana. "That's strange."

"That's fucking peculiar." Cooper put the Valiant in reverse and backed against the car behind him, then twisted the wheel and put it in drive and eased out of the parking space. He rolled up to the end of the block and made a right and went south for two blocks, in silence. Then he turned right. "He might have just stepped out for a cup of coffee or something." Cooper crossed Ashland, went another block west to Paulina, turned right and pulled over behind a Sentra with a broken tail light. He switched off the ignition but left the keys in.

"Stay here," he said. "I'll go back and check again. If he's there I'll bring him down here, we'll all go for a ride." He was already sliding out of the car.

"Be careful," Diana said.

"There's nothing to worry about. You keep the doors locked and wait." He slammed the door.

Walking back toward the bright lights of Howard Street, Cooper decided there was no reason to worry. They'd made good time on the way, and they'd caught Barry still out for a quick dinner.

He turned onto Howard and made for Barry's door. A train rumbled on the El tracks above him, heading south for the heart of the city. Beyond, the sky was orange. Cooper stopped at Barry's door again, tried the latch, knocked again, swore again. He stepped back, took a quick sweeping look around.

It was frustration more than worry that made Cooper want to try the back, knock loud enough to get Barry out of the bathroom or wherever the hell he was. The building was flush with the El tracks to his right, and he had to retrace his steps to an alley and go south to get to the rear of the block. He crossed a vacant lot behind a massive old theater and worked his way up the side of the theater, wondering how he was going to identify Barry's back door. He reached a little triangular yard bounded by the El tracks, the back of Barry's building, and the side of the theater. There were overfilled trash dumpsters and litter that hadn't made it to the dumpsters and a ravaged Dodge Charger that had been repainted in different stages and none too competently a number of times in its long career. Above, another train creaked into the station.

He calculated that the second door from the wall of the El station would be the back door to Barry's office. He stepped around a puddle to the door. Beside the door was a window, guarded with rusting burglar bars. Someone had painted over the panes years before but the paint had flaked off in places and Cooper could see light through the patches of filthy glass that were revealed. He put his hand on the knob of the door and turned.

The door came open an inch or two and Cooper pushed harder. The door swung back and there was a hallway. Cooper looked all the way up to Barry's desk, lit by the desk lamp Cooper had seen that afternoon. Beyond the desk was a litter of papers on the floor.

"Barry?" The silence that answered his call and the sight of the papers on the floor set off a faint internal alarm. Cooper stood still for a stretch of seconds. Finally he stepped into the hallway, leaving the door open behind him. The light he had seen through the window was spilling out of a doorway to his left.

Context was everything, Cooper was to think later. In another setting long ago Cooper had become utterly inured to the gaudy effects of high-powered projectiles on human flesh. But seeing Barry sprawled in the bathroom with a smear of his blood down the evil-looking green paint on the wall gave Cooper a kick in the chest it took him a moment to recover from. When the old psychic armor was in place, he thought simply, people are meat.

The insight that people are just meat had gotten Cooper through the worst of the weeks in the A Shau Valley, but he had considered it a milestone on his road to recovery when the incantation had faded out of his everyday consciousness, sometime in the mid-seventies.

Cooper leaned with both hands on the door frame, looking at the body and hearing the seconds tick off. The first thought he had was that someone could have killed Barry for reasons entirely unrelated to Cooper's call, but that it wasn't very likely. The thoughts that followed that one in quick succession were enough to send Cooper right back out the door.

The alley on the other side of the theater led south to Rogers, and it was a quick cut down Rogers over to Paulina. Cooper made tracks. He turned a few heads as he went but he kept running, through the descending dusk, until he reached the place where he had parked the Valiant and saw the Sentra with the broken tail light and the empty parking space behind it.

"What exactly would you say was the hard part about this job?" Wes said. "A couple of hard cases like you and Jimmy versus one broad? Who's gonna put their money on the broad?"

Fudge stared at him through swirls of tobacco smoke, nearly rising to the bait but keeping a hold on himself, taking a long drag on the cigarette to cover it. "I didn't even get there till it was all over," he said. "Talk to fuckin' Jimmy. He's the one she got the drop on."

"And you couldn't run her down?"

"I would have except for those two assholes." Fudge put the tips of his fingers to the mottled purple swell at the side of his left eye.

Wes shook his head, his gaze going out over the restaurant. An old man limped over the tile floor and sank into the booth behind Fudge. Wes leaned across the table, his voice lower. "I'm getting tired of making excuses to the midget," he said. "He's starting to doubt my judgment. Hell, I'm starting to doubt my judgment."

I wonder if this guy ever looks in the mirror, Fudge was thinking. I wonder how it feels to have a face like that.

"You could fire me," he said aloud.

Wes leaned back and took a sip of coffee. "No. I gave you the job, you're in for the duration. I need you. But I don't need any more mistakes."

Fudge aimed two fingers at Wes's face, the cigarette held between them. "Don't lecture me, Wes. I don't take instruction real well."

Wes smiled, tossing a dollar on the table. "That's the mood. Keep that feeling. I want you mean and nasty like this. From now on."

Fudge watched him all the way out the door.

Cooper lay on the couch in his living room, lights off, hoping his place looked uninhabited from the street and waiting for the phone to ring. He wanted badly to turn the lights on because in the dark there was no escape from Barry's reproachful stare. Given a choice, he would have been almost anywhere else. But he was confined to the couch by the crumpled and torn map of the city of Chicago which lay on the steamer trunk two feet from him in the dark.

Cooper had found the map lying in the parking space where he had left the Valiant. His eye had lit on it in the moments after the first rush of panic, and he had recognized it as the one he kept on the dashboard. He had scooped it up and seen the words scrawled in blue ballpoint across the back: *Cooper—will call—D.* The writing was unmistakably Diana's.

An hour later now, Cooper lay on the couch with the Louisville Slugger on the floor within easy reach, aware that the bat was a poor defense against the weapon that had killed Barry. Cooper was contending with a variety of unpleasant feelings that had replaced the panic: anxiety, bafflement, irritation. Most of all fear. And a distinct and persistent vision of Barry's corpse.

When the phone finally rang it startled Cooper so badly he nearly pitched onto the floor, and he had to regain his balance before he could pick up the receiver. "Yeah," he breathed.

"I have your car keys," Diana said from a million miles away.

"Christ." Reeling, Cooper settled back on the cushions. "What happened?"

"I saw one of Wetzel's men."

"Where are you?"

"I'm at a gas station just off the Eisenhower somewhere, Oak Park maybe."

"Are you all right?"

"I'm fine. Sorry I took off like that. But I've been sleuthing."

"Diana, listen to me. Barry's dead. Somebody shot him."

Cooper heard electrons hissing over the wire and then, "My God."

"And if it was Wetzel's men, then the only way they could have marked Barry was to follow me. Which means the Valiant is marked. So stay the hell away from it."

"Oh my God."

"You understand? Ditch the car. Now."

There was silence again, and then, "But I'm in the middle of nowhere."

Cooper thought. "All right, if you're still alive then they probably haven't picked you up. But don't drive any farther than you have to. Drive the thing to an El station, take the train back. I'll meet you at the church."

There was a pause, for a couple of heartbeats. "Cooper, I'm not going back to the church."

"It's the best place to hide."

"I can't go back there, I'll go nuts." Cooper could hear the strain in her voice. "Listen, I'll go to Rachel's."

"I'm not sure that's safe."

"How could they know about her?"

Cooper exhaled into the phone, unable to answer. "Fine. She'll be harboring a fugitive. Will she mind?"

"She's my best friend. She'll help me."

"OK, it doesn't matter anyway. Tomorrow we get another lawyer and go to the cops first thing."

"Oh God. Barry. Cooper, listen. The man I saw . . ."

"Look. Get off the phone and go stash the car someplace. Then you can tell me what the hell you're doing out there."

"All right. I'll call you when I get to Rachel's."

"I won't be here. They have to know where I live, and if they've started whacking people, I don't want to hang around. You get to Rachel's, I'll call you."

After a brief silence she said, "Christ, what have I done?"

"Get rid of the car. I'll talk to you in an hour or two."

After he hung up, Cooper made his way through the dark to the front window. He looked around the edge of the blind out into the street. Then he took his jacket off the closet doorknob and went back to the kitchen, dodging familiar shapes in the dark. He stood at the back door for a moment, listening. Finally he unlocked the door and stepped out onto the porch, stepping immediately to the single light bulb and unscrewing it, grimacing as he burned his fingers. In the dark he locked his door and made for the ladder at the end of the porch that led to the trap in the roof.

The block consisted mainly of three-flats, flush with each other or separated by narrow gangways. Cooper stayed well away from the street side of the roofs and was able to creep quietly down the entire block, twice leaping six-foot gaps that tested his old paratrooper's nerves, but otherwise without obstacle. At the end of the block he listened, then raised his head above the low border to the roof and watched, and finally lowered himself over the edge to a back stairway and descended to the alley.

Ten minutes later he was in Burk's, hiding in the twilight at the back of the bar beyond the pool table, clutching a cold wet bottle and thinking. He stayed there for an hour, watching the pool with a critical eye, and then went to the pay phone. One ear plugged against the jukebox, he punched Rachel's number into the phone and talked for a minute, then left the bar.

He got on the El at Morse and went three stops down the line to Thorndale and walked west until he came to Rachel's. He thought he was clear but he had little confidence left in his judgment, and just in case, he went on past Rachel's and slipped into a gangway and waited for ten minutes for someone to come down after him, ready to avenge Barry's killing with his bare hands. Finally, he doubled back to Rachel's.

Diana's hair shone in the light from the globe in Rachel's living room, but her face was pale. She's thinner, Cooper thought. It's starting to twist her and tie her in knots. He held her briefly and released her. "Tell me about Barry," she said.

"Somebody shot him in the head." He looked for a reaction but saw none. She's getting hard or she's getting numb, he thought.

"Were the police there?"

"No. I found him. Not too long after it happened."

Diana drew back then, closing her eyes on it all for a second or two, and turned slowly and walked to the couch along the wall. She sat down, folding her legs under her, looking at nothing. Cooper was seeing Barry's shattered head again, much too vividly for comfort.

He looked at Rachel. "She fill you in?"

Rachel nodded, arms tightly clasped. She looked dazed, as if someone had just clapped her on the back of the head with a two-by-four. After a moment she said, "She can hide here."

"Tomorrow we're going to the cops. We won't mention you."

"I know who killed him," Diana said from the couch.

Cooper stepped to the rattan chair and sank into it. "What happened?"

"About two minutes after you left me in the car, a guy came walking down the street, on the other side, and got into a car, just across and a little ways up from me. I recognized him."

Cooper blinked. "Who was it?"

"A guy who was sitting at the bar in the Palmer House when I met Wetzel."

"And you recognized him?"

"I'm a waitress. You get in the habit of noticing individuals. Sitting there in the bar waiting for Wetzel, I watched the other people. When this guy showed up on the street he rang a bell. It took me a few seconds to place him, but I did. And I thought it would be good to follow him."

Cooper passed a hand over his face. "They knew by that time what my car looked like. He could have spotted you."

"He wasn't looking for me." She blinked at nothing. "He must have just come from killing Barry."

Cooper stared across the room at her. "Maybe. I hope you didn't follow him too close."

Her eyes refocused on him. "He was easy to tail, I just fixed on the pattern of the tail lights. It was getting dark by then, and he would have had a harder time seeing me behind him. He let his car warm up for a while and I had time to write you the note and drop it out the window."

Cooper shook his head slowly. "Did you get his number?"

"I wanted to, but I was afraid to get too close. I followed him down Sheridan to Morse and over to George's"

"George's?"

"Yeah. He went halfway down the block and parked and then came back and went in the restaurant. I pulled into the Jewel lot across the street and watched him go in. Then I got out and went into the Jewel so I could hide behind the posters in the window and watch. I could see him sitting in a booth by the window. And guess who he was sitting with."

"I give up," said Cooper, closing his eyes.

"The guy who chased me down the alley today."

"Huh."

"That took care of any doubts I had. I stood there looking at them for a while and I decided the thing to do was to get his license number. I went out of the store and walked down toward where he had parked, but as I was about to cross I looked up and saw the guy coming down the sidewalk. He'd only been in the restaurant for maybe five minutes. I ducked into the video store there and watched. He got in the car and turned around and went back down Morse, so I ran back to the car and took off after him. I picked him up again waiting for the red light at Sheridan."

"And you followed him to Oak Park."

"Farther. All the way to Oak Brook. Until we got onto quiet streets where I did get worried about being spotted.

But I followed him as far as a street called Tudor Lane. Big rich folks' houses. Estates. Then I drove back to Oak Park, stopped to get gas and called you. Your car's parked by the Austin El station."

Cooper rubbed his temple. "I'm going to try not to lecture you. You know these guys are killers."

Diana's head sank. "Yeah," she said quietly.

Cooper wanted to go across and take her in his arms. "You can describe the guy?"

She shook herself. "Five-nine or ten, stocky, gray wiry hair."

"What kind of car was he driving?"

"Cooper, I don't know cars like you do. I didn't get close enough to read the trademark. It was sort of silver-colored, and a recent make, that's all I can say."

Cooper looked out the window and said, "Wetzel lives in Oak Brook."

Diana nodded slowly, drained, her voice and gaze distant. "So we have them then. All we have to do is tell the cops."

"And it's high time. Knowing what we do about Barry's death we're probably in violation of the law every minute we delay talking to them."

Something passed over Diana's face like a breath of cold wind over water, and the look she sent Cooper showed numb denial of something beyond endurance. Then her face was hidden in her hands and the silence in the room was heavy. Just as Cooper was thinking it was time to go over and hold her, she took her hands away, her face composed. "I got him killed," she said simply.

"Look, if anybody did, it was me, 'cause it was me they tailed."

In the silence that followed, Cooper could not hold her gaze. He looked away out the window, numb with the vision of Barry's death, paralyzed with disgust.

"I'm ready to go," Diana said. "Let's go talk to the police."

Cooper closed his eyes, drawing a slow deep breath of relief. He was tired, suddenly bone-weary. He turned back to Diana. "It's probably too late tonight to scare up another lawyer. Tomorrow we'll get one, have him meet us at the station." We'll keep this one alive, he added silently to himself.

Rachel had quietly vanished. Diana sat unmoving, head bowed and face hidden, and it was only from the silent shaking of her shoulders that Cooper could see she was weeping.

Moss gently swirled the ice cubes in his tumbler of scotch and looked across the low mahogany coffee table at Annette curled up with *Cosmo* in the gray silk-upholstered armchair by the fireplace. He tried to remember the last time he'd screwed her. As far as he could remember it had been more than a month ago, on the sectional sofa in the parlor across the hall, by the French windows that opened onto the terrace. He also tried to remember why he had been so taken with her as to bring her out to the estate to join his stable, as he sometimes liked to refer to his harem. Looking at her now across the room, he could appreciate the spectacular tumble of glowing brown hair about her head and the swell of her ass under the tight stone-washed jeans, but he could not for the life of him imagine why that face had looked so sexy to him when he'd spotted her serving drinks at the Ambassador East. It was a bit of a cow's face, he decided now, a bit . . . bovine, he thought the word was. In ten years she'd be an old cow.

Of course, she'd be long gone by then. She hadn't lasted nearly as long as some of his girls. With Kristen, for example, the pleasure, the enticement, the enthusiasm had been there for a couple of years before he'd sent her off wherever former prostitutes go with a generous lump sum payoff. Moss took a drink of the scotch and sighed audibly. It was time, he supposed, to be generous to Annette, send her packing. She had already settled in too much here, started to get domestic and let her appearance slide a little, forgetting the makeup and the fancy underwear. God knew what she spent her allowance on; it sure as hell wasn't clothes anymore.

Every member of his stable had been told the terms; when Moss got tired of you, out you went, though with enough cash to cushion the blow. Moss was a generous man. There would be plenty of candidates to replace her.

Looking at Annette and thinking that tomorrow was a good day to give her the farewell talk, Moss started thinking that now was a good time for a farewell tussle. The way she was sitting in the armchair thrust her hips out at him and Moss remembered that the last time hadn't really been what you'd call boring, and there was a little stir way down in his guts. Oh, yes.

Annette had finally looked up, conscious of his staring at her, and he put down his scotch on the mahogany table and said, "Come over here." She looked at him insolently for a full three seconds before putting down the magazine, and Moss thought how good it was going to be to show her he was still boss just before turning her out. She put her feet on the floor, smiling just a little now in that smart-ass way, starting to rise.

There was a knock at the broad oak door. Moss swore under his breath and called out "Yeah," glad at least that Sancho had finally learned to knock. The door opened and Sancho leaned into the room in his white coat, hoping, the bastard, to see something, and said, "Mr. Wes is waiting in your study."

Moss sighed again. He looked at Annette, halfway out of her chair, and said, "Wait right here." He levered himself off the couch and scooped up the scotch and headed for the door. "Don't you have any work to do anywhere?" he said to Sancho, who was lingering by the door.

"Yes, sir." The Mexican butler gave him a rented smile and stood aside to let him pass.

Moss headed down the long passage over the blood-red runner toward the business wing. The business wing contained his paneled study and what he called the communications room, with the phones and the IBM computer and the fax machine and the gray steel desk for the accountant. Moss worked there when he didn't feel like going downtown. There was a separate entrance to the wing and the accountant and Wes could come and go without farting around with the window-dressing butler. Women were barred from the business wing; Moss had found them too much of a distraction after the novelty of sex on the broad desktop had worn off, and besides he didn't want any of his women poking around where he dealt with money.

Moss grimaced as he went through the door at the end of the passage and closed it behind him. He had managed to forget about The Problem for the last half hour or so, and he was irritated to have to deal with it just as he was getting interested in sex again for the first time in four or five days. He made for the door to the study. Through it he could see Wes standing at the window, broad back to him, staring out at the foliage. Wes turned as he came in and Moss was freshly irritated by the sight of the pock-marked face and the reptile eyes.

He'd look bored if somebody was cutting off his nuts, Moss thought. I guess it's too much to ask him to look worried just because my life is falling apart. "What's the good news, Wes?" he said.

"I wish there was some, Mr. Wetzel." Wes came away from the window and sat in the oxblood tub chair as Moss slid behind the desk.

"What now?" said Moss, plunking down the scotch and sinking into his chair.

"I gotta confess to you, I thought these two guys were better when I hired them."

"Oh shit. What are you trying to tell me, Wes?"

"They almost had her this afternoon. In fact they had her. But she pulled a fast one on them, put the kid in the hospital in fact."

"You're bullshitting me, Wes. Tell me you're bull-shitting me."

"I'm not. This is turning out to be one tough lady."

"What happened?"

"The janitor called about two this afternoon. She had come back to her place, just like I thought she would eventually. I got the kid over there because he was closest, and Frank dropped the guy he was watching and hustled over to help. I was on my way when she pulled the fast one. Frank says she threw boiling water in the kid's face and then took off out the back. He went after her but she flagged down some good-citizen types and they held Frank up long enough for her to get away."

"Aw, for Christ's sake, Wes."

Unperturbed, Wes went on. "Frank went back and took the kid to the emergency room. He said he's got first-degree burns all over his face but he's basically OK. I think he's going to want some sick leave, though."

"Sick leave? What'd you do, give these guys a union contract?"

"It's a figure of speech, Mr. Wetzel. I don't think he's gonna want to help for a day or two."

"Terrific. So what is this kid going to tell the police about all this?"

"Absolutely nothing, Mr. Wetzel. It was an accident, as far as the hospital's concerned."

Moss shook his head, lips pursed. "So what now?"

"We're still on the job. Frank's looking for the guy again."

"You lost the guy."

"Had to. Like I said, Frank dropped him when the broad showed up at her place. He was only watching him 'cause we hoped he'd lead us to her. But he went back after he left the hospital. Trouble was the guy's car was gone from his place. But we'll find him again. We got his license number, we know where he lives. He'll lead us to the lady again."

"When? I gotta have this resolved, Wes."

"It takes patient work."

"And competent work."

Wes just stared for a moment, like a granite statue somebody had left on the chair, and Moss wondered if he'd been just a mite rude. Wes said, "Mr. Wetzel, if you don't like my work you can fire me."

There was a mini-staredown that lasted for maybe three seconds. Moss lost, as he had known immediately he would. He heaved his third audible sigh of the evening and said, "I don't have a whole lot of choice, do I Wes?"

"Not a lot, no."

Moss nodded slowly, wearily. "OK. You know what you're doing. Keep me posted."

"You'll know everything you need to know, Mr. Wetzel." Wes stood up and made for the door.

Moss watched him go, wondering what else there was he didn't need to know. He waved Wes out of the study, and then he started thinking about how deep he was in with Wes.

When he got back to the parlor Annette was gone.

With Waylon wailin' from the stereo Wes started to feel a little better. He took a beer from the mini-refrigerator in the corner and went to the workbench. When Wes was pissed off he liked to work at the bench; it was therapy.

And he was getting pissed off for sure with these two guys. Wes liked to think that he hadn't earned three stripes and a rocker without knowing something about leadership, and his leadership was starting to look bad here. Leadership not only meant giving the right orders, but giving them to the right people, picking the right people for the job. He took a long swallow from the bottle and plunked it down and pulled the box of brass cartridge cases toward him.

Fudge was OK but the kid was a fucking disaster. Fudge must have dug him out from under a rock. Wes seated the case on the die and pulled the lever of the turret press to decap and resize it, popped it off and reached for another. It was too late to get new help; just like the midget was stuck with him, he was pretty much stuck with Fudge and the moron.

When he had done fifty cases he rotated the priming die into place and started inserting the primers, each pull of the lever pressing the primer into place and flaring the mouth of the case. When the tape ended he turned it over and got himself another beer.

It would all work out. He would get the job done and take care of the loose ends, like he always did. Wes wasn't too worried about the law; he was careful and he'd pulled off thirteen confirmed kills so far with no trouble. Wes didn't give a shit anyway; anybody who tried to take him to jail would have to kill him first. Wes prided himself on taking a very hard-nosed view of life. There were things he wanted from it, some creature comforts, but there wasn't that much to it. Life for Wes consisted in doing the most professional job he could and staying as comfortable as possible and waiting for it all to end. There just had never been too much to life for Wes, ever since the evening Dad had put three .22 long rifle slugs into Ma's head and been hauled away by the cops. Whenever it ended Wes would be ready to go, as long as he could go with his boots on and guns blazing.

He measured out five and a half grains of powder from the meter and seated the 124-grain jacketed bullet with a pull on the lever. Wes held up the round and looked at it in the lamplight. It shone, a thing of beauty.

Wes loved the sight and feel and smell of machined steel and brass and copper. He loved the smooth working of a bolt, the click of a magazine sliding home, the easy trigger pull of an automatic, the sharp crisp report. For Wes, there was nothing truer or finer in life.

DIANA AWOKE TO the faint luminescence of early morning beyond the rice-paper shades. For a moment she was at peace, aware only of Cooper's breathing beside her, of the unaccustomed quiet of the city streets beyond the shades. Then she remembered why she was on a futon on Rachel's floor, and closed her eyes as the tide of pain swept slowly through her, finally sinking into numbness.

Muted bird noises reached her from outside and she remembered mornings in Miramar, winds off the bay and birds rioting in the foliage beyond the terrace. Cooper stirred beside her. Diana lay still; she and Cooper had both tossed uneasily through most of the night, and she feared waking him now that he was finally asleep. Herself, she deserved to lie awake.

Whatever happens to me now, I deserve it, she thought. I bring death to my friends. Again the chill took her.

Cooper's breath was even and slow, and Diana rolled onto her side, her back aching from the hours on the thin hard futon. She wanted her bed; she wanted to rest in her own bed in her own home, whole again. She shivered as she remembered the destruction, shivered remembering the broad man with strangler's hands. She fought down a sudden urgent need for tears, knowing her home would never be safe again.

Calmer, she walked through the place in her mind, touching all the bases. Kitchen to dining room to living room, into the hallway with the bedroom to the left, bath to the right, back into the living room.

A car passed in the street outside. Diana lay rigid, her heart beating quickly. She raised her head from the sofa cushion and listened. It had grown lighter. At her back Cooper thrashed, shifted, jostled her. An exhalation, almost a sigh, leaked slowly from his mouth.

"Cooper?" she whispered, praying he was awake.

"Mm." His hand sought her and came to rest on her hip. She twisted around, flailing at the blanket, to bring her face near his. He opened his eyes, the furrow between his brows deepening, unshaven and unrested.

Diana let him blink until she was sure he was awake. Something kicked in at last, alarm probably, and he tried to sit up. She placed a hand on his chest.

"Shh. It's all right, baby."

"What is it?" His voice was a quiet rumble, thick with sleep.

"I think I know."

He blinked some more and said, "Know what?"

"I think I know where Tommy hid the evidence."

Moss woke up with a dry mouth and a full bladder. And a hint of a headache. There was just a little bit of light coming in around the brocade curtains. Five o'clock maybe, guessed Moss, and looked at the luminous dial of the clock. Ten past. Moss relapsed onto his back and swore softly. Beside him Janine's breath whistled faintly.

Moss levered himself out of bed and trod wearily over the plush velvet carpet to the bathroom. He pissed and then ran water out of the gold-plated tap until it was cold and took a long drink. He set the cup down and caught sight of himself in the mirror, looking a hundred years old. The hair was going on top and what was left was starting to look like steel wool and the face looked like it was melting. Moss turned hurriedly from the mirror.

Not even the cognac had helped him sleep through the night. Not even the wad he'd shot into Janine. He stood at the door of the bathroom and looked at her still shape under the covers. He should have sent her back to her room, kicked her out and had the bed to himself. This sleep situation was getting desperate. Either he lay awake till three or something woke him up at five; it got him at either end of the night.

Moss stood looking at Janine, wishing he could work up a little excitement, running over who else was in the house. Kareema, Jessie, Kelly, Brandy. Annette the Cow, of course. He could go jump in bed with any of them, wake them up with a good-morning poke.

Moss took his robe from the back of a chair and put it on, shaking his head. He was too tired, tired of all of them. He wondered why it was that even with the most beautiful women in the world, after a while all you had left was a sleeping broad with bad breath who farted in her sleep and snored. Nothing lasted in this world. You used up women the way you used up gasoline or wore out a pair of Ferragamo shoes. You used them up and had to replace them.

Maybe it was time to recycle this whole lot, Moss thought. Toss 'em out on the street. He went to the window and pulled the curtain aside. It was getting light outside, but it was going to be another lousy day, with a sky full of dirty wet clouds. Moss had been thinking it might be nice to get out on the golf course, swat the thing around for a few hours and try and forget all this shit. It was all this shit with the Torres woman or whatever her name was that was keeping him awake, of course.

Moss's eye fell on a lighted window in the south wing of the house. Wes's room. Son of a bitch, he's already up, thought Moss. Either that or he never went to bed. The son of a bitch is down there scheming.

Moss let the curtain fall back and found his way to an armchair. He sank onto it with a grunt. He couldn't decide whether the sight of the lighted window cheered him or not. He knew on the one hand that if there was one person who could get him out of this mess, it was Wes. Wes had saved his ass in Trinidad and he was going to save his ass now. Hiring Wes was the best investment Moss had ever made.

But Moss knew on the other hand that pretty soon it was going to be time to give Wes a nice little raise, start treating him nice, real nice, because Wes sure as hell knew a lot about Moss that Moss would just as soon never got around. It had never occurred to him to doubt Wes's loyalty, because Moss knew that money could buy a whole lot of loyalty, and he paid well. But Moss also knew that people had a way of wanting to move up the career ladder.

And that bothered him vis-à-vis Wes, just a little.

"I just saw it suddenly, remembered it," Diana said. "When I went back there yesterday, Tommy's guitar was gone."

Cooper chewed toast and looked at her across the table. "It wasn't just lost in the shuffle?"

"I don't think so. It's too big. If it was there I'd have seen it, and it finally filtered through to my conscious mind that I hadn't seen it. His duffel bag was there, ripped open, a few of his clothes were lying there. In the bay window, where he kept his stuff. But the guitar was gone."

On the heels of a swallow of coffee, Copper said, "I guess it's a possibility. So where's the guitar?"

"I think I know that, too. He sent it out for repairs."

Cooper looked at her for a moment. "This is where I ask how you know, and you say, 'You know my methods, Watson.' "

"I know because he was complaining about it. He said he needed to get something adjusted. And another thing. He kept a bunch of sheet music in the bottom of the case. I saw it when he had the guitar out playing it. Now think about it. If he wanted to hide the stuff from me and from anyone who might search the place, what better idea than to put it in with the sheet music in his guitar case and send the thing out?"

Cooper nodded, finished off the coffee and set down the mug. The mug was Rachel's, and on it was written in large letters BITCH. Cooper stared at it for a moment and said, "OK. How does that change things?"

"Doesn't it make you want to try to find it, to have something to hand the police?"

"Let the cops find it. Right now we're obstructing justice. I'd like to put an end to that as soon as possible."

Diana nodded, somberly. "There's one more reason I'd like to find it before I talk to the police."

"What's that?"

"The stuff Tommy had on me. That's probably in there, too. And if we can avoid it, I'd just as soon the police didn't see it."

Cooper nodded, then put his head in his hands, rubbed at his eyes. He sighed. "There's got to be a claim check or something. He probably had it on him when he died. I won't be able to get a hold of it. In fact, the cops may already have checked it out. They'd be interested in something like that."

"Maybe not. Why assume they've already got it? There's a phone book in there."

"There's a lot of guitar shops in this city."

"How many can there be? He probably took it to that one on Sheridan Road, anyway."

Cooper shook his head. "They won't give it to me without the ticket."

"Tell them something happened to Tommy, tell them you're his best friend or something. Pay the bill, they'll give it to you."

"Maybe. What happens if I can't find it, or they won't give it to me?"

Diana sagged on the chair. "Then I'll just have to take my chances, I guess. But let's try, for God's sake."

Cooper frowned and stood up, gathering dishes and taking them to the sink. He leaned on the sink for a while and then turned. He spoke quietly, his voice under control. "They damn near got you yesterday. They did get Barry. They blew his fucking brains onto the wall. I saw 'em there. And now you want to stall some more. On a hunch."

Diana's hand was trembling as she set down the coffee cup. She laid both palms on the table and looked up at Cooper. Her voice was husky and the accent was showing.

"You told me once to never ever let myself be stampeded into a bad deal. So all right. I know as well as you do it's time to go talk to them. I didn't have to see Barry to lie there half the night crying for him. But I also know that the police are going to want to see what Tommy had before they believe anything. And chances are, then they'll see what he had on me, too. And that is disaster, Cooper, that's the end of the world. The police don't scare me anymore but the drug thing does, what they're doing to people now. So all I'm saying is, if I can possibly avoid that, let's take one last chance on finding the stuff and pulling out what Tommy had on me."

"Diana."

"Quiet. Last night all I could see was Barry. If you'd said let's go eight hours ago I'd have gone. But this morning I can see what has to be in that guitar case too, and I'm trying hard not to let myself get stampeded. Give me one last chance. Give me this morning. If we don't find it by noon we go to the police."

Cooper swung away from the table, looking for things to smash. He wound up staring out the window over the sink, clutching the sill, nausea stirring. He knew she was mad and he knew she was right, and there was no middle ground. Every minute they stayed away from the police would be harder to explain, but taking her in now was laying her wide open to the worst the law could do. "We can't do it. It's too flimsy," Cooper said to the squirrel on the power line outside.

"It has to be there. All of it. Give me four hours, for God's sake. If you won't do it, I will." Her chair scraped on the floor.

"Sit down," Cooper said, whirling on her. He stared at her, frozen on the chair, and suddenly, for an instant, it was her he wanted to belt. He wanted to knock her off the chair, send that auburn hair flying. He exhaled, letting the poison out. He looked into her startled eyes; she had seen it. "Stay put," he said, quietly. He leaned back on the counter, losing again. He looked out the window; the squirrel was gone.

"I'll try," he said after a long moment. "But meantime, I want you looking up lawyers. Noon comes, whether or not I have it, we go to the cops. I'll drag you by the hair if I have to."

She looked at him, a tear hanging at the corner of an eye. "I guess I'd deserve that, wouldn't I?"

On the long train ride out to Oak Park, Cooper stared out the window at the colorless cityscape and made plans. He found the car where Diana said it was, half a block from the Austin station, with a fifty-dollar parking ticket pinned under the windshield wiper. Cooper tossed it on the seat and drove back into the city.

He cruised up Lake Shore Drive and onto Sheridan Road and went home. He made no attempt to look for anybody watching as he parked the car on his block and marched straight to his front door, hoping he was right in thinking they weren't ready to kill him, not yet.

Upstairs, he made a pot of coffee in the old percolator and sat at the end of the couch next to the telephone. He pulled out the yellow pages and looked up a number and dialed.

"This is Tommy Thorne," he said into the phone. "I'm wondering if the guitar I left last week is ready."

"What kind was it?"

"The Stratocaster," Cooper said, glad Diana had remembered.

"Uh . . ." There was a pause and then, "What was the name?"

"Thorne. Tommy Thorne."

"We don't seem to have any record of it."

"Shit, you know what? I think I got the wrong place. I wrote down a list of 'em here and I think I got mixed up. I left it at a different place. Sorry to bother you, partner."

Cooper had to go through the act twice more before he hit it. The place was called Blakely Custom Guitar and it was on Broadway. "She's all fixed up," the man at the other end of the line said.

"OK, I'm gonna send in a friend to pick it up, OK? I'm kind of laid up here."

"Long as he's got the ticket."

Cooper moved to the chair at the front window and put his feet up on the sill. He watched the new leaves tossing against a background of dirty gray and thought about the claim check and wondered how important it would be to the police to pick up the guitar if they had found the check. After a while he began to think about all the other problems he had. He was trying to resist the temptation to look out at the street when the telephone rang.

"MacLeish. Rise and shine," said Moreland over the line.

"I been up for hours, Mel."

"Not as long as I have, I bet. I've been working on our story."

"Our story?"

"Ours, partner. And a good one it looks to be, too."

"I'm listening."

"Well, you know I'm at the center of an all-seeing international information network here. I got feelers out all over the globe."

"Meaning you can read a Teletype."

"Meaning I can work the phone lines with the best of 'em. You should see my Rolodex, pal. I got numbers in here Henry Kissinger would kill to have."

"Maybe Henry could help us."

"Hey, we don't need him. I spent some time on the phone this morning, running up the bill."

"And?"

"And I had a very interesting talk with a Harry Belafonte sound-alike who works for Reuters down in Port of Spain."

"I bet it was interesting. What'd he say?"

"Are you sitting down?"

"Mel, just give me the story."

"OK. Remember Gladstone Drake?"

"Yeah."

"Well, somebody shot ol' Gladstone the other day. Gladstone is worm meat now."

A couple of seconds went by and Cooper grunted. "What's the other day?"

"Sunday, the guy said."

"Huh. Well, Wetzel didn't kill him, then."

"What is it with you and Wetzel?"

"I told you, I don't know. I'm just interested."

"Yeah, well here's the interesting part. My colleague says Drake was widely rumored—I think that's what he said, or maybe it was 'reputed', I don't know—to be a rather important figure in the distribution of cocaine on the fair island of Trinidad. Probably Tobago, too, for that matter. The word is he died in a turf war. They're mighty close to the mainland there, you know. My guy says they're having big fun with various clans and subclans, Colombian and Venezuelan and Trinidadian and God knows what else, all slugging it out for market shares in the islands. And Gladstone wasn't careful enough. Apparently the knowledgeable money is on one Wilson Melendez, another local squire with some dubious business interests and Gladstone's big rival. Melendez is lying low and the cops profess to be baffled. How about that?"

"How about that." Cooper was staring out the window. "What do you think that means with regard to Moss Wetzel?"

"I couldn't say. You're the one with the Wetzel obsession. But just to play along, if you think there's something shady going on behind Wetzel's Empire of the Rising Dick, maybe it has something to do with Colombia's major export. War on Drugs and all, there is still an awful lot of money in the white stuff."

Cooper frowned at the trees outside. "Maybe."

"I asked the guy if he'd heard anything about Moss Wetzel and he said he vaguely remembered when he was down there for the shoot but hadn't heard anything in particular about him. He said he'd keep his ears open. I probably started a rumor down there, you know. That's the power of the press for you."

"Yeah. OK Mel, thanks. I'll keep you posted."

"You better. I want the works on this Wetzel business, whatever it is."

"If it turns out to be anything at all, you'll get it."

"But promise me now, MacLeish. You'll go carefully here. You know about libel laws and so forth, right?"

Cooper laughed softly and bitterly into the phone. "Yeah. I know all about that."

Cooper hung up the phone and sat on the couch for a while, thinking. Then he looked at his watch. It was getting into late morning and he decided the hook was probably baited. He grabbed his jacket and went out to the car.

Cooper drove the Valiant over to Sheridan Road and headed south, not going too fast or too slow. Where Sheridan slewed east he kept going south on Broadway, looking in the mirror. He pulled into the parking lot of the Dominick's just north of Thorndale, went in and bought a pound of coffee, then got back in the car and went on.

He stopped at a hardware store at Bryn Mawr, made a right and went up Ridge to Clark, came back north. He stopped at his bank to get cash he didn't really need, and when he came back out and looked in his side mirror and saw the Imperial double-parked a block behind, he was sure.

Cooper pulled out onto Clark again and went north. He turned onto Morse Avenue and went east almost to the El tracks, then pulled over and parked. He crossed the street and got a *Tribune* out of the newspaper box on the corner, then crossed back, taking one look down the block, and went into the diner.

It was nearly empty, in the slack time between breakfast and lunch. Cooper tossed the paper on the counter and slid onto a stool. "What do you say, Duck?" he said to the mournful Korean man in the long white apron slouching on a stool behind the counter.

"Business no good. Everybody eat Greek food." Duck nodded at the competition across the street. "Business no good."

"Well, you can give me a cup of coffee and a doughnut. And if your wife can mind the store for a minute or two you could do me a big favor."

Duck shrugged, brought the coffee and the doughnut and blinked at the ten-dollar bill Cooper laid on the counter.

"Keep the change. You know what a Chrysler Imperial looks like?"

Duck slowly picked up the ten. "Sure."

"Well, there's a blue Imperial parked on the north side of the street about half a block back. I'd appreciate it if you could walk down to the drugstore or something and just look at the license number for me. Without the gentleman inside noticing."

Duck's square Korean face was split by a smile. "Just see number?"

"Just the number."

Duck put the ten in the cash register, still smiling. "Bad guy?"

"Yeah, a bad guy."

Duck yelled something in Korean back into the cramped kitchen, taking off the apron. His wife's face appeared in the kitchen door, then vanished again. "I come back," said Duck, and left the diner.

Cooper scanned the paper. He'd drunk half the coffee and finished the doughnut when Duck came back in and slipped behind the counter. He picked up a pen and an order pad and wrote a number on a ticket. He tore off the ticket and set it beside Cooper's saucer.

"Thanks," said Cooper.

"Look like bad guy," said Duck. "Smoke too much."

Cooper went to the pay phone by the door. He punched a number into the phone. "Twenty-four," a man's voice said after two rings.

"Can I talk to Lieutenant Valenti?" Cooper said.

"Just a minute."

When Valenti came on and identified himself Cooper said, "It's MacLeish. How busy are you today?"

"The usual. If you're trying to make me busier, forget it."

"Can you do me a quick favor?"

"Ah, here we go. Your favors never turn out to be small."

"This is a small one. For a top cop like you it's a minute's work."

Valenti said, "What's the favor?"

"Check out a license number for me."

"What the hell for?"

"I think somebody's following me."

Cooper thought he heard a grunt over the phone, faintly. "You're playing cop again. Cops don't like it when people do that."

"Look, I just want to know who the hell this guy is who's following me."

"Flag him down and ask him."

"Listen. You've known me long enough to know I don't fuck around with stuff like this."

A moment passed and Valenti said, "What's the number?"

Cooper read him the number on the meal ticket.

Valenti breathed something inaudible into the phone. "Give me an hour. I have real work to do here, you know."

"I appreciate it. Can I call you back in an hour?"

"Give me a number where I can get you."

"Sorry. I'm going to be on the run."

"Oh yeah? Who from?"

"Don't worry, not you guys," Cooper said with less than total conviction, and hung up.

He went back to the counter. "You got a back door to this place, Duck?"

Duck smiled and cocked his head toward the rear. "He smoke a lot more cigarette today, huh?"

"I'm hoping for at least four more before he gets suspicious," said Cooper.

Cooper went up the back stairs to Diana's place, hoping to find the door unlocked. If it wasn't he would have to try the janitor again, and he wasn't certain how much credit he had left there. He had taken the back-alley approach again, figuring if anyone was watching it was likely to be the cops, but preferring to avoid them for another hour or two.

Diana's back door opened to his touch. He was used to the litter and hardly noticed it as he stepped through it, carefully, listening. He paused at the doorway to the dining room and again at the living room, not wanting any surprises. When he was confident there would be none he stepped across the living room rug to where Diana had thrown her jacket on the sofa. He picked it up and felt in the pockets for the keys.

He took one quick look out the window and then went to the back door. He locked the dead bolt and then came back through the apartment and left by the front door. He locked it and went down the stairs. treading softly over the worn carpet, Diana's jacket under his arm and her keys in his pocket, hoping this idea was the right one, because he didn't have any more.

The mailboxes were in the little entrance hall. The little strip of paper that said FROELICH had begun to peel off at a corner. Cooper fished out Diana's keys and fitted the smallest one into the lock. The box was jammed with an accumulation of junk mail. Cooper sorted quickly, stuffing envelopes back in the box, finally pausing to look at an envelope addressed in block capitals to T. Thorne with a return address in Ft. Lauderdale. Cooper's frown slowly relaxed into a smile as he saw that the envelope bore a Loop postmark dated four days before.

He tore open the envelope. The ticket slid out from the blank sheet of notepaper which enclosed it. At the top it said BLAKELY CUSTOM GUITAR—SALES AND SERVICE with an address on Broadway below it. Cooper put it back in the envelope and slipped it inside his jacket into his shirt pocket. He closed the mailbox and put away the keys. Then he pushed out the door.

"I want to hear a little more," said Valenti.

"A little more what?" Cooper spoke from a quiet pay phone in a drugstore on Devon Avenue.

"A little more about why somebody's following you."

"How the hell should I know? That's why I want to know who it is, so I can figure out why."

Valenti made a noise into the phone that could have been a laugh. "You just can't imagine, huh?"

"I've got an idea or two, sure. Listen, I'll make a little deal with you."

"What's the deal?"

"Help me out here, and when I've got something to interest the law I'll bring it to you. Nobody else. Lieutenant Valenti cracks another case."

"If you've got something that would interest the law I want to hear it now."

"I don't have it yet. When I do, I'm coming straight to you. Now who's the guy in the Chrysler Imperial?"

For perhaps five seconds Cooper waited. Finally Valenti said, "Frank Fudge."

"What?"

"That's his real name. Frank Fudge. You do meet the most interesting people, MacLeish, I gotta hand it to you."

"And who the hell is Frank Fudge?"

"Frank Fudge is an ex-cop. He handed over his star about four years ago after there were some unpleasant rumors about less-than-enthusiastic police work on some disappearing trailer loads down on the Southwest Side. Nobody ever proved anything, but Fudge was asked to find another line of work."

"And what was his new line of work?"

"He set up as a private investigator, believe it or not. The word is he always manages to keep his license, somehow."

"Huh."

"So whose wife is it, MacLeish?"

"Listen, there's a lady's reputation at stake here."

"All right MacLeish, keep it to yourself. But let me tell you one thing."

"Shoot."

"You use this to embarrass me in any way, and I will personally nail your fucking pelt to the wall."

When Wes came into the office Moss was at the window, watching a freighter far out on the lake, right at the horizon line, barely visible. Moss turned around and grimaced at Wes. "Tell me something good," he said.

"Our man's out of the hospital." Wes stood in the middle of the room, immobile.

"Terrific. What's his next trick?" Moss stalked to the desk and sat down.

"He won't fuck up again."

"Sit down, will you?" Wes obeyed and Moss snatched the fountain pen from the desk and began twirling it in his fingers. "How soon do we get some results?"

"Soon."

"You've been telling me that for days."

"It's not an easy job, Mr. Wetzel. The boyfriend is a complicating factor. He knows we're on to him. Just this morning he gave one of my men the slip. But we'll pick him up again. And he'll lead us to her. We think he spent the night with her."

Moss shook his head. "Why don't you just grab him, make him tell you where she is?"

"That's always a possibility. We'll do that if we have to. But it's messy, it's risky. We'd prefer to get 'em both together, with the material, in one operation."

Moss brooded, staring out the window at the mottled sky. "Sooner or later they're going to skip town."

"Maybe. But sooner rather than later we're going to find them. We haven't exhausted all our resources yet."

"Well I'm fucking exhausted, let me tell you that."

"You're not the only one, Mr. Wetzel."

Moss cast a sharp look at him, impassive in the chair opposite. "No, OK, I know you're doing your best. But you gotta understand how this weighs on my mind."

"If you don't like my work I'm sure there are other people you could hire."

Moss stared at Wes but lost again, tossed the pen back on the desk and stammered a little. "I never said that, Wes. And let me tell you another thing. If you, maybe I should say *when* you get this taken care of, there will be a very nice little bonus in it for you."

"That won't be necessary. I'm not complaining about money."

"Hey, I reward competence around here, Wes. Wrap this thing up once and for all and you'll be taken care of."

He met Wes's unblinking stare for a moment and then nodded once, with finality.

"Is that all?" said Wes.

"Unless you have something else to report."

"Not yet. I'll keep you posted."

Watching Wes leave the office, Moss wondered if he was imagining things or if there was a touch less deference in Wes's manner these days.

When the telephone rang, Nathan Longstreet was in the bath. It was ten o'clock in the morning and he was bored. He had gotten up because he was bored with lying in bed, taken a bath because he was bored with showers. In a while he would fix himself breakfast at home because he was bored with eating the Bonanza Breakfast Special at the Golden Nugget down the street.

When the telephone rang he said "shit" out loud because he had just settled into the steaming water. In the next instant he remembered the answering machine he had bought secondhand for thirty dollars so that he wouldn't miss any more job offers, and relaxed. When the telephone rang the second time he said "shit" again because he remembered that he had unplugged the answering machine to plug in the espresso maker. Waiting for the third ring he tried to decide how important the call could be. When the phone went off again he said "shit" three times consecutively and hauled himself out of the bath water because he had finally gotten bored with being unemployed and this might be another job offer.

Not bothering with a towel, he made for the phone, leaving a trail of puddles with a light steam rising off them. He got to the phone just after the fifth ring and said, "Yo."

"Mr. Longstreet?"

"Yeah. Uh, that's right, that's me." Nathan regretted leaving the towel behind, not only because he was cold but because he felt obscurely that this personage could sense his nakedness over the wire and he might lose the job.

The voice at the other end of the wire was masculine, measured, patient. "Mr. Longstreet, this is Sergeant

McDowell of the Chicago Police Department, and I'm trying to locate a woman named Diana Froelich."

"Diana Froelich?" Nathan's incredulity rang in his voice.

"That's right. You do know a Diana Froelich, don't you?"

"Uh, sort of, yeah. I went out with her a couple of times, if that's knowing her. But that was four or five years ago. Why in the hell are you calling me?"

"We found your name in her address book, sir, and we're just doing the legwork."

"What's going on? What are you doing with her address book?"

"She can't be found and we're looking for her, that's all."

Nathan sucked in his paunch and looked down at the puddle forming at his feet. "Well, Officer, I'll tell you. Like I said, I went out with her a few times, but it never went anywhere. We were on different wavelengths, like. She's kind of a rare bird."

"I see. Well, she has your name in her book, anyway."

"She never erased it, huh?"

"It's written in ink."

"Jeez, that was optimistic of her. No little stars penciled in beside it, I take it?"

"Uh . . ."

"Sorry. Just kidding around. She disappeared, huh?"

"Yes, sir. I was wondering if you could maybe tell me who her closer associates were, people who might be able to help us a little more than yourself."

"To tell you the truth, I really hardly know her. I'd forgotten all about her until just now." Nathan frowned as he told the lie, since his failure to make headway with Diana still rankled as one of his bitterest failures.

At the other end of the line the voice was still patient. "You wouldn't be able to tell me, for instance, who her closest friend might be? Someone who wouldn't be listed in the book here? Someone she might have mentioned to you on one of those dates?"

"And you expect me to remember? That was years ago."

"We have to check, sir."

"Sure. Well, you're in luck, because I just happen to know who her best friend is, because it was more or less through her that I met Diana."

"That's great. Can you give me a name?"

"Yeah. Rachel Leeds. I used to work with her. She introduced me to Diana at a party or something. But I haven't seen either of them in years. I don't work at the same place anymore, see."

"Rachel Leeds? That's L-E-E-D-S?"

"Yeah. Like the Who 'Live at Leeds.' "

"I beg your pardon?"

"Nothing. Leeds like you spelled it. I don't know where she lives or anything, but she's probably in the phone book."

"OK, we'll give her a try. Thanks for your help."

"Hey, no problem. What happened to Diana?"

"We try not to speculate, sir. We just want to find her."

"Well, I hope she's all right, because if she's not the world is poorer by one very fine-looking woman. Can I go back to my bath now?"

"As far as I'm concerned," the policeman said placidly.

Nathan sank back into the hot water and said "shit" once more, softly, as he remembered that he still hadn't plugged the answering machine back in. Meanwhile, several miles away, Fudge looked up from the phone and said, "Bingo."

A woman on the bus had told Cecil that blacks and whites didn't mix in Chicago, but he saw plenty of both walking through the tree-lined streets away from the lake. The city was very different here. Until he had come looking for the address on Fargo Avenue, Cecil had thought the entire city was skyscrapers and expressways. He liked it here; it was quiet. Chilly, though; Cecil had been chilly since he'd stepped off the bus.

He asked a white woman the way to Fargo Avenue and she told him, looking at first a little suspicious when he approached her but answering civilly enough. Cecil heard Spanish coming from an open window above him; half the city seemed to be Spanish.

The numbering system on the buildings was easy to follow and he found the 1600 block just beyond the overhead train tracks without trouble. It seemed a pleasant block, composed mostly of three-story apartment buildings made of dark-red brick, some arranged around courtyards with ragged gardens. Cecil thought it would all look better in sunny weather. There were children playing, the first children Cecil had seen in Chicago.

He spotted the address near the end of the block and walked on past it, just looking. At the end of the block he turned left and walked toward a park he saw opening out to the west, five or six acres of bright green grass. As he passed the mouth of the alley that ran behind the building he was interested in, he looked left and gave the back stairs a quick examination. They were a trifle exposed, he decided.

Cecil walked into the park and sat on a bench that faced the mouth of the alley. He watched until the chill got to him, thinking that Chicago didn't seem like such a terrible place to live, except of course for the weather.

Cooper watched as the Valiant rolled into the metered parking lot at the edge of the park. He was perched at the end of a bench that faced out over the lively waters of the lake, collar raised against a stiff breeze and twisted so he could look back at the parking lot. He saw Emilio pull into one of the slots and immediately get out and walk briskly away. He was going to owe Emilio a nice dinner at least when this was all over.

He watched for one minute to see if a Chrysler Imperial would creep into the lot. When there was nothing, he rose and shook the stiffness out of his limbs and trod directly over the grass to the car. Cooper had doubted that Fudge or anybody else would still be watching the Valiant, but he wanted to be certain he was clear, above all now. If somebody was trailing, hanging back just out of sight, Cooper hoped they were unaware the lot had a second exit onto Lunt Avenue. The keys were in the ignition and within a minute Cooper had the Valiant out on Sheridan Road, heading south.

Blakely Custom Guitar was a modest storefront on

Broadway south of Belmont, squeezed in between a used bookstore and a pastry shop. The window was filled with guitars on display stands, both acoustic and electric, along with a few music books: *Joe Pass on Guitar, Chet Atkins' Favorite Tunes, Basic Rock Chords.* Inside, guitars hung from the ceiling, rich wood hues of acoustics and bright plastic tones of electrics. A display case held an array of strings, picks and paraphernalia Cooper didn't recognize.

Blakely himself was fortyish, bald on top with long hair streaming down the sides and a big handlebar moustache. He looked as if gravity were inexorably pulling his hair down off the crown of his head.

Cooper handed him the ticket. "Tommy Thorne left a guitar here last week. He sent me to pick it up for him."

Blakely picked it up and peered at it, then at Cooper. "Oh yeah, he called this morning. What happened? He was supposed to pick it up Monday morning."

"Tommy had a little accident in his Volvo. He can't get around real well right now."

"No kiddin'. That's too bad. He all right?"

"He's got a hell of a headache."

"I was wondering what happened to him. He said he needed it for a job on Monday."

"Well, he got hurt on Sunday night."

Blakely shook his head and went back through the door. He came back in a minute with a thin guitar case, which he laid reverently on the counter. "That's a nice instrument," he said, opening it. The guitar inside was sleek and black, with a neck of blond wood. "This is one of the older Strats. Been taken care of, too. This here guitar's worth a lot of money."

"Yeah, well, Tommy's a pro."

"Tell him I just had to adjust the truss rod a bit, strobe-tuned it. The intonation's perfect now. It should play fine."

"Great. How much do I owe you?"

Blakely shoved the ticket across the counter. "Forty-five bucks. Tell Tommy he's got a nice axe there. If he ever wants to sell it, have him call me."

"I'll tell him," Cooper said, pulling bills out of his wallet.

Outside, Cooper put the guitar on the back seat of the

Valiant and headed back up to Belmont and then out toward the Drive. He got on the Drive going north, but when he got to Montrose he took the exit. He parked in the vast lot beyond the soccer fields, among a few scattered cars.

Cooper knelt on the front seat and reached into the back to wrestle with the guitar case. He got it open and pulled the guitar out by the neck and lowered it to the floor. The inside of the case was lined with purple velvet. The sheet music Diana had seen lay at the bottom. Cooper snatched the sheaf of papers and shuffled through them quickly. There were several sheets of handwritten music, hastily scribbled eighth- and sixteenth-notes and other notation Cooper didn't recognize, in pencil on a treble staff. At the top of some of the sheets were titles Tommy had scrawled: *Bonebreaker Blues, Shuffle On Again, Dog My Cats.* There was nothing else.

Cooper went through it again, in frustration. When he was sure there was nothing else mixed in with the music he slapped it back into the case, twisted around and slumped onto the seat behind the wheel. He stared out across the park and pulled at his moustache and thought.

They weren't going to find the stuff. Cooper felt relief first, then a whiff of Diana's fear. But it was time. It was time to start thinking about the nuts and bolts of getting Diana safely from Rachel's place to a nice secure room with a couple of policemen in attendance and a smart tough lawyer. A vision of Barry crumpled in the bathroom came to Cooper, and he felt the world go sour for a moment.

He turned to the back seat again. Reaching for the guitar, his eye fell on the case. He was still for a time, just scowling at it. She wouldn't let me give up now, he thought. Cooper let go of the guitar and swore viciously. He took out the sheet music and tossed it on the seat. He looked at the purple-lined interior of the case, which hugged the shape of the guitar. Halfway up the neck was a small rectangular compartment nestled against a divider that supported the neck of the guitar. Cooper pulled on the leather tab on the cover and it came up to reveal a jumble of extra strings and picks. He rummaged through the contents, looking for photos or maps, but found neither.

His eye went the length of the case. Look for a seam, he thought. He began to probe with his fingers around the edges of the case. The velvet apparently covered foam rubber or some similar padding material. After a minute Cooper was satisfied that the velvet was securely anchored everywhere, and he had felt nothing anomalous beneath it. He looked again at the divider which formed one end of the little compartment. It was nearly an inch thick. He gave it a firm wrench with strong fingers, and it gave a little.

Cooper leaned farther into the back seat and worked on it with both hands. He pushed on the wall of the case and pulled on the divider and abruptly it came loose. Cooper eased it up out of the case, seeing how the screws in the side had been sheared off to leave pegs that fit into the holes in the end of the divider. He turned the piece over and saw that it was hollow. He inserted a finger and thumb in the underside, pulled hard and extracted a tightly folded six-by-nine manila envelope.

"This is the one we've been looking for," said Fudge. "The best friend. The one you don't have to write down in your address book because you call her all the time. The one you go to when you're in deep shit." He tapped the notepad with two fingers.

Wes pulled the pad across the table and read the name and address on it. "Not too far from here," he said.

"No. I bet that's where's she been."

"But is she still there?"

"Fuck if I know. We can find out."

"OK, let's get on it. How's Jimmy?"

"Pissed off."

"What's he want to do?"

"What do you mean?"

"I mean is he still in?"

"He's in. He's OK. His face looks like a baboon's ass but he's rarin' to go."

"All right. Call him. How do you want to set this up?"

"We'll need a van. No markings. Just a plain old van."

"OK. I'll need maybe an hour."

"I'll get over there and look at the place. I'll have

Jimmy meet me over there. Page me when you get the van."

Wes had started to slide out of the booth. "Got it."

"One thing," Fudge said.

"Yeah?" Wes halted on the edge of the seat.

"Once she's in the van, I'm out. I'm gone. You understand? Have my money ready."

Wes stared at him, gray eyes unmoving. "OK, Frank. Suit yourself. I think maybe Jimmy'll want to stay in."

"I don't wanna know nothing about it," said Fudge.

The map had been folded and refolded many times, until it had begun to tear along its creases. The paper was limp and the colors faded and there were stains in a couple of places where coffee or some other dark substance had been spilled on it. It was a detailed topographical map veined with contour lines and scattered with tiny symbols of vegetation. Along the top and in the lower left corner was the clear light blue of the sea. The city was ruled off in an intricate grid of fine black lines, sprawling away from the patch of water in the lower left corner and clearly labeled: PORT OF SPAIN. The legend at the bottom of the map gave a scale of 1:25,000 and said PUBLISHED BY DIRECTORATE OF OVERSEAS SURVEYS FOR THE GOVERNMENT OF TRINIDAD AND TOBAGO 1970.

The X was in red ink, in the center of a carefully drawn circle about half an inch in diameter. It lay in what the map indicated was broken forest, in very hilly country, some miles to the north of Port of Spain. The nearest labeled feature was what appeared to be a village called Morne Chaleur. The name Maraval was appended to a smallish town some miles to the east. The X was well removed from any marked road; Morne Chaleur appeared to be accessible from the main road north from Port of Spain.

Cooper laid the map on the seat and picked up the scrap of cloth. It was unmistakably the bottom six or eight inches of a necktie, cut off with some sharp instrument but along a purposeful zigzag. The cloth was rotted with damp and stained dark brown. It gave off a faint odor of rich tropical earth. Cooper rubbed at the monogram with his thumb, finally deciding it was an intertwined W and M.

He frowned at it, then out at the clouds lowering over the lake. He laid it on top of the map.

The last thing he pulled out of the envelope was a plastic ID card with a blank deposit slip folded around it. Diana's face looked up in blurry surprise from the card. The card and the slip said NORTH BAY NATIONAL BANK. Cooper put them in his shirt pocket.

Cooper stared out the windshield for several minutes and then slowly replaced the map and the piece of the tie in the envelope. He put the envelope in the right-hand pocket of his jacket and then leaned over the back of the seat again to replace the guitar in its case. He started the car and made his way back toward the Drive, still frowning, but knowing it was almost all over.

"She's in there." Fudge nodded at the red-brick three-flat a half block away. "I called asking for the Leeds woman and she took a message."

"You sure it's our girl?"

"Yeah. She's got just that tiny bit of an accent."

"OK. How you want to play it?"

"Jimmy's with the van?"

"Yeah."

"Have him put it in the alley. By the back stairs. He drives. With his face nobody's gonna trust him an inch."

"Us they'll trust, huh?"

"They'll have to. You don't monkey around when there's a gas leak in the building."

"You got the gas company IDs? People want to see that these days."

"In an emergency you don't need ID. You got a hard hat and a flashlight, you tell 'em the building's about to go, they don't wait to look at ID."

"Where you gonna get a hard hat?"

"That's basic equipment, pal. I carry one in the trunk. Equipment's half the battle in this job. You got the tools, it's easy."

Wes looked at him blankly for a moment. "So we get her out on the sidewalk. Then what?"

"No. We get whoever else is in there out on the sidewalk. That's the point. We knock at the other two doors first."

Wes nodded. "And once the building's empty . . ."

"Then we got maybe ten minutes. Before people get suspicious."

"Should be enough to get inside."

"Should be. I'll go in the front door from the hall. I'll knock first, try the gas company thing, but if she's suspicious she may not answer. So then I'll force it. She'll probably head out the back. Then she's all yours. The back porch is pretty well hidden but you probably want to drive her back inside and see what's what." Fudge stared sourly out the windshield. He fished inside his jacket for a cigarette. "If she's got the material in there . . ." He lit the cigarette.

"Then the job's pretty much over."

Fudge nodded. "I don't want to know. I found her for you. Once you're in there with her, I'm gone."

Wes pulled out a white business-size envelope, stuffed to a thickness of half an inch and sealed, and tossed it on the seat. "If it bothers you, Frank . . ." He shook his head, opening the door. ". . . don't think about it."

Diana sat with her hands clasped between her knees, paralyzed. The yellow pages lay open on the coffee table in front of her. She had counted seventy-two pages of lawyers in the book and found strident half-page ads for offices specializing in criminal law. The phone was in easy reach on the table, and still she sat unable to move.

Barry had been the only lawyer she'd known, and she had killed him. She wished she had called one of these faceless shysters from the book first, killed him instead of Barry.

She wished she had shoved Tommy Thorne off the stern of the *Bismarck*, into the swirling phosphorescence, long ago.

Again she stretched out her hand to the phone, then mechanically pulled it back again, as she had known she would, and suddenly her face was in her hands and she was collapsing sideways onto the couch. "*Mamá, te necesito,*" she breathed, barely aloud. Sobs came through her fingers, bursting out against all her efforts, matching the rhythm of her shaking torso.

There was the rock, and there was the hard place. Legions of policemen and lawyers and judges on one side and on the other two or three quiet ruthless men with nothing showing in their eyes. In between was Cooper.

Diana took a deep shivering breath and took her hands from her face. After a moment she sat up, looking out the broad front windows at the dark brick facades, the heavy stolid northern buildings. Go, her voice told her again. The world is a big place and a jet airplane can take you a long way fast. You can make it very hard for people to find you. With your three languages you can cover half the globe. There are other lives out there waiting to be built.

And Cooper? Diana wondered if Cooper could possibly ever come with her, knowing it wasn't fair to ask him. And leaving Cooper behind was unthinkable.

She rose from the couch and went to make tea, postponing another confrontation with the phone. She stood huddled with arms folded in Rachel's cluttered kitchen, yearning for the recent past that was already lost, the world of petty triumphs and sorrows and waiting for better things, of solace in friends' kitchens and fading youth and the slow crystallization of a maturer self. Diana knew it was all lost now, that nothing Cooper was going to find out there in the city could bring it back, that unimaginable disruption was imminent whatever the outcome.

She stood with the mug of tea held in both hands, looking out the front windows. The fear lay cold in her, not the fear of death now but the fear of long corridors and windowless rooms and the legions of uniformed men. Somewhere in the building a buzzer sounded faintly, followed by the distant sound of the front door opening below. Diana looked reflexively down at the sidewalk but saw nothing. Her eyes went to the phone again and she knew she was finally ready to talk to a lawyer, because she was going to need someone to walk down those long corridors with her. She came away from the window and set the mug on the coffee table.

Before she could reach for the telephone, it rang, making her jump.

* * *

"I got it," Cooper said. He had his free ear plugged with an index to keep out the roar of the traffic on Montrose. "It was hidden in the guitar case—the tie and the map. And the bank stuff with your name on it."

"Thank God," said Diana, a tinny voice in his ear.

"Did you get onto a lawyer?"

"Not yet. I was just nerved up to it when you called."

Cooper was surprised by a sudden urgent need to see her, hold her. "OK, I'm on my way. I'm at a gas station on Montrose. Give me ten minutes. I'll ring three times."

"All right. I'm not going anywhere."

"It's over, Diana," Cooper said, willing it to be so. "It's just about over."

"Yeah. It's all over," she said.

Nobody answered Fudge's knock on the top floor, and he went softly back down past two to find the old lady coming out of the first-floor apartment with an obese tabby cat clutched to her breast and a harried open-mouthed look on her ravaged face. The old lady had on emerald-green slacks and thick glasses. Her eyes were surreally large as she looked up at Fudge and said, "I didn't smell nothing."

"Well then, you're lucky somebody did. We got quite an accumulation of gas down there."

"You mean the place could blow up?"

Fudge shook his head, ushering her out the front door. "It's not likely but with gas you gotta be careful. We got a crew on the way and we'll have it taken care of pretty soon."

"Everything I own's in that apartment," the lady said, her voice straining at the upper end of its range.

"If nobody does anything stupid, nothing's gonna happen," Fudge said in quiet reassuring tones. "Just stand well clear of the building. I'd suggest you get across the street there and just wait."

"I think the girl's home in the place above me. I heard her moving around. Did you get her out?"

"She didn't answer the door, but I'll go back and check again. Now just calm down, get across the street and wait.

Nobody's gonna get blown up." Fudge waved her across with the flashlight and went back inside.

On the landing in front of the second-floor apartment, he stowed the flashlight in the left-hand pocket of his windbreaker. He stepped to the door and listened. He mouthed a silent curse because he could hear her talking in there and he feared she was not alone. Then he heard the clack of a telephone being replaced on a cradle. There were steps, then silence. Fudge raised his hand to the door and planted three sharp raps on it. "Gas company," he barked.

He waited with his hand inside his jacket on the rubber grip of his S&W Police Special. He waited thirty seconds by his watch, but there was no sound from beyond the door. He let go of the pistol and from the right-hand pocket of his windbreaker he drew out a pry bar and a linoleum knife. He took one deep breath and spread his feet and wedged the blade of the knife between the door and the jamb. He shoved the pry bar in just above the knife, where the bolt would be, and pressed down, spreading the door. He pulled up with the knife, forcing the bolt back into the lock. A shove opened the door.

The chain stopped it after eight inches, but Fudge could hear the movement in the living room. She would be rising from a chair or a couch, scared out of her wits, and while he could undo the chain with the old thumbtack-and-rubber-band trick, he didn't think he'd have to. Most likely she'd take off out the back.

Sure enough, he heard her take off, running.

Wes felt the burst of adrenal energy all through him as he heard footsteps coming fast, back through the kitchen. He heard the frantic scrabbling at the chain and the dead bolt and he hooked a finger through the handle of the screen door. When the inner door came open Wes tore open the screen and swung into her face, cutting off the scream with a hand over the mouth, the dark eyes showing wide above his broad fingers. He pushed her back into the kitchen and knocked her hand aside as it came up to claw at his eyes. He snarled as she bit hard into his palm and pulled his hand away, catching her with his other hand as she twisted, and then put an end to it, driving his right fist hard into her slender midsection.

She crumpled in airless agony on the linoleum and Wes turned calmly to close and lock the door. She had rolled over in slow motion, her ass in the air and her face on the floor, and he grabbed the auburn hair and jerked her upright and pushed her back into the dining room, where he flung her across the table, scattering chairs. She went down to the floor again, still feeling for the first desperate gasps of air, her face frozen in that comical dead-fish look, arms held tight to her belly.

Wes walked into the hall and looked at Fudge, visible through the partly open door, the yellow hard hat on his head. Fudge nodded once and pulled the door shut. Wes walked back to where Diana lay finally taking in air with a raking helpless sound. He stood over her and watched until she was able to sit up, supporting herself on one hand with the other to her stomach, her eyes still wide but starting to focus on him.

"You got something I want." Wes was very conscious of seconds ticking off the clock.

The eyes closed and she sank back against a leg of the table. "No," she managed, just audibly. "It's not here."

Wes reached down and put a hand on either side of her face, thumbs over her eyes, and started to press. She went rigid and tried to knock his hands away, but he held her and slowly increased the pressure.

"It's not here!" This time it was a full-throated scream.

Wes took his thumbs away from her eyeballs and grabbed another handful of hair and pulled her to her feet. He forced her against the table, bending her over backward with her butt against the edge, her back arched painfully, feet just off the floor, head pinned to the table by its long auburn hair.

"Let's talk, huh? Where is it?"

She was sobbing now, hands to her eyes. She struggled for control of her voice and said, "In Tommy Thorne's guitar case."

"And where's the guitar case?"

"In a shop, I don't know which one."

"Tell me about it." Wes gave her head an encouraging

bang against the table. She took a swipe at the arm holding her head to the table, eyes squeezed shut in a grimace. Wes put his free hand to her throat. "Don't piss me off, girl. Talk."

Her eyes came open and focused on his, wide open and darting back and forth across his face. She gasped a couple of times, blinking. Her hands fell back on the table on either side of her head. Wes had a thigh wedged between her legs and he could feel the tension running up and down her body. Finally she said, "That's my best guess. I never had the stuff. Tommy hid it someplace, the guitar is all I can figure." Her words came in fast breathless rushes.

Wes held her fast against the table and thought. "Your boyfriend looking for it?" he said. Her eyes flared even farther open for a second. He could see her cooking up a lie and he gave her head another bang. "Huh?"

"Yes," she said, eyes screwed shut again, tears leaking at the corners.

"He coming back here?"

"If he finds it. He's gonna call first." She gave vent to a sob and her hands went to Wes's chest and she strained with all her might, not budging him.

He backed away suddenly and brought her upright by the hair. She gained her balance and stood giving him a weepy cockeyed look, her head pulled to one side. "You're gonna give me a quick little tour of the place, OK? I want to see all the rooms." He released her hair and she staggered back a step. "Move. That way. I'm right behind you. Walk don't run."

As soon as she turned, Wes started calculating. When she went through the doorway into the living room and looked over her shoulder, he motioned to the right, toward the hall. When she turned that way, Wes picked the spot at the base of her skull and wound up. She had no time to turn or flinch before the tensed blade of his hand slammed her there, and she went sideways against the wall and slid to the floor, taking a couple of shelves full of books with her.

Poulos sat behind the wheel of the van, pulling irritably at a flap of dying skin on his cheek. Everything was quiet in the building, but he was still nervous. Poulos didn't like the plan at all; he kept waiting for a squad to come screaming up with cops piling out and waving guns at him. He hated the pants-down, shit-eating feeling of getting caught.

Poulos wasn't even sure she was in there; he had a sneaking suspicion Fudge was basically a fuckup. He sure hadn't been any help yesterday. The guy Wes seemed to know what he was doing, but they were both dependent on Fudge for their information here.

Poulos shifted on the seat, his eyes glued to the back door on the second-floor porch above him, having trouble containing the nervous energy in his thick muscles. There was only one thing that had kept him on this job, and if that didn't pan out here he was fucking gone.

The back door came open and Poulos watched open-mouthed as Wes came out and descended the stairs. Poulos wondered how the hell he had done it; there she was sure enough, limp in Wes's arms, one arm dangling loose and her head lolling against his shoulder.

Poulos smiled.

19

COOPER SAW THE old lady standing forlornly across the street from Rachel's place with a cat in her arms, but paid her no notice until he was going up the steps and she shouted "Don't go in there," in her high thin quaver.

He turned and gave her a patient look and yelled, "Why not?"

"There's a gas leak. They're kicking everybody out of the building."

Cooper stepped back down onto the sidewalk and looked up at Rachel's windows. Then he walked across the street. "Who's kicking everybody out?" he said to the woman.

"The gas company. A man came and said there was lot of gas built up in the basement and it could go sky high and we had to get out. He said a crew was on the way to fix it but I'm still waiting. Been out here fifteen, twenty minutes. Shush." She struggled with the cat in her arms.

"Where's the man?"

"I don't know. He walked off that way and got in a car and left."

Cooper stared at the building, thinking, No, no, no. "The woman in the second-floor apartment. Did she come out?"

"The man from the gas company said she went out the back. He missed her at first but went back to look for her."

Cooper went back across the street at a lope and down the gangway to the back. There was a cement-floored yard behind the building, giving onto the alley. There was nobody in the alley and Cooper took the steps up three at a time. The back door was shut and there was no broken glass or smashed panels and he had a moment of hope, a brief image of Diana waiting safely just around the corner. The door opened when he turned the knob and he burst into Rachel's kitchen.

"Diana?" There was no answer and he pushed through to the dining room and saw the overturned chairs and swore. In the living room he saw the books tumbled onto the floor and then his eyes went to the bright red scrawl across the mirror in the hall and his stomach turned over.

It wasn't blood, as his first visceral reaction screamed; the lipstick that had written it stood on the table beneath the mirror. The block capitals were six inches high.

DON'T CALL US, WE'LL CALL YOU
NO COPS, NO GAMES
WRONG MOVE = ONE DEAD LADY

Cooper sat down on the wicker chair because his legs were suddenly trembling under his weight. He stared at the words, reproaches running in fevered sequence through his mind. He fought them off, knowing he had time only to think hard and fast. He rose from the chair and made a quick tour of the apartment, finding nothing else disturbed. He wondered how they had gotten in; whatever they had pulled had been wicked and smart. The whole time, his heart was in overdrive but his mind had settled into an arctic calm.

He went back into the hall and stood facing the message on the mirror, examining and discarding options one by one. When he had sifted down to a single hard clear choice he said, out loud but softly, "All right."

First things first, thought Cooper. He went into the kitchen and tore open doors until he found a bottle of Windex and a rag. He spent a precious five minutes cleaning the mirror in the hall, getting the message off and the drips of water wiped up. He wasn't sure where the lipstick had come from, but he put it in the medicine chest in the bathroom and put the rag and the Windex back in the kitchen. He righted chairs and slapped books back onto shelves. He gathered Diana's few effects and stuffed them into her bag. He locked the back door and left by the front.

Outside, he said to the old lady, "I think you can go back in now. They got everything squared away."

Bewildered, she said, "I didn't even see nobody from the gas company."

"They went in through the back. They're gone now."

"You mean they woulda let me stand out here all day?"

"That's the gas company for you," said Cooper. "The only time they want to talk to you is when you don't pay the bill."

Newborn, Diana knew nothing. Her face was pressed to something rough and the darkness around her jolted her and rumbled. She raised her head and there was light there, above. She didn't even know enough to be bewildered. The first thing that could be called a fact that she became aware of was that she could not move her arms.

Her head sagged back to the hard, vibrating floor. It didn't occur to her to wonder what floor it might be. Not being able to move her arms was irksome, and she struggled again. Her stomach muscles strained, her shoulder ground into the hard surface beneath her. Struggling, she began to learn about the world; arms and legs could not be moved.

It finally struck her that this was extraordinary, and she began to learn rapidly. She was moving, or this thing that she was in was moving; thus the rumbling, the vibration.

And she was not alone. Twisting, she could bring the source of light into view. That is a windshield, she was suddenly aware. With a wrench she swung her legs around and rose to a sitting position. And that a head, silhouetted against the gray sky outside.

Her knowledge of her world was almost complete. She knew what a van was, and she knew she was in one. She knew she was bound somehow, quite securely, not comfortably. But still she did not know enough to be afraid.

The fear came back along with understanding, with the voice she made out over the rumble as the vehicle slowed and Diana was pitched onto her side.

"Good morning, sweetheart." The head was still only a silhouette, but she could see eyes in the rearview mirror.

When it came, the fear froze her and left her yearning for the brief infancy that had preceded it. Diana's muscles tensed against her restraints, and as she drew breath through her nose she realized she was gagged as well. The last cavities in her memory filled with a sudden flood.

The van eased to a halt. Diana lay on the floor, her heart a frantic drumbeat in her chest. She lay perfectly still, thinking wildly that to move was to invite harm. There was a rustling and a squeak of springs and the voice said, "Now don't go back to sleep on me, baby. The fun's gonna start soon."

Then her reaction was to haul herself upright and get as far away as possible, because she knew that voice. She rolled, scooted, thumped her way to the back of the van, bruising her back on the wheel well, losing her balance and crumpling against the doors at the rear. She looked to the front to see the man craning to watch her, backlit by the windshield but with just enough light from the side to show the weird, mottled, inhuman face. When she was still he turned without a word and settled himself on the seat.

The van began moving again. Through the windshield

Diana could see traffic lights, dirty clouds, stone cornices on old brick buildings. She closed her eyes.

Cooper. If they had waited for Cooper, ambushed him, then it was all over.

I should have protected him. I should have lied. I was too weak.

Devastated by her failure, she squeezed her eyes shut against tears of despair, defeat. After the effort of suppression, she let out an explosive breath through her nose, sending out a little spray of muscus. Her head rolled from side to side; she contracted all her muscles in a futile rage against the tape that held her limbs. Finally she shot a look of hatred toward the man in the front of the van.

She tried to see Cooper, coming back to the apartment. They would have been waiting. Where? Would Cooper have had a chance? Did they shoot him, club him, stab him?

Or: did they miss him?

For if they had killed Cooper, why hadn't they killed her, too?

Hope, almost joy, suffused her. Cooper was alive. If Cooper was dead there was no reason for her to be alive. And Diana knew suddenly that she could and she must stay in control.

Diana knew what Cooper would tell her. Cooper would say *keep your head.*

Keep your head. The incantation alone served to calm her. Her breathing was fast and noisy, wheezing through her nostrils. Her heart was still pounding, but she squared her shoulders against the side of the van and listened to Cooper's voice: keep your head.

Cooper had told her once of his own closest brush with terminal panic, lost in the elephant grass in the wake of a catastrophically bungled night ambush, waiting out the darkness only to hear muttered orders in Vietnamese coming through the grass with the dawn. He had almost bolted but somehow, by some obscure grace, kept his head. And Diana remembered now the words Cooper said had saved him as he repeated them to himself, while the NVA patrol stepped around him: the calmer I am, the harder I am to kill.

* * *

In a phone book in a restaurant on Broadway Cooper found the number of the art-supply store where Rachel worked.

"We're out," he told her. "Forget we were there last night."

"What happened?" she said.

"Nothing happened. We're moving, that's all. We found another place to hide."

"Where are you going?"

"Diana will fill you in. I'll have her give you a call."

Cooper was a bit brutal in cutting off the conversation, but clocks were ticking. Hoping he'd bought enough time to work with, he got back in the Valiant and went north. He parked on Paulina a couple of blocks north of Lunt and got out and quickly walked away from it, feeling suddenly that time had run out on the car.

Cooper walked over to Clark and down to Lunt, watching people go about their business and desperately groping for all the old reflexes and instincts and armor, hoping he could still find the attitude. At Lunt he went around the corner to the garage where Emilio worked.

Inside the garage everything was black. Emilio had grease on the overalls and blackened hands and smudges shading into his thicket of beard. He looked up from the bowels of a vintage jet-black Corvette and teeth shone white through the beard. "Hey, Mr. Badass. Still walkin' tall?"

"So far. You got yellow pages I could look at?"

"In the office. Whose ass gets kicked today?"

"You don't want to know, friend. Just keep the bail money ready."

Emilio's laugh followed him into the office. There had been no Frank Fudge in the phone book at the restaurant. Cooper thumped the dog-eared disintegrating directory onto the desktop and quickly found two columns of *Investigators*. There was a FUDGE FRANK D AGENCY with an address on Irving Park. Cooper noted it and the phone number and went back into the garage.

Emilio waved a socket wrench at him. "Hey, I looked for you last night. They ain't no competition around no more. I played for two hours and it was just run 'em out every time."

"I've been having a busy week," said Cooper.

"My old lady thinks you're Al Capone or something. She tryin' to tell me now she don't want me to play with you no more."

"Tell her I'm sorry. I'll come over and bring her some flowers or something."

"Ah, she'll get over it. She was sheltered like, growin' up down there in Sonora. She still don't like it here."

"Her instincts are sound."

"She'll get used to it."

"Maybe. Listen. You got a car I could borrow for a day or two? The Valiant's coughing up blood today."

"Shit, bring it in. I'll fix it."

"I can't move it and I don't have time to deal with it right now. If you could let me have one of your string for the rest of the day I'd appreciate it. Hell, I'll pay you for it. I just need wheels."

Emilio shrugged. "Sure. I got an old Firebird back in the alley I can let you have."

"Perfect. I owe you a big one, partner."

"Hey, *somos hermanos.*"

While Emilio went to the office to get the key Cooper's eyes scanned the garage, looking for salvation.

"Here you go. Treat her right," Emilio said, holding up the key.

"Thanks. Two more favors."

"What?"

Cooper slid the manila envelope out of his pocket. "Keep this for me for a couple of hours. Keep it in a pocket. Don't put it in the office or anything. Keep it where you keep your folding money."

Emilio had just a notion of a smile on his lips as he took the envelope and put it inside his coveralls. "And what's the second favor?"

"Let me borrow this." Cooper swung the iron bar up from where it rested in a corner. It was about two and a half feet long.

Emilio blinked at him. "What for?"

"I got a dent in the Valiant I want to pound out." He

hefted the bar, gripping it like a baseball bat. It weighed about twenty pounds, he judged. "You'll get it back today."

Cooper could tell Emilio didn't believe him for a second, not for an instant. He gave Cooper a calculating look, head to one side, impassive. "Am I gonna have to go to the bank again?" he said.

Cooper smiled. "You ought to know me better than that."

The tape that bound her limbs and covered her mouth was white athletic tape, tough and unyielding, better than rope. Her legs were held tightly together; she could barely separate her knees. Her wrists were crossed at the small of her back, immovable under several turns of tape.

Her heart had slowed a bit and she was breathing without trouble. Her upper back was against the side of the van, near the rear doors, allowing her to keep her balance as the van accelerated and turned. The words from the driver's seat came at intervals, loud enough to be heard over the engine, directed out the windshield, eerily detached from her situation.

"Are we gonna have fun, you and me . . . Oooooeeee! Yes baby, I am gonna show you a hell of a time. . . . Nice fucking signal, asshole. . . . Diana, baby . . . You are gonna have the time of your life in a little while." Diana listened and repeated the words Cooper had told her and looked at her surroundings.

There was a handle recessed in the right-hand door at the rear of the van. Diana stared at it and flexed her toes in the wool socks that were all she had on her feet. To bring her feet up to the handle she would have to first position herself in the center of the floor and not too close or too far from the doors, then swing her legs up and fall back. It would be difficult to scoot or roll across the floor without attracting notice, and the timing would have to be right. The van was apparently on a long straight street now; there were no turns and only occasional stoplights. The trick would be to start getting in position as the van slowed for a light.

"You know . . . I wish you were still wearing those

jeans, Diana, those nice tight jeans you had on the other day. . . . Oh, would I love to cut those off you with a pair of shears, peel 'em right off your ass. . . ." The van began to slow, and Diana wriggled away from the wall, pushing with her shoulders, contracted her stomach muscles to bring her into a fetal position and spun on her buttocks, bringing her feet to bear on the rear doors, pushing on around until she could shove out from the wall with her feet. "Comfortable, sweetheart?"

The van had almost come to a stop when Diana swung into position and raised her feet to the handle of the rear door. She wedged her toes under it, the steel pressing painfully through the socks and the thin flesh into the bone, and strained to lift it. The purchase was inadequate and she withdrew her toes, breath whistling out her nose, and tried with the balls of her feet. The van rocked to a halt.

"Oh now Diana." The voice was louder, as if the man at the wheel had turned. "You don't really think I'd be stupid enough to leave the doors unlocked, do you?" Panic surged back as Diana jabbed fiercely at the handle, bruising her feet. Blood throbbed in her temples.

"You're wasting energy you're gonna need in a little while, baby." Diana gave up and let her feet fall away from the door, taking her over onto her left side. *Keep your head,* she said distinctly in the cool empty sanctuary inside her. She lay and panted through her nose while the van was put into gear and picked up speed. "You're gonna wear yourself out and you won't have nothing left for the fun stuff."

Diana raised her head and shifted enough to look at the back of the man's head as he drove. She could see trees now, passing in rank beyond the windshield. The automatic transmission kicked up another notch.

Diana pulled her knees to her chest again, tensing her overworked stomach muscles again. She pushed out an elbow, straining against the tape on her wrists, pressed her face to the floor, raised a hip, struggled to gain leverage with her shoulder. She got both knees under her, her forehead against the steel floor and her neck muscles straining, and pulled into a kneeling position. She knelt with her head on the floor and rested, seeing the sequence clearly. The van was moving at a steady fast pace.

Diana rose to her knees, then rocked back, wriggling her toes to get a grip on the floor. She gained it and rose precariously to her feet. Through the windshield she could see the street, full of cars and people unaware of her. Without hesitating she began to hop, head low, careening forward.

The man's head came around just as she lost her balance and pitched forward between the seats into his lap, knocking one of his arms from the wheel. The van lurched hard to the left.

"Jesus . . ." There was a screech of brakes and a long peal on a horn. ". . . Christ!" A thick arm hurled her back into the depths of the van. Diana rolled one way and another as the vehicle swerved madly and then braked. More horns sounded.

The van stopped abruptly and the man was coming out of the seat, swinging a leg back toward her. Diana had stabilized on her back by the time he reached her. For a moment she fixed on the blotched red face hanging above her, and then flashes went off as a thick hand slammed her briefly out of her senses.

When she could focus again, he said, "Nice try, bitch." He was scrabbling in a pocket. The puffed red face was close above her and more tape was coming off the roll. This time it went around her throat.

He wrapped a couple of turns around Diana's neck and then one of the strangler's hands caught her under the arm and dragged her forward toward the seats. Her head slammed into the back of the passenger seat and he was very close to her, working feverishly, his arms going around her as he fastened the other end of the tape to the base of the seat. Diana closed her eyes. Another car honked, long and loud, nearby.

He was back in the seat quickly. "All right, all right!" he roared at someone outside. He shoved the van into gear and they began to move again. "Son of a bitch."

Diana opened her eyes and tested her new bonds. There was very little give; she was securely held by the neck, her head against the back of the seat. The tape was tight but not enough to keep her from breathing. She squirmed until she was on her side, more comfortably, her head dropping to the floor.

Somebody has got to have seen it, she was thinking.

"Oh baby," the voice said from above her, remote now. "She's pissed me off good this time." The voice was more detached and unreal than ever. "I'm gonna have to teach the girl a lesson." The van swerved, then accelerated. A siren sounded, too far away to offer hope.

"I'll tell you what I'm gonna do," said the man at the wheel, voice raised to the world at large. "I'm gonna make this cunt sorry she was born a woman."

THE FIREBIRD HAD its hardest charging days behind it and the brakes were on the soft side, but it worked. Cooper took a deep breath and pointed it down Clark Street.

The fastest way he could think of to find the people who had Diana was also the most dangerous, because he would be finding them on their terms. The other ways he could think of were much less certain and would consume more time. Cooper wasn't sure how much he had to worry about the time factor, except that the longer they had her, the more likely it was that impatience and irritation and random mishaps would put her in danger.

Of course, thought Cooper, stuck in the Clark Street traffic, she may be dead already.

If so, somebody else was going to die too.

Cooper turned east and went over to Glenwood, then south. He double-parked in front of the old folks' bar. It was open, but there was nobody there besides the barkeep, who had time only to look up blankly as Cooper ducked in for a look and out again. He went on down over the old bricks in the shade of the El embankment until he reached his street.

What passed for his plan was quite simple: cruise the block and look. Then park and watch. If they were there, he ought to see them first, because they would presumably be looking for the Valiant. He didn't know what kind of car he was looking for, but he would count heads in the cars along the street. If necessary he would get out and walk, trolling for sharks. That would be the scary part, because he was fairly certain that a simple exchange was not all Wetzel's men would have planned.

Cooper turned left and began the pass. Even at an unnaturally slow pace it was hard to drive and check for heads in parked cars at the same time. He went all the way to the alley just short of Sheridan Road without seeing anybody. He turned into the alley and reversed onto the street, went back to the first open parking space and dropped anchor at about the limit of feasible surveillance range. He figured if anyone was watching, they had to be in front of him.

He waited, uncertain, for a minute or two. The iron bar lay on the seat beside him. He wondered if it would help to carry it down the block with him and decided probably not. Cooper took the key out of the ignition and got out of the car. He crossed to the other side of the street and walked toward his door, a hundred yards away.

Walking the point had never been his favorite thing, and walking it without a weapon didn't improve it. He looked into cars and onto porches and told himself, without much assurance, that they wouldn't simply try a hit. The sidewalk was deserted.

When he reached his door he turned up the walk, hair rising on the back of his neck, and went into the foyer. He pulled out his keys and opened his mailbox and cleared it of junk mail, keeping an eye on the street.

Cooper let himself in and went up the stairs. When he reached his door he unlocked it, stood to one side and pushed it open hard enough that it swung back and banged against the wall. He tossed the junk mail onto the living-room floor and then waited, just listening. After a few seconds he stepped quietly up the stairs to the landing above, leaving the door to his place open.

He took a look out the window at the still empty street and then sat on the landing and waited. Cars passed by outside without stopping. Nobody rang, nobody opened the door below, nobody made soft footsteps inside his apartment. No telephones rang.

Cooper gave them fifteen minutes and then decided they had something else in mind. That was all right, he told himself; so did he.

Wes checked his watch; twelve minutes before it would be time to try calling the boyfriend again. He wondered if he should shorten the interval from half an hour to a quarter, but decided that was just impatience talking. Wes had learned the value of patience long before.

He had also learned the value of good subordinates, and he knew he had a problem with Poulos. Wes figured he should have seen the white van by now. It should by now be parked in the far corner of the vast lot, near the K Mart. It wasn't, which led Wes to think about accidents and sharp-eyed cops and other things he'd rather not think about. He shook his head and fished in the plastic bin on the dash for another tape.

He had just shoved Merle Haggard into the slot when the car phone buzzed. Wes picked it up and heard Poulos's voice.

"Hello, yeah, listen. I ah, I had to change things a little bit."

Here we go, thought Wes. "What do you mean?"

"I had to get the van off the street fast."

"What happened?"

"I almost had an accident. The bitch woke up and tried to jump me."

"I thought you tied her up, for Christ's sake."

"I did. She got up on her feet and kind of flopped on me. I damn near hit another car."

"That's great, that's just terrific."

"Listen. I took care of it. I got clear and got to a place I could stash her and then I ditched the van."

"Why didn't you bring her over here like I said?"

"You kidding? A zillion people saw what happened. I was right in the middle of Western Avenue. If anybody saw her through the window and called the cops, they're looking for the van right now. I had to bail out."

Wes put a hand to his brow and said, "OK, so where the fuck is she?"

"In my garage."

"WHAT?"

"I said she's in my fuckin' garage. I was in the neighborhood, lucky for us. Took me ten minutes to get there. It would have taken a half hour to get to where you are. And I never would have made it."

"So she's in your garage, screaming her head off."

"She's rolled up in a rug. She can't move. She can't make any noise. Nobody's gonna see her. She's safe till you get something else to move her in."

"How many of your neighbors saw you drive the van in?"

"Nobody, probably. It's in the alley out back. And if they did, so what? I borrowed a van to move some shit, big fuckin' deal."

"So what'd you do with the van?"

"It's in the parking lot of a Dominick's, on Broadway. That's where I'm calling from. I'm gonna walk over and pick up my car and go back."

"All right, where's your garage?"

"Look, she's OK there for a while. You work on getting another van."

Moron, thought Wes. "Where is your fucking garage?" he said slowly.

"4823 Monticello. It's my ma's house. Make sure you come around through the alley."

"You took her to your mother's house?"

"Look . . ."

"How's your ma going to react when she goes out and finds her? You going to tell her it's an old girlfriend?"

"She never goes out to the garage. She don't drive. Listen, you got a better idea, let me know. I had to get her off the street."

"All right, all right. I'll handle it. You get back there and keep her from raising the roof."

Poulos's voice crackled in Wes's ear. "Hey, I'll take good care of her, don't you worry."

The address of the Frank D. Fudge Agency turned out to be a dilapidated one-story office complex along one side of a corner parking lot far out on Irving Park. At the end, fronting on Irving, was a Polish travel agency. There was a red-lettered sign in the window that said WARSZAWA $300. Beyond the travel agency a covered walk ran past windows of offices. On the wall by the door in the middle of the walk was a board with names posted in removable letters. The three names on the sign besides Frank D. Fudge were South Asian. Fudge was also the only one without MD or DDS after his name. The windows all had blinds drawn and the parking lot was empty except for an aged Ford Torino and a dark blue Chrysler Imperial.

Cooper had gone past the place and had to turn around and come back east. He looked at the offices for a while from across the street and decided it didn't look like Frank D. Fudge was making a very good living being a detective, which he didn't find surprising. It also looked like business could be better for Indian dentists, but Cooper was less concerned with that. He put the Firebird in gear and pulled out into traffic again.

He took the next left and looked for the alley he had seen beyond the parking lot. He rolled slowly up the alley, coming almost to a halt as he neared the office mall, looking for back doors, holes in the fence, anything that might help. There didn't seem to be any back doors to the offices; there was a trash dumpster with the address of the complex on it at the end of the walk. Cooper braked and rolled down the window, then took the iron bar from the seat and chucked it into the weeds at the end of the walk. He rolled on up to the street and went right, away from Irving, and parked a hundred yards up a block of small tidy houses.

There were people about, but Cooper couldn't think of any way of doing things that didn't involve, at this point, considerable risk. He walked back down toward Fudge's office trying to keep an unhurried pace. He went up the alley, retrieved the bar and stepped onto the walk, holding the bar close to his side.

The door opened into a lobby with frayed chairs and a building directory behind cracked glass that reproduced the one outside. There was a reception counter to the right but it was firmly shuttered. Cooper stood listening and heard only the sound of failed practices. Someone had taken in patients as recently as three months ago, judging from the magazines on a side table, but if there were any here today they were suffering in silence.

FUDGE INVESTIGATIONS 5, said the directory on the wall. Cooper stepped into the hallway that ran the length of the building and looked for numbers. Even to the right, odd to the left, it seemed to be. To his right, at the end of the corridor, he could see through a glass door into what looked like the travel agency. He saw no one in there, but it had looked open from the street and Cooper hoped the Poles weren't curious by nature.

He went softly down the hall to the left. Number five was the next-to-last office on the right side of the corridor. Cooper paused at the flimsy plywood door, considering scenarios: locked, unlocked, knock or just try the knob. In the end he tried the knob, and the door swung open.

The man from the motel sat at a desk ten feet from the door. He was in shirt-sleeves, with his tie loosened and awry. There was a bottle of Early Times on the desk, and beside it a glass with a half inch in the bottom. Frank Fudge looked at Cooper with his lips slightly parted, unblinking.

Cooper had kept the bar out of sight outside the door. Now he took a step into the room and brought the bar inside, closing the door behind him with his left hand. He brought the bar up like DiMaggio stepping to the plate. "You got a piece, now's the time to go for it," he said.

Fudge came out of his stupor and dived for the right-hand desk drawer as Cooper started to move. Fudge had the holster halfway out of the drawer when Cooper brought the bar down on his wrist.

Fudge's choked-off scream almost covered the sound of the bone breaking, but not quite. His head went down on the desktop and the holster thumped to the floor. Cooper shoved Fudge's wheeled chair away from the desk with his foot and stooped to grasp the revolver by the rubber grip. He shook off the holster and held the gun loosely at his hip, the bar hanging at his side, while Fudge recovered, pushing himself upright in the chair with his intact hand on the far corner of the desk.

"How's the motel business?" said Cooper.

Fudge flopped back in his chair, cradling his right arm in his left. The contraction of his features eased very slowly. When he opened his eyes, tears spilled out. "Jesus," he said.

"Where is she?" said Cooper.

"I don't know what the fuck you're talking about," Fudge squeezed out.

Cooper looked at the .38 Police Special in his hand and then slipped it into the side pocket of his jacket. He brought the bar up with both hands. "I don't think you're an idiot," he said, "and I don't much like this kind of thing. But if you're going to play stupid I'm willing to throw my principles out the window and take you apart bone by bone. Your call."

"I don't know where she is." Fudge was listing to port, eyes closed again.

Cooper shifted his feet and swung through the bottle on the desk like Bobby Thomson burying the Dodgers. Bourbon and glass went everywhere, much of it onto Fudge. When the tinkling stopped Fudge opened his eyes, looked at Cooper and sighed in desolation.

"Chop has her," he said.

Diana had finally kicked and writhed into a position in which she didn't take in too much dust when she breathed and wasn't bearing all her weight on her right shoulder as before. Her panting had subsided after a while and she lay with her eyes closed, sparring with panic in her cool dark inner spaces, keeping it at bay. Now that her breathing was calmer she was no longer worried about suffocating; her nasal passages were clear and she was getting ample air. Her muscles were on the verge of massive cramping but she could ease the discomfort somewhat by periodic flexing and shifting. She had made several attempts to unroll the carpet that enclosed her but had been unable to generate sufficient momentum in her confinement. She had finally turned her attention to preparing for what she knew was to come.

Pain is survivable. Cooper had told her that more than once, and he should know, thought Diana. Unless there is too much of it, he had added, but Diana preferred not to think of that now. Instead she concentrated on the world that would come after the pain. She was convinced now that she would not die, not as long as Cooper was alive. As long as Cooper controlled the envelope, Diana knew she would not die.

But she also knew that before anything could deliver her, the man with the scalded face would come back.

Even rape is survivable, Diana thought. She remembered her Aunt Berta, the stolid Teutonic matron who alone of all her father's mysterious clan had sought out the offspring of a distant exotic marriage and claimed Diana as family. Berta had lived through the obliteration of Berlin in 1945. Diana remembered listening as her aunt, steel to the core, passed lightly over mention of the Russian soldiers who had come creeping through the ruins. For Berta there had been a world after the pain.

He cannot touch me, not where it really counts, unless I let him, Diana told herself.

The words could not hold back the images, and panic surged inside her. She held it off for a moment but then the fight was lost, and spasms shook her as she thrashed against the filthy carpet. Eyes squeezed shut against the tears, she forced as much of a scream as she could muster out through her nostrils, until her head throbbed with the effort. Exhausted, she shook with sobs.

I am not strong enough, she thought. *No puedo, no puedo.*

Control returned with the thought that nostrils blocked with mucus would kill her. She sniffed hard to clear them, then was shaken with a violent sneeze that did the job more effectively. Survive, she thought, suddenly fiercely in command of herself again.

And, suddenly, finding words and a certainty lost long

ago. *Padre nuestro, que estás en los cielos . . .* Diana prayed.

A car engine purred as it drew to a halt outside the garage.

"What the fuck is Chop?" said Cooper.

"Chop is his name. C-Z-O-P. Czop. He's a bohunk or something."

"Where did he take her?"

"I don't know."

There was a framed picture on the wall behind the desk. It showed a younger and tidier Officer Frank Fudge shaking hands with a man in the uniform of a Very Important Cop. Cooper drove the bar through the glass, the photo and a layer of wallboard. He brushed shards from his jacket and turned to Fudge again. "You don't have much furniture in here. I'm going to run out of things to hit soon."

"I'm out of it, for Christ's sake. Once I found her Czop took over. I just tracked her down. That's what I do, I find people." Fudge straightened his legs, pushing farther away from Cooper across the gray rug. He was still cradling his arm but his eyes were roaming the office.

Cooper took a step after him. "And you didn't have any idea what he was going to do with her."

"He didn't tell me," Fudge brought out in a rush.

Cooper came overhand this time, like splitting logs, and hit Fudge just above the right knee. Fudge pitched onto the floor, strangling another scream in his throat, and took most of the fall on his left shoulder, trying like hell to save the right arm and knee. He wasn't entirely successful and what came out of his mouth as he lay on the rug sounded like a slow boiler leak. Cooper stepped over him and grabbed the knot of his tie. He jerked Fudge's hundred and eighty pounds upright till Fudge started helping with his good leg and then tossed him back on the chair. When Fudge's eyes came open again Cooper said, "If you don't know, you got to have an idea."

"Czop got a van." The words were barely audible.

"A van. OK, a van. Where'd he take her?"

"Don't . . . hit me." Fudge's features were screwed up

tight again and Cooper waited while they unwound, a little with every hissing breath. "I'll tell you what I know. Don't fucking hit me again."

"Don't fucking lie to me again."

"Czop was gonna have Jimmy drive her around in the van while he got in touch with you. He was just supposed to keep moving."

"What's the van look like? What's the license number?"

"I don't know. Czop stole it or something. He said it wouldn't be missed for a while. He was gonna get in touch with you, set up a meet. Ahh, Christ." Fudge's head sagged sideways and then he rocked forward until Cooper forced him back with the end of the bar.

"How do you get in touch with Czop?" Cooper said.

"Car phone."

"Dial it." Cooper reached back and brought the phone to the edge of the desk. He grabbed the arm of the chair and hauled Fudge to it.

"My fuckin' hand."

Cooper picked up the receiver. "Dial it with your left, asshole."

Cooper held the receiver to his ear with his left hand, swinging the bar in his right, standing clear of the desk in case of surprises, while Fudge laboriously punched out the number with his left hand. Cooper watched and committed it to memory. When he could hear the phone ringing at the other end, Cooper put out his foot and shoved Fudge away from the desk again.

The phone was answered immediately. "Yeah."

Cooper said, "I got something you want. You got something I want. Talk."

There was a silence. At the end of it the voice said, "Who the fuck are you?"

"You don't want to know. All you want to know is how to get a manila envelope back."

"How'd you get this number?"

"And all I want to know is how comfortable the lady is. You read me OK?"

"I read you."

" 'Cause if she's got any complaints, you're going to wish you never laid eyes on her."

A whiff of laughter came over the line. "Oh my. You certainly sound like a tough individual."

"Just a minute." Cooper handed the phone to Fudge. "He wants to talk to you." Fudge grimaced and took the phone. As he put it to his ear Cooper flicked the bar out and tapped him on the right kneecap, not too hard. Fudge screamed into the phone and doubled over.

Cooper picked the phone up off the rug. "Czop? You listening?"

"Who was that?"

"That was your ace detective. Listen to me, Czop. When I see her again she better be smiling. You understand? She better be one satisfied customer, or the days when you could sleep at night are over. Now when and where?"

The silence this time lasted only a couple of seconds. "Let me get back to you."

"Forget it. All we need is a time and a place. A public place. Very public. Any time you're ready. I don't give a shit about what's in the envelope. Once you have the one hard piece of evidence, your boss has nothing to worry about even if I did try to make something of it, so there's no call to hold a grudge. The lady was pressured into it in the first place. If you want I'm willing to show you two air tickets out of the country when we meet, hers and mine. You get the envelope, I walk off with her, and we're even. Deal?"

"I'll have to confer with my principal."

"About what? You're supposed to take care of it for your principal, aren't you? You can have it taken care of in an hour."

"I'll need more than an hour."

"What the hell for?"

"You know, I can hang up this phone and let you worry a little more. I don't think I want what's in the envelope quite as bad as you want the lady back."

"Maybe. But you still have to have it, and the only way you're going to get it is if she's safe."

"What I'm saying is you need a little spirit of compromise here. We got business, we work it out in a businesslike fashion. You can leave out the threats."

Cooper's grip on the phone eased, just a bit. "So what's your proposal?"

"Nine o'clock tonight. Place to be determined."

The phone hissed in Cooper's ear as he thought frantically. "Nine o'clock's OK. But I choose the place."

More silence. Then, "So name a place."

Cooper drew a deep breath, feeling it all hanging in the balance. "Do you know a restaurant downtown called the Carousel? On State Street just north of Adams?"

"I can find it."

"It's on the west side of the street. That's Carousel like merry-go-round."

"We don't really need an audience, do we?"

"I want people around. That's the best guarantee for both of us."

"For you maybe, not for me. You could get a whole tac unit in there, mixed in with everybody else."

"If there are any cops in there you'll see 'em, believe me. That time of night there'll be people but not too many. But I don't think you really understand where I'm coming from. I'm not a professional here, I'm not in this to carve a hunk out of your boss. I don't give a fuck about him or his problems, like I said. I want the lady back, period. The last thing in the world I'd do is risk trying to screw you. You have to know that's straight because I haven't brought the cops into this so far, right?"

There was a pause of a beat or two. "Keep talking."

"What's left to say? I won't fuck you over, you don't fuck me over. I'll be sitting in the Carousel at nine. You walk in with the lady, and I mean she walks in on her own two feet, I give you the envelope, and we're long gone. We got a deal?"

"How do I recognize you?"

"You don't have to. The lady knows me."

Five seconds went by like hours and then the voice at the other end sounded almost jaunty saying, "All right, partner, you got yourself a deal. I'll see you at nine tonight." The line went dead.

Cooper put the phone back on the cradle. He became aware of muscles knotted tight through the center of his torso. He stared at the phone, sensing ripples already in motion from the stone he'd dropped in the pool, hoping he'd thought it out right. He looked at Fudge. The detective sat with a wide grimace locked in place, broken wrist cradled in his lap, good leg flexing against the floor, trying to ease stress on the broken one that flopped a little to the side. His breath was shallow and audible. His shirt had wet splotches on it and the odor of bourbon hung in the air.

"Czop won't fuck you over," he said, forcing the words out.

"You better hope not." Cooper shoved the phone aside and slid a haunch onto the corner of the desk. "We're not finished. Is Czop the one that killed the lawyer up on Howard?"

"I don't know what you're talking about."

Cooper raised the bar, just casually resting it on his shoulder. Fudge's eyes followed it. "Look," Cooper said. "I'm tired of this, you're tired of this. Let's get it done. Now I know you followed me to the lawyer's office. If Czop didn't kill him, you must have."

Fudge met Cooper's look, his eyes watering but steady now. "I didn't kill him."

Cooper stared at him for a moment. "How about Thorne, the guy down on Oak Street? Did Czop do him too?"

Fudge closed his eyes. "You figure it out."

Things stirred far down in Cooper's stomach. "So you knew Czop was taking out anybody that might know about Wetzel's little problem. But of course all you do is find people. You're not responsible for what happens afterwards, huh?"

Fudge opened his eyes and they went away across the room. He had gone white and he looked exhausted and half a dozen heartbeats away from shock. "What the fuck you think the whiskey's for?" he breathed.

Cooper's lips tightened. After a moment he said, "Wetzel must be scared shitless. You know what's in the envelope?"

Fudge wheezed a little more and shook his head. "I never fuckin' saw Wetzel. This was Czop's job from start to finish. He needed help, he came to me."

"How about Czop? Does he know what's in the envelope?"

Fudge wheezed for a moment before answering. "I guess he'd have to, to be sure he was getting what he paid for."

Cooper nodded. "Tell me about Czop. Before you pass out. Or before I decide to wake you up a bit."

The words came quickly. "Wesley Czop. He's worked for Wetzel about four years. Before that he was in corporate security. I don't know for who. I think he was in the military a while. I ran into him when I was a cop."

"I bet that's an interesting story. He likes to shoot people, huh?"

"He likes to do his job. He's a pro. That's why I say he won't fuck you over."

"Unless his job includes guaranteeing Wetzel all the loose ends are tied up."

Fudge closed his eyes again. Cooper stared at him, all the knots inside him slowly getting tighter. He'd made what he thought was the best deal, conceding the delay in exchange for the privilege of choosing the ground. Now it was waiting time. And thinking time. He slid off the desk.

"You know how to get in touch with Wetzel?" he said.

The eyes came open. "I told you. I never set eyes on Wetzel. Czop's running the show."

Cooper nodded. "All right." He turned to the desk. He started pulling drawers open. In the top one there was paper, pencils, clips, trash. In the second there was a tangle of black wires, a minuscule cassette recorder, earphones, tiny microphones, something that looked like a stethoscope attached to a hearing aid. In the third one down Cooper found the cuffs. He pulled them out and turned back to Fudge. "Give me your keys."

"Aw shit, they're in my pocket." Fudge was already grimacing, eyes screwed tight, waiting for the pain. Cooper had no sympathy left. He caught Fudge by the tie again and hauled him off the chair. Fudge's good hand went to Cooper's arm in a show of resistance but it died an early death as the groan came out between clenched teeth. The groan opened into a sigh of agony as Cooper laid him on the floor. Fudge didn't move as Cooper plunged his hand into the trouser pocket. He pulled out a ring of keys and stepped away, quickly identifying the key to the handcuffs and opening them. Earlier he had spotted the pipe running from floor to ceiling in the corner and now he dragged Fudge across the floor to it by his good arm, bringing more noise from the tightened throat. Cooper put one cuff around Fudge's unbroken wrist and the other around the pipe. He stood up and threw the ring of keys across the office to clink on the far wall and drop in the corner.

"You can't . . . leave me here." Fudge's eyes were wide.

"Nine-one-one will get a call about you. In a few hours."

"Ah shit." The head sagged to the floor.

Cooper retrieved the iron bar and left the office quickly, knowing corruption was contagious and fearing he'd taken on a good dose already. He shut the door softly behind him.

DIANA HEARD THE man grunt as he tugged at the rolled-up carpet. She was turned over three or four times, jerkily, and then spilled out onto the dirty concrete floor of the garage. She rolled against the right front tire of the car and lay still, cheek to the floor, as the man hauled the bulky carpet to a corner of the garage and stuffed it awkwardly against the wall. From the corner of her eye she could see the cardboard he had taped over the window. The garage was illuminated by a single naked bulb.

Rapid footsteps came back toward her and she was yanked violently upright by a grip on the tape that bound her hands. The sudden strain on her shoulders brought a cry through her nose. The other hand took her under one arm and pulled her up until she got her feet under her. She swung around in the process and was brought face to face with the man. She caught her breath at the sight of the face so close. There was no expression on the mottled features beyond a tight-lipped concentration. He dragged her forward to the front of the car and threw her facedown across the hood, facing the windshield. A hand dug in the hair on the back of her head and pulled it painfully upright and to one side.

"Look at me, Diana." She opened her eyes to see the scalded face two feet from hers, two dark eyes in a blotched peeling mass of flesh. Something cold washed through Diana's entrails. "I look like hell, huh? I look scary, do I?" He paused, awaiting an answer, and when Diana made no response he slammed her face back onto the hood, hard enough to stun her for an instant. She began to slide off the car but the grip on the tape forced her up again. When she regained her footing the man spoke. "You're gonna pay for that, cunt. You're gonna pay me back big-time."

The grip was released suddenly. Diana twisted to look as the man strode to the corner to her right and behind her. He was moving with rapid clumsy strokes, in the grip of an irresistible haste. He tugged at something out of the line of her sight and pulled it free: a tangle of bright-yellow nylon rope. Her head dipped to rest on the cool smooth finish of the car as the man moved behind her.

She felt the rope go between her arms, around the tape that held her wrists. She felt the man knot it, test the knot. Then he stepped up on the fender of the car, depressing it beneath her, and she heard him passing the end of the rope over a beam. She shuddered, anticipating.

He stepped down and pulled the rope taut and she let out another muffled cry as her arms were pulled painfully toward the ceiling, forcing her forward against the car to avoid the dislocation of her shoulders. The man gave a couple of tugs on the rope to test it and then there was a scrabbling noise as he tied it somewhere behind her. Then he was at her feet, digging at the tape there, peeling it off, freeing her legs. When the last of the tape came off she spread her feet, relieved to have the stability but shaky on her feet.

Her haunches were high in the air, exposed; she was forced to keep them that way to lessen the strain on her arms. Diana began to cry again, face down on the hood, trying to find the words to the prayer, starting to understand just how far she was to descend before she could glimpse the world after the pain.

A hard slap on the buttocks stopped her sobs and opened her eyes. "Comfortable?" the man said behind her. His voice was a purr. "You look good enough to fucking eat, you know that?"

A growl began deep in Diana's throat as one of the thick strangler's hands lighted on her buttock, squeezing, moving down, probing. She growled and brought her legs tightly together.

"Open up." He forced her legs apart with three short kicks. Suddenly his hand had what it sought, and Diana screwed her eyes shut and kept growling, deep in her throat.

"That's it, baby. That's what we want." The purr was quieter. There was a hiatus, a complete absence of movement, just long enough for Diana to open her eyes, and then he was tearing at the thin sweatpants that covered her, ripping them off her, sweeping her feet from under her and increasing the strain on her shoulders as she scrambled not to fall. Her panties went next and then she was naked, the last defenses gone. Every muscle in her was rigid, waiting, her breath whistling in and out.

His face came into view, just above the hood of the car, near hers. A vile grin had taken possession of it, stretching the tender scarlet skin around the eyes and mouth. "You're gonna have to wait a little bit. We're not quite ready yet. I'm gonna let you think about it for a couple of minutes here." A hand rested on her head, caressed her hair, then abruptly bounced her face off the hood of the car. "While you're waiting I want you to think a little bit, Diana. I want you to adjust your attitude here. I want you to enjoy this, huh?" He patted her cheek. "Because you know what they say when rape is inevitable." He pushed away from the car and Diana heard him go to the door with that uncontainable haste. The door opened and closed, and she was left trussed and exposed, shaking and wheezing through her nose.

But calmer, for she had found the cold hard fury she knew she needed to survive.

Because whatever anyone else might say, Diana knew that the only thing to do when rape was inevitable was to lie back and wait for a chance to claw the bastard's eyes out.

Cooper came out of the Reyes Travel Agency stuffing the ticket folder into his jacket pocket. Step one, he thought. He stood for a moment watching traffic go by down Ashland Avenue, honking, weaving, braking, oblivious of him and his troubles. There were high ragged clouds out over the lake, remote and wind-borne and clean.

Steps two through *n* would be harder. Cooper stood wound tight, wishing he could go back to the Firebird and get the bar and start laying about him, smashing things. Instead he knew he had to wait, and plan.

He wandered into a coffee shop, making sure there was a pay phone in back, and sat in the window ignoring a cup of coffee while he tried to whip his thoughts into line. He shuffled the things he could postpone and the things he couldn't and the things that would be bonuses and the things he had to be damn sure about. Finally he thought about Barry Frank lying dead in the toilet and decided it all had to be part of the package.

The place had no phone book, so Cooper had to go through information. They had no listing for *Maverick* magazine, so Cooper had the patient operator run through the Wetzels, deciding finally Wetzel Enterprises was what he wanted. She gave him a number and he punched it in, hoping the boss would be in.

When a female voice cooed the name of the company into his ear Cooper said, "Get me Mr. Wetzel. This is Wesley Czop and it's urgent." He listened while the woman spluttered and then leaned on her a little, and she went away with a click. While he waited for someone higher up to talk to him, Cooper went over his talk with

Frank Fudge and wondered about all the things he didn't know and whether they would make any difference.

In a surprisingly short time a man's voice came on the line. "Yeah Wes, what is it?"

Cooper took a breath. "Mr. Wetzel, I'm afraid I got through to you on false pretenses. This isn't Wes actually. My name is Frank Fudge and I've been working with Wes on a job he's doing for you. I used Wes's name because I didn't think mine would get through to you."

There was a silence and then Wetzel said, "Frank what?"

"Fudge, like chocolate. Wes may have told you about me."

"I don't think so." The voice was very deliberate, wary.

Hesitation was failure, Cooper knew. "I'm calling because I believe I can save you a good deal of trouble. Has Wes informed you that we found the woman?"

More silence. "Uh, listen," Wetzel said.

Cooper began to think it might come off. "Perhaps it would be better if we discussed this in person."

"Or perhaps it would be better if I got in touch with Wes first."

"I wouldn't do that if I were you. You see, Wes hasn't been entirely straight with you." The silence went on so long that Cooper finally said, "Mr. Wetzel?"

"I'm still here. Maybe we should talk. Where are you?"

"I'm at Ashland and North. Name a place and time."

"All right." Wetzel muttered something inaudible. "You know where Miller's Pub is, in the Loop?"

"On Wabash. When?"

"When can you be there?"

"Fifteen, twenty minutes."

"Give me half an hour."

"Fine. I'll be at one of the seats in the window. I'll be the one without a tie."

"See you," Wetzel said, and the line went dead.

Diana had been alone for half a minute when she realized that she could get a foot up on the fender of the car. The sock on her right foot had come off with her pants, and the bare foot had better traction. She got the foot up and then straightened against the limits of the rope and her own flexibility and heaved off her left foot, stepping up onto the fender.

She made it with an explosive effort and then collapsed onto her knees, winding up in a kneeling position on the hood with enough slack in the rope to ease the killing tension in her shoulders. She tottered, gained her balance and came upright. Her arms were still forced backward by the rope, but at a less drastic angle.

And from here she could rise to her feet. She tried it gingerly, panting through her nose, coming up to a crouch with her head at the roof beans, moving back a step to gain slack on the rope. Don't lose your balance, she thought. Fall off the car and it's all over. Two dislocated shoulders will more than distract you from being raped.

Steady on her feet, the ache in her shoulders easing, she knew that whatever happened, she was going to make him fight her. The sock was still on her left foot, presenting a danger of slipping. Gingerly she brought the toe of the sock near her bare right heel and clamped down on it. When she was sure of her balance she tugged with her left foot, the loose woolen sock sliding off easily. Her footing assured, her eyes darted around the garage. The roof of the car looked like a better base to fight from, but the rope would not let her reach there. She extended her arms down as far as she could, testing whether she could possibly bring her hands past her buttocks and around to step through and bring her hands to the front of her body, but they were bound too close together.

She turned to see how the nylon rope was secured. It had been tied to a bracket screwed into one of the wall beams, six and a half feet above the floor. Diana saw at a glance that she could reach it with a foot, but the knot looked efficient and she could never undo it with her toes.

At the second glance she saw she wouldn't have to. She could slide it off. The bracket had once held lumber perhaps; it was a piece of steel with a right-angle bend in it and the rope had been tied to the horizontal arm. Diana saw that if she could move the knot with her toes she might get it around the bend and up the vertical arm and off. Keeping her balance would be the hard part.

She was able to turn completely around and face the bracket. The car was a good three feet from the end wall of the garage, so it would be a stretch, but it was feasible. The car rocked slightly beneath her as she shifted position, balancing carefully. Slowly she put out her right foot and rested it against the wall, steadying herself. The problem became evident.

She could reach the knot, but she was overbalanced so that her weight naturally took her toward the wall, not away from it. It would be impossible to get the leverage necessary to bring the knot out along the bracket toward the bend.

Diana pushed off with her foot and regained her balance on the hood, her panting an audible whistle. She had no idea why the man had left her or when he was coming back, but she had to be ready. If worse came to worst she would make him stand on the hood, kick until he caught her.

She looked at the bracket again. Just to the left of it was a shelf that ran along the wall, five feet high, ending a foot from the bracket. On the shelf was an accumulation of junk: moldering cardboard boxes full of fertilizer, bits of rusted chain, old garden trowels. The shelf was about ten inches wide.

If she could step onto it, maybe sit on it, she could bring her hands to bear on the knot. Her range of movement allowed her to move to the corner of the car, opposite the shelf. She could easily put a foot on it, but she wasn't sure it would bear her weight. It had to, she decided, and shot out her foot to begin sweeping the junk off the shelf. She nearly lost her balance, reminded herself of the consequences of that and tried again. It took all her concentration to balance on one foot while using the other to kick at the shelf.

She was able to clear a space on it, things clanking to the floor. She rested, swaying a bit, listening for footsteps. She saw that it was best to try to sit, just get a haunch on the shelf, her back to the bracket. She would have to step into the void and hope she hadn't utterly misjudged the physics of the thing.

Simply waiting for the man to come back would be

worse than two dislocated shoulders, she knew. She gathered the slack in the rope with her hands at her back and stepped onto the shelf with her right foot. She hung precariously for a moment, afraid she'd gotten hung up halfway, and then steadied herself with the help of the rope. She began a slow transfer of weight toward the shelf, turning her right side toward it. She shifted her foot farther down the shelf, went past the point of no return and landed her bare flank on the pitted board. It groaned and shook and she waited for the collapse, but it held. She was sitting on the shelf, if barely, the toes of her left foot still touching the car, steadying her.

She felt behind her for the bracket. Seconds passed, and she had not found it. Despairing, she strained to shift her thigh along the shelf. A splinter pierced it. She was at the very end of the shelf, its edge cutting painfully into her bare flesh. Eyes screwed shut, stretching her arms to the utmost, she hit the bracket. Grabbing it, she nearly unbalanced herself, but she held on. She felt the turns of nylon rope around the steel.

She heard a door somewhere open and shut, then footsteps coming down a walk. She could not get a grip on the knot; she switched hands and her fingers closed on it and it began to slide. The footsteps were coming at that anxious hurried clip.

Diana had to lean forward, nearly toppling off the shelf, and strain her arm and shoulder muscles to their limits, but the knot came slowly up the vertical arm of the bracket. It slipped off and Diana pitched forward, shoving off from the car with her left leg and clearing it to land on both feet on the concrete floor. She stumbled into the wall, gained her balance and turned. The trailing rope had cleared the beam and fallen to the floor. The footsteps rang louder.

Diana started for the corner of the garage opposite the door, the eight-foot length of rope trailing behind her. As the footsteps slowed just outside the door, she saw that all he had to do was catch the rope and he had her. She pinned the rope under her foot and squeezed it between two toes. As the latch rattled she jerked her foot backward and twitched the rope into a tangle at her feet. She ducked into a crouch, hidden from the door by the car, and felt for the rope with her fingers.

Hinges creaked and then everything stopped for a second except the thumping of Diana's heart. "Fuck!" the man said, under his breath. For an instant Diana dared to hope he might think she'd fled and look elsewhere, but then the footsteps came inexorably around the front of the car.

Diana had a fistful of rope, maybe enough to keep him from catching her. She shot to her feet and looked. The man stood wide-eyed at the front of the car, mouth open, hair standing up, his lobster's face frozen in surprise. In his right hand was a dome-shaped kettle, the kind with a cap over the spout that whistles. Steam rose gently from the spout.

And Diana fled. She scuttled to the rear of the car and turned again to see him come around the right front end, his features settling into a smile. "You're cute, ain't you?" he said. He took another step and Diana moved again, keeping the maximum distance between them. She was at the left rear of the car now, near the overhead door that gave onto the alley. She shot out a heel and kicked the door twice, hard, hoping for noise.

The man set the kettle gently on the hood of the car. The smile was gone. He opened his mouth to say something and then closed it again and started down the side of the car. Diana moved with him, heading up the opposite side, toward the door to the back yard of the house.

"Smart, very smart," he said, reversing direction. "But I ain't stupid." He was speaking in that low raspy purr again. He stood at the front fender again, ready to head her off. Diana backed to the main door and kicked it again, hurting her heel but barely feeling it.

He was moving again, coming toward her clockwise around the car, passing the open door to the yard, shoving it closed and reaching the side she was on. She went back around the rear of the car, seeing that she could not get to the door as long as he stayed at the front or on the right side of the car.

"I can wear you down, Diana," he said. "I can do this

longer than you can. Sooner or later you're gonna get tired."

Not bloody likely, Diana thought.

Cooper knew Wetzel immediately when he walked in and made for the window seats, scowling. He was no more than five-six, a bit stocky but expensively taken care of, graying hair well groomed, gray silk suit, monogrammed scarlet tie, spit-shined pointy shoes. He picked Cooper out at once and bore down on him, hands in trouser pockets and chin rising as he approached.

"Fudge?"

"Mr. Wetzel." Cooper put out his hand and Wetzel shook it.

"Let's go back to a booth," he said curtly.

Cooper picked up his stein and followed him back into the dimmer recesses of the place to a plush leather-upholstered booth. Waiters nodded at Wetzel as he passed. Wetzel slid into the booth, facing the front of the place, and Cooper sat opposite.

Wetzel had a broad round face with a hawk's nose and light brown eyes beneath impressive brows that enhanced his frown. When he had ordered a vodka martini he looked at Cooper and said, "Now what the hell's going on?"

Cooper groped for his lines. "So Wes hasn't contacted you about the lady?"

"No." Wetzel's eyes flicked away for an instant, then back.

"We got her around one this afternoon."

"And?"

"She didn't have the stuff. But apparently her friend does. Wes contacted him and set up an exchange for this evening, the lady for the stuff."

Wetzel exhaled and sagged just a bit. "The stuff."

"Yeah, the stuff. Wes did *not* tell me what it is, by the way. I've been assuming it's something that could uh . . . compromise you, but that's all I know and all I want to know, because I know how these things are played."

Wetzel nodded, with a grim tight smile. "So? What do you mean Wes hasn't played it straight?"

Cooper frowned at his beer, twirling the stein slowly on

the table. "Aren't you wondering why I'm telling you this?"

Wetzel looked briefly as if he had swallowed something that tasted bad. "OK, I'm wondering. Why are you telling me this?"

"Because I don't make very much money. Being a private eye isn't all it's cracked up to be."

Wetzel nodded, once. "I see. And what would I be buying?"

"Advance knowledge of just how Wes is planning to sell you out."

Wetzel's martini arrived during the silence that followed. He took a sip, set the glass back on the table with great caution and said, "Wes would not sell me out."

"Why wouldn't he?"

"Because I pay him top dollar and because he's a pro."

"I know he's a pro. But what's a pro loyal to? And who's to say someone else couldn't top your dollar?" Cooper let that hang in the air for a moment before he went on. "From what I've been able to gather, Wes knows a hell of a lot about your affairs. Doesn't that ever bother you?"

Wetzel stared at him and said, "What do you have?"

"Wes would, could and is selling you out." After a beat Cooper added, "Of course, you don't have to believe me."

Wetzel looked like a man who has just stepped in filth. Seconds ticked away and he said, "How much do you want?"

"Enough to get me the hell out of Chicago and set up somewhere else. I've had enough of the place and you won't want me around. Say ten thousand bucks."

"Ten thousand," Wetzel repeated in a quiet voice.

"I think that's reasonable for something that could save you the kind of trouble you're looking at."

Wetzel blinked, several times. "And how do I know what you're going to tell me is reliable?"

Cooper drank beer, swallowed, set the stein down. "It will have the ring of authenticity."

A slow smile creased Wetzel's face. "It fucking better."

"I'm prepared to tell you right now in exchange for a written IOU. Just a little note in your handwriting. If you consider what you hear worth it, you slide it across the table."

Wetzel drank and then sat with lips squeezed tight, brows lowered, looking at Cooper, a man disgusted with the world. Finally he went for his jacket pocket. He pulled out a small leather-bound notebook and a gold pen.

"Make it out to Frank D. Fudge," said Cooper.

Wetzel scribbled on a page of the notebook and tore it out. He held it so Cooper could read it. Cooper saw the letters IOU and the correct figure and Wetzel's signature. He nodded.

"Talk," Wetzel said.

Cooper put his elbows on the table, leaning toward Wetzel. "Word is you've had some unpleasant dealings with a man named Victor Casalegno."

Wetzel froze like ice, like marble. After a moment he said, "Yes."

"Well, earlier today Wes had a long conversation with Victor Casalegno."

Wetzel blinked several times rapidly. "How do you know?"

"I'm a very curious man by nature. And by trade." Cooper smiled. "With the right equipment it's extremely easy to monitor calls on a car phone."

Wetzel grunted. "You're sure it was Casalegno?"

"Wes addressed him by name and it was his voice. See, I know Casalegno. Not just from TV, either."

"And what did they say?"

"They were a bit oblique, but the gist of it was that Wes is going to have something for Casalegno tomorrow."

Wetzel sat for a long time just looking at Cooper after that. Finally he took another drink of his martini and then looked past Cooper's shoulder again, the IOU held lightly between right thumb and forefinger, his lips still tensed. "Son of a bitch," he said quietly.

"If you want my advice," Cooper said, "don't do anything until after the exchange. When Wes gets the stuff back, that's when you have to start to worry."

Wetzel's eyes were back. "He'll go straight to Casalegno with it."

Cooper took a drink of beer. "I'd say there's a real danger of that."

For the next minute neither of them spoke. Wetzel sat still, looking far away, not drinking. Cooper leaned back in the corner of the booth, watching him and trying to stay a move ahead. Finally Wetzel stirred.

"Where's the swap supposed to happen?"

"That I don't know. Wes paid me off and I'm out of it. You'll have to find out from him."

"How does he plan to do it?"

"I'd guess it'll be a fairly straightforward exchange. Except . . ."

"Yeah?"

"I imagine Wes has special plans for the lady and her friend. That would pretty much be in line with your orders, wouldn't it?"

Wetzel polished off his martini at a gulp. "I don't know what the hell you're talking about."

"OK, I was just speculating. You want my advice?"

"For ten thousand bucks, I'll take all you got."

"Don't monkey with the exchange. Wes will do that part of it right. You want to get him once he's clear."

Wetzel glared at the empty glass, then up at Cooper. He nodded a couple of times. He turned over the IOU, looked at it, sighed and slid it across the table. Cooper folded it across and slipped it inside his jacket.

Wetzel watched him as he started to slide out of the booth. "You wouldn't want to come work for me, would you?" he said. "I think I'm going to have an opening soon."

Cooper halted and gaped at him for a moment, then smiled. "I appreciate the offer, but I think I'm ready for a warmer climate. Where I can lie in the sun and forget things."

Wetzel grunted. "Perhaps that's wise."

"Yeah. If you could have the money ready in used bills by say, next Monday, I'll give you a call and stop by. All right?"

Wetzel looked at him as if he weren't really thinking about him, then slowly stuck out his hand. "All right." He looked like the big loser in a poker game, trying to be a good sport.

Cooper shook his hand and stood up. "It's been a real pleasure," he said.

"LET ME TELL you what's gonna happen, Diana," said the man with the scalded face. "You're gonna go on playing keep-away for a while, but you're gonna run out of gas before I do. And you're gonna keep trying to cut through the tape by sawing it against the beams like that, only they ain't sharp enough to do you any good and even if you do start to make headway all I gotta do is take a couple of steps to stop it. Same goes for trying to tear the cardboard off the windows. Or trying to get the door up. You'd need thirty seconds to get it open with your hands tied like that and I won't give you three. All you can do is keep running, till you trip or cut your foot open or just plain get tired. So give it the fuck up." He was panting a little, leaning on the car, talking to her across the roof. His fury at being held off this long was pushing at the lid of the pot.

Diana stopped rubbing the tape against the board at her back, knowing he was right about that and realizing she was wasting energy she would need to keep moving, keep her concentration. Diana knew that it was move or die.

"Of course there's another possibility," the man said. "I can cut you off." He smiled. His eyes went to the carpet still piled in the corner and Diana saw that if he crammed it between the car and the door to barricade the way around the back of the car, all he would have to do was to come around the other way and get her. She started to move toward the door to the yard, calculating time needed to move the rug versus time needed to get the door open.

The door to the yard opened.

Diana and the man with the scalded face froze and watched as it swung inward and the man with iron-gray hair stepped in. Diana recognized the implacable pitted face and sagged back against the wall, her legs suddenly yielding.

The gray-haired man stopped just inside the door. His expression never changed as he took in the other man, Diana opposite him, her clothes on the floor, the teakettle still steaming gently on the hood of the car. He closed the door behind him. Finally he looked at the man with the red face and said, "Looks like you got a Mexican standoff here."

"It's under control," said the other man.

"Yeah." The gray-haired man stood with his hands in his pockets. He looked at Diana again. Diana leaned against the wall, numb, heaving with her exertion, and looked for something she could read in the stone-colored eyes. The man took two steps, stooped to pick up her sweat pants and panties, shook dust from them, and tossed them on the hood of the car next to the kettle. He looked from the kettle to Diana's face and shook his head.

He turned back to the other man. "Go in the house and get a washcloth," he said.

"Keep the fuck out of this, Wes. This is between me and her." The low purr had given way to a husky growl.

"Go in the house and get something to clean her up with." The voice was flat, the stare even.

"I deserve a chance to take a piece out of this bitch." One thick finger was leveled at the man named Wes.

"You deserve a tire iron across the back of your head. Now go in the house and get a rag."

The only sound for a few seconds was the panting of two people on opposite sides of the garage. Then the man with the scalded face shifted his feet with a scraping sound and looked across at Diana. He gave her a look full of wishes, shook his head once and made for the door.

As the sound of his steps faded up the walk, Wes came slowly around the corner of the car to stand in front of Diana. He gave her a look that started at her feet and ran up her bare legs, lingered for a moment, and then came on up to her face. Diana had started to tremble, her knees on the point of giving way. Wes's eyes were blank.

"What can I tell you?" he said. "He's an asshole."

He turned away and went to stand at the open door to the yard. He stood there until the other man came back. Wes took the washcloth from him and picked up the teakettle. He poured steaming water over the cloth, waved it around to cool it, wrung it out and brought it over to Diana. He wiped her face gently, clearing away tears, mucus, grime. He went back to the kettle and rinsed the cloth, wet it again. He passed the cloth over her face a second time and then tossed it on the hood of the car. He took Diana by the elbow and turned her around. Turning, she saw the murderous look on the other man's face. She lowered her head and felt Wes disengage the rope from her fingers and then dig at the tightly wound tape between her hands.

"You're not gonna let her go, are you?"

Wes did not answer. Instead he said, "Check to see the alley's clear, then move your car out. Back mine in here in its place." He paused to pull his keys from a pocket and toss them across the hood. "It's parked down to the right." The other man did not move. "Go," said Wes.

The door slammed. Tape was coming off Diana's wrists in one long strip. When the end of the strip was tugged free Diana turned and rubbed at her wrists, flexing cold swollen hands. Wes was wadding the tape into a ball.

Diana reached for the strip of tape across her mouth. Wes stopped her with a hand on her forearm. "That stays on for a while," he said. He pulled her toward the front of the car, released her arm and handed her her clothes. "Get dressed. We got places to go."

Cooper wrote feverishly, his hand starting to cramp. A half-empty cup of coffee sat in front of him on the counter. The sizzle of flesh on a hot grill came from the kitchen behind the counter. Two stools down, a man in a plaid wool jacket and fake-fur Alpine cap watched him, a cigarette burning dangerously close to his fingers. When Cooper paused, the man said, "Love letter?"

Cooper spared him a glance. "My last will and testament," he said.

The man nodded and drew on the cigarette, half an inch of ash falling to the counter. "You need a witness, let me know," he said.

An anorexic waitress who looked as if she hadn't seen the sun in fifteen years stopped in front of Cooper with the coffeepot. "Warm you up a bit?"

"No thanks. But if you could get me an envelope from somewhere you got a friend for life."

"Lucky me," she said, going away.

Cooper scrawled the last couple of lines, signed his name and folded the two advertising flyers so that his message on the reverse side faced out. A business-size envelope with a crease in the middle and a brown stain on it dropped onto the counter. "The boss was keeping the bills in this but I guess he finally paid 'em all," the waitress said.

Cooper stuffed and sealed the envelope, got a stamp out of his wallet and then carefully addressed the envelope to Melvin Moreland, with the name of the paper and Chicago, Illinois. He paid his bill, thanked the waitress and made for the door. "You forgot to have me witness it," said the man in the plaid jacket to his back.

The garage was closed and Emilio was at the sink in the back lathering his hands when Cooper came in. Emilio gave him a blank look as he leaned the iron bar against the wall in the corner.

"Take care of it?" said Emilio.

"Part of it. I'm going to need the car for a few more hours though."

"Keep it till tomorrow. I ain't gonna need it."

Cooper wandered into the office while Emilio finished. He stood at the window, looking out at the littered street. The sooted clouds had thickened again and the light was fading. Screws were being tightened at the base of his skull and the coffee lay in the pit of his stomach like rain in a pothole. He watched the clouds drift slowly and thought about the earth turning and wished it would turn faster.

When Emilio came into the office he watched him strip off the overalls and hang them in a corner. Emilio pulled the manila envelope out of the waistband of his jeans and held it out to Cooper. "This is what you came for, right?"

Cooper nodded and put the envelope in his jacket pocket, slipping it down beside the revolver he'd taken from Fudge. "I'll trade you." He produced the envelope addressed to Moreland. "Keep this for a day or two. Mail it if I don't bring the car back or if you read about me in the newspaper."

Emilio tossed the envelope in the desk drawer. "You better try for the TV. I don't read the papers."

"I'll see what I can do."

Emilio was pulling on a denim jacket. "Listen," he said. "Pull the Firebird in the garage. I got some plates I can put on it that won't get traced back to me."

Cooper smiled. "Don't worry. You won't get splashed on."

"I got eyes. Whatever's going on with you, it ain't safe and it ain't legal."

"Well, you got that right. But trust me, man, I didn't go asking for it."

"Shit, I trust you, Coop." Emilio's Pancho Villa grin lit up the office. "I just want to be able to say I never heard of you."

Wes parked at a Jewel three blocks west of Fudge's office, down at the far end of the big lot, figuring no one else would park close enough to notice any thumping that might be coming from the trunk. He walked back along Irving to the little mall where the Imperial was still parked in the otherwise empty lot. He went on past, noting that the Polack travel office was closed, then circled around through the alley. He went into the little lobby and stood listening until he was fairly sure the place was empty. He moved cautiously to the hallway and listened again, then went left toward Fudge's office.

When he was halfway there he heard the voice, muffled by intervening walls, a little unsteady. He thought he heard someone say "hey," then maybe "help." He paused outside number five, and now he could hear it clearly. "In here," said Fudge through the door.

Wes opened the door. Fudge stared at him, blanched and

motionless. He had pulled himself to a sitting position in the corner. Wes closed the door and came slowly over the carpet, looking at the limp leg stretched out, the hand cradled in the lap, the handcuffs. He smelled the bourbon and swept broken glass aside with his toe.

"He didn't kill you," Wes said.

Fudge's head lolled back against the wall. "The keys are over there." The voice did not have a lot of breath behind it.

Wes stood above him, hands on his hips, shaking his head very slightly. "How the hell did you let him take you?"

Fudge's brow furrowed. "He's fast. He doesn't fuck around. Now get the key and get me to a doctor."

Wes stopped shaking his head but kept on looking at Fudge until the detective's face went blank and wary.

"Wes," he said. "Get me the fuck out of here."

"What are you going to tell them at the hospital?" Wes said.

"I'll make something up. Come on."

"There'll have to be a police report."

"So I'll tell 'em a story. Jesus, Wes."

"I don't think I can risk it, Frank."

Fudge's jaw slacked and his eyes widened just a little. He blinked at Wes, rapidly. "Wes, don't fuck around," he said.

Wes brought the Beretta out from under his jacket. Fudge's eyes went to it and then back to Wes's face. His mouth worked, he swallowed, his lips parted. Instead of speech, a dry wheeze came out.

"Sorry, Frank. You fucked up." The gun came up.

"I won't talk, Wes."

"You already did."

Fudge looked into the muzzle of the Beretta and closed his eyes, just for a second or two. "Don't shoot me in the head," he said, starting to shake all over.

"It's quicker that way, Frank."

Fudge's eyes bulged and he sucked in a quick lungful of air. "NOT IN THE . . ." The shot nailed Fudge in the center of the forehead. His head bounced off the wall, spotting it red. Wes watched the body settle, head hanging to the left with the eyes open, then stooped to pick up the cartridge and made for the door without looking back.

Diana rested, then resumed driving her heels into the side of the trunk. She had started kicking soon after the car had halted, calculating that she had nothing to lose. Either she would attract attention from someone able to help, or she would force the gray-haired man to move the car. After a minute she had been convinced that he was gone and begun steadily, methodically thumping the inside of the trunk, ten hard blows at a time with intervals to rest.

The intervals grew longer as she grew tired. There was no panic now, only a sense that her sanity depending on fighting, to the last ounce of her strength. The last moment of near panic had come when the man had taped her hands and feet again and put her in the trunk. She had tried to twist away, but he had held her by the hair and told her he would just as soon club her again, and she had submitted. She did not, however, consider that submitting once had bound her to continued submission.

She drew a deep breath through her nose and prepared to lift her legs again. She froze as she heard steps scraping outside, then the dull click of a key in a lock and the opening and slamming of a door. The engine started. The car began to move, in reverse at first and then forward, and Diana relaxed and tried to track their path in her mind. There was a wait with the sound of traffic going by and then a turn and increasing speed; Diana knew they had pulled onto a street.

She gave up after a time; it was impossible to tell which direction they were traveling in, too difficult to estimate how much distance they were covering. The car slowed, halted at lights, accelerated, turned, navigated a world invisible to Diana. She lay in not too great discomfort on the floor of the trunk and moved carefully around her inner spaces, a step or two ahead of despair. She thought of Cooper, alive and free. On occasion Diana had doubted, from simple human frailty, the depth of Cooper's love for her, but in the present situation she was certain of one thing: as long as Cooper breathed, he would fight for her.

That comfort was balanced by the awareness that the

people who had her were very capable of stopping Cooper's breathing. That brought the worst pangs: the thought that Cooper might die for her. That brought the tears welling and the rush of despair, thinking that her sins, old ones she had thought long buried, could kill Cooper. She would rather die herself. *En vez de él, que me muera yo,* she pleaded to a God that spoke only the language of her childhood.

The car moved steadily as Diana prayed and thought of a future that with luck she might see. If she and Cooper survived, it would be time to invent a new life. Again. She had reinvented herself before, thinking each time it was for good. She could see San Juan, Miami, Chicago, falling astern in the wake.

Whatever and wherever it was, let it only be with Cooper. Diana had grown inured to loss in the course of a fragmented life, but that was a loss she could not face. Let them grind her possessions into dust, leave her with only the clothes on her back, banish her from all the places she had loved, but let her have Cooper.

Diana was snapped back from her thoughts by the engine being switched off. She had hardly noticed the car coming to a halt. The door slammed and footsteps receded, and she waited. A long time passed in the darkness, and then suddenly there was a key scratching at the lock of the trunk.

She squinted against the light as the lid was raised, making out the shape of the man above her. She saw a roof above, fluorescent lights. The man removed his keys from the lock and put them in a pocket and leaned with both hands on the back of the car. Diana blinked and focused on him, standing above her stone-faced in the glare of the lights.

"Here's the deal," he said. "You want to be treated like a human being, that's OK by me. But you're smart enough to know that if you try anything, you jeopardize that. I'd just as soon throw you back in here. You understand me?"

Diana nodded, her neck stiff from craning to look up at him.

"All right then." The gray-haired man reached in and cradled her in his arms and hauled her out of the trunk, setting her gently on the cement floor. They were in a garage, she saw. Black grease spotted the floor and a clutter of hoses, toolboxes and overloaded shelves lined the walls. He had parked the car at the back, next to a hydraulic lift. The place was silent.

Diana tottered on her tightly bound feet and the gray-haired man steadied her. When she had her footing he took his hands from her arms and said, "We're to the point now where we just wait for things to happen and there's no reason we can't be civilized about it. I'm going to take the tape off and you're going to keep your temper. Everybody's gone home, so making noise won't help you anyway. Fair enough?" Again Diana nodded. The man reached up and peeled the tape off her mouth.

"Thank you," she said.

He stooped to deal with the tape around her ankles. It came off and then he stood and turned her around to remove the tape that bound her hands. Diana saw light through the glass in the lowered doors at the front of the garage. She was surprised; she had thought night must have fallen long since.

When her hands were freed she turned to the man, starting to feel like a human being. She was shivering, whether from cold or something else she wasn't sure. The man pitched the wadded tape into the open trunk and then closed it. He cocked his head toward the side of the garage. "Come on," he said.

He led her to a room partitioned off from the garage by a wall with a large window in it. It was lit by a fluorescent tube in the low ceiling. Inside were two folding chairs, a low table with an ashtray on it and a television set. It was floored with cracked linoleum. The man opened the door and ushered her in. "The TV works if you plug it in, but it's kind of loud," he said. "The controls are broken." Diana saw that the knobs had all been removed. "I'll be back," the man said, and before Diana could respond he had shut the door and was locking it with a key she had not seen him produce. He strode out of sight without another word and Diana heard a door open and close somewhere nearby. She stared out at the garage, empty except for the white car she had come in and a dark-blue one parked against the far wall.

When he had been gone for a couple of minutes she tried the doorknob. It would not turn. She wheeled and began to pace, glad to be able to move. She was still shivering, and she realized that she had been cold all day, hauled around the city in the sweatsuit and socks she'd put on in Rachel's apartment in the morning, several ages before. She clasped her arms and paced faster, trying to generate heat. She was glad to be out of the trunk but the room was only slightly larger.

After a few minutes she plugged in the TV, just to have something to do. The high volume assaulted her immediately; peals of laughter rattled the little room. She jerked the plug out of the wall and sank finally onto one of the chairs.

She heard the unseen door open, heard familiar footsteps. The gray-haired man appeared at the door, carrying a white paper bag. He unlocked the door and came into the room. He set the bag on the table. "Coffee. Ham and swiss. The best I could do." He pulled two covered Styrofoam cups and two cellophane-wrapped sandwiches from the bag. He upended the bag, and napkins, plastic cream containers and packets of sugar spilled out. "Help yourself," he said.

They sat opposite one another across the low table. Diana had no appetite but the coffee warmed her. She loaded it with cream and sugar, smothering the rank taste. Knowing she should eat something, she picked up the sandwich and chewed mechanically, making a physical exercise of it. Her eyes went from the floor up the wall to the ceiling, out over the man's shoulder into the garage, everywhere but into the pale unblinking eyes in the pockmarked face. Two currents contended in the wash of her emotions: there was a rush of gratitude, which she knew was false and dangerous, and, underneath, the memory of his hands on her face in Rachel's apartment.

He stuffed trash into the bag and leaned back on the chair. She could feel him watching her. Finally she risked a look at his face. He sat with one leg crossed over the other, hands resting on his hips, staring at her with no great apparent interest. "I'll get you some shoes and a jacket," he said.

Diana swallowed and set down the remnants of the sandwich. "That would be nice."

"There's a restroom here where you can wash up before we go. I missed a couple of spots."

Diana nodded, eyes on the floor. She knew the rush of gratitude was false, but her need for any remotely human contact made her raise her eyes to the empty face again. "I should thank you for getting that guy off me," she said.

He neither nodded nor shrugged; he made no gesture of response. He merely stared, and after a couple of seconds he said, "It wasn't a personal favor."

And Diana's eyes were away again, the cold settling deeper into her bones. She remembered reading what the snake charmer had said about cobras. He had said that you could learn to coexist with a cobra, but you must never forget for an instant that it was a cobra.

Cooper lay on Diana's couch and listened to muted sounds beyond the windowpanes as night approached in the city outside. Children's cries rose in the twilight, incoherent, as easily indicating terror as pleasure. Cars passed, trailing snatches of brassy Mexican songs. Tires squealed, horns blared. El trains rumbled faintly in the distance. Light faded slowly in the silent apartment.

Cooper had taken refuge in Diana's place because, with three hours to kill and his own home blown wide open for police and hired killers, he had wanted aspirin and a place to lie down in quiet without having to explain anything to anyone. He trusted his calculation that the police would have lost interest in the place.

And it was full of Diana's things. Cooper wanted to lie in the midst of her possessions, scattered as they were, and imagine futures inhabited by Diana. The present was an open wound he had to avoid touching. As for the other possible futures, Cooper had looked them in the eye and taken their measure. He had survived enough in his life to know that the very worst short of his own death could be survived in some fashion or other, but he knew also that you could survive only so much before you simply got too tired. Cooper had a feeling that if he survived without Diana the fatigue would be permanent.

Thoughts of his own survival, however, had been fleeting. What had brought him to the apartment was the need to beat with her heartbeat, breathe with her breath. Long ago Cooper had successfully armor-plated his heart against an extraordinary degree of ambient cruelty; now at the brink of middle age he found he vibrated more to Diana's sorrows and joys than to his own. Sharing in the painful beauty of her life had expanded his; protecting that life was the first thing in twenty-odd years he would die for.

Without hesitation, thought Cooper.

Cooper, however, had been a soldier, and while soldiers may be willing to die, it is never their own deaths they plan for. Cooper ran patiently through it all again, calculating, planning for deaths other than his own. He was picturing move and countermove, probing for weaknesses, when the scratching at the front door of the apartment began.

Cooper lay still, hidden from the door by the back of the couch, and listened as the faint clicking of metal on metal came through the room in the fading light. He tried to remember if he had heard anyone come in the door downstairs. Some time ago, a long time ago, there had been a ring on a distant doorbell and voices in the stairwell, but then the door below had slammed again.

Someone had been very clever. And someone, Cooper realized, was picking the lock. This was not a key he was hearing; this was neither cop nor janitor. Slowly, silently, Cooper reached for his jacket on the floor. The clicking stopped as Cooper located the side pocket and felt the rubber grip of the revolver and began to ease it out of the pocket. There was a final, louder click, and then the rattle of the knob and the creak of hinges as the door swung open.

The distant street noises were the only sound for at least fifteen seconds. Cooper lay breathing through his mouth, listening. His arm hung off the side of the couch, the muzzle of the revolver resting on the floor. The person at the door made no sound. After the long silence the hinges creaked again as the door was carefully pushed shut.

The second pause was shorter. Cooper heard a rustle of clothing, a creak of the floor, and then footsteps. Cooper brought the revolver up as they approached. A man stepped around the end of the couch into the light from the bay windows and Cooper pointed the revolver at his head and waited to be noticed.

The man was black, somewhere near six feet tall and slender. His eyes moved around the tumbled room and after a second lit on Cooper.

"Easy," Cooper said.

The man did not start, flinch or gasp. He looked at Cooper for three seconds, unmoving, and then smiled. His teeth shone very white in contrast to his face. "I'm as easy as a mouse," he said. The soft voice was foreign, with a lilt very different from American Black.

"Take your hand out of your pocket."

The man withdrew his right hand from the pocket of the light-colored sport jacket he wore over a white shirt without a tie. He raised both hands, palms out, to about shoulder height.

Cooper kept the gun trained on him as he swung his feet off the couch and stood up. "Put your hands on the wall there," he said, motioning. The man turned and went slowly to a spot by the doorway into the dining room. He put his hands flat on the wall and spread his feet. Cooper put the revolver at the base of the man's skull and searched him, patting, probing, missing nothing. A faint odor of sweat rose from the man. In the jacket pocket Cooper found a narrow strip of flat steel about six inches long with a right-angle hook at the end, and another strip about half an inch wide with a kink in the middle. "Tools," the man said. In his waistband, with the shirt tucked over it, was a large wallet. Cooper flapped it open and saw money and the edge of a passport peeking out of a pocket. "Where are you from?" he said.

"A place you never heard of."

"Try me."

"Trinidad."

"I've heard the name." Cooper moved the gun to the man's spine and patted down his legs. He found no weapons. At last he stepped back six feet and said, "Turn around."

The man came off the wall and turned to face Cooper.

His complexion was medium dark, his hair in a moderate Afro, his features cut from mahogany with bold strokes. On his chin was a little fringe of goatee. He smiled again. "Can I put my hands down?" he said.

"No. Who are you?"

"I'm Cecil," he said simply.

Cooper raised the muzzle a degree or two. "Am I supposed to know you?"

"You haven't been listening to your telephone messages," the man said.

Cooper blinked at him. Out of a sudden flood of data, one word leapt at him: Trinidad. "Sit down," he said, waving at the couch with the revolver and tracking the man all the way there. "You can put your hands down," he said.

"Thank you." The man settled onto the couch and rested his hands on his thighs.

Cooper kept the revolver aimed while he made his way to the telephone stand in the corner. The tiny red light of the phone-answering machine was blinking. The flashes came in groups of five, indicating five messages. Cooper pressed the button and stood watching the man on the couch while there was a whir and a hiss and the messages began, thin tinny voices in the darkening room.

The first was from a woman who identified herself as Sherry and said she was wondering if Diana was all right; she had seen her name in the paper. In the second message a man called Douglas said in faintly effeminate but emphatic tones that Diana had better call Mario if she wanted to keep her job. There was a click and then three seconds of silence, and then the soft voice with the accent began.

"My name is Cecil and I am looking for Tommy Thorne. I was told you might know where he is. Please call me at the Garfield Hotel, 426-9973." The fourth message was a shorter version of the third, repeating the phone number. The fifth was a hang-up. The hiss ended and there were five quick beeps and the tape rewound itself.

Cooper walked slowly to the armchair by the bay windows and hauled it around to face the couch. He sat with the revolver resting on his thigh and said, "You a friend of Tommy's?"

"No. I never met him."

"You came all the way from Trinidad looking for him?"

"Yes."

"Well, you're not going to find him."

"Why not?"

"He's dead."

The black man opened and closed his mouth, saying "ah" silently. "So who kill him?"

"It's a long story. How did you get the phone number here?"

"Tommy have ah friend in Florida. He give me a name . . . Miss Diana Froelich. I thought this was her house."

"It is. What did you think gave you the right to break in here?"

"I didn't *break* in, man. I picked the lock. Professionals don't break in."

"Professional what?"

"Burglar, man. I'm the best damn burglar in Trinidad."

"All right, give me a reason I shouldn't call the police. Or shoot you."

White teeth shone as he smiled. "You won't shoot me, so don't even bother making stupid threats. You could call the police if you want, but I doubt you really want to, from the way things look here. I think you should ask me some more questions."

Cooper stared, the gun still aimed. "So what did you think you'd find in here?"

"I didn't know, but it looked damned interesting. I been calling for two days and got no answer. Today I came and looked in the kitchen window. It didn't look as if anybody was home. And I really wanted to find Tommy Thorne."

"Why?"

The man on the couch stared at Cooper, the dark face impassive. After a moment he said, "I want to find out what happened to my sister."

Children screamed in the park outside. Cooper stared back at the man on the couch and nodded slowly as things fell into place. He raised the revolver from his thigh, released the grip and let it pivot on his finger until it was no longer pointing at the other man. "I think I can tell you want happened to your sister," he said.

"I HAVE TO tell you, Mr. Wetzel, I think you'd be going out on a big limb with the Maverick Ranch idea. That's one hell of a competitive market, the Club-Med type resort, and there's all kinds of reasons you won't make it. There's a limit to the number of beaches and ski slopes that haven't been bought up, for one thing. And the initial capitalization is staggering, let me tell you. But then you're not listening to a damn thing I'm saying, are you?"

Moss looked up sharply from his fountain pen to the accountant with the single steadfast sprig of sandy hair left on a freckled dome. "I hear you," he said. "You're right. You're right again. Congratulations." Moss flung the pen onto the desktop, where it spun across the broad blotter and came to rest against the bronze nude.

The accountant's lips tightened and he closed the folder. "So there's no need to meet with Delgado tomorrow then, is there?"

"No. Screw Delgado. Screw the whole thing. Sell off everything and give the money to the Women's Temperance League."

The accountant shrugged, drawing another folder across the desktop. "I'm just the messenger, Mr. Wetzel."

"Don't get testy. I get a little hot, I shoot off my mouth. Don't take it personally. What's the next disaster we have to look at?"

"There's no disaster. But I would like to talk about that half million."

"Excuse me." Moss reached for the buzzing phone. "Yeah." Moss listened for a second and leaned forward in the seat. "Where the hell you been?" he growled into the phone. "Just a minute." He waved at the accountant. "I'll look at this shit with you tomorrow, Dave. First thing, I promise. But I got some important things coming down here right now. Can this stuff keep?"

The accountant gave a decorous accountantly sigh. "It will keep. But I did make a special trip in to go over this with you."

"Look, buy yourself dinner at L'Escargot, put it on your account. Stay at the fuckin' Whitehall tonight, see me tomorrow at nine. But I gotta deal with this now, OK?"

Moss watched the accountant stuff papers under his arm and execute an orderly, disciplined retreat, then returned to the phone. "I been trying to reach you," he said.

At the other end of the line Wes said, "Can we talk?"

"Yeah, yeah. I sent everybody home. What the fuck's happening?"

"We got her."

"That's . . ." Moss almost said *That's what I hear* but checked himself in time, his heart leaping at his near mistake. He said lamely, "That's good."

"There's just one problem," said Wes.

"Let me guess," said Moss. "She doesn't have the stuff."

"No. But the boyfriend has it. I've talked to him and we've set up an exchange."

Moss exhaled into the phone, clutching an arm of his chair with a suddenly slick palm. *What would I ask?* he thought frantically. "Where are you now?"

"I'm at a gas station on Roosevelt Road. The lady's in what they call the customer lounge. She's as comfortable as I can make her and she's not going anywhere."

"Uh-huh. Ah . . . what about the people at the gas station?"

"The owner owed me a favor. He thinks I'm hiding a boosted car or something and he won't ask any questions. Or answer any."

"I see." Now you'd ask it, Moss thought. "When and where's the swap supposed to be?"

"I don't think you really need to know that, Mr. Wetzel. I'll take care of it."

"I'm sure you will Wes, I'm sure you will." Moss

leaned back in the chair, looking out at the gray watercolor sky hanging over the lake. "Look, I'm just asking because after all, it's my nuts in the wringer. I've been left out of the loop here and I'm just trying to keep a handle on things. It's not a lot of fun to sit in here talking to a bunch of robots with briefcases, wondering what's going on with my life out there. Just fill me in a little, will you? At least so I can live a little, vicariously like?"

Moss held his breath while he waited for the voice at the other end of the line to answer. Finally Wes said, "Sure. We're making the exchange at a restaurant called the Carousel, on State Street downtown, at nine o'clock this evening."

"Mm. Nine o'clock." Moss exhaled and clenched the phone tighter. "Sounds good, Wes. Ah, listen . . . I'm assuming that . . . um, the principals for the other side will . . . let's say they'll be getting out of the business after tonight. Am I right?"

"I'll take care of it, Mr. Wetzel."

"I'm sure you will, Wes. Thanks for checking in. I'll see you out at the house tonight, then? After the exchange?"

"I'll be there."

After he hung up, Moss went to the window and stood looking down at the creep of cars in the sunless streets, fists balled in the pockets of his carefully tailored suit, his knees wobbling just a little. Moss knew that he was alone on this one, as solitary as the pigeon perched on the cornice of the building across the way. It had to stop somewhere, Moss knew. If you kept paying people to sweep up your messes, you kept leaving people who knew about them, and that left them open to temptation. Fucking Wes, he thought.

Moss knew that it was stand-up time. He wasn't a tough guy, never had been, but he'd held his own a few times when he was backed into a corner, and this was not just a corner but the end of a deep dark alleyway. Moss took a deep breath and thought about what it would take to walk out of that alley. Across the way, the pigeon took three steps along the cornice, head bobbing back and forth idiotically, and leapt off into space.

* * *

"Even the best can get caught. Yvette came to see me once, and I could see she wasn't coming back no more. After that I heard news of her when an old mate of mine was put in with me. He told me he'd seen her on the street."

In the twilit dining room Cecil shook his head once and reached for his glass. Cooper watched as he took a delicate sip of the clear rum. Cooper had rescued the bottle and a couple of glasses from the kitchen and put them out as a peace offering. They had turned on no lights because Cooper wanted no attention from the street. The inch of rum in his own glass was untouched.

"When ah come out ah went looking. Ah couldn't find she on the street corners, but I had mah mates around town and finally ah found somebody who told me she'd been lucky. She was working in a nice house, working for a big man. He had nightclubs, bars and things." With the rum and the course of the story the island accent was reasserting itself.

"Gladstone Drake?" Cooper said.

Cecil sat motionless for a moment and said, "Thorne tell you everything, man."

"Thorne told me nothing. I learned a little from a newspaperman and guessed a lot. You know Drake's dead too?"

Cecil nodded. "I know." Cooper thought for a moment he was going to elaborate, but instead he went on. "Drake use to keep a half dozen of his best girls for the best clients. They went to the hotels or they got sent up to those nice quiet villas up on the hills. And that's weh mah sister end up."

Cecil drank more rum, and then he thrust his hand inside his jacket and withdrew a wallet-size photograph. He slid it across the table toward Cooper. The light was almost gone, but Cooper carried the picture to the window, where he could make out the radiant face of a young black girl, in a dark blue sweater and a blouse with a white collar. It looked like a school uniform and the girl looked about fourteen.

"The picture is five years old," said Cecil. "But yuh could see why she was tops with him."

Cooper frowned at the lovely dark features and nodded. He came back to the table and handed the picture to Cecil. "How did you find out what happened?" he said.

"Ah didn't. Like you, ah learned a little and guessed a lot. It wasn't easy getting close to the girls who worked for Drake—he kept them in grip like the bloody Crown Jewels. But ah managed to corner one of them one day and she tell me Yvette was gone. She disappeared a week before. The story was that she went up into the hills with a rich American, and then she run off in the night with his money."

Cecil paused to drink. He sighed after a hard swallow. The whites of his eyes shone in the dark. "Drake threaten to kill her if he ever put his hands on her. But he couldn't find her. The American was gone. And the girl I talked to didn't believe Yvette would have done that. It would have been stupid. Unless it was a lot of cash, we talking real cash."

"What did she think had happened?"

"She didn't say. But she was afraid. Whores are always afraid."

Cooper nodded slowly, his fingers resting on his glass, trying not to drink.

"She tell me how to find the villa. She'd been sent up there a few times. It belongs to Drake but he lends it to friends. Or customers. There's an old couple that lives in a cottage behind and takes care of the place. They were afraid, too." Cecil drained his glass and reached for the bottle. There was only a splash left in the bottom and he drained it into his glass. "Somebody had killed the gardener a week before."

"The gardener?"

"Ah man named Nestor. Somebody shoot him in the head and left him by the side of a road, up in the woods. Two days after Yvette was up there." Cecil paused and looked at Cooper, waiting for him to catch up.

"I'm waiting for Tommy Thorne to come in here somewhere," said Cooper.

Cecil nodded. "In the village they tell me about Nestor.

And about the American who used to live in a little bungalow at the edge of the village. He and Nestor were friends. And they told me that the night before Nestor was found, he had come asking all over the village for the American, Tommy Thorne. And the day when they find Nestor, Thorne left. For good. For America. With his suitcases. Hopped the bus and left."

Cooper nodded. "But he left an address."

"Ah got it from papers he signed with the Hindu in the village who rented him the bungalow. An address in Fort Lauderdale, Florida."

Cooper gave in and raised his glass. The rum burned all the way down his throat. "And here you are," he said.

"And here I am. And you say you can tell me what happened."

"I can make some more guesses. But they're based on what Tommy had."

Cecil stirred in the dark. "What's his name, the man who killed her?"

"Moss Wetzel. He's a magazine publisher. I met him today. He's scared to death he'll be found out."

"And what did Tommy have?"

Cooper let out a long, slow sigh. "He had a map showing where she was buried. And half of the murder weapon."

"Half of it?"

"I think Wetzel strangled her. With his tie. He was wearing one like it today. And he, or probably Nestor, buried her with it."

"Dat was stupid."

"He probably panicked. Roused Nestor, paid him to do the dirty work. And then had Nestor killed to shut him up."

"He wouldn't do it himself?"

"I couldn't prove it, but I think he probably had his bodyguard do it. Gunplay is not Wetzel's style."

"But Nestor tell Thorne what happened."

"And took him to where she was buried, probably. And Tommy dug her up, cut off half the tie and buried her again. He knew that scrap of cloth could make him rich."

For a long time the two men sat and listened to the dying street noises and tended to their thoughts. Finally Cecil broke the silence. "She must make him angry, man. They beat her once because there were some things she wouldn't let them do."

Cooper looked out the window at the deepening blue of the sky. "Could be. Having met the guy, and considering what he does, I don't find it too hard to imagine."

Cecil leaned forward, the chair creaking under him. "You can call the police now," he said. "Or you can let me walk out the door."

Seconds passed. "Or?" said Cooper.

"Or you can help me."

Cooper tapped a finger lightly, silently, on the rim of his glass. He took a quick drink, shook his head and said, "You've come a hell of a long way on a thin chance of finding him."

Cecil shoved an empty glass away from him. "Ah remember almost nothing of mah mother, because ah was only eight years old when she died. But ah remember the last thing ah told her."

"What was that?"

"Ah tell her I'd take care of baby sister."

"You want a chance to redeem yourself?" said Wes into the telephone.

"I don't need to fucking redeem myself. Two more minutes and I had the bitch trussed up like a turkey." Poulos was talking low and fast, as if there were someone nearby he didn't want to hear him.

"The only turkey I saw in that garage weighed two hundred pounds and had a moustache. You had a job to do, and you fucked it up."

"She didn't get away, did she?"

"She should never have gotten out of the van. I had to scramble pretty good for an hour or so there to sort things out."

"You don't like my work, you can get fucked. After you pay me the seven-fifty you owe me."

"I'd like to see some work from you, I really would. Now I'll ask you again. You want to show me something? For the seven-fifty plus a hundred-dollar bonus. Plus a chance to convince me you're not brain-dead."

There was a silence. Wes sat looking out the window of the darkened office at the pumps outside. Finally Poulos said, "What's the job?"

"Same job. Tonight we finish it. You in?"

"If you think I can handle it."

"If you can't handle this there's no hope for you."

"Hey . . ."

"I'll need to meet you somewhere."

"You . . ."

"I got a piece for you."

A few seconds ticked off and Poulos said, "A piece."

"A nice clean one that won't ever be traced. After you use it you throw it in the river. You read me?"

Through the silence Wes could hear Poulos salivating, thinking about using the piece. Wes smiled as Poulos said, "Loud and clear, chief."

Cooper found Stumps at the old folks' bar around eight o'clock. The old man was alone about halfway down the bar, with the visor of the Cubs cap low over his eyes and a death grip on the handle of a beer stein.

"Cooper," he said when he turned his head. "Thought you left town."

"Wish I had," said Cooper, laying a hand on the old man's shoulder. "I got to talk to you."

"Climb aboard and start talkin'." Stumps slapped the seat of the barstool beside his.

"Not here, man. Come out to the car, we'll go for a drive."

Stumps blinked at him, head tilted back unnaturally so he could see out from under the cap, and then nodded once. "Lemme finish my beer," he said.

"Kill it fast. People are waiting on us."

Stumps drained the stein in two gulps, grabbed a pair of crumpled bills off the bar and slid off the stool. "Lead the way."

In the Firebird, Cooper turned the ignition key and gunned the motor. "I need your help again," he said.

"She ain't out of trouble yet, is she?" Stumps said.

"Worse than ever, bad as it could be. They got her."

"Who got her?"

"The bad guys, the assholes." Cooper swung out onto the street. The car throbbed as it rolled over the bricks, branches passing overhead. "It's a long story but the punch line is short. They want something I got. They'll swap it for Diana but I'd bet the farm they won't let us walk away from the table."

Stumps was silent as Cooper swung around under the viaduct and headed back north. "You need more help than I can give you, boy," he said after a moment.

"I need the cavalry coming over the ridge. But they're not going to make it in time, so I need that shotgun you got under your mattress."

Stumps shook his head once and whistled. "You're hip deep in it, ain't you?"

"Neck deep. What do you say?"

"I say you go talk to John Law."

"John Law can't move fast enough or light enough on his feet to help me here."

Cooper went left, heading for the church. Stumps was still shaking his head. "What the hell you gonna do, stick it in your belt?"

"No. The shotgun's the ace up my sleeve. The shotgun's for when we make it back to the car, 'cause I think that's when they'll try it. I want something to grab when I open the door to the car."

Stumps was silent all the way down Lunt to the church. As Cooper turned, Stumps said, "You need more than the gun. You need an extra pair of eyes."

"I got an extra pair of eyes. But I want all the insurance I can get."

"OK, two extra pairs of eyes. And an extra trigger finger."

Cooper eased to a stop by the door of the church. He looked across the seat at Stumps. "I'm talking about a shootout here, Stumps. I mean I think it's going to come down to that. I'm talking about professional killers."

The old man's eyes shone faintly in the light from the street lamps. "You think I'm scared of professional killers?" His jaw worked briefly. "What do you think the Japanese Imperial Army was? You forget who you're talkin' to, boy? I'm a gyrene. I took my licks in the biggest shootout the world's ever seen. And if you think I'm just a broken-down old drunk you got another think comin', 'cause if you wasn't my friend you'd be a sorry son of a bitch right now."

Cooper hadn't seen where the knife came from but he'd heard the flick of the switch and flinched as the tip of the blade touched his neck. Stumps held the switchblade to his neck for a couple of seconds and then flashed his gap-toothed smile and folded the knife and stowed it away under his jacket. "You're gonna need somebody like me, Cooper."

Cooper stared hard at him. "How much have you had to drink tonight?"

"I ain't hardly started. Hell, what makes most people drunk just gets me runnin' smooth. Look, I can see straight, and it don't take a fuckin' marksman anyway to operate that howitzer I got in there."

Cooper made a fast decision, desperation greasing the wheels. "All right, you just re-upped. Can you get that thing out here without getting arrested?"

"I got an old overcoat in there. The lining's torn and the gun fits down in there. If I walk funny and you don't look too close nothing shows."

"Go get it."

When Stumps reemerged from the side door of the church he was wearing a long wool overcoat, a dark dull green with big brass buttons. It looked like an old army coat vintage 1930s. His hands were jammed in the pockets and held close at his sides, preventing the tail of the coat from swirling freely around his legs. He walked with a stiff short stride. Looking hard, Cooper could tell something was funny about the coat, but he didn't think it would scream out to a passing cop.

Leaning into the car, Stumps reached inside the coat and wrestled the gun out. He pointed the muzzle at the floor and climbed in after it. With the gun between his legs he closed the door.

"Christ," said Cooper. The shotgun was two and a half feet long even without the stock and half the barrel. The barrel had been sawed off an inch beyond the fore-end. What was left of the stock was wrapped with black friction tape. The gun looked big enough to stop a tank. "Can't you keep it under wraps? We get stopped with that thing in the car, we're history."

"I can't sit down with it inside my coat. Just drive careful."

Cooper put the car in gear. "You got it loaded?"

"It's got five rounds in there ready to go. I hope it ain't gonna take more than five, 'cause you need time to reload this thing."

"If you get five rounds off and we're not finished, there's no hope for us anyway."

"Who am I gonna be shootin' at?"

"With luck, nobody. If our luck runs like I'm afraid it will, anybody that jumps up and says boo. We got time, I'll show you the layout."

"Who's your other pair of eyes?"

"Nobody you know. You won't even see him."

Topping a rise on Lake Shore Drive, seeing the lights stretching south into the night, Cooper said, "You ever practice with that thing?"

"Practice," said Stumps. "With this? You can't practice with this. You just point it and hope you got the guts to squeeze the trigger."

Cooper shook his head. "I'm worried about everything in the world right now except your guts, old man. Guts I believe you got."

Moss dabbed delicately at his lips with the spotless linen napkin. Around him waiters moved with dispatch; silverware tinkled gently and warm discreet lighting shone on crystal. Moss shoved the plate away from him, the quail ragout hardly disturbed. His stomach seemed to be trying to climb up his throat.

Stand-up time. Moss took a sip of the Pinot Noir to quell his innards, and his gaze became lost in the distance as he sat back and folded his arms, alone against the world. Moss sighed, thinking how you could pay an entire fortune to other people hoping they would protect you, all for naught.

The waiter hovered, a deferential hand moving tenuously toward the platter, his face showing deep concern. Moss waved the plate away. "Gimme a check," he said.

There was one way to do it, Moss had decided. One way to do it and be left the only one standing and the only one who knew. It was a risk, but then life was a risk from womb to tomb. Moss had taken risks before. Maybe that was the problem; he'd started paying other people to take his risks for him.

It was going to be scary, that was for sure. It was going to mean brazening things out, hanging tough for a while. But it should put an end to things. Moss drained his wineglass and thought longingly of brandy, shining amber in a fat round snifter. With a consciousness of his new role, the need for a new lean mean Moss Wetzel, steely-eyed and alert, he rejected it.

When the waiter eased the red leather folder and the pen onto the tablecloth at his elbow, Moss said, "There's one more thing you could do for me."

"Yes, sir?"

"You could get me a potato. A raw potato."

The waiter froze halfway out of his grovel, eyebrows creasing the forehead as they rose. "Sir?"

"Could you get me a raw potato from the kitchen or someplace? One raw Idaho potato. I'll pay you for it, for God's sake."

"Certainly." The waiter ducked back toward the kitchen and Moss picked up the pen. He took a deep breath and let it out slowly, looking around the restaurant where people sat unaware of him and his troubles. Moss smiled, for he felt powerful suddenly, immensely potent.

24

DIANA HAD TAKEN to pacing, three steps across the floor and back again, when she was startled to see the gray-haired man appear at the door of the little room. She had not heard the garage door go up and the white car had not reappeared. The gray-haired man was pulling the key from his pocket. From his left hand hung a plastic shopping bag. He opened the door of the lounge and said, "Time to go."

Diana stood with heart thumping and managed to say, "OK."

The gray-haired man reached into the bag and pulled out a pair of white deck shoes and a denim jacket. "Compliments of the management," he said. "There's a bathroom where you can wash up a little. Move. We're in a hurry."

Diana put on the shoes and picked up the jacket. She followed the man out into the garage and through the office at the front to a small greasy restroom where she washed her face and hands. She looked into the cracked mirror and saw a pale stranger with familiar eyes. Over the stranger's shoulder, the gray-haired man stood in the doorway. She dried her hands and face gingerly on the soiled length of towel that hung from a broken dispenser on the wall. She turned to the man and said, "Do you have a comb?" He pulled a comb from his pocket and handed it to her. Diana ran it through the worst tangles in her filthy hair and handed it back. "I take it I don't have to ride in the trunk anymore?" she said.

"Not unless you want to. We're past all that now."

She nodded and put on the jacket. She followed him back through the office and out into the night. She had no idea where she was but it didn't look like a nice part of town: the storefronts opposite were all barred and padlocked and the street was deserted. Two blocks away she could see men standing in front of a bar. She felt a little light-headed stepping carefully through the cool night air.

The white car was parked at the side of the station. The man unlocked the passenger side and held the door for her as she got in, then closed it and went around to the driver's side. He started the car and reversed away from the building, then spun the wheel and eased out onto the street.

"Where are we going?" said Diana, starved for human speech.

"Downtown. Where the lights are brighter. You're smart enough not to jeopardize things at this point by doing anything stupid like waving at cops out the window, right?"

Diana closed her eyes and let her head fall back against the headrest. "Yeah. I'm smart enough," she said.

Cooper cruised slowly west on Madison. The Loop was sparsely populated; darkened facades disappeared into the black sky above well-lighted empty streets. Ahead, a squad car turned lazily off Madison onto Dearborn, going north. Cooper barely noted it; police were irrelevant now. He pulled over to the curb and pointed across the street.

"That's the alley. Two blocks south it ends at a construction site. The last door on your left will be the restaurant."

"Got it." Stumps wrestled with the shotgun and pulled the door handle. "Lemme get the thing under my coat before you drive off," he said.

"Remember, you're just for emergencies. If everything goes right we go out the front and you never hear a thing. Give us a half hour before you leave. I wish we could come back and pick you up but I don't think we can chance it."

"I've walked out of worse places than this."

"Don't try and get the gun home. Ditch it back there somewhere."

"Let me worry about that. You get her out and take her someplace a long way away." Stumps pushed open the door and slid out, then leaned back into the car to pull the shotgun off the seat and slide it into the lining of his coat, looking, Cooper hoped, like a man getting the final word in with the driver or taking a package off the seat. Stumps shoved the gun inside his coat and then, withdrawing, pulled something from a side pocket. Whiskey sloshed inside a clear glass bottle.

"You really need that?" said Cooper.

Leaning back into the car, Stumps said, "Camouflage, son. Why else would a broken-down old man be sitting in an alley?"

"OK, it's your show." Cooper pulled away and left Stumps behind, seeing him shuffle across the street in the rearview mirror.

Cooper circled back to Wabash via Dearborn and Washington, watching. It was coming up on eight forty-five and there weren't too many people out; since they'd torn down the big movie houses and the old Greyhound station, there was even less activity than before in the north Loop. He turned south on Wabash, under the El tracks, and when he passed Monroe he started looking for a place to park. Such getaway plans as he had did not depend on finding the ideal spot—he knew better than to make plans like that—but he would be grateful for any favors chance dealt him. He found a place half a block south of the Palmer House that would fill the bill.

Cooper sat behind the wheel for a moment after he shut off the ignition, watching cars go by, hearing a train rumble overhead, checking off the steps to his plan. Remembering the dictum of a competent but long-dead lieutenant, he'd tried to keep it simple but flexible. He wavered for a moment, thinking of how he'd changed the plan to incorporate Stumps but decided it was a net gain. Drunk or not, Stumps had walked through the valley of death before, and that was the kind of man Cooper wanted holding the gun when the game broke up. Cooper thought of the guns he'd handled that day and wished he'd run across one more.

Cooper had the attitude back. An old and familiar thought came to him, the thought that he could be living the last fifteen minutes of his life. And the response was equally familiar: if that was the way it was going to be, he was going to take as many of them as possible with him.

He got out of the car and walked south toward Adams, allowing himself a single optimistic thought. There was, of course, always the chance they'd play it straight.

Moss had given it some thought. Wes would need to park somewhere close to the restaurant. He would avoid parking garages, needing a quick getaway. That meant leaving it on the street somewhere, probably on Adams or Monroe since State Street was closed to cars. Maybe Dearborn, behind the place. Moss had seen that there was an alley that ran along the side of the restaurant back to Dearborn. In any event Wes would have to drop it on the street, illegally parked maybe, somewhere within a block or two of the restaurant.

So all Omar had to do was cruise, patrol a two- or three-block area in the minutes leading up to nine o'clock, and the LeSabre would have to be there. Moss checked his watch and leaned forward to slide the panel open. "Start 'er up, Omar. We're looking for Mr. Czop's LeSabre, OK? It'll be somewhere on Adams, Monroe or Dearborn within a block of State Street, and it could pull up just about any time now. Let's go find it."

Omar nodded and Moss closed the panel and leaned back on the seat. There were two things he was worried about. The first was whether Wes would recognize the limo and be suspicious if he saw it. Moss thought not; he'd have a lot on his mind. The second thing to worry about was what Omar thought of all this. It would be pretty obvious that Moss was maneuvering Wes into the limo, and he hoped Omar didn't put that together with what was going to happen later. But then Moss had decided that if the scenario was tight enough later, they wouldn't ever be able to touch him. Omar could suspect what he wanted; he would know nothing.

Moss's stomach fluttered as he looked anxiously out the window at the files of parked cars creeping past. New experiences, he thought. That's what keeps people young.

Cooper pushed through the door and nodded at the watchful Greek who presided over the cash register. The Carousel was long and narrow, with two booths in the front window and a couple of dozen others on the left-hand wall going all the way back to the kitchen. Along the right wall was the lunch counter; a door at the end of it led into a narrow hallway. A sign over the door said RESTROOMS–TELEPHONE. The tables were of white Formica with gold sparkles, and the booths were upholstered in brown plastic. The lighting was subdued inside yellow glass fixtures. The effect was aquatic, producing the ambience of the bottom of a stagnant pond on a bright summer day.

Cooper walked slowly back to the third booth on the left-hand wall, carefully paying no attention to the black man sitting alone in one of the booths by the front window, staring moodily out at the street. There were three solitary customers at the counter, all of them males who could certainly remember Roosevelt's administration if not Hoover's. A booth toward the back was occupied by two young black couples having a good time, and in the distant rear sat an elderly woman in an elaborate hat, carefully tackling an enormous sundae. That took care of the customers; in addition to the Greek by the door there were two haggard waitresses and an aging Mexican busboy. Cooper sat facing the front of the restaurant, ordered coffee and waited for somebody to walk in the door.

He had chosen the Carousel on the basis of hasty calculations under pressure. He'd chosen it because it was public, had a front and back door and was right next to a subway entrance on State Street. He had wanted as many choices of exit as possible. He had also wanted anonymity. He'd been in the place but it wasn't one of his regular haunts and he was unlikely to see anyone he knew. He sat over his coffee and listened to the laughter behind him and thought of things that could go wrong.

Just about anything, he thought. You set up a position and hope you're quick enough to adjust to what they throw at you. His eyes flicked to the black man with the fringe of goatee on his chin. He had lit a cigarette and was blowing smoke toward the ceiling, still staring out the front window. Cooper thought he'd covered himself about as well as he could, given the circumstances. His watch said nine-oh-one.

He took a token sip of coffee and regretted it. His stomach wasn't going to stand much more coffee or much more immobility. Don't keep me waiting, he pleaded silently, and then looked to the door, because a man with iron-gray hair was pushing in, with Diana in tow.

"Just pull up right alongside it," said Moss. Omar obeyed and Moss, his heart suddenly doing quick time, felt for the potato in the pocket of his overcoat. He was fairly sure Wes hadn't seen him; from two blocks away Moss had seen the LeSabre slide to the curb and Wes and the woman get out. They had ducked down the alley off Dearborn without a look back. Moss reached for the door handle. When the limo came to a halt, he stepped out onto the pavement and shot a quick look up and down Dearborn, seeing a couple of pedestrians on the other side of the street but nothing closer.

Boldness, he intoned to himself. Moss stepped quickly to the rear of the LeSabre, shielded by the limo from the view of the people across the street, and pulled the potato out of his pocket. He stooped to the exhaust pipe and with a forceful motion jammed the potato over the end of the pipe. He gave it a thump with the heel of his hand to make sure it was secure, and then he straightened up and strode back to the car without a sideways glance.

"Go around the block," he barked at Omar as he pulled the door shut. "Back to where we were." Omar nodded and put it in gear, and they were away.

Heart pounding, Moss grinned like a jackal as the limo crept up the block.

Czop escorted Diana down the aisle with a hand on her elbow, like a kid showing off his new girlfriend. He wore a silver windbreaker with the sleeves pulled up to reveal thick forearms. Cooper's heart had turned over at the sight of Diana and his eyes locked with hers as she came toward him; he looked for signs of distress, duress, fear, whatever, but saw only the steady self-possession he usually saw there. She had on an unfamiliar denim jacket and her auburn hair fell loose about her face.

Czop stopped at the booth and motioned for Diana to

slide in ahead of him. She sat down and scooted over next to the wall. She was pallid but she was moving with her usual grace. "Hi," she said quietly.

Cooper's eyes flicked to Czop as he lowered himself to the seat, then back to Diana. "Are you all right?" he said.

"Yes." She nodded, her lips tightening in what might have been a good try at a smile. "I'm fine." Cooper looked into those bottomless eyes for a second longer and then looked at the man beside her.

Czop looked back with the studied blankness of complete unconcern. Cooper took in the pitted face with its stubby nose and chin, the cropped hair and the stone-gray eyes. People that stared at you like that were used to getting their way, he knew. Cooper wanted to pitch the coffee into his face.

A waitress appeared. Czop said, "Nothing for me. These two might want something to eat."

"We're on our way out. Just give me a check for the coffee," Cooper said. The waitress shrugged and took the menus away. When she was behind the counter Cooper said, "Step one."

He pulled a slip of paper from his left-hand jacket pocket and slid it across the table to Czop, who unfolded it. "That's a Visa card transaction slip. You can see I paid a lot of money to a travel agency today. You don't get to see the destination but it should prove to you that we're leaving. As of tomorrow we're taking a long vacation and we never heard of you or your boss. And you never heard of us, OK?"

Czop refolded the slip and handed it back. He nodded once. "OK."

"Step two." Cooper replaced the slip in his pocket. "This is what you want." He pulled the manila envelope from his right-hand pocket and tossed it across the table. Czop picked it up and opened the flap. He looked into the envelope, holding it open with two fingers. "I might have made a Xerox of one of those items, but without the other one I couldn't do a thing to you. You're free and clear. Agreed?"

Czop closed the envelope and slipped it inside his windbreaker. "I guess so."

"Guess so isn't good enough. We got a deal or not?"

Czop blinked once, slowly. "Looks to me like we got a deal," he said.

"OK, then, you get up and let her out and we'll make tracks."

"Not yet," said Czop. "You don't get to leave yet. I go first."

"The hell you do. You got what you want, you got no reason to stand in our way. Our safe-conduct guarantee is for you to sit here and have a nice leisurely cup of coffee."

Czop shook his head. "What's my guarantee? You could walk out that door and wave your hand and send half a dozen cops through that door. I want five minutes to get clear before you leave."

Here's where it goes wrong, thought Cooper. If Czop didn't want to move, he wasn't going to get Diana out of there without a commotion.

"Five minutes," said Czop. "If you try and walk out of here before that, you'll die when you step out the door."

Cooper met his stare; he looked at Diana and saw her staring, too. "Wait here," he told them both and stood up. He walked to the front window and looked out. He saw a man at the end of the Plexiglas shelter over the subway entrance, leaning on the *USA Today* newsbox and looking in his direction. The man was short and thickset and had a mottled face, discolored by what looked like a birthmark. Cooper turned from the window, making eye contact in passing with the black man in the booth. He shook his head once and went back to the booth.

He sat down slowly. "All right, move. Five minutes. It's been nice knowing you."

For the first time Czop smiled. He stood up and said, "They have pretty good pie here. You ought to try some." He walked to the door, not hurrying, and went out. Cooper watched him turn left, away from the front window, and disappear.

Diana said, "We wait?"

"I don't know." Cooper felt things wobbling underneath him. He stared at Diana for a moment, then looked at the black man in the booth by the front, who was staring at him. "Shit," said Cooper quietly. The black man had slid to the edge of his seat. Cooper made a very slight motion to the left with his head and the black man stood up and made for the door. Cooper watched, his stomach knotted, visualizing a dozen or so things Czop could do.

"Hey." The Greek at the cash register was waving at the black man. "You pay me." The Greek pointed at the booth where he'd been sitting.

"I left money on the table," the black man said, a hand on the door.

"You pay here, bring me the money," the Greek said, his voice rising.

"For Christ's sake," Cooper hissed. Diana twisted to see. The black man made it back to the table in two strides, swept check and money off it, and slammed them on the counter by the cash register. The Greek glared at him as he pushed out the door.

Diana sat still, watching Cooper, who was looking out the front window. "What's happening?" she breathed.

"I don't know." Cooper thought furiously, thinking of doors and alleys, of what Czop might do with five minutes, of how likely it was he would come for them.

Keep it simple, keep it flexible, and take the initiative, Cooper thought. There was only one asset whose position he knew at this point. Clocks were ticking all over the world, all over the universe, and suddenly Cooper was sure. "Let's go," he said, reaching for Diana's hand.

Cecil stood outside the restaurant, scanning the street. There weren't too many people about, but the man in the silver jacket had disappeared. Cecil was fairly certain that the man with the burned face whom he'd been watching through the window was there for a purpose, but Cooper had seen him too, and Cecil couldn't worry about him. As far as he could see, there were two places the man in the silver jacket might have gone: down the steps here, into what must be the underground, or across the street into the arcade.

If he's gone into the underground he's out of it, Cecil decided, though not with a great deal of confidence. He began to walk across the street toward the entrance to the arcade. The fallback was clear; Cooper had told him that if they were going to try something, it was most likely they would try it at the car because that's how they had done it with Tommy Thorne. That was why he had insisted Cecil park the Valiant as close as possible to the restaurant; the Valiant was the decoy.

Cecil stood at the glass doors and looked down the long arcade that ran through the Palmer House. He saw half a dozen people, none of them the man he was looking for. All right, we go for the car, thought Cecil.

Behind him, the man with the silver jacket came out of the subway entrance, not the one in front of the restaurant but its twin a hundred feet south, and made for the mouth of the alley beside the restaurant.

Wes hauled on the reins going down the alley, resisting the urge to hurry. Nothing caught attention like a man in a hurry. To his left lay a half block of razed construction site beyond a chicken-wire fence, to his right the high brick wall of the restaurant. The alley was brightly lit and wide open to view from anyone on the upper floors of the buildings on the south side of Adams, but Wes knew that the one that intersected it from the north, behind the restaurant, would be narrower and darker.

When he reached the rear of the building he stepped into the narrow passage like a man who knew exactly where he was going. There was a single bulb in a wire cage over the back door of the restaurant, but it wasn't enough to chase the shadows from the nooks formed by dumpsters and doorways. Wes looked north up the alley toward Monroe, just making sure nobody else was prowling tonight, and started calculating.

He smelled the whiskey before he heard the voice and made out the shape in the darkness of a recessed doorway opposite the restaurant.

" 'Fraid this seat's taken," rasped an old man's voice, full of years and emptied pints. "Unless you got a cigarette you could spare."

"You go up and pay for the coffee," said Cooper. "Then you follow me through to the restrooms." He slid the check and a dollar across the table to Diana. "Watch the front window. He won't come back in, but he might try to slip around to the back." Diana nodded and they rose together. Cooper had trouble turning his back on Diana to head for the door at the end of the counter, not wanting to lose her from sight, but it had to look natural. He didn't want anyone to remember anything.

He stepped past the end of the counter and pushed open the door. There was a long featureless hallway with walls painted beige and woodwork dark brown. Cooper let the door swing shut behind him, listening. A faint clank of pots in a sink sounded somewhere behind a wall. He turned to look through the window in the door. Diana was at the cash register, waiting for change. When she took it and started back toward him, Cooper pushed on down the hallway, slowly, looking for convincing reasons why Czop couldn't have stationed anyone back here.

He passed a disused elevator and then a stairhead on his right with a hand-lettered cardboard sign saying RESTROOMS and pointing down the stairs into another silent empty hall. The phone was in an angle where the hall jogged right, and then there was a clear shot to the back door. Cooper heard the door behind him open and looked to see Diana coming quickly after him. He extended a hand for her, seeing her almost break into a run, thinking that beyond that brown-painted steel door was their escort, and just maybe the beginning of a long and healthy life.

Wes put the muzzle of the Beretta to the old man's forehead. "I said move," he breathed.

He could see the old man's watery eyes blinking in the faint light. "Just trying to be friendly," the old man said. He lowered the hand containing the flask of whiskey.

Wes didn't want to give his position away by shooting anyone yet. If he couldn't get the old buzzard to march out of there fast he was going to have to club him. He stepped back and jerked the pistol toward the construction site. "Go find another hole to piss in," he said.

"I bet you don't have many friends," the old man said, moving now, coming out of the doorway into the glow from the light bulb, a wreck in a baseball cap and a long overcoat, holding his left arm to his side as if it were in a sling.

"I don't need friends," said Wes. "March."

"How about this way?" the old drunk said, pointing north up the alley with the whiskey bottle.

"Wrong." Wes waved the pistol again, shooing him south. He was going to have to kill the old man after he did the other two, and passing him along his escape route would be easiest.

"Okay, partner, you're the boss. Take her easy." The old man raised the flask in salute and made for the mouth of the alley, putting the flask to his lips as he went. "I guess the town's big enough for me and you both," he said.

"Faster," said Wes.

Fuck this, thought Poulos. The guy Wes was jacking him around. First of all, putting him out front here, telling him to pop the bitch and her boyfriend if they tried to come out the front. Even if he did like Wes told him and got them in the little foyer, before they got out on the street, it was stupid to do it in the open like that, a block and a half from the car. Wes had told him to run down in the subway, but fuck that. Poulos knew that what Wes wanted was for them to see him out front and try the back way, where Wes would be, after his own cute trick with the subway. And second, who the fuck knew they wouldn't just sit in the place, call the cops and have them come pick him up? Wes had left him hanging out here.

Poulos looked up and down the street and came away from the newsbox, stepping toward the window of the restaurant. The booths inside came into view and Poulos saw that the whole front part of the place was empty. His eyes went to a booth full of niggers way in the back and then he saw her, moving down the counter on the right, toward the door to the john. Poulos watched for a second, seeing her slip through the door, seeing his last chance to get a piece of her walk away, and then rage shot through him like an electric current and he was charging through the door into the restaurant.

* * *

Things happened very fast when Cooper wrenched back the last stiff bolt and pulled the door open against the tension of the automatic closer. There was the crack and tinkle of glass on concrete and then a growl out of the darkness. "Cooper!"

Cooper looked left and saw the tails of the overcoat flying as Stumps leapt into the mouth of the alley, shotgun coming up. Cooper's reflexes had just managed to halt his forward progress, Diana pressing against his back, when Stumps fired. The BOOM of the blast lit the alley and was followed immediately by two sharp cracks and muzzle flashes from the shadows to the right, and Cooper saw Stumps jerk backwards. He saw no more because he was frantically pushing Diana back inside. There was a third pistol shot and the steel door clanged as a round slammed into it where Cooper's head had been.

Mercifully they had both kept their feet. Cooper wasted no time trying to fight the automatic closer on the door; he knew there was time only to run. Diana was already taking long strides back down the hallway; Cooper followed, hoping they could make it to the jog in the corridor before that pistol came in the door behind them.

Diana made it around the jog and cried out, and Cooper cannoned into her as she pulled up abruptly. Over her shoulder he saw why: the man with the discolored face was coming through the door to the restaurant, hand coming out of a pocket.

Cooper caught Diana by the arm and saved her from falling, then threw her the only way there was left to go: down the stairs. She bounced off the wall and regained her balance after a leap of four or five steps, and Cooper was right behind her, hearing footsteps and knowing they were going to run out of places to run.

The downstairs hallway was like the upper one but with more doors. Cooper put his shoulder into the first two, hoping one would give. He could hear feet on the stairs.

The door that said MEN on it was open, and Cooper swept Diana through it. He shoved her past the urinals toward the stall at the rear of the squalid little room and she hit the door and swung it inward, but caught herself on the frame and kept her balance. Cooper and Diana traded one quick glance that had no room for all the things there was no time to say; it was last-stand time.

He got the door to the hall closed again and heard the footsteps outside. They reached the bottom of the stairs and stopped, but there couldn't be much mystery about what door to try. There was one thing Cooper could do to make things harder for the man with the gun; he reached for the light switch and with a flick of a hand put the bathroom into complete darkness.

After a few seconds the footsteps came closer, at a trot now. They halted outside the door and there was another pause during which Cooper thought of all he could do to a human being with his bare hands, and then the door burst inward, bringing light.

Cooper froze against the wall, letting the door swing slowly shut again, the light fading. The same foot that had kicked it open stopped it with a gap of six inches left and then a hand came through the gap, feeling for the switch.

Cooper grabbed the wrist with both hands and pulled. The man grunted as his face was rammed into the door frame and then Cooper was through the door, driving him across the hall into the far wall with a forearm across his throat, trying to crush it. The impact brought strangled noises from the throat and distorted the red face, but the reaction was immediate and violent. A fist and a knee drove Cooper back and the gun in the left hand was coming up.

Cooper pitched forward, twisting to the right, and clamped down on the arm, pinning it to his left side under his arm and grabbing the barrel with his right hand. A blow on the back of his head nearly detached him, but he was fiercely concentrated on keeping his grip on the gun. The man at his back was immensely strong, and Cooper had no way to resist being swung around into the wall, headfirst.

He bucked and managed to take part of the impact on his shoulder and keep hold of the pistol. The next blow fell on his kidneys and he cried out, but his grip held and he saw Diana's legs in the doorway.

She was just coming out of the bathroom as Cooper was whipped against the wall again and lost his grip on the gun. He bounced and picked himself up, woozy, to see Diana flying at the man's face. She was going for his eyes, no quarter given, and he had to bring both arms up to protect himself, forgetting the gun for an instant. She raked his face and he bellowed, but he peeled her off him in a second, sending her sprawling down the hallway, and the gun was still there.

Cooper's tackle caught him off guard but he was a tree trunk, a mountain, and he wouldn't go down. Cooper planted a foot and jerked, and the man's leg gave way and he slid partway down the wall but then the gun was swinging toward Cooper's head. He knocked it aside with a forearm and kicked upward into the man's crotch. There was a grunt of pain and Cooper was on his back on the floor and Diana was getting set for another rush and then suddenly the man lurched away from the wall, disentangling himself and switching the gun back to his right hand, and Cooper knew it was all over: two quick shots.

Except that the man froze suddenly, the horror-show face turned to the stairway, and brought the gun up in that direction. Behind him, Diana dropped to the floor, face to the concrete, hands over her head.

Cooper understood nothing until the roar of the shotgun filled the hallway and most of the pattern caught the man in the chest, punching fragments of his leather jacket into his heart and lungs and knocking him backward. His skull cracked on the concrete as he hit the floor. Blood welled and a cry trailed off into a gurgle.

Cooper twisted to see Stumps at the foot of the stairs, falling back against the newel post, legs giving way. Cooper stared at the old man uncomprehending; the shotgun drooped to the floor and then the bare head with wisps of white hair started to droop too. Cooper heard steps behind him; Diana had recovered first and was stepping quickly past the corpse on the floor, that vacant look of denial on her face. Cooper rallied and scrambled to his feet and they reached the old man together.

He sat on the bottom step, starting to list, eyes open. Cooper caught the lapel of the coat and pulled him upright. Stumps looked up, opened his mouth and coughed blood onto his stubbled chin.

Cooper let him slump over. He knew what a dying man looked like. He picked up the shotgun and started up the stairs. There was blood on the steps, marking the long hard trail Stumps had hauled himself along. Three shots left, thought Cooper. Come in that back door, Czop. Stumps missed you but I won't.

Halfway up the steps he halted, thinking that if Czop had come in the back door, he would have been there long before Stumps. If Stumps had lived to come down those steps, it meant Czop had not been around. There were voices in the hall above now, excited voices in Spanish. Cooper froze for a few seconds, hearing them come, paralyzed. Then he thought about police and wheeled and went back down far enough to toss the shotgun across Stumps's body. He came back up and caught Diana by the wrist and pulled her upward.

The busboy and a cook were at the head of the stairs, staring at the trail of blood that led from the back door. They watched Cooper and Diana with wide eyes, backing away.

"There's a couple of maniacs down there shooting at each other," Cooper said. "Go call the cops." Cooper took one look at the back door and then made for the front of the restaurant at speed, Diana in tow. The Greek was hovering in the doorway, having dispatched the help to brave the bullets. "Call the cops," Cooper told him. "They're shooting at each other down there." The Greek seemed to be having trouble understanding. Cooper and Diana brushed past him.

The Greek called after them as they left the restaurant, but it was too late. Cooper stopped briefly in the doorway and scanned the street, looking for Czop, looking for Cecil, looking for cops, and then took Diana across State Street at a run. If any part of his plan was still in operation, he hoped it was the decoy part. All Cooper could think of to do was to get through the Palmer House and into the Firebird and drive till the road ran out.

From the bus stop on the northeast corner of Adams and State, Cecil could look through the corner store windows and see the entrance to the restaurant, but the mouth of the alley was obscured by a news kiosk. Cecil pitched his cigarette into the gutter. When he heard the distant shots he turned to look. The man who had been in front of the restaurant was no longer there. Cecil wandered away from the bus stop and went up State Street until his view was unobstructed.

Cooper was wrong, he thought. Cecil kept on walking, waiting for someone to come out of the alley or the restaurant. When he drew even with the alley he looked across and saw a silver jacket up at the far end, moving fast. Cecil shook his head and turned abruptly and walked back south. He crossed Adams and got in the Valiant, thinking it was too bad about Cooper and the lady, but that it didn't really matter much, because he knew what he had to know.

Wes made tracks, still shaken. He could still feel the boom of the gun and the pellets whistling by him, tearing the sleeve of his jacket. Thank God the old fucker was a lousy shot, he thought. I should have clubbed him right away. But that was good shooting, taking him down like that. Wes knew he should have put one into his head to make sure, but he'd been a little rattled. In eight years in the Army and twelve years of cleaning up people's messes, nobody had ever actually shot at Wes before, and he hadn't enjoyed the sensation at all.

Wes swore again, replaying things and reviewing his call. He'd decided not to go in the door after them because you just didn't go charging into buildings full of people if you wanted to get away unidentified. It hurt to let them go, but there was always the chance the kid at the front would nail them. That meant the big worry was to get to the kid before the police did. Wes had watched the kid park the Trans Am in a deep dark alley, making it easy for him.

He resisted the urge to look over his shoulder, but he kept listening. He hadn't heard any more shots by the time he reached Dearborn, and he figured the kid had fucked it up or chickened out. A real hit was a big jump up for a cheap musclehead like Poulos, but then Wes had never intended Poulos to do the job.

"Goddammit," Wes said out loud, pulling out his car

keys as he made for the LeSabre. This meant there was one more chance to get them, but he would have to move fast. He'd have to get to the Valiant right away and hope they hadn't gotten there before him and that there was nobody very observant at the bus stop. He got the door open and slid behind the wheel and stuck the keys in, and then swore again as the engine turned over a few times and died.

He tried it again, and the same thing happened; the engine wouldn't catch. It wasn't battery trouble; the engine just started and died. Wes was seriously pissed off by this time and after a few more tries he tore the keys out and started to get out of the car. The operation had gone all to hell and if he was going to salvage it now, it would be at great risk.

Wes had just slammed the door shut when he saw the big silver limo gliding toward him like a great white shark, veering across two lanes and slowing. He recognized Wetzel's limo and said softly, "What the fuck now."

The limo eased to a stop beside him and the back door came open. There was Moss, leaning out and saying, "Jump in, Wes. Good thing I came along."

THE ROAD RAN out at a one-story cinder-block motel in a town a hundred miles from Chicago and twenty miles off the interstate, over roads where Cooper could be sure no one was following. Cooper made sure to note the number on the license plates Emilio had put on the Firebird before he went in to register; he knew he would arouse enough suspicion limping and bruised without having to confess he didn't know his license number. The gray-haired lady had seen worse, evidently; she gave him the key to room number six without comment.

Inside the room, with the chain on and all the lights blazing and an armchair backed against the door, they lay on the bed in silence for an eternity, holding fast and waiting for the trembling to go away.

When they were deep into the wee hours and the only sounds outside were small-town sounds of insects and distant freight trains, Diana said, "I want to take a shower. A very long, very hot shower. But I want the curtain open and I want you sitting there so I can see you. I'm not going to feel safe for a long time."

Moss sat behind his desk, in all his baronial splendor. The lamp on the desk was on, but the rest of the room was lit mainly by the fire which Moss had ordered by phone from the limo, calling ahead to tell Sancho to build it. Shadows danced as the fire hissed in the grate.

"Well, here's to you Wes, Jesus." Moss hoisted his Scotch. Wes sat on the edge of the oxblood tub chair, a dark green bottle of beer in his hand.

"The job's not finished," he said.

"Bullshit. Here's what we wanted, right?" Arrayed on the desktop were the manila envelope, the map, the scrap of tie and a single sheet of white paper.

Wes nodded. "But the lady and her friend got away. That was part of my job."

"Can they hurt me?"

"No. Not seriously."

"Then fuck 'em. You said they're leaving town, right?"

"That's what they claim."

"Then we don't have anything to worry about, do we?"

"I don't think so, Mr. Wetzel. I'm just sorry not to finish the job."

"Forget it, Wes. You did a hell of a job. And now it's time to do the honors."

Moss rose and picked up the tie and the map and the envelope. He came out from behind the desk and strode across the Persian rug to the fireplace. The tie dangled from his fingers for a moment, and then he pitched it onto the flaming logs.

"You don't know how glad I am to see that go," he said. The tie curled and blackened and was consumed. Moss stared at it and shivered a little. After a moment he roused himself. "This'll make a fireball," he said, crumpling the map and the envelope together. They followed the tie onto the fire and the room was brightly lit as they caught and the fireball ensued. Wes watched from the chair, like a statue.

Moss went back to the desk and picked up the sheet of paper. It had been folded in half and taped shut; Moss had cut the tape. "This was in there. I think it's the boyfriend, being cute." Moss glanced at it again. On the outside were written the words *To Mr. Czop.* Inside was one sentence. It said *You shouldn't have killed the lawyer.* Moss handed it across the desk to Wes, who read it and refolded it.

"What does it mean?" Moss said.

Wes put the bottle on the corner of the desk and stood up. He wadded the note up, walked to the fire and threw it into the flames. "It means I shouldn't have killed the lawyer, I guess."

"Something else I don't want to know about," said Moss.

"That's right." Wes was staring at the floor now, looking like a man with a problem.

Moss came away from the desk. "Well, Wes, I want to tell you I'm happy with the job you did. So the people got away, I don't care. You saved my ass again, and I'm gonna reward you. Just like with ballplayers, you're the best, you ought to get paid like the best. So I've got a little bonus for you here." Moss was holding up his index finger and smiling, looking like a magician about to pull a rabbit out of someplace. He walked to the cabinet in the corner and opened the double doors, revealing the safe. "You remember that half million in cash?" he said, starting to spin the dial. "How could you forget, right? Well, before I get it reinserted into Wetzel Enterprises' usual channels, I thought I might spread a little of it around. I can't think of anybody who deserves a little tax-free under-the-table bonus more than you. How's that sound?"

"Sounds just fine, Mr. Wetzel." Wes's voice behind him was as flat as ever. Not even money gets him excited, Moss thought. He put the dial on the last number and pulled the handle and the door swung open. We'll see if this gets him excited, he thought, taking a deep breath.

When he turned from the safe, Moss was holding the Colt Python. He pointed it at Wes's chest eight feet away and cocked it. "Put your hands up, Wes," he said, glad to find he could speak normally.

Wes showed no sign of surprise or dismay; he merely raised his hands to shoulder height, slowly. Moss kept the gun trained on his chest, holding it with one hand like Clint Eastwood, too close to miss. "This is a trick old Gladstone Drake told me about," he said. "The gun in the safe."

Wes stared back at him and said, "Why?"

"Why, the man says. Because you're a scumbag, Wes. Because you sold me out like a fucking whore. How much are you getting for me, Wes?"

"I don't know what you're talking about."

"Of course you don't. You never talked to Victor Casalegno."

Wes blinked. He blinked! thought Moss. "Who says I did?"

"Your old friend Frank Fudge says you did. You sold me out, he sold you out."

"Fudge? Fudge said I sold you to Casalegno?"

"Yeah. You ought to choose your friends better, Wes."

Wes looked puzzled for a moment, just an instant. "I guess you're right, Mr. Wetzel," he said.

"Yeah, I'm right Mr. Wetzel all right. OK, here's what we're going to do, Wes. It's a robbery. You got a little greedy knowing about the money in the safe and you tried to take it." Moss shifted his feet, nerving himself up for it, bringing his other hand up to steady his wrist, sighting on Wes's chest. Christ, he was actually going to do it.

"And you pulled the Gladstone Drake trick on me, is that right?" Wes smiled.

"That's right, Wes. Funny, huh? You don't think I'll do it."

"I think you'll try." Wes lowered his hands, still smiling.

Moss knew it was time; Wes still scared him to death. "Good night, Wes." He squeezed the trigger.

The click was loud but did nothing to erase Wes's smile. A second went by, maybe two, and Moss squeezed again.

Click. Click, click, click. The cylinder turned, the hammer fell, and the solid click of well-machined steel filled the room.

I loaded it. I know I fucking loaded it, thought Moss, his knees starting to go like strings on a bass fiddle.

"Yes, it's loaded," Wes said, bringing the automatic from behind his back. "You can see the rounds in there. But you left it in your desk. And I reloaded it for you. With my own special loads. Look like the real thing but just go click." The black automatic was pointing at Moss's belly.

Moss squeezed off three more frantic clicks and then threw the revolver at Wes's head. Wes dodged and the gun sailed across the study and hit the thick curtains over the window and fell to the carpeted floor with a soft thud.

"Here's what we're going to do," said Wes, no longer smiling. "Sit down at the desk." He waved the pistol. "Go on, sit down."

Moss could no longer speak and he wasn't sure his legs would carry him to the desk, but the involuntary reflexes go a long way toward following an order from a waved pistol, and he took a couple of steps. On the way he found his voice, and he said, "You can't do it, Wes. They'll nail you."

"I'm not going to do it," Wes said. "Sit down and put your hands on the desk."

Moss sat, his heart on the brink of a coronary, his guts about to loosen, seeing hope in Wes's words. He put his hands palm down on the desktop. "OK, what now?" he got out in a reedy voice.

"I think we'll make it a suicide," Wes said. He backed toward the window, keeping the gun leveled at Moss. He found the revolver where it had fallen and brought it back to the desk. "All you need is one real round," he said. He laid the automatic on the corner of the desk. "Go ahead, if you think you're fast enough," he said.

Moss knew he should go for that gun; he couldn't just sit here and watch Wes replacing one of the dummy rounds with one he'd pulled out of his shirt pocket, but every time he even started to think about leaning, he met Wes's eyes and saw he would never make it. "Wes," he said. "All the cash in the safe. It's yours. Take it and go."

Wes snapped the cylinder home. "I plan to," he said, and Moss knew it was over.

He lunged for the automatic but Wes was too quick for him and Moss sprawled out across the vast desktop and came up empty-handed. He slid slowly back into his chair, seeing it all, just like they said it did, flash before his eyes. Daddy, he wanted to scream. Don't hit me again.

"Sit up," said Wes. Moss sat up, tears starting to well. Wes had put the automatic back in the holster under his jacket and was bringing the revolver forward. "Open your mouth," he said.

Moss's voice had quit working; he leaned back in the chair to get away from the muzzle of the gun.

There was a click and the connecting door to the communications room swung open. Wes snapped his head to the left to look, but beyond the open door was darkness. "Drop it," said a voice from the darkness.

Wes wheeled toward the doorway. He brought the Python up and snapped off a shot but two shots cracked from the darkness and he stumbled back and fell into the oxblood tub chair. He sat there slightly askew with a red blossom growing low on his abdomen, blood soaking through the tan slacks just above the groin, spreading fast. His light gray eyes were wide with astonishment but then started to crinkle with the pain. He worked like hell to train the gun as the man walked into the room. He pulled the trigger and there was a loud click.

"All yuh needed was one real one, you said." The man was black. The gun in his hand was a revolver. He walked to the chair and watched as Wes dropped the gun and started to curl up in agony, hands to his groin. "Yuh missed with it." The man shot once more, from a foot away, and much of Wes's head went onto the back of the oxblood tub chair. The black man looked at Moss and said, "Ah sorry 'bout the chair, man."

Moss looked from what was left of Wes to the man, his ears ringing from the shots. The man was tall and thin and very black and he had a fringe of whiskers on his chin.

Moss was bewildered about everything, but through the haze he knew immediately and certainly that this man was from Trinidad.

"How the hell did you get in?" he said finally, still reeling.

The man smiled, showing ivory teeth. "Dat's a trade secret, man."

Starting to appreciate the great and bounteous gift of life, starting, he thought, to see the light, Moss said, "Did Gladstone send you?"

"You might say that," the black man said.

Moss blinked, shook his head, flexed his arms, astounded to be alive. "Well, whoever you are, I sure am glad to see you."

"Ah don't think that's going to last," the black man said, the smile gone.

And Moss froze again, looking up at the face and thinking where in God's name have I seen that face before and starting to get the answer even before the man reached into a pocket and pulled out the picture. He put the picture on the desk and shoved it toward Moss, and Moss only needed one look to be sure.

"It was an accident," he said, just audibly. The shades were descending over Moss's vision now, much worse than before, because this was all the nightmares coming home. "She panicked. I never meant to kill her. She lost her head and I was a bit too rough. For Christ's sake . . ."

"Open yuh mouth," the black man said, leaning toward him.

"YOU CAN BE at the airport in forty minutes," Cooper said. "Just leave the car in the lot somewhere. I'll find it."

Cecil nodded, steam rising into his face from his coffee. "OK," he said. Behind the counter, a black girl yelled orders back into the kitchen.

"There's a guitar in the trunk," Cooper said. "A nice guitar. Take it. I can't have it in the car. Sell it, keep it, whatever you want. It's worth a lot of money, I'm told." Again Cecil nodded. He took a sip of coffee. "Good luck," said Cooper.

"Thanks, man." Cecil set down the cup and reached for the white Burger King bag at the edge of the table. He pushed it across to Cooper. "Here," he said.

Cooper took the bag and hefted it. It weighed about a pound. He looked inside it. He saw banded stacks of green bills, the figure 100 showing at the corners. He snapped a look at Cecil. "What's this?"

Cecil smiled. "That's your cut," he said.

Cooper sat in the Firebird, looking across the rain-splattered street at the mini-mall on Irving Park, looking at Frank Fudge's blue Chrysler Imperial. The police van parked next to it said EVIDENCE TECHNICIAN on the side. They'd carried out the body half an hour before, the man at the Citgo station behind him had said.

Cooper sat with the engine idling and dealing with the effects on his conscience of a purposely neglected telephone call. Frank Fudge was going to haunt him a little, he feared. But there were other things to think about; it was time to deal with the final problem. Cooper put the car in gear and pulled out into traffic, dreading the meeting he'd set up over the phone at the gas station.

"Don't bother to sit down," Valenti said as Cooper approached the booth. "You're coming with me." The lieutenant wasn't smiling. He had been tracking Cooper all the way from the door with that look, the look of a big mean cop you didn't want to piss off.

"You're pissed off," said Cooper.

"And you're in shit so deep you're still sinking."

"Am I under arrest?" Cooper slid onto the seat opposite Valenti.

"Don't tempt me." Valenti started to scoot off the seat.

"You think I did Fudge, huh?"

"What I think is you better walk to that squad out there before I have to put the cuffs on you. There are two dicks down at Area Six who are very very anxious to talk to you."

"You'll be mighty embarrassed when you have to let me go because they find out the weapon I supposedly used belonged to a professional killer named Wesley Czop."

Valenti stopped scooting. He looked at Cooper without blinking for a long moment. "You're not under arrest. Not yet. Save your stories for the detectives. I'm sick and tired of listening to you."

"I've got a hell of a good story this time. You hear about the double killing out in Oak Brook last night?"

Valenti stared, brows lowering, and said, "The *Maverick* guy?"

"Yeah. He shot his bodyguard. Then he shot himself. That's the way it looks, anyway, according to a guy I know on the news bureau. I heard the first report on the radio, I called him and he had some details. You want the name of the dead bodyguard?"

Valenti let out a sigh, the sigh of a long-suffering cop. "The guy you mentioned just now."

"That's right. Wesley Czop. Now here's why you're going to be thanking me instead of booking me. Check the ballistics."

"The ballistics."

"Yeah. I will bet you the farm that the gun they found on Czop was the gun that killed Thorne, the lawyer up on Howard Street, Fudge, and one more I haven't told you about yet. Check it out."

Valenti's look would have withered flowers and sent children running to Mama's skirts. "OK, no handcuffs," the lieutenant said finally. "But the dicks are waiting."

"Lead the way," said Cooper.

Peck leaned back on the creaking chair, exhaling. He looked fatigued but still hostile, his bald head shining in the fluorescent lights. "Let me see if I got this all straight," he said. "It's kind of a lot to take in, you know?"

"It was kind of a lot to figure out, too," said Cooper.

Peck looked at him with distaste. "So stop me if I get

anything wrong. Now let's see. Moss Wetzel goes down to Trinidad for this magazine layout, and down there he does something he'd just as soon keep a lid on, and Tommy Thorne finds out about it. You don't know what Wetzel did or how Thorne got on to it. OK, Thorne comes up here and looks up your girlfriend because he used to know her in Miami. He crashes with her and puts the bite on Wetzel. Except Wetzel's no patsy and he sics Czop on Tommy. Czop spots Tommy last Sunday night and shoots him, but somehow he finds out about Diana and finds her place and tosses it looking for the stuff Tommy's peddling. Diana comes home and almost walks into it, but she sees what's going on and splits, takes the first Greyhound out. Right?"

Cooper nodded. Across the table Hunt was shredding a Styrofoam cup, limp in a limp white shirt. "Why didn't she report it?" he said.

"I told you. She was scared. She knew the kind of people Tommy ran with. She just wanted to disappear until she could talk to me."

Peck held up a hand. "OK, OK. So she leaves town. Fine. Now where was I? Czop finds something at her place that puts him on to you, and he tells Fudge to follow you around. You go into the lawyer's office to talk about this battery case of yours, Fudge thinks you're taking him the stuff on Wetzel, and Czop goes back and caps the lawyer. Right? Great. Now by this time you have spotted Fudge in the rearview mirror, and you go talk to him. You tell him you don't know what the hell Thorne's up to and you and Diana don't want any part of the action."

"And he just believed it, because of your honest face," Hunt said.

Cooper sighed. "He believed it because I told him where to find Tommy's stuff."

"Which you had figured out because of the guitar being missing."

"That's right."

Hunt crumbled Styrofoam and glared at Cooper. Peck rocked forward on the chair and went on. "All right, fine. You told Fudge where to find the stuff and he told you about Wetzel. That was the deal, a straight swap. He gets the stuff, you get Wetzel and Czop's identity, just enough information to deter Wetzel from having you killed, since you can leave a letter for the newspapers or whatever." Cooper nodded. "Now comes the part you deduced."

"Or made up," said Hunt.

Peck scowled. "Whatever. You think Fudge went and got the stuff and didn't tell Czop, because he decided to squeeze Wetzel himself."

"Yeah."

"Except Czop found out. He found out when he walked in on you and Diana at her place later."

"Funny coincidence he should find you both there," said Hunt.

Cooper shook his head. "I think he'd bribed the janitor. When she showed up, the guy called Czop. I was waiting there 'cause I expected her to come back eventually."

"Could be," said Peck, impatient. "Anyway, you told Czop about talking to Fudge and he realized Fudge was fucking him over, since he'd just talked to him and Fudge hadn't mentioned you."

"Only thing I can figure," said Cooper.

"So Czop takes Diana as security, marches her out of there with a gun at her back, puts her in the trunk of his car and goes to see Fudge. He finds the stuff, shoots Fudge for being a bad boy, and then calls you and tells you you can pick up Diana at nine o'clock."

"Why didn't he just drop her off at a street corner?" said Hunt.

Cooper's tone was patient. "Because he wanted to kill us. She was bait to get me downtown so he could do us both."

Hunt and Peck exchanged a brief glance. "And when you showed up he offered you money to keep quiet and get out of the country," Peck said.

"Fifty thousand dollars," said Cooper. "In a brown paper bag."

"Except it was all a trick. He was laying for you when you left the restaurant and he would have got you if it hadn't been for the old man."

"That's right," said Cooper. "Did you find out who the other dead guy was?"

"Yeah, we know him. Why did you run away instead of calling us?"

"Czop was still around. We made tracks. You would have, too."

"And Diana dropped you off and drove out to O'Hare and you don't know where she is."

"San Juan would be my guess."

"Why didn't you go with her?"

"We had a fight. I wanted her to come talk to you guys."

The two detectives exchanged a long pained look. Peck turned back to Cooper, a man nearing the far edge of exasperation. "So what the hell happened out in Oak Brook?"

Cooper shifted stiff limbs, frowning. "Your guess is as good as mine. Maybe Czop tried what Fudge was going to try. And Wetzel was tired of being squeezed, so he shot him. Then maybe he realized that shooting him hadn't solved the problem, because Czop had put the evidence out of reach or something, I don't know. Maybe it was a lovers' quarrel."

"It doesn't make any sense," said Hunt. "How did Wetzel get a hold of Fudge's gun?"

"I guess Czop took it when he killed him."

"Why? And why did Czop use Wetzel's gun instead of his automatic?"

Cooper kneaded the bridge of his nose, tired eyes squeezed shut. "I never said I had all the answers. I said I could tell you who killed Thorne, the lawyer, Fudge, and the old man, and why. Did the ballistics all check out?"

Peck nodded silently, staring sourly at his thumbs. "They checked out," he said. He raised his eyes to Cooper's. "That's one hell of a story, all right. That's one I'm going to have to think about for a while. I'd like it a little better if I could go over it with your lady friend."

"I'll let you know when she calls," Cooper said.

The silence which ensued was broken when Valenti stirred in the corner where he sat dangling his gold-banded lieutenant's cap from a finger. "I have a question," he said.

"What's that?"

"What happened to the fifty thousand dollars?"

Hunt laughed suddenly, almost hysterically. "Yeah. What the hell happened to the money? I suppose you're going to tell us she took it with her."

Cooper nodded. "Some of it. I grabbed a handful out of the sack and threw it on the seat when I got out of the car."

"And the rest of it?" said Peck. All the hereditary skepticism of nameless generations of policemen showed on his pallid face.

"It's right here." Cooper reached into his right-hand jacket pocket and pulled out a brown paper bag. He held it by a bottom corner and shook it, and banded stacks of hundred-dollar bills spilled out across the top of the table. Everyone looked at the bills for a long moment. In the corner Valenti smiled, very faintly.

Cooper said, "I've told you all I know. I've told you the truth. Check it out."

In the silence, Peck looked at Hunt and Hunt looked at Peck and they both looked at Valenti, sitting on a chair in the corner, his smile gone.

After another very long moment Peck pushed away from the table with a scraping noise. He stood up and said, "Get the fuck out of here." He made for the door. Hunt tossed the remains of the cup on the table and started to follow.

"Wait a minute," said Cooper.

"What?"

"Do I get to keep that?" He pointed to the money on the table.

Hunt looked to Peck in the doorway. "We'll give you a receipt," Peck said, bitterly.

Outside in the vast parking lot, it was raining. Valenti stopped at the squad car, stopped dead in the rain, and faced Cooper. He said, "Even if it all checks out, I think if I look hard enough, I'll find holes."

Cooper hunched his shoulders against the rain. "But you won't, because you've got everything you need. You've got a story that explains all the physical evidence. You've got all the bodies and the bullets accounted for. And you've got one other thing."

"What?"

"You have my word of honor I didn't kill anybody."

Valenti looked at Cooper for a long time, rain running off the bill of his cap, and said, "No more favors, MacLeish. Never."

Cooper nodded slowly. "I'll hop a bus. See you around."

Father Doyle had heard from the police, who had found keys tagged with the name of the church on Stumps's body. Cooper found the priest in the red-brick rectory next to the church and heard the first, uninformed police version: God knew what the old drunk was up to or where he got a cannon like that, but it was probably a fouled-up heist, a falling-out among thieves. Cooper didn't tell him how he'd heard of the death and the priest didn't ask.

"I thought the old son of a bitch was harmless," Father Doyle said. The priest had pointed the police toward a sister out on the West Side, and Cooper followed in their tracks.

The neighborhood had been white but was now almost all black, a tired street of worn houses with patched roofs and tiny ragged lawns, all growing sodden under the rain. The diminutive but brisk woman who answered Cooper's ring was past seventy and had been crying.

"I had to learn to accept a lot of things about Norman," she said in a 1950s living room preserved as if under glass. "But I don't believe he was a hoodlum."

"He wasn't," said Cooper. "I don't know what happened either, but your brother wasn't a crook."

"How did you know him?" she asked, clutching a handkerchief, fiercely dignified on a square gray-blue sofa.

"We told each other war stories. In a bar."

She nodded, yellow-white hair done up in a bun with a net over it. Her frown went away out the window into the rain. "The war," she said. "That was what broke Norman."

"Him and a lot of others, too. But it never broke him entirely."

"The drinking did that. That took him the rest of the way."

"He wasn't a write-off," Cooper said. "There was a man still there."

She nodded, distantly, forgetting Cooper. Then she rose and said, "Would you like to see a picture?"

She was gone for a minute and came back with a framed photo about five by eight. She put it in Cooper's hands with reverence. The photo showed a boy, a boy with bright eyes in old-fashioned Marine khakis, the globe and anchor on the cap. He looked about sixteen years old. He looked ready to grab the universe by the tail.

"That's the Norman our father always wanted to remember," the woman said. Cooper nodded, imagining. The woman reached into a pocket of her dress and pulled out another photo. This one was an ancient black-and-white snapshot with serrated edges. It showed a blond boy of four or five with an older sister of maybe ten. They were holding hands, squinting into the camera, on a long-ago summer day. "And that's the Norman I want to remember," she said.

After a moment Cooper handed back both photos. "That was a long time ago."

"It was indeed." She looked at the snapshot for a second or two, then slipped it back into her pocket, folded the framed photo to her breast and went out of the room.

While she was gone Cooper took the crumpled white Burger King paper bag from his jacket pocket and opened it and looked inside. There were still a good many banded stacks of bills inside, even though Cooper had transferred most of the bills to the brown bag he'd taken to the police station.

Cooper thought back, making sure he hadn't told the woman his name. When she came back into the room Cooper rose and held the bag out to her. "I owe your brother for saving my life," he said. "I figure this is about right. If you feel bad about taking it, give it to charity. But use some of it to bury him." She took the bag, bewildered, and looked inside. When she looked up Cooper thought he was going to have to catch her. When she steadied a little he said, "And when you bury him, make sure you buy a flag for the coffin."

He let himself out and walked back to the car in the rain.

* * *

Cooper nearly fell asleep to the drumming of the rain on the roof of the Firebird. In front of him, beyond the trash can which held the pieces of his letter to Moreland, Moss Wetzel's IOU. and a lump of burned plastic that had once been a photo ID, beyond the strip of grass and the narrow beach, the lake danced under the weeping heavens. The world was gray and close about him, sheltering. When he snapped back from his doze he passed a hand over his face and reached for the ignition key. He said aloud, "Keep the job, God. It's too much for me." He started the car and backed out of the slot.

When he let himself into the apartment he called softly to Diana and she answered from the bedroom. He found her under the blankets, on her side, two pillows tucked under her dark golden head. He kissed her on the cheek and sat on the edge of the bed.

He watched raindrops die and merge into rivers on the windowpane for a time and then said, "They won't ever find out."

Diana raised her head from the pillows. "What?" she breathed.

"There's no way they can ever know about it," Cooper said.

Her head went back down but her eyes stayed open. Her voice was hollow as she said, "About what?"

"About how you set Tommy up."

When next he looked at her she was crying, face in the pillow and shaking silently. He caressed her head, working his fingers gently into her hair. "He deserved it," he said.

She gasped for air and said, "You knew all along."

"Not all along. Early enough to work hard to keep you out of a police interrogation room. That's the only thing that could make me lie to the cops—protecting you."

"When did you figure it out?"

"I wondered from the start." Cooper caressed her and looked out the window, thinking. "The first thing I wondered, other than your general reluctance to go to the police, was why you split right away, before they searched your place. You headed right out to Rachel's before there was any reason to believe you were in danger. If it was just a dry run that Tommy had aborted, there was no reason to think your place wasn't safe."

She shook with the smothered sobs, and he bent closer to her. "It's over," he whispered.

"I knew they'd kill him," she managed between sobs. Cooper waited. When her breathing was steady she raised her face from the pillow and said, "When I was supposed to call and set up the exchange at the bus station. By that time I was scared to death."

"That'll do it every time."

"In the car, on the way to make the call, I thought of it. It really stank as a plan, didn't it?"

"It got Tommy killed. I'd say it worked OK."

"It got Barry killed, too. And Stumps. And almost us."

"Tommy would have gotten *you* killed if you hadn't done it. And Barry wasn't your fault. He was mine. Forget it now. What did you tell Wetzel?"

Diana strove to control her breathing. "Instead of giving him the instructions for the exchange at the bus station, I told him Tommy would be waiting in the bar on Rush Street at eleven that night."

"The place where he was going to meet you for a drink after work."

"Uh-huh. I told Wetzel what Tommy looked like and what he was wearing and said he would have what Wetzel wanted. I blew him sky high."

"I'd like to have been there to see Tommy's face."

She shook again, fighting the sobs. Finally calm, she said, "I used to love him."

"Don't let it eat you up. He tried to trade your life for his. Till the very last. He could have told them where the envelope really was and maybe saved his life, but instead he tried one last scam. He told them you had the stuff in your apartment and gave them the key."

"I know. I didn't expect that. I didn't think of that possibility until I was sitting in my place with that empty folder in my hands, realizing I had misjudged everything. Then I was really scared."

Behind the drumming of the raindrops Cooper could hear the faint distant chorus of the lake. The anger stirred in him again, briefly. "Why did you lie to me?" he said softly.

She raised a tear-smudged face, urgently searching his. "That was one thing I couldn't do, make you share my guilt. I couldn't make you help me get away with murder."

"It wasn't murder. Not by my standards."

"I couldn't tell you. I came close, but I couldn't admit it, not even to you."

"Don't ever lie to me again."

She shook, weeping into the pillow. "Forgive me," she said at last.

"You're forgiven. It's over." He held her for a time, listening.

Diana stirred and said, "When were you sure?"

"When I talked to Cecil. The way he told it, Tommy had never met Wetzel or anyone connected with him when they were down there in Trinidad. So there was only one way they could have spotted him that night. Somebody had to finger him. And you were the only somebody."

After that he held her while she cried some more, feeling the weight of her grief and her guilt lifting slowly. The rain never stopped. After a long time, lying quietly beside him, she said, "I feel like I've been living at the bottom of a toilet."

"You have. You've been living in a world where people are just meat. When people take that attitude, it gets pretty grim."

"I'd never really seen it before, that grimness I mean. I'd never had to walk in it, smell it and taste it and feel its hands on me before. It's spoiled everything."

"That's how it feels for a while," said Cooper. "But then the rains come."

He looked out at it, lashing the tired brick. "The sun comes out, the moon goes up, the Earth goes around enough times, and you start to see colors again. It happens, believe me. Especially if you're not alone."

He'd never known she had such strength, to crush him to her like this.

"We'll make it down to those beaches someday," Cooper said, feeling suddenly that with her the grimness could never really touch him again. "I don't think it's real wise to use those tickets in there right away, but we'll make it."

"Cash in the tickets. I don't need beaches," Diana breathed. "We could be on the moon, we could be at the North Pole, right here in this room, as long as we're together I'm whole."

"Yeah," said Cooper, his heart swelling with the murmur of the rain. "That's it, isn't it?"